ISOLDESSE

ISOLDESSE

BOOK ONE IN THE
AEVO COMPENDIUM SERIES

KIMBERLY GRYMES

TRACTOR BEAM PUBLISHING

ISBN-13: 978-1736179321 (Hardcover)
ISBN-13: 978-1736179307 (Paperback)
ISBN-13: 978-1736179314 (eBook)

Library of Congress Control Number 2020922939

Tractor Beam Publishing
P.O. Box 261, Rose Hill, KS 67133

www.kimberlygrymes.com

To Jim, my husband and best friend.
I couldn't have done this without your love and support.
Thank you.

THE WORLDS OF
ISOLDESSE

EARTH'S
MOON

SENDARA'S
MOONS

PRIOMH

EARTH

SENDARA

ANUMINIS **OBARD**

ANUMEN
✦ TERMINOLOGY ✦

Amula – (ah-mew-lah) Incantations that involve speaking certain words of the Anumen language that are encoded with instructions to manipulate the energy of the Eilimintachs.

Anumen – (ah-new-men) A race of beings that live on a world called Anuminis. The women of this species have a magical connection to the Eilimintachs.

Anuminis – (ah-new-min-is) The home world of the Anumens.

Arcstone – A powerful stone found on Anuminis that has the capability of holding the essence of a single Anumen woman after her physical life ends. The arcstone can also form a permanent bond, a connection, to a living person, who can then see and hear the Anumen occupying the stone as well as utilize the magic of the arcstone.

Daramum – An Anumen term for *grandmother*.

Eilimintachs – (el-im-in-tocks) Believed by the Anumens to be powerful beings with a connection to the elements who have blessed Anumen women with the ability to cast amulas.

Essence – Similar to a soul, but it's also a form of energy with strings or mechanics that keeps the soul and body alive. An essence is fueled by the elements.

Ittums – (it-tums) An Anumen term for the Hiccum flower.

Iya – An Anumen term for *hello* and *goodbye*.

Obard – A race of hostile beings. They invaded Anuminis, forcing Anumens to flee their home world.

Pioras – (pie-or-us) An Anumen term for unexpected side effects during an arcstone bond; usually because an Anumen casts a secondary amula on the arcstone prior to bonding.

Séara – (say-era) An Anumen term for a powerful Anumen who can sense amulas, communicate with Anumens in the Unforeseen World, and sometimes get glimpses or premonitions through visions or dreams.

Transessent stone – A smooth white stone, flat and oval in shape. Originally mined from Anuminis. The Sendarians use the stones as batteries, whereas the Anumens use the stones to amplify their amulas.

The Unforeseen World – The place where an Anumen's essence ascends to after their physical life is over, and where they live out their second life before final rest.

Youthen – An Anumen term for *young child.*

SENDARIAN
TERMINOLOGY

Aevo Compendium – (aye-voe | com-pen-di-um) Also called Aevo C; an observation project left to the Sendarians by their goddess, Isoldesse, who instructed them to continue her work observing and documenting the evolutionary progress of the worlds she mothered and influenced.

Anumen Doctrine – Sacred scriptures and charges left by Isoldesse for the council and royal family to use as they rule over Sendara.

Athru – A Sendarian rebellion group who intends to remove the governing forces of the royal family and Elemental Council from Sendara.

Beannaith – (bay-nayth) A Sendarian term for *hello and goodbye.*

EarLincs – Temporary ear translator implants that allow the recipient to instantly hear what others are saying in their own language.

Elemental Council – An overseeing agency that monitors and enforces the consumption of natural resources on Sendara.

The Endless Forest – A thick wooded forest that covers most of Priomh's moon surface.

Essence – Similar to a soul, but it's also a form of energy with strings or mechanics that keeps the soul and body alive. An essence is fueled by the elements.

Gróntah – (groan-tah) A Sendarian slang word that means *fucking-asshole.*

Hegah – (hey-gah) A Sendarian term for *hell.*

Hiccum flowers – Small green flowers found in Hiccum trees, and when you pick them, they instantly turn a bright yellow color.

Imperilment – A Sendarian term for when someone is acting beyond the means of being helped or arrested. The only way to stop them from harming themselves and others is to use force by whatever means necessary. Only a Rhaltan Enforcer can call Imperilment.

Lasher – A Sendarian weapon. Similar to a baton but longer and with a tapered, more flexible end that whips your opponent.

Lead – A supervisor of departments within a community. She or he reports to the Leadess or Leader of that community.

Leadess/Leader – An overseer of a designated community. Assigned by the Queen of Sendara and reports directly to the queen, the Elemental Council, and the Rhaltan Enforcers.

Live InterNeural Connection – Also known as a **Linc**, is an artificial assistant implanted into a Sendarian once they've entered the predult stage of their life. Lincs are wired directly into the nervous system and become a part of the Sendarian. Lincs are more like personal assistants as well as resources for information, as they are all connected to the Sendara Main Network.

Loggie – A Sendarian slang word that means *idiot*.

Mount Nocholus – (mount | nock-oh-lus) A lone snowcapped mountain on the Priomh moon.

Paralytic restraint – A snug, semitranslucent silicone device fitted around the neck like a collar. When it's activated, the brain and muscles of the wearer can be controlled through a plac.

Pinship – A special, and secret, transport spaceship that uses space-pinch technology to travel between worlds.

Plac – A portable computer device used by the Sendarians. It has the ability to morph into a soft, pliable silicone material for convenient storage.

Predult – A Sendarian term that describes the years that come after the teen years and before adulthood.

Priomh – (pre-ohm) Sendara's third-largest orbiting moon. It's a habitable moon and is home to the research community also called Priomh, which is dedicated to the Aevo Compendium.

Rhaltan Enforcers – (rawl-tan) The Sendarian military/police force.

Scout – A Sendarian term for *spy/assassin*.

Sendara – The home world of the Sendarians.

Sendara Network – The main online Sendarian computer network.

Sendarians – A peaceful race of humanoid beings. They have advanced technology and are capable of traveling through space to other worlds.

South Sendara – Also known as the Isle of Awry, or the land of the lost. Sendarians believe those who've lost their faith in Isoldesse reside on the isolated island. The Sendarians there have broken away and declared independence from the royal family, Elemental Council, and Rhaltan Enforcement.

Spiaire – (spy-ir) A Sendarian who lives a double life on an alien world during an Aevo Compendium trial. There are four total Spiaires assigned to four different regions of whatever world is undergoing observation. A Spiaire's job is to befriend the subjects without revealing their true identity and prepare the subjects for extraction to Priomh.

Tarais – (tar-ess) The main transport spaceship that travels between worlds, bringing Spiaires and subjects to and from the many worlds observed.

Taut – (taught) A Sendarian slang word that means *bitch*.

Transessent bracer – A metal wristband that monitors an individual's health and tracks their location. It's powered by a transessent stone.

Transessent stone – A smooth white stone, flat and oval in shape. Originally mined from Anuminis. The Sendarians use the stones as batteries, whereas the Anumens use the stones to amplify their amulas.

The Waking – The procedure in which the Sendarians on Priomh wake the subjects from deep-space sedation.

PROLOGUE

It had been seven hundred and twenty-two days since Geevi disappeared. Almost two years of searching and still no word. Though Breyah's Leads had insisted she stop looking, she'd refused to give up. She only wanted to know that Geevi was okay.

Breyah stepped farther into the empty home. She'd ordered everything to remain as it was, furnished and vacant, ready for whenever her friend decided to come home. Living quarters within their little moon community were limited, but Breyah didn't care. This was Geevi's home.

Breyah prayed to Isoldesse every day that her friend would return, but it had been two years.

"Linc," she said while admiring Geevi's vase collection she'd brought to Priomh from their home world, Sendara.

Her Live InterNeural Connection responded deep within her ear, *"How can I be of assistance?"*

Breyah surveyed the abandoned home, and how everything was exactly where Geevi had left it. It had taken a little more than half a year for Geevi's replacement to arrive, and another year for Breyah and her team of Leads to train and prepare the new recruit for the duties of a Spiaire—to live a double life on an alien world, without revealing her identity, while befriending the subjects for the Aevo Compendium assessment.

"Linc, I'd like to send a communication."

"*And to whom would you like to send a message?*"

Before Breyah could answer, a woman spoke from behind her. "Breyah, what are you doing in here?"

Breyah turned to see her second-in-command, Rian, enter. The top of her pale blue hair grazed the underside of the doorframe.

"Beannaith, Rian," Breyah greeted her. "Is everything all right?"

"Yeah, yeah, everything's all right. Is everything all right with you? Because we're supposed to be at a meeting with the other Leads right now. Everyone's waiting to finalize the upcoming Aevo C's mission agenda before the *Tarais* sets out tomorrow. I think they're all a bit nervous since it's the first away mission for our newbie Spiaire."

Breyah wasn't worried. If there were ever an easy world to assess, it was Earth. A trip to Earth would be more of a vacation than an assignment for the Spiaires. Besides, Breyah was fairly sure the humans hadn't evolved much since Earth's last assessment fifty years ago.

"I'm quite confident that she'll be fine." Breyah crossed her arms and rubbed the edges of the yellow stone embedded in an elegant arm cuff. A family heirloom from her mother. She glanced around the abandoned home and recalled the strange feeling she'd woken with. A sensation so strong, she'd convinced herself that her childhood friend had finally returned. "I needed to check on something before the meeting."

Rian's porcelain skin blended with the white fabric of her knee-length dress. She crossed the narrow sitting room and stood gazing out the expansive glass wall. "I can't believe how amazing the view is from this home. I'd be tempted to downsize and move in here just for this view."

She was right. The view was amazing. The Endless Forest that covered most of the Priomh moon stretched out, butting up against Mount Nocholus. After her friend's disappearance, Breyah used to come here before her day began for a quiet place to collect her thoughts. She'd sit and admire first light as it rose from behind the south side of the mountain, but over time her visits dwindled, until one day she'd stopped coming.

Rian rested her hands on the fitted fabric sculpting her hips and faced her Leadess. "I think it's time you let go. She's not coming back. This is a perfectly good home, and you've waited long enough. And it's time—"

"I know, I know."

Rian glared at Breyah, her sapphire eyes glinting. "Do you, though?"

Her second-in-command had grown to know Breyah almost as much as Geevi had, though their childhoods were nothing alike. Breyah couldn't help but sympathize with Rian's life before Priomh. How on Sendara, Rian grew up feeling out of place and isolated from the others in her community. But here, on Priomh, she'd been given a fresh start, and it hadn't taken her long to move up the ranks to Breyah's second-in-command.

"We should go." Breyah turned to leave.

"If you insist."

Breyah stopped midway and recalled the strong sense she'd felt earlier that Geevi was nearby. "Actually, tell the Leads I'll be there shortly."

"*Breyah*," Rian groaned. "Let it go."

"I will. I promise. I just need a moment."

Without another word, Rian left. She ducked under the doorframe and closed the door behind herself, leaving Breyah alone in the open space of Geevi's old home. She approached the exterior glass wall and admired the view once more. The outline of her thick red hair and orange eyes reflected against the dark treetops of the Endless Forest. "Linc," she addressed again. "I'd like to send that communication now."

Her Linc replied, "*Of course, Leadess. Based on your location, I can assume the recipient, but to be sure, whom are we sending a message to?*"

"Your assumption is correct. Now, let's pray to Isoldesse that this will be the one Geevi responds to."

PART

ONE

EARTH

1

Kenna slammed her laptop shut and cursed.

From across the kitchen table, Meegan lowered her book. "Everything okay over there?"

"No," Kenna moaned and dropped her head onto her laptop. She slid her fingers under her glasses, rubbed her temples, and willed herself not to cry.

How did this... I mean... Why didn't they pick me?

Meegan leaned forward, elbows resting on the wood surface of the round table. "What happened?"

"I didn't get in." Long strands of mahogany hair draped over the sides of her face, muffling her voice. "I didn't get the summer internship at the observatory."

"Oh. I'm sorry."

The internship would've given her some one-on-one time with her dream telescope at the observatory. The thirty-two-inch Ortega was a major-league player in the world of telescopes, *ten times* more powerful than the two telescopes she owned. But it was so much more than just the opportunity to gaze through an amazing telescope. She'd also be missing out on shadowing the observatory staff as they documented and analyzed celestial phenomena. Oh, to be at the forefront if there was ever first contact... Not that it would happen during her internship, but she could dream.

She turned her head on the laptop and brushed the hair from her face. "I guess I should've kissed more ass or offered to tutor more freshmen. Ugh, I've barely slept this past semester! I even volunteered all those extra hours after classes hoping to impress the Head of the Department of Physics. Shit, was I supposed to sl—"

"Whoa! Hey, now." Meegan snapped her fingers, breaking Kenna from her rant. "Let's not go there, because *ew* that's gross, and yeah, it sucks, but let's be real... It's not the end of the world."

Kenna sat up and pouted while sliding her glasses back on. "But I really, *really* wanted—"

"I know, I know, and I'm kind of surprised they didn't pick you. You're like one of the department favorites. I would've bet my lucky ring you were going to get the internship." She tapped the small, round mood ring on her middle finger.

"You do realize how pissed your mom would be if you lost her old ring, right? Broken or not, she would've totally blamed *me* for you losing it." Over the years, whenever they hung out at Meegan's house, that was one thing Mrs. Prinor became known for. Constantly asking Meegan if she was wearing *that* mood ring, even though Kenna had never seen it any other color besides purple.

"She doesn't blame you for everything," Meegan countered with an eye roll. Though her grin hinted there might be some truth to what Kenna was saying. "Besides, I'd never actually bet my mother's ring. I'm just saying that's how sure I was you were going to get the internship." Meegan removed an elastic band from her wrist and tugged her black hair into a low, sleek ponytail. "Listen, we'll be college graduates in less than three weeks, and you've worked your ass off these past four years. One summer off with no classes, no internships, and no tutoring sessions won't throw your space career plans. Besides, now you've got more time to spend with your mom up at the museum. You're always complaining you don't see her enough."

"Yeah, I guess." Kenna tucked her dark hair behind her ears and tried to focus on the positives. "The gift shop's always calling me and asking if I want more hours, and it would be nice to see Mom more often."

"Exactly." Meegan lifted her book, but then lowered it. "You really need to stop saying yes all the time. You're constantly piling too much on your plate. Look at you... You can barely keep your eyes open!"

"I can't help it. It's hard for me to say no." Kenna cupped her hand over her mouth, covering her yawn. Her gaze wandered out the kitchen window to the street below. *Maybe I should take the summer off.* Though, taking it easy never came naturally. Her mind was a speeding train that rarely eased on the brakes.

"I don't know where I'd be if it weren't for your no-bullshit pep talks." Flipping her phone over from next to her laptop, she checked the time and notifications. "Seriously, you know exactly what to say when I have one of my freak-out moments."

"That's what best friends are for. To slap some sense into you when you're not thinking straight," Meegan said with a chuckle and flipped open her book.

Kenna stared at the worn edges of the dustjacket. "Why do you insist on reading that in front of me?"

From behind the open book, Meegan teased, "I like this series. It's written by one of my favorite authors."

Kenna didn't need to see Meegan's face to know she was smiling ear to ear. "Well, in that case maybe I can see about getting you a signed copy."

Without lowering the book, Meegan said, "Nah, that's okay," and then after a few seconds, she tipped the book forward. Her brown eyes stared over the top. "Besides, I can drive over to your parents' house and have your dad sign it for me at any time. I'm like his second daughter."

When the doorbell rang, both girls stopped laughing and looked through the kitchen doorway.

"You expecting someone?" Meegan asked.

Kenna shook her head before getting up to answer the door.

Out in the living room, the floor-to-ceiling curtains were drawn open and the warm Florida sun flooded the entire third-floor apartment. Kenna opened the front door, and immediately a surge of excitement feuded with her exhaustion. She smiled and leaned her head against the edge of the door. "Darci! You're back!"

A woman with strawberry-blonde hair loosely braided across the top of her head like a crown stood out on the third-floor landing. She was wearing one of her typical flowing, bohemian-style tops with pale pink shorts, brown leather ballet flats, and her favorite military-green canvas bag slung over one shoulder.

"Hey, girls!" Darci exclaimed. "I wanted to surprise you by coming home a few days early. *And* I was so excited to see you that I drove straight past my apartment to your place!"

Kenna enjoyed hanging out with Darci. Though, she couldn't say Meegan felt the same, but Kenna liked how Darci's social-butterfly persona brought some balance to their friend group. "Well, we're surprised. How was your trip?"

Meegan crossed her arms and in a semi-snarky tone said, "I'm impressed. You didn't post one picture of your trip back to Florida on Insta. That must've been super hard for you."

"Ha-ha. You're hilarious." Darci hung her bag on the coat hook and then turned to Kenna. "I had such a good time. I got to tour, shop, and eat out all over Boston. Oh, and the air! I can't believe how crisp and cool the air is up there. It was amazing! Like, ten times better than how all those articles I read online described it."

The moment Darci mentioned Boston, Meegan drifted toward the sofa. She'd been avoiding any conversation having to do with her boyfriend, Nick, ever since he'd moved to Massachusetts a few weeks ago. All she'd said was they weren't together anymore.

Boston also stirred up old feelings for Kenna about a childhood friend she'd recently reconnected with on Instagram. A middle school friend from when she and her parents used to live out in Kansas. Liam, now living up in Boston, had at one time been her best friend but also that guy she secretly crushed on. When Kenna found out her family was moving to Florida, she'd figured she'd never see him again, so what was the point in pursuing a relationship? Who knew they'd reconnect via social media almost a decade later?

Darci hadn't taken a breath from her rambling about Boston when Meegan finally interrupted. "How many coffees have you had already?"

"Ignore her." Kenna threw her arms open and hugged her friend. She knew her body probably felt like dead weight, but she leaned in anyway. "I'm glad you're home."

Darci pushed Kenna to arm's length and eyed her over before asking Meegan, "What's with Droopy here? No, wait. Let me guess. She was up all night studying for finals or stargazing through one of those telescopes of hers?"

"Might've been a little of both." Meegan sat in the oversized beige armchair while picking up the *Magnolia* magazine from the coffee table. "She was wide awake when I got here early this morning. Rewriting class notes, making flash cards, and God knows what else."

"Hello! I'm standing right here."

Darci narrowed her glare at Kenna. "You look like crap, you know that, right? It wouldn't hurt to get some sun too." Darci paused before waving a dismissive hand. "Never mind that, you can take a nap later. Though, speaking of naps, I'm curious—are you still sleeping in that stupid geriatric chair?"

"Are you calling my favorite chair *old?*" Kenna gasped in a playfully offended tone. Then she turned away from Darci and scooted past Meegan to the couch. "But if you must know… yes, I slept in my chair last night. It's a recliner, and it's super comfortable."

"You realize you have a perfectly good bed two feet away from that clunker, right?" Before Kenna could answer, Darci continued spouting, "I read online that it's not healthy to sleep all curled up like that for long periods of time. It'll ruin your posture. I'll send you the article." Before she could take another breath, she continued, "I also read an interesting article this morning on the plane about eating chocolate before bed and how the taste of chocolate sets your mind up for, well, *good* dreams. I'll send you that one too. Oh, and this other article about—"

"Seriously, Darci. How many cups of coffee have you had?" Meegan lowered her magazine. "You remember what we talked about? Limiting your coffee?"

Darci's shoulders dropped, and she groaned. "Yeah, yeah. One cup. Anything more... decaf only."

"Do I really look that crappy?" Kenna rubbed her eyes from under her glasses. "It's the end of the semester and I've got a lot—"

"Stop! Do not finish that sentence!" With her hands out and head shaking, Darci plopped herself down on the floral sofa next to Kenna. Her big smile lit up her bright green eyes as she said, "We so need a social day. A fun day. A day without talking about school, work, term papers, et cetera, et cetera."

Meegan closed her magazine and agreed. "We should hit the outlets. I could use some new sandals."

It took them about twenty minutes to convince Kenna to come out shopping with them, if only for a few hours.

"I promise we won't keep you out late," Darci said. "Besides, I'm flying out to California tomorrow. And before you say anything"—she pointed a lightly freckled finger at Kenna—"it's only for a few days. I'll be back in time for finals."

"California?" Kenna scoffed. "Graduation is less than four weeks away and you want to take another trip, this time to California? Can't it wait?"

"No, it can't. There are some things in this universe that are more important than school!" Darci snapped with a little more sharpness than Kenna was used to. Darci shook off the tension lingering between them and continued, "Listen, while I was visiting my friend, Eryn up in Boston, we decided we needed to take a quick trip out to California to check on our friend, Grace. She hasn't been answering any of our calls or texts, and we're worried about her. It's probably nothing, and I promise I'll be back before finals."

When Kenna heard her phone chime from the kitchen, she excused herself. She needed a time-out before she said something she'd regret. Lack of sleep usually meant the filtering part of her brain was on vacation.

She found her phone on the kitchen table. The notification bar told her it was a new message from her dad. She slumped into one of the kitchen chairs and wished it had been from Liam.

I don't know why I'm so hung up on him. He's like ten states away from me, and that's not going to change anytime soon.

One tap to her phone and the full message from her dad opened. He wanted to know if she could stop by the house later. Kenna adjusted her glasses and typed a quick reply.

Sorry. Can't today. Maybe tomorrow or Tuesday.

She scrolled through her messages. She'd meant to reply to Liam's late-night text last night, but she'd gotten caught up in a puzzling issue while searching the sky for Arcturus. Normally, it would've taken her less than a minute to spot the star in the sky, especially because it was the brightest star in the northern hemisphere, but oddly, Kenna couldn't find the red giant. She chalked it up to something wrong with her lens and spent her Saturday night up on the roof thoroughly cleaning her rooftop telescope.

A mixture of butterflies and nervous knots tangled in her stomach as she opened and reread Liam's last message.

Hey, I need to talk with you. Can I call you sometime this week?

I wish he'd just tell me what the heck he wants to talk about. He knows I hate wondering about things.

She typed a response and then deleted it. This went on for a few minutes until she was satisfied with her response.

> Sure. Whenever. Because I love when you leave me hanging like that.

With her phone, she walked back into the living room right as her roommate walked in through the front door. Ally was juggling two reusable grocery totes along with a fresh bouquet, her purse, and yesterday's mail. Kenna could see her roommate's brown skin pinching beneath the straps of the totes and quickly hurried over to help.

"Oh, thanks," Ally said. "I've got more in the car."

"I can help!" Meegan jumped up from the armchair, tossed the magazine onto the coffee table, and headed out the door. A few seconds later, Ally returned from the kitchen and headed back outside.

Kenna watched her roommate leave the apartment in long strides. *She always buys so much food.* Silently, she wished she had Ally's appetite while having her rock-hard abs too. If she hadn't opened her own catering business last summer after she graduated college, Kenna swore her roommate could've been a supermodel. Five-foot-ten, radiant brown skin, and a headful of gorgeous curls.

"Hey, I forgot." Darci hurried over to her shoulder bag hanging by the front door. She pulled out a manila envelope and handed it to Kenna. "I found it on the driveway, by your deck stairs. I got distracted with a text and shoved it in my purse. I probably would've forgotten about it if I hadn't seen Ally carrying all that mail."

Kenna flipped the manila envelope over and stared at her full name, neatly written in black Sharpie.

McKenna Adalyss Towmann

"There's no return address," Kenna observed while tearing one side of the envelope open. "Who do you think dropped it off?"

Darci shrugged and moved closer. "I didn't see anyone when I found it."

Kenna tipped the envelope and shook out a small rectangular white box about the size of a deck of cards, along with a card. Darci held the box while Kenna opened the card.

"What does it say?" Darci asked.

Kenna held the card open and showed Darci. "It says, *Hold and Read.*"

"What the heck does that mean?" Darci opened the box, and both girls stared at the yellow crystal-looking stone inside. It was slender with shallow points on both ends. Darci dropped the crystal into Kenna's hand, and an ultrathin silver chain dangled between her fingers.

"It's a necklace." Kenna held the crystal in her palm. "Why would someone give me a necklace?"

"Beats me. Maybe you have an admirer?" Darci cooed.

"What are you guys doing?" Meegan asked from the front doorway.

"I got a package. I'll be right there to help unpack." She shot Darci a nervous yet excited smirk before repeating the strange words on the card. "*Banna idir dufiur et gohdeo.*"

In an instant, Kenna's vision went dark, and the room went silent into nothingness.

2

A t the word *gohdeo*, Meegan's fingers uncurled. Both grocery totes slipped from her fingers to the floor. Pieces of fruit bounced and rolled along the hardwood. In the two minutes she'd gone to help Ally, her best friend had somehow gotten a hold of Anumen magic.

There was nothing she could do. Even though she couldn't see the arcstone, she was attuned to the magical amula taking effect. An intuitive awareness that only certain Anumens like herself possessed.

The amula surrounded Kenna like wavering heat rising from a hot road. From behind, a current of air swept into the apartment and rushed at Kenna. Time had slowed for everyone but Meegan as the wind carrying the energy of the Eilimintachs enclosed and compressed the quivering amula into her friend's body.

There was nothing she could do. The amula had been cast. Meegan watched in horror as the essence of the arcstone and Kenna became one.

Darci glanced over at Meegan and the mess of apples, plums, and pears scattered on the floor. "Meeg, what's wro—"

"Catch her!" Meegan shouted, arms outstretched.

Kenna's body swayed. Darci reacted and tried to catch her but struggled to hold her tilting body. Meegan dashed forward and barely caught Kenna from behind. Carefully, she dragged her unconscious friend to the sofa.

This can't be happening. Where is it? Where's the arcstone? Shit! Shit! Shit!

It didn't take her long to find it. An ultrathin chain draped over Kenna's thumb, and Meegan knew the arcstone had to be in there, hiding in Kenna's fist.

The last time she'd seen an arcstone had been over a century ago, before her days on Earth.

I should call someone. I should call—

"What happened? Why did she faint like that?" Darci frantically asked, breaking Meegan from her thoughts.

Meegan wasn't sure how to answer.

In her mind, she played out that conversation. *Oh here, let me explain... So, Kenna read a magical incantation, or amula, that activated a sacred bond between Kenna's essence and the essence of the Anumen contained inside that arcstone.*

Oh, and since I'm being honest, I'm a three-hundred-and-eighteen-year-old refugee from a world called Anuminis that was invaded by a hostile alien race called the Obard.

Meegan bit her lower lip and blankly stared at Darci.

Yeah, I don't think that conversation would go over well.

Luckily, Meegan didn't have to explain anything because Ally strode in with more groceries. "Hey, what's going on? And why's my fruit all over the floor?"

"It's Kenna! Something's wrong with her!" Darci jumped to her feet and rushed by Meegan. Meegan sat on the arm of the sofa, next to Kenna's feet, as Darci helped pick up the fruit. With a shaky voice, Darci explained about the manila envelope and how there'd been a card and a necklace inside. "It was addressed to Kenna, so I gave it to her. I-I didn't know!"

"She's fine," Meegan somewhat lied. "She's just super tired, that's all. You know how she's been pushing herself way too hard these past few weeks."

"Yeah, I guess. Everything happened so fast! Ugh, sometimes I'm so oblivious." Darci bit her lower lip and hugged the fruit in her arms.

"She was up before me this morning," Ally recalled. "That's usually a sign she didn't sleep well. Or at all. Plus, I can always tell when it's getting close to the end of a semester. That's when Kenna turns into the Walking Dead."

"Zombie Kenna, I may have to start calling her that," Meegan said, forcing a smile. "I'm not even kidding you guys when I say she was falling asleep at the kitchen table this morning. I should've told her to go back to bed." Meegan couldn't read Ally's face because it wasn't the most believable lie, but it was the best she could think of right now. "You should put that stuff away before it goes bad. I'll sit with her." Meegan gestured to the grocery bags. "I'd hate to see all that food go to waste."

Ally nodded, slowly moving toward the kitchen while staring at Kenna. "Yeah, okay. But I think we should call her parents if she doesn't wake soon. Maybe they know something about her that we don't. A medical condition or something."

"Maybe," Meegan agreed even though she knew Kenna didn't have any strange medical conditions. "But let's wait a bit before calling them."

Darci followed Ally into the kitchen, offering apologies and promises not to touch their mail anymore. Meegan took advantage of their absence and looked for the card Darci mentioned. She spotted a white corner peeking out from under the coffee table. Picking it up, she noted the handwriting was elegant yet simple. Without speaking the words, she recited the phrase in her head, *Banna idir dufiur et gohdeo*, and then whispered, "The bond between sisters is forever."

This isn't good. Stay calm—keep your cool. Now isn't the time to freak out in front of Ally or Darci. An arcstone bond is one of the oldest amulas and... uh, shit! Of course, I can't remember the specifics. That means going home and searching through one of my mom's old journals.

Oh, no! My parents! If they find out that someone's messing with Anumen magic and a human, my best friend, has bonded with an arcstone, they'll send me to my aunt's house in North Carolina for the next fifty years!

Ally was quick to return with an ear thermometer and Darci on her heels. As they walked by, Darci shouted and pointed to the piece of cardstock in Meegan's hand. "That's the card. The one she read before"—she redirected her hands toward Kenna—"this happened!"

Meegan couldn't help but feel somehow responsible, even though she had no idea who gave it to Kenna or why, or where the arcstone had come from. Somehow a piece of her past had found its way back into her life. Instinctively, she glanced at her finger and noted how the stone in her "mood ring" was still purple. A small relief in the bigger picture. The enchanted ring would've warned her otherwise if there were Obard close by.

It had been over two centuries since the Obard invaded Anuminis, forcing her people to scatter across the universe. But years before the Obard invaded, Meegan had secretly witnessed an arcstone ascension. She had been a young child, a youthen of a hundred and twenty years, when her daramum, her grandmother, ascended her essence into an arcstone. She'd never gotten to ask her daramum why she chose to live her second life in the arcstone rather than ascend to the Unforeseen World with the rest of their people, because Meegan had never gotten to say goodbye. Something else her mother had taken from her.

She missed her daramum and often wondered what happened to that arcstone. Every night she'd pray to the Eilimintachs that her grandmother was safe and hadn't ended up in the hands of the Obard.

"Maybe we should call her parents? What time is it?" Ally asked, more to herself than the others. "I betcha her mom's working at the museum."

"I'm telling you, she's fine," Meegan said. "And she's not running a fever, so you don't need the thermometer. She's over-exhausted to the point of—well, this." Meegan lowered the card onto the coffee table, picked up one of Ally's magazines again, and got cozy in the nearby armchair. "What we should do is let her sleep."

She stared at her sleeping friend. Kenna's clenched fist resting on her stomach. Meegan knew things weren't ever going to be the same. Before she could figure out where the arcstone came from, she first needed to uncover the identity of the Anumen who had ascended into that arcstone. Whose essence was Kenna forming a bond with? She sent a silent prayer to the Eilimintachs that the essence contained inside that arcstone had good intentions and not some Anumen out for vengeance or power. Because there was no undoing the bond of an arcstone. It could only be undone through death—Kenna's death.

3

Kenna opened her eyes to a dark room. She sat up from the sofa and saw Meegan a few feet away, glaring at the white card that had accompanied the crystal necklace. Darci's muffled voice came from the kitchen, but everything beyond a five-foot radius had a shadowy overcast.

Was I that tired and fell asleep? And now what? It's the middle of the night.

"Meeg, what the heck is going on?" When her friend didn't respond, she asked again while waving one hand in front of Meegan's face. But still no reaction.

"Okay, now you're freaking me out!" She gently shoved Meegan in the arm, except her hand didn't stop and somehow passed through Meegan's shoulder. The motion threw Kenna off balance, and she stumbled forward, her own body passing through Meegan's.

She spun on her toes, faced her best friend, and yelled, "Holy shit! What the hell was that? Am I dead or something?" and then gasped when she noticed her body lying on the couch.

"Oh my God—oh my God! I *am* dead!"

"No, your essence has not separated from your physical body," a woman's hoarse voice replied from within the air.

Kenna wanted to run and scream, but her body—or whatever this projection was—wouldn't budge. Across the room, in front of Kenna's bedroom door, a reddish-orange cloud of smoke appeared. From within, an old woman materialized, wearing a stunning floor-length gown with a golden beaded top that covered her chest, shoulders, and arms. Soft, sheer fabric the color of clouds at sunset flowed to the hardwood floor. But what really caught Kenna's attention was the woman's visible, soft golden aura. The same color as the crystal Kenna held a few moments ago.

"You're glowing?"

"Well, yes. My essence is one with the arcstone."

"*Ark-what?*"

"I understand you have questions, and we'll have plenty of time to answer those questions, but for now our time is limited until the bond has been completed."

Did she say bond?

Before Kenna could ask, what little light remained in the room began to fade. More curious than afraid as the darkness closed in on her, she asked, "What's happening? Will I see you again? How do I find you? Can you tell me anything else? Please!"

"It's time to wake, and we'll talk again soon, I promise. But for now, protect the arcstone and keep it close." The woman's voice trailed off as the voices of her friends got louder.

※ ✧ ※ ✧ ※

After blinking several times, Kenna focused her eyes on Ally and Darci standing over her. She tilted her chin toward the ceiling and saw behind her was the bright blue sky outside their apartment windows. The sun filled the room, and she turned her attention back to her bickering friends.

"I think we should call her parents now." Ally reached for her cell phone.

"No!" Meegan and Darci shouted in unison.

"Hey, I'm awake. No need to call my parents." Kenna groaned and wiggled her way into a sitting position. "I'm fine, really." Not wanting to get into the details of her weird dream, or whatever that was, Kenna went with exhaustion. "I was tired and upset about—"

"You were upset? No one mentioned you being upset. What happened?" Ally glared at the two girls standing by as if they were misbehaving children. Before Kenna could answer, Meegan jumped in and explained about the observatory internship.

"Oh," Ally sighed. "I'm sorry, Ken."

"It's my fault. I shouldn't have pushed myself so hard this last semester. They probably don't even let any of the interns near the Ortega. I should've been paying more attention to my health instead of trying to impress my professors."

Kenna scooted over on the floral sofa, making room for Darci. "We're all stressed," Darci said with her naturally cheery tone. Her friend moved closer and rested a hand on Kenna's arm. A faint scent, one she hadn't noticed before and something she hadn't smelled in years, tickled her nose. Kenna was about to ask what perfume Darci was wearing when her friend continued her spiel. "Another good reason for a social day! Shopping is a great way to de-stress your mind. A time-out to refuel the soul. I read that in an article someone posted on Twitter."

"You and that damn Twitter," Kenna joked and stood from the sofa. Her body no longer felt weighed down with grogginess, but instead a strange, warm energy hummed beneath her skin. Like a caffeine buzz encouraging her to get up and get moving. She glanced at the wall clock. "Huh, I swear it feels like I slept for hours."

"Well, you didn't. It was more like two or three minutes," Meegan guessed. "You're sure you're good?"

"I don't know what happened, but yeah, I feel good. Like I got a full night's sleep, *good*." She twisted her wavy hair into a low pony with a scrunchie from the coffee table. "I'm ready for that social day whenever you are."

Ally picked up the manila envelope from the other side of the square coffee table and held it up to Kenna. "And you don't know who sent you this?"

The stone, what did that dream lady call it? Shit, I can't remember. Something-stone. Kenna opened her hand and looked down at the yellow crystal with the silver chain threaded through one end. The whole thing wasn't any bigger than a pen cap.

I'm not into holistic crystals and stones, but it is pretty.

"Here, let me help." Meegan looped her finger through the thin chain, unclasped it, and then reclasped it around Kenna's neck. "It's a little bigger than what you usually wear, but I like it."

It was true. Kenna did prefer small-scaled jewelry. Undecided if she wanted to wear it, she didn't stop Meegan from putting it on her. The crystal rested above her chest, layered beneath a simple silver disc smaller than a dime, engraved with a cluster of circles. A gift from her mother.

Kenna turned to Darci. "Hey, when you found the package, you're sure you didn't see anyone leaving the driveway?"

Darci shook her head. "Nope, no one." She grabbed her canvas tote by the front door and slung it over her head. "Should we stop and pick up Prue?"

"No." Ally let loose her tight brown spirals from their high ponytail. With one hand she flattened any stray curls before redoing her ponytail. "She's still wallowing about her boyfriend, or ex-boyfriend, whatever he is, and I'm not in the mood to hear her whining about that asshole." Her voice trailed off as she walked into the kitchen.

"Is she okay?" Darci whispered and turned a thumb in Ally's direction. "What did I miss while I was away?"

Kenna and Meegan quickly filled Darci in about the assumed breakup between Ally's sister and Xander. "Prue's been pretty upset," Kenna explained. "I think it's the not knowing what she did or what happened that's killing her."

Darci looked more concerned than upset. "So, has he gone missing or something? Like kidnapped or dead?"

"What? No!" Meegan said while shaking her head. "How did you get kidnapped or dead? Are you even listening to me?"

Dead.

The word reminded Kenna that a few minutes ago, she'd thought she might've been dead. Seeing herself lying on the sofa and having her hand pass through her friend's body wasn't exactly normal. She would've sworn she had died if it weren't for the mysterious woman telling her otherwise.

"He's not dead," Meegan explained, breaking Kenna from her thoughts. "I saw him two days ago with some redheaded woman."

"What?" Ally called from the kitchen. With a green pepper in one hand, she stood in the doorway and asked, "Why didn't you say something?"

"Slipped my mind," Meegan said with a slight cringe. "Honestly, I didn't want to get involved. He's a jerk and Prue's better off without him."

Ally's silence implied she couldn't argue with that. No one in the room could.

"Sorry," Meegan said and then promised that the next time she saw him, she'd tell Ally right away.

"We should get going," Darci cut in. "I haven't eaten since before my flight and I'm starving."

Ally disappeared into the kitchen again while Kenna excused herself to grab her sandals and purse. In her bedroom, she stopped in front of her dresser and stared at the crystal pendant in the mirror. The dream woman's words, *until the bond is complete*, echoed in her mind. What did that mean? Then again, it probably didn't matter. It'd only been a dream. What she did know was that she'd pushed herself too hard these past few weeks with term papers, tutoring sessions, shifts at the museum, studies for her finals, and grad school planning. Her mind had officially cracked.

Weird bonds and magical stones? It was the kind of stuff her father would write about in his science-fiction fantasy books. Now wasn't the time to entertain fantasy delusions. Yes, she'd go have a social day. A well-needed break with her friends. But after…

After.

For the first time in a long time, she decided not to worry about or plan what would happen *after* today. And she wasn't going to let anything stop her from having the best summer ever with her friends.

4

A woman in a designer red bikini and a white sarong stood out on the back deck of a secluded beach home. Gemma welcomed the cool breeze against her skin, a brief escape from the Florida heat. Loose strands of dark ginger hair gently blew across her face while her sarong rippled against her legs. She stared out into the ocean and watched the waves roll in over the gritty sand.

One more day. I can tolerate this planet and these humans for one more day.

As a former Spiaire, Gemma had been away from Sendara before, but this was her first off-planet mission for the Athru.

"*Gemma.*" A woman's soothing voice spoke deep within her ear canal. "*My apologies for initiating conversation, but you've received another communication from Leadess Ganecht. Would you like me to dictate the message now?*"

She's relentless. I'll give her that.

She glanced over her shoulder to the other side of the deck, to the patio table where her siblings, Micah and Cahleen, sat. Gemma could only assume they were discussing this evening's plans to apprehend their two marks—the Sendarian Spiaire assigned to this region and one of the human candidates selected for the upcoming Aevo Compendium.

The Aevo Compendium used to mean everything to Gemma. A project entrusted to the Sendarians by their goddess, Isoldesse, wherein they were to continue her work in documenting the evolution and social behaviors of the worlds she mothered.

To Gemma, and most of Sendara, Isoldesse was their savior. Her divine intervention over two millennia ago had changed the fate of their world from what Gemma imagined was similar to Earth's— planet resources being carelessly consumed and governing forces battling for power and control. Isoldesse had written the Anumen Doctrine, sacred scriptures outlining a new way of life. She'd formed the Elemental Council to oversee that the Anumen Doctrine ways were being followed. She'd also selected one bloodline to rule over Sendara.

For generations, the royal family had been a humble, hands-on family, but more recently there were rumors, discreet incidents, about the queen straying from Isoldesse's word. Nothing public, but enough notice for a few to form the Athru, a rebel alliance with intentions to end the royal family and Elemental Council's control over Sendara. To lift the restrictions and laws set by both ruling forces that over the years had twisted Isoldesse's words for their benefit. Gemma's eyes had been opened to what Sendara had become—bland and monotonous, with no allowance for growth. The Athru planned to change all that... in the name of Isoldesse.

"Spiaire Gemma, please confirm you'd like me to recite Leadess Ganecht's message."

"Stop calling me *Spiaire*, and yes, recite the damn message," she whispered to her interneural assistant.

"Transcribing the communication sent from Breyah of the Ganecht family, Leadess of the moon community Priomh:

Beannaith, my friend,

Geevi, it has been over two years since your disappearance, and as usual, I pray to Isoldesse that you are happy and content with your chosen path, whatever it may be. I will never judge you and I will never speak ill of your actions to leave our charge with the Aevo Compendium. I only wish you would send word that you are well and in no danger.

May we meet again one day,

Breyah

End of communication. Shall I discard or archive?"
"Archive," she quietly instructed.

Live InterNeural Connection technology was forbidden, and one of the first things deactivated after a Sendarian pledged their loyalty to the Athru. But Anora, one of the three Athru leaders, had permitted Gemma to keep her Linc in secrecy. No one else could know. Not even Cahleen or Micah, and especially not the other two Athru leaders, Quaid and Biryn.

Phase one of Anora's plan began here on Earth, to sabotage this world's current Aevo Compendium. As a former Spiaire, and one of Breyah's closest confidants, Gemma had inside knowledge of Priomh that kept her useful to the leaders of the Athru... for now. Information like how there were always four Spiaires, one for each of the four regions to whichever planet was undergoing observation. How it was the Spiaires' responsibility to seek out and befriend the preselected candidates before extraction. And now, it was Gemma's responsibility to spy on the Spiaires.

Anora had assigned Gemma and her siblings to Florida, while Sabine and her companion were sent up north. Abastian had been stationed out west in California, while the Beast was left to watch the Spiaire in the Midwest of this region.

Quaid—the Beast—is unpredictable and immoral in every possible way. I don't know how so many are willingly following his orders. Anora and Biryn, I understand. They're both devoted believers in change for Sendara. But that Beast wants nothing but destruction.

Tonight was the night they'd been waiting for these past six months. Soon they'd be heading back to Sendara space with eight captives—four Spiaires and four human Aevo C subjects. One from each region.

That's if all goes as planned.

A loud *thud* broke Gemma from her thoughts. A short blade, curved like a predator's claw, had slammed deep into the wood of the painted blue railing, inches from Gemma's fingers. Without so much as a flinch, Gemma wiggled the black blade free and faced her sister.

"Seriously? What?"

"Did you not hear me?"

"I only need to hear you when the Spiaire has changed her position."

With two fingers, Cahleen slid a smartphone toward the empty seat at the head of the patio table. "See for yourself," she said and then sank back in the wooden patio chair.

Gemma lowered her oversized designer sunglasses and discreetly narrowed her bright orange eyes at her elder sister soaking in the sun. Her black two-piece halter bathing suit exposed the recent tattoo trailing her left oblique. A poem Cahleen had written, questioning the faith and the existence of their goddess, Isoldesse.

Something they'd agreed to disagree on long before their mission to Earth.

Gemma never regretted her time as one of Breyah's Spiaires. For the longest time, she'd thought her service on Priomh, to the Aevo Compendium project, was the best way to prove her devotion to Isoldesse. But that all changed when Anora approached her two years ago. The Athru leader had convinced her of all the good they could bring to the Sendarian people. Why sit around and watch all the other worlds Isoldesse molded evolve and grow with luxuries Sendara would never see? Anora had told Gemma, *"If you want to prove yourself to Isoldesse, then help me remind Sendarians of what the Anumen Doctrine really means, and not what the Elemental Council and the queen tell us it means."*

A loud groan from her brother veered her back to the present. "How much longer do we have to sit out here? Can't we take this conversation inside?" Micah asked from beneath his baseball cap. Unlike Cahleen, he sat hiding under the patio umbrella protecting his pale skin from what he called *deadly rays of poison.*

Some days she wondered how the three of them were related. Micah, antisocial yet brilliant with tech, Cahleen, one of the best Athru Scouts with her stealthy tactics and unfailing composure, and she with her persuasive social skills.

Gemma sauntered over to the table and tossed Cahleen's dagger onto the teak surface. The weight of the hilt hit hard and startled Micah from behind his portable Linc device.

Technically, no Athru were to have portable Linc devices either, but Micah had lifted the plac while they were in the docking station on Priomh. Right before they snuck aboard the *Tarais* heading to Earth. He assured Gemma and Cahleen that he'd deactivated the tracking element and uploaded one of his cloaking codes to hide his presence when accessing the main Sendarian Network. *"We need to keep tabs on what the queen and Rhaltan are up to,"* he'd insisted.

"Geez, Gemma." Micah lowered the book-sized piece of black glass and scowled at his sister standing at the head of the table. "Why do you always have to be so dramatic?"

She shrugged one shoulder and smirked at her younger brother as she picked up the cell phone. "It's in my beautiful, shimmering blood to be *dramatic.*"

"You're unfocused and ridiculous," Micah muttered.

If he weren't my brother, and the smartest Sendarian I know, I might consider leaving him here on this malnourished and abused planet.

"I know that look," said Cahleen, interrupting Gemma's internal plans to abandon their brother. "Leave it be, Gemma," she said while twisting the tip of the claw dagger into the arm of the patio chair. "We've got way too much riding on this mission for you two to get into another one of your who's-got-the-bigger-ego arguments. Stay focused."

Gemma could sense her sister's stare boring into her. She lowered the cell phone and locked eyes with Cahleen, the corner of Gemma's lip curling up. "What? I'm not arguing with him anymore, so you can stop staring." Secretly, she admired how intimidating Cahleen could be, yet at the same time she worried how much of her sister's essence had turned black from her duties as a Scout.

"Besides," Gemma added while spinning the cell phone on the table, "I am focused. I'm trying to figure out what that little gróntah's up to."

"Language, language. Even I don't go around calling Sendarians gróntahs." Cahleen tried to keep a straight face but couldn't. "You need to let it go. Whatever that pain-in-the-ass Spiaire is doing outside her Compendium orders is none of our concern."

"But—" Gemma tried to argue.

Cahleen cut her off. "You're taking *her* job way too seriously. You're not living on Priomh, and you're not one of Breyah's Spiaires anymore. Let's just do what we came here for and then focus on getting home. I don't want to be here, and he"—she pointed the tip of the dagger toward Micah—"sure as hegah doesn't want to be here. So don't screw things up or get sidetracked."

"I'm not," Gemma insisted. "She's been meeting with humans outside her assigned subjects. Something's up, and I want to know who they are and why she's meeting with them. There might be something going on that we can use as *leverage*." Gemma emphasized that last word, hoping to entice Cahleen's predatory instincts.

Cahleen nodded in defeat. "Fine. We'll look into it, but only because we have hours to spare and I'm bored."

"Says the assassin," Micah muttered from behind his plac.

"You say *assassin* like that's a bad thing," Gemma snickered with a pang of guilt. "Anyway, tell me, Cahleen, are we set for tonight? Are the holding cells equipped and secure?"

"I'm waiting for Micah to finish connecting the last of the security cameras, but otherwise, yes. We're prepared for our guests."

Micah swiped the sweat collecting under the brim of his cap. His reddish-blond hair looked dark and wet. With an exaggerated sigh, he assured them both that he'd finished connecting the feed from the cameras to his plac last night.

"I also received a communication from our inside guy on the *Tarais*, which is currently in orbit, cloaked from the human satellites. He's secured us the same spare quarters for the journey home. All glass surfaces have been rerouted to avoid any live recordings. If anyone tries to view activity logs from our quarters, they'll see video logs from the adjacent empty suite."

"Excellent!" Gemma cheered. "See, now we have plenty of time to spy on that treacherous little Spiaire before tonight."

With one hand, Cahleen ran her fingers through her overgrown pixie haircut and asked, "Have you heard from Quaid? Because, you know," she said and picked up the smartphone, "he's out to get you, and if that brute got word about this little deviation, he'd surely use it to convince Biryn you're a liability—that all three of us are *liabilities*."

That was the last thing Gemma wanted to do—bring unwanted attention from Quaid to either Cahleen or Micah. Regardless of how much Micah annoyed her, she wouldn't want Quaid punishing him because of her curiosity.

"We don't tell that gróntah a thing. Whatever we discover," Micah stated in a tone Gemma appreciated. "I don't care if he is one of the Athru leaders."

"Agreed, and besides, I spoke with the Beast yesterday," Gemma said while briefly looking up at the sky. "I think he's bored. He's been calling and checking in with me a lot more over the past week. I got the impression he might have killed his Spiaire."

Though, I pray to Isoldesse that Seph isn't dead. We might not have been close friends or always agreed on Spiaire tactics, but he doesn't deserve to die here so far from home.

"What do you mean *killed*?" Micah held his finger over the top right corner of his plac for a few seconds. The solid surface of the black glass morphed into a flexible silicone material, allowing him to roll up the device. He secured the plac, then dragged one finger along the rolled seam, locking it into place. "Anora specifically said no killing. We're under orders not to draw any unnecessary attention from the humans." Micah's gaze shifted to Cahleen.

"I wasn't planning on killing anyone!" Cahleen exclaimed and stabbed a second dagger, one with a straight blade and hollowed-out center, hard into the teak tabletop. "Not yet at least."

"Micah, when does the Beast ever follow anyone else's orders? He's an animal." Wanting to change the subject, Gemma asked Cahleen, "What's the status of the Spiaire?"

Cahleen glanced at the open GPS map and said, "Looks like she's shopping," before passing the phone to Gemma.

An idea formed. Gemma tapped the edge of the phone against her chin. "You know…"

Cahleen leaned forward and rested her elbows on her knees, her blue contacts concealing her orange irises. "Ah-ha, I'm listening."

"We need a backup plan. I'll head over to the outlets and do some last-minute shopping with Xander," she said while texting, "while you run out and invite one… or both… I don't care… of the two mystery humans our Spiaire keeps meeting with to come over for a chat. They're not part of her subject group, we know that, so maybe one of them can explain what's going on and how they know each other. I'm sure we have a few extra holding cells you can throw them in until it's time to leave tomorrow, yes?"

Cahleen confirmed they had two extra holding cells. "I can check the cameras before I leave."

"The cameras are fine," Micah grumbled.

"Good." The phone vibrated in Gemma's hand. "Oh, for the love of… It's Xander. He'll be here in ten minutes." Gemma tossed the phone onto the table and cursed.

"Be nice," Cahleen forewarned her sister. "We need him."

Without saying a word, Micah retreated inside. Cahleen also stood, collected her sharp toys, and reminded Gemma to put her contacts in before Xander got there.

"Ugh, another thing I loathe about this planet. That I have to *hide* my beautiful eyes!" she dramatically shouted as Cahleen walked away toward the house.

Before heading inside, Gemma returned to the end of the deck and stared out at the ocean. Their childhood home was by the ocean on Sendara. She closed her eyes and took in the sounds of the waves rolling in. She longed to visit her parents' home, but even more she longed to prove herself to Isoldesse. She was hours away from discovering why Darci was going against protocol and meeting with two humans outside her Spiaire subject group.

Gemma wanted answers, and if there was anything she excelled at, it was figuring out how to get the things she wanted.

5

G emma unhooked the blouse from the store rack and pretended to admire the design while keeping a careful watch out the storefront window. Over the past two hours, she'd trailed behind Darci and her three assigned humans at the outlets.

"Linc," Gemma whispered, "any new communications from Anora?"

"*None,*" her Linc replied, "*but you should know I have detected an active search query within the Sendara Network seeking your location.*"

Interesting.

"And?"

The artificial voice explained, "*The request is a low-level priority. Plus, our connection to the main network spreads thinner the farther we're away from Sendara space, which is why I believe our location has yet to be detected.*"

"Who initiated the search?"

"*Leadess Ganecht of the moon colony on Priomh.*"

Breyah.

"And what happens when we get closer to Sendara space?" Gemma asked while pretending to browse shirts hanging against the wall in the front corner of the shop.

"Our signal will return to one hundred percent."

"And how long until my location is reported?" Gemma whispered, her fingers clenching the hanger beneath the shirt.

"Twenty-eight hours."

Shit. Less than one day.

"Once the search query has pinned your location, the initiator of the search application, Leadess Ganecht, along with the Rhaltan Enforcers, will be immediately notified."

Gemma yanked the shirt from the hanger and twisted it as if to suffocate the life out of it.

Breyah I can handle. Drawing the attention of Rhaltan Enforcers wouldn't go over well with the Athru leaders. Not after years of planning and patiently waiting for the right Aevo Compendium to sabotage.

"There is something else you should be aware of," the organic voice continued in her soft, informative tone. *"Anyone with a plac who happens to monitor search queries could..."*

Gemma only partially heard what her interneural assistant had said because about halfway into Linc's advisory, a hand cupped her shoulder and sent her nerves into a tizzy. She shrieked and yelled at the man behind her. "Damn it, Xander! You scared me!"

"Sorry, babe. Didn't mean to startle you." He flashed his signature cocky smile and pointed to the dark sunglasses perched at the end of his tan nose. "What do you think of these?"

Her feelings for him over these past months had teetered between annoyance and amusement. There were brief moments she found his company entertaining, like spending time with a pet, but they were often short-lived.

Xander pivoted in his white canvas sneakers and returned to posing in the mirror. "I mean, I don't *need* another pair, but you can never have too many sunglasses, right, babe?"

Humans and their incessant need for more.

Oblivious to her stern look, he lifted the frames and winked at her. He seemed pleased that she was finally giving him some attention. Not that he wasn't a good-looking man, because he was attractive. She appreciated his height and toned muscles, common features in most Sendarian men. But unlike the men she was used to courting back home, Xander had a puppy-dog disposition that oddly appealed to her. The power she held over him, and how easily he submitted to her, excited her in a way she hadn't felt before. She often contemplated keeping him—as a pet, of course—after the Athru were done with him.

She plastered on her best fake smile and beckoned him with one slender finger. Continuing her role of doting girlfriend, she batted her eyes and tugged at the collar of his navy-blue polo shirt. Their proximity was closer than she liked, but she needed some time alone and flirting was her best weapon. "Could you be a dear and get us some iced lattes?"

He placed the sunglasses on a pile of folded shorts and nodded. "Iced lattes do sound good." He wrapped his arms around Gemma, pulling her in even closer. "How can I say no to those big, sexy green eyes?" He leaned in to kiss her, but she raised a finger to block his lips.

"I'll wait here until you get back with those refreshing lattes, okay?"

But Xander didn't budge. Instead, he frowned and stared at her. Slightly amused, she rolled her eyes and turned her cheek out. "Okay, fine."

Instantly, the gloom on his face shifted into a wide grin. He nuzzled his lips against her cheek and between pecks, he whispered, "*Ti amo.*"

Oh goddess, he's speaking Italian again.

"*Would you like me to translate?*" Linc's voice cut through her thoughts.

She cleared her throat and discreetly made an *uh-uh* sound.

"*Understood,*" Linc complied.

"All right, all right. That's enough." She giggled and stretched her arms out, pushing him away. "Lattes!"

Xander started for the door but rushed back for one last kiss. "Sorry, couldn't help myself. Be right back, babe."

A heat she hadn't felt for some time flushed through her. *Idiot. He's a puppet—that's it!*

Once Xander was out of sight, Gemma stopped browsing and surveyed outside through the front store window. No sign of the Spiaire or her assigned human subjects.

Whatever that phony taut Darci was up to, she'd figure it out one way or another.

Darci will be banished, like our beloved prince. But before that happens, I need to know what she's up to.

The queen had ruled that interacting with alien species outside their Aevo Compendium subjects was forbidden. Going against her word wouldn't result in just a slap on the hand, but banishment from Sendara and Priomh. Which was exactly what the queen had done when her only son fell in love with a human during the last Earth Aevo Compendium assessment fifty years ago. Gemma didn't know the prince personally but knew of his reputation. He was kind, open minded, and approachable. The complete opposite of his mother. Under the prince's rule, Gemma could imagine the Sendarians evolving and possibly the planet's resources being opened up for more opportunities. Nothing like in the days before Isoldesse, but enough to allow Sendarians the opportunity for personal growth without restrictions. To have a fraction of the luxuries found here on Earth would be better than what was allowed on Sendara now.

When Isoldesse returned, and she did promise in the Anumen Doctrine that one day she would return, she'd be proud of their independence and prosperity without draining or killing the planet.

Why shouldn't the Sendarians be allowed to evolve too? To take what works and make it better. Isoldesse will bless those in the Athru for removing the Elemental Council and that taut of a queen. The suppression over Sendara is coming to an end.

The moment Gemma decided that this shopping trip was a waste of time, her cell phone rang from inside her purse. The gold chains of her designer handbag jangled as she set it down on the display table. She dug out the cell phone Micah had given her and saw Quaid's nickname, the Beast, lit up across the screen. Not in the mood to speak with the brute, she let the call go to voicemail.

But he didn't leave a message. A few seconds later, she received a text instructing her to call him. That was when she also noticed a new text from Cahleen letting her know she'd secured one of Darci's mystery humans and wanted to know what she should do next.

"Well, that's good news."

She considered waiting to call Quaid but decided to get it over with. She pressed the Call icon and held the phone to her ear. When Quaid answered, Gemma bluntly asked, "What do you want?"

His voice was low and throaty. "Beannaith, Gemma."

She pictured the Beast on the other end. A brawny man of almost seven feet, with broad shoulders and the strength of twenty Sendarian men. But it wasn't his towering appearance that she feared. No, it was the unnatural malevolence that swelled in his essence. His brutality and selfishness disturbed her. He was always preaching to anyone who would listen about how he'd been chosen to save Sendara through the Athru by any means necessary, that his strength, endurance, and determination would prevail, but all Gemma saw was arrogance, hostility, and a need for destruction.

Only a few months before this Earth mission, Anora had approached Gemma and confided her growing concerns about Quaid to her. Gemma and Cahleen offered to go to Earth to help execute phase one, but also to keep an eye on the Beast. Something Gemma was beginning to regret.

Gemma glanced out the storefront window and snapped, "Don't *Beannaith* me. What do you want, Quaid?"

"Watch your tone," he growled. "I'm wondering if you've heard from Sabine?"

How did this gróntah ever become one of the leaders of the Athru?

She reeled in her anger but calmly replied, "I have. I've arranged a private plane from a small airport outside of Boston to fly her and her companion down here once they've captured the Spiaire up north and their human mark. But I haven't heard from Abastian out in the California region in weeks. What about you? Have you spoken to him recently?"

Quaid grumbled into the speaker. Chills ran down Gemma's spine. Even through the phone, the man disturbed her. His raspy breathing filled the silence over the line until he finally said, "Don't worry about Abastian. I'm asking about Sabine and—and why you haven't checked in with me today. Makes me wonder—"

"Wonder what?"

His voice—no, everything about that gróntah—made her blood boil. But she'd made a promise to Anora that she intended to keep.

"You're questioning my loyalty? Why? Because I didn't call you the second I rolled out of bed this morning?" she scoffed into the phone. "I don't have time for your pointless inquisitions." It probably wasn't the smartest idea to cop an attitude with a man who could snap her neck faster than she could sneeze. But she knew her confidence was the only thing going for her when it came to Quaid.

Feeling as though she had the upper hand, she pushed her luck a bit further. "And what have you been doing these past few weeks? Because I can't recall the last time you mentioned your Spiaire. How is Seph doing?"

A low chuckle echoed over the line. "Clever, clever. But fortunately, I do not answer to little bugs." He then stressed a venomous reminder to her—"You answer to me. You obey me."

For a moment, Gemma was relieved that he was hundreds of miles away in the Midwest of this land, because taunting him for information wasn't going in her favor like she'd hoped. "Quaid, I don't have time for your shit," she snapped and disconnected the call. Consequences be damned.

Her hands trembled, and for a second, she thought she might throw up in the store's corner. But then her phone vibrated in her shaking hand. It was another text from Cahleen:

You're coming home, yes? Or should I begin questioning the woman?

Gemma took a breath and welcomed the distraction.

Wait for me. On my way now.

She hit the Send button just as she spotted Xander walking toward the store. The need to regain a sense of power coursed through her veins. Lucky for her, a remedy was coming straight to her, flashing his clueless smile and carrying two large iced lattes.

6

"**H**ey, Mom. Before you ask—yes, I'm fine. I'm out shopping with Kenna, Darci, and Ally." Meegan tapped Kenna on the shoulder and gestured toward the front doors of the store. The eye roll Kenna responded with made Meegan smile.

Everyone knew how overdramatic and overprotective her mother was, but to be fair, they didn't know the truth about why.

"Fawness, sweetie, I received a call from your aunt." She spoke the word *aunt* with her usual hint of you-know-who-I'm-talking-about tone.

The dramatic change in temperature didn't faze Meegan the moment she stepped outside the air-conditioned store and into the sauna of heat outside. Her sole focus was to make this a quick and painless phone call.

"She called to check on us," her mom continued. "She—well, I guess she sensed a powerful amula in this area this morning."

"There's no way Aunt Bea sensed an amula all the way from North Carolina. Come on, Mom."

"Aunt Bea is never wrong—never! Now tell me, you didn't see or sense anything recently, did you?" Before Meegan could answer, her mom blurted, "Never mind. It doesn't matter. I want you to come home. We don't need that kind of atten—"

"Mom! Relax. Nothing's happened." Meegan spit out the words before her mind had finished debating whether to tell the truth or not. "And please, stop calling me Fawness. It was cute when I was a kid and before you allowed me to have friends."

"It's not a pet name, Meegan. It's your title and you need to accept— Oh, you did it again! You changed the subject! I hate when you do that."

Meegan's so-called Aunt Bea rarely called with premonitions anymore, and when she did it usually sent Meegan's mother into a state of emergency for weeks. The stories her parents would tell her about powerful Anumen women were just that—stories. The few memories she had of her home world were vague flashbacks from a youthen's perspective.

"Mom, seriously. I didn't see or feel anything," she lied. Telling her mom about Kenna and the arcstone would only do more harm than good right now. *Harm* meaning she'd be forced to move three states up to Aunt Bea's house without a goodbye or explanation to her friends. No. Meegan needed to figure out what the hell was going on without her parents' interference.

Her mother stuttered a few words, attempting to convince Meegan to come home. "You can hang out with your friends tomorrow, I promise."

"Actually, I'm staying..." Her voice trailed off mid-sentence when she noticed Xander walking four stores down in her direction. *What the hell is that douchebag doing here?*

"You are most definitely not staying at your friend's tonight."

Meegan sidestepped and hid behind the outlet directory board. She snuck a quick peek to see if he was looking her way. He wasn't.

"Mom, I've got to go."

"You're coming home!"

Meegan turned and pressed her back to the plexiglass. She stared at her mother's old enchanted mood ring. The one thing her mother forced her to wear.

She means well, she reminded her flustered nerves.

"Mom, I love you, but I'm staying at Kenna and Ally's tonight whether you like it or not." Before her mother could throw a hissy fit, she quickly added, "You've already forced me to break up with my boyfriend, which was unnecessary, stupid, and heartbreaking. I won't let you keep me from my friends too!"

Meegan tried to lower her voice, but anytime she thought of Nick, her anger fumed. She'd broken Nick's heart and felt horrible doing so. It had been her parents who saw an opportunity when he'd been accepted into a competitive pharmacy program up in the New England area. They insisted it was time to sever ties with the human boy. Meegan eventually gave in to their pressure and broke up with him.

"Meegan, no! I want you to come home."

"And I said I was staying at Kenna's place tonight. End of discussion."

Her mother didn't say another word. A tiny feeling of guilt butted heads with the frustration boiling over inside Meegan. She knew her mother was only trying to protect her, but it was too much of a risk to leave Kenna alone. So, for now, she needed to stay close to Kenna and find out more about the arcstone's origins. Hopefully, the arcstone wouldn't draw the attention of the one thing that her parents were trying to protect her from—the Obard.

7

After the call with Quaid and the disappointment of wasting her time spying on Darci, all Gemma wanted to do was go home. She tossed her cell into her purse, slung the leather straps of her purse over her shoulder, and hurried out of the store. The moment she stepped outside, a wall of humidity engulfed her. Beads of warm sweat formed beneath her silk tank top and trickled down her skin.

A few feet away, Xander held up her iced latte and said, "I made sure they didn't fill the cup with too much ice. I know how much you hate that."

In a rush, she took the latte and sucked the cold beverage up through the straw. At that moment, all that mattered was the taste of caramel mixed with chilled coffee and how it coated her throat and cooled her stomach.

"I guess I should've gotten you a Venti." Xander cupped his hand over his dark brown eyes, scanned the row of stores, and asked, "Which store now, babe?"

It was hard to release the straw, but she did. "Thank you." The sincerity behind her words felt odd, but nonetheless, she appreciated his kindness. "Now, let's get out of here. My head is pounding from this heat."

Xander's face lit up, and he rambled off options for what they could do next. Gemma only heard the first suggestion, something about swimming, before she remembered Darci. She glanced over her shoulder and searched the walkway. It took less than a second to recognize the two humans gawking at her. They were from Darci's assigned group. But no sign of Darci.

Are they— Oh, Isoldesse, they are pointing that cell phone at us!

A tall brown-skinned woman held her phone out in Gemma and Xander's direction, as though she was recording or taking pictures of them. Next to her stood a shorter young woman with a light-olive complexion and long black hair draped over one shoulder. The shorter woman had her arms crossed and a vexed stare directed at Gemma.

"Shit!" Gemma blurted out and shielded her face. She touched her temples and realized she'd forgotten to put her sunglasses on. "No, no, no! Where are my glasses?"

Her stomach dropped, and she begged Isoldesse for help in settling her nerves and keeping the latte from coming back up. She spun on the balls of her feet and shoved the plastic cup into Xander's chest. "Hold this!" she barked, and then frantically searched for her sunglasses in her oversized purse.

"What? What's wrong? It's this heat, isn't it? You're not going to pass out, are you? Oh God, please don't pass out!" He circled Gemma with his arms stretched out wide, ready to catch her if needed.

After sliding on her sunglasses, she yelled, "Just go! Get the car! I'll be right behind you. You can pick me up by the curb."

This was because of Xander. She needed to get *him* out of here. She'd been so concerned about Darci possibly recognizing her that she'd forgotten about the humans and their connection to Xander. It was him they were taking pictures of.

Xander reached in for a hug, which was the absolute last thing Gemma wanted. She shoved his arms away, on the verge of losing it, and snapped, "Xander! Go. Get. The car!"

She glanced to see if they were still there, and they were. They'd put the phone away, but they were still standing there, talking and pointing at Xander. When they took a few steps in her and Xander's direction, Gemma swore her heart was halfway up her throat.

Oh, you've got to be kidding me!

"Why are you still standing here? Go get the car, Xander!"

He recoiled, and she watched the soft features of his face tighten. He pursed his lips and readjusted his stance. She needed to act fast before those two stupid humans got closer and confronted Xander about his previous relationship—the one Gemma had intentionally severed. She'd come too far in this mission to lose Xander.

She swallowed her pride and frustration and tried again, but this time with sincerity. "Please, Xander. My head is killing me."

The muscles in his face relaxed. Her apologetic tone worked. "Meet me by the curb in two minutes." He obviously didn't care about the sweat along her hairline when he leaned in and kissed her forehead before jogging off to fetch the car.

Gemma retrieved her phone and pretended to be on a call. She then casually followed Xander to the parking lot. It wasn't until there was enough distance between her and the two girls that she picked up her pace and texted Cahleen:

> Messed up. Darci's humans spotted Xander and took pictures of us. Spiaire timetable possibly affected.

Within seconds, Cahleen responded:

> I'll handle. Come home.

When Gemma emerged from within the alley of stores and reached the parking lot, Xander was approaching the curb. She clutched her phone and stepped out in front of the two-door Audi convertible. The top to the convertible was up, but Xander had his window down. He slammed on the brakes and yelled, "Whoa, babe! I almost hit you!"

She rushed over to the passenger side, opened the door, and hopped in. "Go now!"

"Your head's not getting any better?"

"What?" she snarled at him. "My head?" She blinked several times while staring past him. The last thing she needed was for her pursuers to round the corner and start hollering for Xander. "Oh yes, my head. Thank you for getting the car so fast." She cringed for effect. "Now, please, let's go."

Xander talked the entire drive to Gemma's house while she sat in silence and cursed herself for her stupidity. When they arrived at her house, he put the car in park, unbuckled, and continued to jabber on. Gemma contained her frustration and begged him to stop. She didn't want to say or do something that she'd have to mend later. Cahleen was right. He had a role to play, and they would need him for later... for phase two of Anora's plan to take down the Queen of Sendara.

"Sorry, babe. Let me get you inside and I can—"

"Stop!" she blurted, cutting him off. *Breathe—be nice.* Calmer, she continued, "I need some time to rest, so no more today. But I want to see you tomorrow. Can we meet up for lunch? Say one-ish?"

He closed his mouth and nodded in defeat. "Fine, tomorrow at one."

He leaned in and kissed her cheek. Still in shock, and unraveled from the scene at the outlets, she didn't contest his advances. She thanked him for taking her shopping, even though she'd come back empty handed, and climbed out of the convertible. Her sandals slapped against the stone pavers and up the wooden steps of the front porch. Once inside, she yelled for her brother. When he didn't respond, she repeatedly hollered his name until he appeared in the entryway.

"I'm right here, Gemma. You can stop yelling now." He must have noticed the tenseness in her eyes and the death grip she had on her purse, because he lowered his plac, stepped closer, and asked, "What happened?"

The bloodcurdling scream that erupted from deep inside Gemma echoed throughout the house. It had been years since she'd felt so infuriated—so defeated and careless.

She pushed past her brother and sat at one of the counter stools in the kitchen. With her forehead resting on the cool granite, she grumbled, "Disaster! Complete disaster."

Micah retrieved a bottle of water from the fridge and handed it to her. He set his plac next to her and turned it so she could see the screen. With her head still on the counter, she glanced at the message isolated in the center of the plac screen. It showed Breyah's search query.

Oh, you've gotta be shitting me!

She sat up on the stool, her gaze fixed to the device. "Advice?" she asked with dual intentions.

"Advice?" Micah asked. "More like, explain?"

But it was the second reply, from her Linc, that interested Gemma. *"Be honest with him. Anora never disclosed why she kept your Linc connection active. Do you trust Anora over your own blood?"*

Gemma inhaled a deep breath and as she exhaled, she said, "No."

"No—what? No, you won't explain?" Micah jabbed his finger on the screen. "Gemma, there's a search query pursuing your location! This is serious. It could lead Rhaltan Enforcers straight to us!" He stared at her blank expression for a few moments until his shoulders dropped and he sighed. "You weren't talking to me, were you?"

The moment of truth, regardless of what Anora had asked. Exhaustion overwhelmed her muscles and with one nod, she confirmed what Micah had pieced together.

"How long?"

"Since Priomh. It was never deactivated. Anora asked me to keep my Linc active but in secrecy."

Micah narrowed his eyes and picked up his plac. "Not even us? Gemma, I could've helped."

The constant bickering between the two of them seemed to fade out of existence. "I wanted to, truly I did. You know I trust you and Cahleen with my life, but I also needed to keep Anora's trust."

Micah chewed on the inside of his cheek, a habit he did when he needed to process a situation. After a deep breath he stated, "Going forward, I don't care who you promise secrets to, you share with Cahleen and me."

Gemma agreed. He redirected his attention to his plac. His fingers swiped and tapped at the screen. When he finished, he pressed and held the side button until the hard glass softened to a flexible material. He rolled up the device and then dragged his finger along the seam, locking it into place.

"I added a few anonymous sightings that will redirect your search query to the South Sendara region. The royal family has no rule there and the southern clans have illegal tech that prevents surveillance and interference from the Sendara Network."

A gasp escaped Gemma's lips as she comprehended what Micah had done. He'd bought her extra time. "Thank you."

"So, they spotted you, huh? I can see how that could cause a problem," Micah said, changing the conversation to the previous issue at hand. "That explains why Cahleen left in a hurry."

"I should've gone alone, and I shouldn't have brought *him* with me."

Oh, I could wring that stupid human boy's neck right now!

But then Xander's words, *Ti amo*, repeated in her mind.

"Gemma, just remember," Micah leaned on the counter and reassured her, "these sacrifices we're all bearing while on Earth will be worth it. When the Athru succeed, Sendara will be a better world." He eyed the wall clock. "Hopefully, Cahleen won't run into any problems."

A wide, confident smile spread across Gemma's face. She patted her brother's forearm and said, "That's the one thing we don't have to worry about. Cahleen never disappoints."

8

K enna waited off to the side, picking through the clearance section while Darci paid for her overflowing shopping basket filled with scented lotions, soaps, and candles. Gifts, Kenna considered, or Darci seriously liked this store.

"Kenna!"

From the front of the store, Meegan and Ally raced between display tables, almost knocking over a tower of candles. As her best friend and roommate approached, their voices competed over one another about whatever they'd seen outside.

"Whoa—whoa! What's going on?"

"Xander!" they said in unison.

"What about Xander?" Darci asked, joining their circle.

"He's here—or he was here," Ally explained. "I think he and his new girlfriend left the outlets after spotting us watching them." She waved her cell phone and continued, "I got a few pictures before my phone died." She shrugged and added, "I guess I forgot to charge it last night."

Meegan jumped in and added, "I saw him while I was outside talking to my mom."

"Oh boy." Kenna cringed. "That must've been an interesting conversation. You'll have to tell me about that later." A small smirk spread across Meegan's face. Never a committed *yes* or *no* when it came to her best friend opening up.

"Meegan was right," Ally said, and then cursed. "He did leave my sister for some fancy supermodel-looking chick! What an asshole."

"God, I hate him!" Kenna released a frustrated groan while pushing open the double doors, exiting the store. "He's such an arrogant, self-serving douche!"

"No one's arguing with that," Darci whispered and then turned to Ally. "After your phone charges for a bit, I want to see what this lady looks like. She can't be that pretty."

"She is. Picture a twenty-something-year-old straight off the cover of *Vogue*. Young yet sophisticated," Meegan attempted to explain. "But then again, she could be older and just look young."

They continued bashing Xander and his new girlfriend all the way to the parking lot. After they lined up all their shopping bags in the rear cargo area of Ally's SUV, they climbed in and headed home.

"Don't forget to plug your phone in," Kenna said from the back seat.

At a stoplight, Ally looped her brown spirals into a low ponytail with a scrunchie before plugging her phone into the charger cable. "Almost forgot, thanks!"

Darci's phone rang from inside her canvas bag. Both thumbs went to work rapidly typing text after text. Kenna quickly lost interest in watching Darci's impressive texting skills and rolled down her window. She took off her glasses and let the cool evening air rush against her face.

The combination of the wind on her face, the low music, and the lull of the road beneath the tires soothed Kenna into a relaxed trance. Behind closed lids, her mind swarmed with thoughts of term papers, upcoming finals, her two evening shifts at the museum gift shop later this week, and Arcturus. Where the hell had that star gone last night? She knew exactly where to look, but yet it wasn't there. She made a mental note to pop up on the roof later and look for that darn star before bed.

Her thoughts shifted, and she pictured the old woman from earlier. Had it been a dream... a mental breakdown... or had she just passed out from exhaustion and imagined the whole thing?

If it had been a dream, it'd been the most realistic dream she'd ever had. She recalled the soft glow that surrounded the mysterious, elegant woman. She also couldn't stop thinking about how the woman had said Kenna's "essence," whatever that meant, was forming a bond.

What the hell was that crazy old woman talking about? A bond? A bond with what? Ugh... I hate not knowing what's going on.

Kenna pulled out the yellow crystal from under her T-shirt. The surface felt warm as she rolled it between her fingers, as though it had been left out in the sun for too long. Something she hadn't noticed earlier.

A foot jabbed into Kenna's calf. "Hey, do you mind if I crash at your place tonight?"

Meegan's voice cut through her concentration, and the warmth of the crystal faded as if it never happened. As if, like everything else that happened to her today, it'd been all in her head.

Maybe I am imagining things.

"So?"

"Yeah, of course," Kenna said and put her glasses back on. "Actually, I already assumed you were sleeping over."

"Why's that?"

"I saw you outside the store talking to your mom. You had your scowly-face on. I've known you long enough to know when you need a break from your mom."

Meegan adjusted herself in her seat and sighed. "Yeah. Well, it's complicated—she's complicated."

Mrs. Prinor's paranoia was something Kenna would probably never understand, and she wasn't exactly sure she wanted to. Either the woman had watched one too many mystery thrillers in which some poor girl gets kidnapped and killed, or she'd had some personal traumatic experience that scared her and left her overly paranoid about who her daughter hung out with. Whatever the reason, over the years Kenna had gotten used to Mrs. Prinor's side glances and suspicious stares.

From the front, Ally squealed and turned the music up. "Oh, I love this song!"

The moment Kenna heard Tom Walker's "Just You and I," she tensed. This was the song Nick sang to Meegan the last time they'd pulled out the karaoke machine at Nick's house, and by the tears welling in Meegan's eyes, she must've remembered it too.

Kenna leaned forward and tapped on Ally's shoulder. "Hey, can you turn the music down?" Ally did, but only a little. Since Meegan's mood was already somber, Kenna nudged her and asked, "So, have you heard from Nick?"

With a slight shake of her head, Meegan said, "We agreed not to contact one another. It's for the best."

"Well, I think that's bullshit!" Kenna snapped. Ally glared through the rearview mirror, and Kenna retracted her confrontational tone. "Sorry. I'm just still in shock about you two."

"I don't want to talk about it, Kenna. Nick and I aren't together anymore and there's nothing more to say."

It was hard to read her friend. If Meeg was holding back tears, and was this upset, then why the hell had she broken up with him in the first place? He'd always said he planned to move back after his residency was over. So, what the hell happened?

Meegan pulled out her phone and began to scroll through Netflix movies. "Hey, you know what we need? One of our movie marathon nights! No books, laptops, or tablets. You pick two, and I'll pick two. I know the perfect sci-fi movie we can watch."

"I guess. I kinda wanted to go up on the roof later, but I can do that tomorrow night." Staying up late the night before school wasn't something she often did, but oddly, she didn't seem as concerned or stressed about class. The load of everything happening in the next few weeks weighed on her, but the overwhelming panic and stress wasn't there. She glanced down at the crystal around her neck. *Maybe this thing does have holistic effects?*

"You guys making plans without me?" Darci chimed in from the front seat.

"Sorry, your invitation got lost in the mail." Kenna laughed and gently nudged Darci's arm from the back. "You up for a movie night?"

"You and your stupid jokes," Darci said with a hint of sarcasm. "Yeah, sure. But I can only stay for one movie. I've got laundry and more packing to do tonight."

"That's right, you're flying out to California tomorrow," Kenna said. "You're not sick of all this traveling or stressed out about finals?"

Darci shook her head. "Nope. But hey, before I forget. Let's meet up at Prue's house tomorrow for a late lunch. My flight doesn't leave until early evening, and it'd be nice to see Prue. I miss her, and I feel like I haven't seen her in weeks. I bet she'd love some company right now."

"I don't know," Ally said, her eyes focused on the road.

Kenna thought about the woman with Xander and how shitty of a situation Prue had been dealt. "I'm not sure she'll be in the get-together mood, especially after Ally tells her what you guys saw earlier at the outlets."

"What!" Ally yelled and glared at Kenna in the rearview mirror. "Why the hell would I tell her? It's over and done. They're broken up!"

"Does she know that? Prue's been wallowing at home for days now, and I think Kenna and Darci are right," Meegan nervously pointed out. "She needs closure, and we should be there for her."

"Well, I think my sister needs some alone time."

"And we disagree," Darci said. "The best thing after a bad breakup is a bottle or two of wine, and some friends to confide in. Sitting home alone and simmering in a depressive state isn't healthy. I read an article—"

Ally shrugged in defeat, cutting Darci off. "Fine! I'll call her later and ask. Just no more talk about whatever you read online, deal?"

Darci smiled, pleased with herself for winning that battle.

Kenna hadn't agreed with the going-over-for-lunch part, only the telling-Prue part, and now she debated on backing out. Her schedule was already busy with attending her morning classes, stopping by her parents' house to say hi, and returning some overdue books at the library. Then she had planned to review her study notes for finals, and she really, *really* wanted to check on that damn star.

The rest of the ride home was quiet, leaving Kenna to her thoughts about her hectic week and how lucky she'd been not to have the boyfriend drama and heartache that her friends had had over these past few weeks. Relationships sucked, and she was in no hurry to find love, which was easier to say since a certain someone didn't live anywhere near her. Maybe Liam going to college in Boston was a bit of a blessing because she couldn't even imagine how she'd find time for a relationship with her crazy schedule.

Darci and Meegan were right. Prue did deserve to know. It wasn't right that they knew the truth about Xander and she didn't. Prue was a good friend, and friends didn't keep secrets. Why would they? What was the point of having people close to you if they weren't honest or there for you when you needed them?

Kenna glanced at her friends in the SUV and a sense of appreciation and happiness filled her, because these girls were some of the closest people she'd known and could always trust.

9

In the driveway, Ally shut the driver-side door and walked to the rear of the SUV while Darci finished her text message to Eryn.

> I think this classifies as an emergency. Seph hasn't checked in for over a week and now Grace out in California isn't responding. But you've got seniority and are the only one permitted to send a Linc communication alert to the Tarais. The Tarais should be in orbit by now. I have to go. I'll call you later tonight.

Per protocol, she deleted the message after sending it. No evidence for the humans to accidentally discover. Darci's knee bounced with nervous energy as she waited in the front seat for Eryn's response. Even if she wanted to bypass Eryn, who was the senior Spiaire on this mission, her Linc wouldn't permit it. Mission protocol was embedded in their Lincs and stated that only the senior reporting Spiaire's Linc had external communication capabilities while off world. All situations were to be reported to Eryn, and she would then determine the next route of action.

Darci's recent trip up north, to visit Eryn in the Boston region, had been a nice break. After six long months, it had been nice to talk face-to-face with another Sendarian. Touring the city was a nice perk too before their departure back to Sendara space.

Tomorrow's the big day. Now I just need to make sure they all show up to Prue's house.

Kenna and Meegan's laughter shook Darci from her thoughts as they got out and followed Ally to the trunk. Darci opened her door to join them when her phone vibrated.

> **Grace and Seph still not answering. I'll send the communication to the Tarais when I get home tonight. Talk more later.**

"Good," she whispered. Again, she deleted the message before tossing the phone into her canvas bag and shutting the SUV door.

One less thing to worry about.

"I don't know about you guys, but I spent way too much money," Kenna noted while sorting through the pile of shopping bags.

"Me too," Darci said and retrieved her bags. She looped her hand through the handles of two large paper shopping bags filled with scented deals from the last store they'd shopped at. It was her last night on Earth, and she wanted to make sure she stocked up on souvenirs and keepsakes for her trip home. Not that there weren't soaps and candles on Sendara, just not the wide variety Earth had. It pleased yet sickened Darci to see the abundance of options humans had. She knew that not all regions of this planet consumed or produced the same product quantities, but she couldn't help but judge the humans for their lack of restraint, especially when it came to needs versus wants. One of many topics she'd researched online during her spare time. Capitalism wasn't always an unfamiliar term on Sendara, but because it'd been banned by Isoldesse over two thousand years ago, it was a thing of the past. Now, Sendarians only produced and consumed what was needed. Not wanted. Of course, there was some flexibility to certain luxuries, but those requests needed to be approved and earned. All a part of the Anumen Doctrine.

"Hey, Meeg, can you grab these brochures for me?" Ally asked and held out a cardboard box.

"Sure." Meegan handed her shopping bags to Kenna and then took the box of brochures.

Darci peeked under the box lid and asked, "Are those your new catering brochures?"

"Yup, and they weren't cheap. Hence me not asking Klutzy over there." She jutted her chin in Kenna's direction. "I can't risk her stumbling over her own feet and dropping them."

Kenna scoffed. "You're hilarious." She turned to Ally and reminded her, "Hey, don't forget your phone. I want to see this redheaded boyfriend-stealer."

"Oh yeah, me too," Darci said while closing the trunk hatch.

Ally hurried to the front seat and grabbed her phone from the center console. "Twenty-two percent!"

"Good enough!" Kenna exclaimed. "All right, now show me this chick."

Ally opened the photo. "Okay. Here she is." She handed her phone to Kenna. "The picture's a bit blurry, but their faces are clear enough."

Meegan started up the deck stairs. "You'll see. She's got that high-maintenance look."

Darci moved closer and looked over Kenna's shoulder. She recognized the guy right away as Prue's ex-boyfriend, but the woman... She looked familiar, but from where? That red hair. Those eyes.

No! There's no way. It can't be her!

Darci's entire body tensed. She slid the twine handles from her shopping bags up her wrist and grabbed the phone from Kenna's hand.

"Hey! I was looking at that!"

Darci muttered, "No, no, no! She can't be here! How is she here?" She stepped away from Kenna with the phone. With two fingers, Darci zoomed in over the woman's face. She'd never met the former Spiaire face-to-face, but she'd idolized her work and studied every one of her Spiaire mission logs. The woman in this picture was definitely Gemma.

"Do you know her?" Kenna asked.

Darci barely registered Kenna's question. Her brain was trying to understand what Gemma was doing on Earth.

How did she get here? Oh, Isoldesse—this can't be happening! I need to do something. I need to call or—or maybe I should send an alert to the Tarais? *No, no. I'm not permitted to do that. I should call Eryn— Oh no! What about Gerard? There's no way she knows about him. I should call Ger—*

"Darci!" Kenna yelled.

Darci flinched and licked her dry lips. How long had she been standing there with her mouth open? "Sorry. Here." She handed the phone to Kenna. Her reaction had drawn Meegan and Ally closer, and now all three of her friends stared and waited for an explanation she couldn't give. With the best smile she could muster, she explained, "Oh, it's nothing. For a second, I thought it was an old friend—but it can't be her. I mean, this girl I know lives nowhere near Florida."

Kenna opened her mouth to say something, but Darci didn't want to get into it, so she blurted out, "You know what?" and tapped her forehead with a light chuckle. "I completely forgot I can't stay."

Kenna narrowed her eyes and asked, "I thought you were going to watch a movie with us?"

"Oh, sorry, I, uh… can't stay. I completely forgot that my friend up in Boston—you know, Eryn—had asked me to call the hotel and car-rental place. You know, to double-check our reservations, and—and well, I think they close in like an hour or something. But hey, I'll see you guys tomorrow, right? Before my flight—at Prue's house for a late lunch, yeah?"

Before anyone could say anything, Darci spun on the toes of her flats and hurried down the gravel driveway, her shopping bags swinging from side to side. With her back to her friends, she hollered, "Great! See you guys tomorrow!" and turned the corner of the multilevel home and disappeared from their view.

10

Darci could barely think straight. Her ballet flats kept slipping along the sidewalk, making it difficult to run. The lot where she'd parked her rental car was only a few more blocks down the road. It had been stupid to park close to the coffee shop and then walk to Kenna and Ally's place. How had she lost sight of the mission and prioritized coffee?

Oh, Isoldesse! That was Gemma! Gemma's here on Earth! How—and why?

"I need to call Gerard—no, not Gerard. Eryn. I need to call Eryn," she said in a panic and slung her canvas purse forward, over her shopping bags. She reached in and rummaged through as she wove between people either walking too slow or standing in the center of the sidewalk, talking and oblivious to the rest of the world.

It was normal for this part of the city, right outside the university campus, to be active in the evening, especially with the beach two streets over. Daylight had dimmed to a soft evening overcast, and more and more Sunday strollers migrated out from their air-conditioned homes, congesting the sidewalks.

Almost there. I can see the side street.

"*Spiaire Darci, your heart rate has increased to concerning levels. I've noted the spike of adrenaline in your mission log.*"

"Great, thanks. How about you patch me through to Eryn?" she muttered while cutting through a group of college girls, but when one of her shopping bags got caught between two of the girls, she jerked to a stop.

Her Linc responded, "*Spiaire Darci, you know communications between Lincs—*"

Turning, Darci tugged her bag free. "Yeah, yeah. Blah-blah. Just shut it—" She stopped when she noticed all five girls were gawking with appalled expressions. "Oh no, no, not you! I'm so sorry!" With an apologetic smile, Darci backed away before spinning and continuing down the sidewalk.

She picked up her pace, ignoring the pain of her scrunched toes against the insides of her flats. One hand dug for her phone in her purse again.

I can't involve Gerard. Not until after I talk with Eryn.

She hurried around a woman walking three dogs.

Maybe I should tell Eryn about my meetings with Gerard?

And past an old couple who were walking arm in arm.

Shit! Where's my phone?

Her fingers finally grazed the smooth screen of her phone at the bottom of her bag.

"Here it is!" Focused on retrieving her phone, she turned her gaze from the sidewalk to the inside of her bag.

What's Eryn going to think when I tell her—

"Ahh!" Darci screamed as she tripped over a guy tying his shoes. One hand caught inside her purse while the other flew straight out in the air. When she hit the ground, her hand skidded along the concrete. The contents of her purse and shopping bags spilled over the sidewalk and along the side of the road.

Besides the ringing in Darci's ears, the world had gone silent. The teenage boy, still kneeling on one knee, leaned toward her. His words were muffled, as if he were talking behind a thick glass wall. She blinked several times before her head cleared and the world refocused.

"Oh my God! Are you all right?" He reached an arm out to help Darci up. "I'm sorry! I should've checked behind me before stopping like that. Really, I'm so, so sorry," he stammered.

She sat dazed. Seagulls soared and cawed from above while cars whizzed by. No one stopped and offered any help. They just gawked and shuffled by. Her attention finally settled on his outstretched hand waiting for her.

"I'm okay," she said.

From deep inside her ear canal, a soft voice confirmed her well-being. "*I detect no permanent damage or the need for immediate medical attention. I've also logged the date and time of the injury on your right hand in your mission log.*"

"Thank you, Linc."

"Come again?"

She smiled at the guy, who appeared to be in his late teens. Most likely new to the university or visiting a sibling. She accepted his hand, and he helped her to her feet. Along the sidewalk, her belongings were scattered everywhere, and she couldn't decide what to do first—help pick up her stuff or grab her phone, which had conveniently fallen out of her purse a few feet from where she stood, and make a run for it.

I need to get to my car. I need to call Eryn.

The young man, who continued to repeatedly apologize, decided for her when he got to his knees and began crawling around and collecting her belongings. He held up a candle in a glass jar and pointed to cracks along the side. "Oh man, this one broke."

"It's fine," she stated while grabbing her phone. "I'm late and I should've been paying attention. This isn't your fault—well, not entirely your fault," she said, and winced at the scrape on her palm starting to bleed. Quickly, she shoved her bleeding hand under her shirt to hide the glittering yellow blood. It wasn't a lot of blood, but enough to see it wasn't red.

With her purse over her shoulder, she picked up one of the large paper bags that hadn't ripped and held it open. The guy carefully placed the broken candle inside while she quickly picked up whatever else was in reach. Everything else was a lost cause.

"Can you clean up the rest for me, please? I'm in a bit of a hurry," she pleaded and then without waiting for his answer, she took off running.

That stuff doesn't matter. What matters is I have my purse and my phone.

Darci rounded the corner of the side street and spotted her blue rental car in the commuter lot across the way. The headlights flashed as she unlocked the vehicle and popped the trunk with the remote. She tossed the shopping bag and her purse inside the trunk and slammed it shut. With her keys and phone, she hurried to the driver-side door.

Not wanting to get into an accident, because the last thing she needed right now was a medical response unit tending to her injuries, she decided to call Eryn now rather than while driving. She opened the car door, leaned against the doorframe, and pressed the power button on her phone. When the screen came to life, she gasped. It was her backup phone. Not the one she used to call Kenna, Meegan, or the other Spiaires.

"No!"

She popped the trunk open again and searched her purse. "Where's my other phone?" She dumped her purse and searched, but no second phone.

With her bottom lip clenched between her teeth, she spun and stared at the main road. "Shit! It must've fallen out." Going back wasn't an option. Her hand was throbbing, and she didn't want to risk someone spotting her yellow blood.

She rested her forehead on the open trunk and pleaded, "Linc, this is serious. Screw protocol. I need you to send a message to Eryn or directly to the *Tarais.*"

"*The* Tarais *has arrived and is cloaked in orbit, preparing the excursion teams for subject tagging. You know protocol states that only Spiaire Eryn is authorized for communications to the* Tarais *prior to tomorrow's transport.*"

"Linc, please! I need to let them know Gemma is here!"

"*My apologies, Spiaire Darci. The protocol program written into my mission commands won't allow me to send any form of communication. Human technology has evolved since their last Aevo Compendium five decades ago, and Priomh's risk assessment team determined the probability of detection was too great.*"

She was left with one option. To dial the one number programmed in her backup phone.

"Fine!"

She selected Gerard's name, the only name listed under contacts, and pressed the phone to her ear. When he didn't answer, she disconnected and tried again. When there was still no answer, she broke protocol again and left a voice message.

"Gerard, please be advised that there is an unauthorized Sendarian, a former Spiaire, here on Earth. You may or may not be familiar with her from your days on Sendara. Gemma of the Vaudd family. I've never met her in person. She's been missing from Priomh for years, but I'm positive it's her. I've seen her public records and recognize her from her profile image. Please be careful. I've lost my primary phone and I'm heading home now to send word to Eryn and the other Spiaires with my plac. It will be an unsanctioned communication, but I need to get word to them. I will call you later tonight with an update. Until then, Beannaith."

Darci had been speaking English for months now, and speaking a single word from her native language felt strange yet comforting. She was excited and sad to leave Earth tomorrow, but it was all part of a Spiaire's job. With how fast the humans were evolving technologically, Breyah was sure to increase Earth's Aevo Compendium from its current fifty-year cycle to something more frequent. Meaning Darci would get to return sooner rather than later.

Some anxious weight had been lifted by the knowledge that she'd called and told at least one person about Gemma being on Earth. Now, on the drive home she could focus on packing and preparing for tomorrow's departure.

She was about to settle into the driver's seat when a slender, muscular arm reached from behind and jerked her back by the neck. Instinctively, Darci dropped the cell and kicked it under the vehicle.

"Stop! What are you doing?" Darci yelled as her hands clawed her attacker's arm, trying to break free. She yelped when a sharp prick stung her neck.

No, this can't be happening. Not today. Not before—

She tried to fight the oncoming blackness that encroached upon her consciousness, but eventually she lost that battle, and her eyes fluttered shut.

11

C ahleen withdrew the needle from Darci's pale, freckled skin. The Spiaire had gone limp against her chest, so she quickly recapped the needle and shoved it into her pocket to get a better grip. No one was in the vicinity, but regardless, Cahleen didn't want to risk being seen. There was barely any hesitation in her movements as she slung Darci over her shoulder and carried her to the SUV parked in the back corner of the commuter lot.

The rear hatch door automatically opened with one foot swipe under the bumper, and she carefully laid the Sendarian in the cargo space before spreading a dark sheet over her. Cahleen closed the hatch door and scanned the parking lot for witnesses before jogging back to the blue car. The mess in the trunk didn't seem to have anything of value. No phones or clues, just clothing, shoes, a broken candle, and random loose junk from Darci's purse.

"Hey," a young man called out from behind Cahleen.

In one swift motion, she turned to face him while reaching for the hidden blade strapped under her shirt. Her hand held steady, wrapped around the hilt, ready to unlatch and use the weapon if needed.

"Hey, did you see a lady with light-red hair and pretty green eyes? She dropped her phone when she tripped over me." The man pivoted and pointed toward the main street. "I wanted to return it."

Cahleen loosened her grip and then reached for the phone. "Oh, you mean Darci. She just ran to the bathroom, but I can give it to her for you."

The man drew out a long breath. "Yeah, uh"—the man's eyes surveyed the open vehicle—"you sure she went to the bathroom?"

Cahleen snatched the phone and raised an eyebrow at the man. "Thanks, I'll make sure she gets this."

When he didn't move, her grin vanished. She matched him in height, but not in build. She eyed his pudgy arms in comparison to her defined muscles and calculated his reaction time if she needed to attack. It was all about who had control and the better advantage, and she knew she had both. In one swift motion, she stepped closer and whipped out the dagger from beneath her shirt.

"Whoa! Okay, we're good." He threw his hands up and took off running.

Once inside the SUV, she set Darci's phone in the cupholder and locked the doors. When she knew she was good and safe, and that the dumbass human hadn't called the cops, she started the engine. But before she shifted into Drive, she sent a quick text to her sister.

Got the Spiaire. I'll be home in twenty.

12

About halfway into their first movie, Ally walked into the living room and started what Kenna liked to call *Ally's evening cool-down routine*. Like clockwork, Ally checked the front-door dead bolt, closed all the curtains and blinds, and then checked the settings on the AC unit.

Kenna paused the movie and asked, "Hey, have you called Prue yet?"

Ally picked up her laptop from the whitewashed coffee table and scowled. "No, Kenna. Not yet." Without another word, she trudged off to her room.

"I'm not trying to piss her off," Kenna said, facing Meegan, who was cuddled up on the opposite end of the couch. "I just think—I mean, wouldn't you want to know? If it was Nick who up and left you without a reason?" The moment the question left her mouth, she realized she probably shouldn't have used Meegan and Nick as an example. Especially since it had been Meegan who ended things with Nick for unknown reasons.

Meegan shrugged and quietly replied, "I guess. But look at it from her shoes. Would you want to be the one who told me?"

"Point taken," Kenna admitted. "But you know I would, right?"

"I would hope so," Meegan said and hugged one of Ally's ruffled baby-blue couch pillows tighter to her chest.

Kenna was about to start the movie but hesitated. She wanted to ask the burning question that had been on her mind since it happened. "So, why did you?"

An awkward silence lingered between them. Something Kenna wasn't used to when talking with her best friend. They'd always told each other everything. She took Meegan's silence as trying to find the right words to explain, and in the meantime, Kenna mentally prepared her rebuttal.

Instead, Meegan asked, "Do you have any ideas about who sent you that stone necklace?"

The unexpected question derailed Kenna's question about Nick. It did, however, remind her about another concerning issue she'd pinned to an imaginary corkboard set in the back of her mind. She looped her finger through the chain, drawing out the yellow crystal from beneath her T-shirt. "I don't have a clue. It's pretty, but not something I'd normally wear."

"I like it." Meegan eyed the stone.

Kenna carefully took the necklace off and placed it on the coffee table. "I would've taken it off earlier, after we got home, but I got distracted by whatever that was with Darci. I can't stop wondering why she freaked out after seeing the picture of Xander and that woman."

"That was odd," Meegan agreed. "It's probably nothing. Don't put too much thought into what Darci does. You know how she can be."

"Yeah, maybe." She couldn't help but make a mental list of all the weird stuff Darci had done, especially when they first started hanging out this semester. Like Darci trying to wash her own dishes at restaurants, or her obsession with the internet—always reading weird articles on her phone or downloading the strangest books. Her oddities hadn't been as bad in the past couple of months, but there was this one thing she'd done last week while they were out for a walk. Darci had been complaining she was hungry and without telling anyone, she walked up to the nearest home, rang their doorbell, and asked them for food. As if it were no big deal.

But she's never lied to us. Well, I don't think she has. I swear she knows that woman. And if she knows that woman, then she may know more about what happened between Xander and Prue. But why wouldn't she—

"Hey, stop overthinking it," Meegan said, cutting into Kenna's thoughts. "We can ask Darci what the heck all that was tomorrow at Prue's house."

"Yeah, I guess. It's just, I hate being left in the dark or lied to."

Meegan readjusted her legs on the sofa and sucked on her bottom lip. "About that," she said. "There's something we need to talk about."

"It's about Nick, isn't it?" Kenna shifted in her seat, eager to hear the truth about what happened with their relationship, but then she remembered something and the second Meegan opened her mouth to speak, Kenna held up her hand and abruptly said, "Wait! Before you say anything, I've got to tell you something about Nick before it slips my mind again. I completely forgot to tell you this morning."

"You weren't yourself this morning. Exhaustion will do that to a person. I'm surprised you didn't pass out sooner while we were sitting in the kitchen."

Kenna glanced at the necklace on the coffee table. There was something about that stupid crystal that affected her. But she wasn't ready to say the word *magical* out loud. But then again, who was she to say magic didn't exist?

Oh, who am I kidding? Magic's not real. Someone's messing with me.

"Hey." Meegan slapped Kenna's leg. "Did you hear what I said?"

"Oh, sorry. Daydreaming."

"I can see that. Now, what do you have to tell me about Nick?"

Kenna draped her mahogany-brown hair over her shoulder and started braiding it. "I only found out yesterday, and I didn't think it was relevant since you two aren't together anymore—and no, it's not an emergency. He's fine." Meegan stared at Kenna, eyes wide, waiting for her next words. "And I promise you I had no idea my friend was going to do this."

"Your friend? What friend?"

"You know, my friend Liam who lives up in Boston. Well, he's been looking for a roommate and Nick was looking for a place, and I guess—well, I guess he asked Nick to move in with him. And Nick said yes."

"Nick is moving in with Liam? Liam, as in your-childhood-best-friend-from-when-you-lived-out-in-Kansas Liam? But how did he—"

"I might have mentioned that a friend recently moved to the Boston area and needed a place to stay." After a moment, she added, "You know how I feel about Liam. He's a good guy. Trustworthy. It's been nice these past few weeks, talking, or more like texting, with him."

Meegan shifted in her seat and faced the TV. Then, as though the conversation had never happened, she leaned forward and picked up the necklace by its thin silver chain and asked, "Are you sure you've never seen one of these before? The stone, I mean."

Again with changing the conversation. Geesh.

The crystal hung from Meegan's fingers. Kenna was curious to know more about what she had seen earlier, with the mysterious old lady, but not right now. Right now, she wanted to know about Meegan and Nick.

"Don't change the subject."

Meegan got up, walked across the room, and set the pendant necklace on the narrow console table doubling as a TV stand before returning to the couch and asking again, "You sure you've never seen a necklace like that one before?"

"Yes, I'm sure! Did you not hear what I just told you about Nick moving in with Liam? He's not going anywhere, Meeg. You need to call—" A sharp pain pinched in Kenna's gut, and she winced while wrapping one arm around her waist. She brushed it off as hunger and was about to demand an explanation for why Meegan had broken up with Nick when the room began to spin, and her stomach dropped as if she were on a roller coaster.

She scooted to the edge of the sofa, hands out in front of her, and steadied herself. She tried to take deep, controlled breaths, but the intake of air only made things worse. An intense nausea swept over her and caused her to gag.

Meegan reached for Kenna and asked, "Hey, you okay?"

With her hand over her mouth, Kenna shook her head and ran to the bathroom. She flipped up the lid to the toilet seat and threw up. Her fingers gripped the toilet seat and tears streamed down her face as she tried to breathe between heaves. A moment later, Meegan's hand came into view and caught Kenna's glasses before they fell into the toilet. She tried to say thank you but couldn't. She could barely breathe. Her friend brushed her hair to one side and tried to lighten the mood by joking. "I'd ask when your last period was, but—"

When Kenna could finally speak, she grumbled, "You're not funny," while wiping her mouth with the back of her hand.

Meegan put the glasses on the counter and picked up the pendant necklace she'd brought into the bathroom. She draped the chain over her friend's head and said, "In the meantime, keep this thing on until bed or something. Just so you don't lose it."

"Yeah, sure, whatever," Kenna slurred. Her head was still fuzzy and focused on the nasty taste of stomach acid lingering in her mouth. While she searched for some mouthwash from under the sink, she asked, "Where the hell did that come from? I can't even remember the last time I threw up like that."

"I'm guessing it's another side effect from being overworked and over exhausted these past few weeks. You've pushed your body too far this semester, and now you're showing physical symptoms. Like when you passed out earlier."

"I guess," Kenna said and blinked several times. "But damn, if that wasn't the worst pain I've ever felt." With her dinner now flushed, she got to her feet, and to her surprise she felt better. Normal. Unsure of where the pain and sickness had come from, she told Meegan, "I'm good now. Really, I'm fine."

"No, you're not fine, and it wasn't something you ate. Seriously, you need to take it easy. Now, not later. Give that exhausted brain of yours a rest." She stood in the bathroom doorway and suggested, "Let's finish the movie, but then that's it. No more tonight, okay?"

Kenna didn't want to argue with her friend anymore and sighed in agreement. She put her glasses on and took her time brushing her teeth while Meegan went to heat some tea in the kitchen. On her way back to the couch, she noted how nothing hurt anymore, as if the moments in the bathroom were a dream.

She curled up on her end of the couch and made a mental note to find out the real story behind their breakup. It wasn't like Meegan to keep something this big from her, which made her wonder if she'd somehow upset her best friend. She knew she had a habit of acting before thinking, and it wouldn't have been the first time she did or said something without thinking things through. Stupid overactive brain. Upsetting her friends, and not realizing it. Whatever she'd done had Darci feeling as though she needed to lie about possibly knowing that woman, while Meegan still refused to open up about what happened between her and Nick. But why?

Was their friendship drifting apart?

The thought of not having either friend in her life hurt almost as bad as the gut-wrenching pain she'd suffered only five minutes ago in the bathroom. A pain she silently hoped was a fluke and something she'd never have to endure again. Ever, ever again.

13

In the kitchen, Meegan blankly stared at her reflection in the black glass of the microwave hung over the stove while the kettle heated on the front burner below.

Her heart swelled at the thought of Nick living with Liam, because that meant there was still a chance she could be in his life. A friendship was better than nothing. And who knows, maybe her parents would reconsider. Doubtful, but she had to hold on to the hope that it was a possibility.

That was the good news. The not-so-good news was that Kenna was showing signs of the arcstone bonding process taking effect. The incident in the bathroom was a textbook definition of what happened when you separated bonded essences. Pain. Excruciating pain for the essence with the physical form.

Somehow, she'd hoped that maybe Kenna's essence might have been one of the few to reject the bond with an arcstone essence. It was rare, but there were records of such instances. But nope. It seemed Kenna's essence was merging with whoever resided in that stupid stone.

What would my parents do? Think, Meegan—think!

When nothing came to mind—other than calling her aunt up in North Carolina for advice, which was a million times out of the question—she cursed at the Eilimintachs.

A rogue Anumen. It could be someone who hasn't formally announced their presence to my parents. Or worse, it could be someone from another world with an Anumen arcstone. What are the chances of that? The only other race our people have ever encountered, besides humans, were the Obard, and I highly doubt they're gifting arcstones to humans. Those monsters destroyed our world for both the arcstone stones and the transessent stones.

I must've missed something. How did this happen right under my nose? There's no way this is all coincidence. No way. Someone wanted Kenna to have that stone. Which means they must be close. They'd want to know the outcome of the bond.

The kettle whistled, drawing Meegan from her thoughts to the task at hand. She lifted the lid from the ceramic jar where Ally kept her bags of herbal tea and placed one in each mug. She poured the hot water into the mugs and then returned the tea kettle to the stove. With her eyes closed, Meegan held one open palm over each mug and whispered, *"Bach masc et gohaf."*

Gently stir the air.

A slow air current swirled beneath her hands, tickling her skin. She opened her eyes and lowered her hands, directing the funnels of air into the steaming mugs. The pleasant aroma of the herbal tea drifted up into the air and eased Meegan's racing thoughts about what to do next.

Watch Kenna, that's for sure, and pay more attention to who's watching us. They've got to be close. But definitely stay close to Kenna. So long as she stays in contact with the stone, she won't have any more occurrences of pain. By early afternoon tomorrow, the bond should be complete. Twenty-six hours. And that's when I'll tell her. I'll explain who I am, where I'm from, and what the arcstone is. Then she'll be able to tell me who she's been talking to, because whoever's in that stone will communicate with her once the bond has been completed, if they haven't already.

And for both our sakes, I need a name.

14

It was perfect timing when Kenna's phone buzzed between the sofa cushions as the ending credits of their second movie scrolled across the screen. She clicked the power button on the remote and the TV screen went black. She pointed the soft glow from her phone screen at the other end of the couch. Meegan lay curled up, her eyes closed. She never even made it to the end of the first movie.

In her notifications, she saw a message from Liam. Eager to read, she sat up and opened the full message.

> Hey stranger! Sorry for the late hello. My friend Brody came over and helped us move Nick's stuff in today. Nick's a great guy. Funny as hell. He'll fit right in. Anyway, about calling you. I still need to talk to you about something. Is tomorrow night, say 9ish good? Let me know. Night Stargirl.

Kenna contemplated calling Liam now rather than waiting until tomorrow. It was killing her not knowing what he wanted to talk about, but before she could dial his number, Ally's bedroom door creaked open. A tall silhouette stepped out into the living room.

"Hey," Kenna said, and the figure shuddered.

"Jesus, Kenna!" Ally yelped.

Kenna stood, stretched, and leaned against the sofa arm. "Did you call Prue and tell her?"

Ally pointed to the kitchen, and Kenna followed. She drew open one of the window curtains before sliding into one of the wooden chairs, while Ally went straight to the fridge. For a brief moment, the fridge lit up the small kitchen space before her roommate sat across the table with a glass container full of leftover grilled chicken.

The moonlight was enough for her to see Ally picking at the chicken. Her slow movements and silent mood hinted to Kenna that the phone call hadn't gone well.

"I know you were against telling her, but did you?"

Ally glanced up, but her eyes didn't meet Kenna's. Instead, she stared out the window. "It's a nice night for stargazing. Do you remember when you first moved in and I used to go up on the roof with you?"

Those nights seemed like forever ago. She understood why Ally had stopped coming up; Ally needed to focus on her catering business, which meant fewer nights stargazing.

But that wasn't what Kenna wanted to talk about right now. She slapped a hand on the table and firmly asked, "Hey, what happened?"

"Shh! You'll wake Meegan." Ally sighed, then continued, "Anyway, yes. I called Prue. It turns out she didn't even know there was another woman. She suspected, but didn't know for sure, and demanded that I send her the pictures." Ally shook her head. "I knew he was a pompous ass, but not a cheater." She pushed the chicken away and her head dropped to the table. Long brown arms crossed over her head, contrasting against the white tabletop.

As an only child, Kenna had a purely speculative view of siblings and their relationships. Ally and Prue were best friends, business partners, and sisters. Something Kenna would never have. The closest person she had to a sister was Meegan.

"Did you send the pictures?"

Ally shot upright with an exasperated glare. "Of course I did! You know how stubborn my sister is. If I hadn't, she would've driven over here like a madwoman demanding to see them."

"Okay, okay. Sorry." Kenna leaned back in her seat. When Ally stood, Kenna tried to sound more comforting than inquisitive. "Well, now she has closure, and that's a good thing. It means she can move on."

"I guess," Ally muttered and secured the lid on the glass container before returning it to the fridge. "I'm going to bed. See you in the morning."

"Night."

Kenna was about to go to bed when she twisted in the wooden chair and stared out the window behind herself. The starry sky tempted her.

Maybe just for ten or fifteen minutes. I am curious to know where that Arcturus star is.

Kenna unlatched the locks on the kitchen window and then carefully ducked out onto the narrow metal balcony. The night air felt warm against her skin. Especially after being cooped up with the AC unit all evening.

At the top of the ladder, she stepped over the brick ledge and onto the open terrace. Three years ago, when Ally first moved into the apartment, the elderly couple who owned the building gave Ally free range to do whatever she pleased up here, and she took full advantage of their offer. It wasn't a large space. Enough for three or four friends to hang out. Soon after Kenna moved in last year and Ally's schedule got busier with her catering business, the space was mainly used by Kenna for stargazing at night.

Ally had decorated the terrace with a few outdoor rugs and a variety of faux plants. In the center were two red plastic lounge chairs, the expensive kind because Ally never did anything on a budget. Toward the back, against a segment of the ledge that extended up into a quaint brick wall lined with vines, was a cast-iron bistro table with two matching chairs. Behind one chair was an extra-large waterproof plastic storage container.

Over by the ladder, Kenna found their battery-operated lantern. She flipped the switch on, and when nothing happened, she banged the bottom until the lantern flickered to life. With the lantern by her side, she opened the container and began setting up her telescope.

This telescope, a refractor model, had become her backup telescope after her parents upgraded her with a more powerful reflector one last October for her twentieth birthday. That beauty was in her bedroom under the window directly below.

Once she finished setting everything up and locating the spot where Arcturus should be, she switched off the lantern and observed the night sky through the magnifying lens.

"All right, let's see where this giant red star is."

Nothing. She knew exactly where to look, and yet the brightest star in the northern hemisphere was MIA. Though, something blue caught her attention in the area where the star should've been. Quickly, she pulled out a box from inside the storage container and opened it to a selection of eyepieces. She carefully removed the eyepiece from the telescope and inserted one with a longer focal length.

With one eye closed, she lifted her glasses and moved in closer to the telescope. She observed the night sky while still twisting the eyepiece into focus. With a higher magnified view, she could see an area of distorted air, a few hundred yards up from the skyline. Whatever it was, it was blocking her view of Arcturus.

"What is that?" she whispered. In the center of the distorted area was a hazy blue glow, slightly bigger than the stars shining in the background. When she stood upright and looked out into the night sky through her glasses, she could barely see the glint of blue. But it was there. Once again, she lifted her glasses and stared at the anomaly through the telescope. After a few moments, an enormous oblong sphere of semiopaque energy wavered over whatever that blue dot was.

Whoa! What just happened?

A bright filament of blue light stretched across the front of the sphere and then curled back toward the top and bottom, revealing a— *Holy shit, it's a ship!*

The hazy blue glow she'd initially seen was no longer hazy or blue, but now a brighter source of white light on the underside of the ship. Bystanders below could have easily mistaken the object for a helicopter overhead. But what Kenna was seeing wasn't a helicopter. She considered the Air Force base a few miles north, but something in her gut told her this wasn't a government aircraft.

Her attention remained glued to the scene through the telescope. The bulk of the ship, with its sleek black hull, looked like the head of a torpedo, but wider and larger. There weren't any distinct wings, but she did notice along the side were three dolphin-like dorsal fins.

"That is *definitely* not one of ours."

The light on the underside of the ship pulsed until four objects jettisoned out the flat end of the vessel. One by one, each smaller vessel appeared to power up with a series of sequential illuminations along the spine of its hull before disengaging and going dark. The night sky outlined the four dark silhouettes that hovered around the larger craft.

"Oh, mother of— This is freaking insane!" She couldn't look away. Her curiosity overpowered the flight part of her brain screaming for her to run inside.

Those are smaller ships, like a dinghy on a bigger boat or—or a dropship like in one of my dad's books. Shuttle ships for away missions! "Oh my God, am I seriously trying to rationalize this with science fiction?"

Through the telescope she watched as one by one, the four small ships flew off in different directions, leaving the larger ship alone in the sky.

"Where did they go?" She jerked up, almost knocking over the bistro chair, and searched the sky for the smaller ships, but all four had disappeared. Seconds later, an immense white light flashed across the sky. She instinctively held her arms up and shielded her eyes. Afraid to miss anything, she peeked over her arms, blinking several times before she caught sight of a long luminous streak that trailed up toward the stars.

Mouth gaping, she lowered her gaze. There, off in the distance, shining brightly in the night sky, was Arcturus.

15

"**W**hat the hell was that?"

Kenna circled the spot she stood and searched for her phone. "I-I should've recorded that!" When she found her phone in the back pocket of her shorts, she decided it was time to go inside. One show was fine, but she had no interest in sticking around for a possible second act. Quickly yet carefully, she put away her telescope and hurried down the ladder.

Once inside, she slammed the kitchen window shut and secured the lock. She shuffled a few steps from the window, then froze with an overwhelming sense of being in the wrong place at the wrong time. How at any moment they would come for her because she'd seen something she shouldn't have. Then the question of who *they* were weighed on her mind. The government, a foreign country, or worse—aliens. Which was a bit ironic because she'd always hoped and believed that there was intelligent life beyond this world. But to come face-to-face with an actual alien—she wasn't sure she was ready for that kind of moment.

But nothing happened.

Her nerves were on high alert. *A secure house is a safe house,* her mother had repeatedly said when she was a kid. *A stranger is less likely to enter your home if your windows and doors are locked.* Kenna had never felt that those words held more truth than right now.

After double-checking the windows in the kitchen, she headed into the living room and quietly checked the front-door dead bolt before setting the swing bar lock into its locked position. Ally had already closed all the curtains, but to ease her mind, she ran her fingers over the window latches to make sure they were locked.

Once she was done, and felt somewhat reassured, Kenna grabbed an extra blanket from the closet and covered Meegan, still fast asleep on the couch.

In her bedroom, she closed the door. Instead of curling up in her so-called geriatric recliner, she opted to clear the textbooks, notebooks, and other miscellaneous items from her bed neatly to the floor. With her phone and glasses on the nightstand, she crawled into bed. She lay on her side and pulled the sheets over her ear as if that would protect her from the imaginary monsters or CIA operatives coming to kidnap her and take her to some secret black ops facility where they would question her about what she'd seen. Her imagination was spinning out of control and wouldn't let up. Fear now trumped her curiosity.

Wrong place. Wrong time.

For the next few minutes, she tossed and turned under the sheets until she finally got comfortable on her stomach. From beneath her shirt, a spot of warmth at her chest pressed between her skin and the mattress, followed by a subtle numbness. Her eyelids fluttered and eventually closed. Any thoughts and fears racing through her mind faded until there was nothing left but a dark, blank canvas.

It was then, far off in the back of her mind, that she heard the woman's trailing voice. *"Sleep, Kenna. Sleep."*

✹ ✩ ✹ ✩ ✹

I'm cold.

Something's not right.

Why is it so cold?

"You need to open your eyes now, Kenna."

But I'm so cold.

"It's okay. Open your eyes."

The first few blinks of her vision were blurry, but eventually her eyes focused. She was outside, standing in the middle of an open field. It was nighttime, yet the light of the moon— "Wait, why are there two moons in the sky?" Her gaze dipped to across the open field. "And where the hell am I?"

She rubbed her bare arms. The long white dress she wore wasn't doing much to keep her warm. The spacious field stretched outward and butted up against the edge of a forest. Glancing behind herself, she saw a narrow clearing with a dirt road that ended at the forest's edge. Though, it appeared as if the road had once continued into the forest, because of the break of trees, but was now closed off by an overgrowth of vines and brush.

"Kenna," a familiar voice softly spoke.

Kenna spun and faced the thick forest again. She tucked her hair behind her ears and searched the field. "Hello?"

Then, there in her peripheral vision, as if her company had been there this whole time, she noticed a woman standing next to her. "Holy crap, you scared me!"

"My apologies," the woman said, still in the same elegant gown from the last time they'd met. "Where are we?" the woman asked, her voice low with concern.

"I don't know. Am I dead?"

The woman's lips curled up and the corners of her mouth creased, revealing a hint of old age. Her voice was soft and raspy, and Kenna wondered if the woman had been a smoker.

"Again, no. Why do you always assume you've died? Is your life that compromised? Should I be worried?"

"What? No." But then Kenna thought about the mysterious spaceships she'd seen earlier. "Or at least I don't think so." She surveyed the field. The greenish-yellow grass bowed in the cool breeze before returning to knee-length height. "I must be dreaming." She bent down a little and brushed her hand along the tops of the grass.

"Maybe. But I think it's something more."

"What does that mean?"

The woman plucked a strand of grass and rolled it between her slender fingers.

Meanwhile, Kenna touched her temples and asked, "Where are my glasses?" while patting her face and searching the ground around herself.

"What are glasses?"

"Never mind." Kenna exhaled a long breath, and then noticed something was different about the woman. With a curious gaze, she asked, "Hey, why aren't you glowing? You had this yellowish-orange glow to you last time I saw you."

The woman lifted her arms and observed them. "Another good question. I've never experienced anything like this before."

"Okay," Kenna said and drew out the last syllable. "How about we start with who are you, and why do I keep seeing you?"

"My name is Ulissa, and my essence lives inside the arcstone you wear around your neck." She pointed a long bony finger at the yellow crystal situated above the low neckline of Kenna's dress.

Kenna lifted the pendant and asked, "You're inside this crystal? But how?"

"It's a stone, not a crystal, and the how isn't important right now. I promise to explain once I know our bond is stable. What Anumen family do you belong to?"

She shook her head and asked, "Ah-new-*what*?"

Ulissa's eyes narrowed. "Are you not Anumen? And yet you've somehow begun the bonding process with an arcstone? How did this happen?"

"Well, I'm from Florida. Not really practicing any form of religion right now, but I won't judge your Ah-new-men faith, or whatever it is you believe in."

"Religion? Faith?"

"Yeah, you know, the stuff that helps people bring meaning to life."

"Ah, I see. I am unfamiliar with religion or faith, but we do appreciate and give thanks to the Eilimintachs."

"El-ay-min-toks? Is that your fancy way of saying the elements?" Kenna rubbed her hands along her bare arms. "Okay, so you're into Wicca."

Ulissa smiled. "You are a strange one, but I like you." Her head tilted up and she stared at the night sky. "I'm not sure where we are. Or how I'm even here with you. I did not fabricate this setting, yet I can sense our minds are connected here."

"So, you're in my dream?" Kenna turned and gazed around the open field. "I've never been this aware in a dream before."

"Kenna," Ulissa began to say as she beckoned Kenna to face her. "Listen to me. I don't know how much time we have here, and our bond is yet to be complete, but it is of the utmost importance that you protect the arcstone with your life. You must always keep it close; otherwise—"

"Pain," Kenna said, finishing the woman's sentence. She wasn't entirely sure how she knew pain was the answer, but it did explain why she'd thrown up earlier.

"You've had your first incident of separation?"

Kenna nodded. "Not a good feeling." She bent over and plucked a single strand of tall grass and twisted it between her fingers. "So, you're telling me I can never take the necklace off?"

"I'm sorry, but yes."

A piercing scream echoed across the field, ending their conversation. Kenna's shoulders lifted to her ears at the unexpected shriek. She spun on the balls of her feet and stared at the peculiar sight across the field—A woman with long hair, kneeling under a stark white tree that hadn't been there moments ago.

Ulissa stepped behind Kenna. She'd expected the old woman to come around and stand on her other side, maybe to get a better view of the mysterious woman, but nope. Ulissa had vanished. "Hey! Where did you go?"

"*I'm here*," she said in Kenna's mind.

"Uh, okay." Kenna lifted the bottom hem of her dress and jogged through the tall grass toward the woman, who was now hunched over, head resting in her hands and sobbing.

Slender leaves dangled from long branches. It reminded Kenna of a giant Willow tree but an albino version. She lifted the end of one of the bowed branches and asked, "Hello? Do you need help?"

At the base of the thick, knotted trunk sat a woman maybe a year or two older than Ally. Her vibrant ginger hair was silky and smooth as if she'd never seen a humid day in her life, and her pale skin was splotched with freckles. The sobbing woman also wore a simple, long white dress identical to Kenna's.

The woman sat upright and sniffled, wiping her... *orange eyes*... and pointing out past the tree toward the forest. Kenna was about to turn and see what she was pointing at when she noticed a decorative cuff clasped around the woman's arm. Embedded in the center of the dark metal cuff was a stone. Not quite the same as Kenna's, but it was cut like a crystal and had the same golden-yellowish coloring.

She has an arcstone.

"Where did you get that—" Kenna started to ask, but Ulissa's voice cut through her mind.

"*Kenna, hurry! Get out of there! It's the Obard!*"

"What? Where? Who are the Obard?"

"*Behind you! At the edge of the forest! You need to run—run now, Kenna!*"

Kenna ducked out from under the branches and saw a long line of towering soldiers emerge from the edge of the forest. A thick fog rolled out in alliance with the beings, swirling around the blades of their broadswords. Their medieval-like armor was covered in black scales. All except the front of their helmets, which hid their faces behind sleek dark visors. Icy-blue strands of hair sprang out from the tops of their helmets, hanging low past their shoulders. From where she stood, they appeared taller than anyone she knew, and she estimated the soldiers to be seven feet or more.

"*Kenna, go!*" Ulissa pleaded.

"But what about—" Kenna pivoted to face the redheaded woman, but she'd disappeared. Along with the white tree. *Oh, you've got to be kidding me!*

She faced the forest again.

This is nothing more than a horrible nightmare.

It's not real!

It's not real!

Panic crept up and lodged itself in her throat. The Obard soldiers were getting closer. She found her voice and asked, "What do they want?"

"*The power within the arcstone. And they'll rip you apart to get it, so please, I beg you, run!*"

The word *run* thundered through Kenna's mind. She gathered up the skirt of her dress and bolted away. The field appeared to stretch out in front of her like rubber, as if the nightmare were making a point to say she had nowhere to run. Regardless of what lay ahead, she didn't dare look back.

"*Kenna!*" Ulissa called, but Kenna didn't stop running. She wanted to wake from this nightmare. To be safe in her bed. To rid herself of this stupid necklace and its curse.

Distracted by her thoughts, she lost her grip on her dress. Heart racing, she fumbled to gather the fabric away from her sprinting feet. She was about to glance over her shoulder to see if the Obard soldiers had caught up to her when she slammed into something hard.

"No, stop! Don't hurt me! Let me go!" Her fists pounded against a solid surface covered in soft fabric. "I need to get out of here!"

"Get out of where?" The man's voice sounded confused and concerned. "Are you hurt? Can I help?"

He released her, and she wasted no time in crossing her arms over her chest. To hide the arcstone. *He could be one of those Obard. This could be a trick. He could be— Wow.* She couldn't help but stare. If this was what the Obard looked like under that scary-ass armor, she might be okay with getting captured. She swallowed the lump in her throat and tried hard not to glance him over, but who was she kidding. Curiosity, once again, got the best of her. He was tall, well over six feet, and either the black long-sleeve shirt was too small or he filled it a little too well with his toned muscles. His hair was short with dark, blond layers and a cowlick above his left eye. She avoided looking at his lips and instead focused on the curiosity in his... *Are his eyes orange too? Definitely a weird-ass dream going on here.* His stance, so attentive like that of an authoritative figure, contradicted the stubble growing along his chin.

He stepped closer and instinctively her guard went up. "Stay away!" She threw out her arm, palm facing him. A quick look over her shoulder revealed that the open field had returned to its peaceful state. No armored soldiers in sight. Only the calm of tall grass swaying in the night.

"*He's not Obard, Kenna,*" Ulissa's voice said, calmer and not as loud in Kenna's mind. "*I don't know where they went, but they're gone.*"

"Do you hear her?" With a grimace, Kenna turned her outstretched hand up and pointed to the sky. "Do you hear that woman talking?"

The man looked around at the field before shaking his head. "No, I don't hear a woman. But..." He paused, narrowing his amber eyes as he inched closer. "...do I know you? I feel like I know you."

It was Kenna's turn to shake her head. She stepped away as he got closer. Unsure of his intentions, she wanted to keep a safe distance between them, even though there was something about him she couldn't quite place. She'd never experienced what people called a *gut feeling*, but here amid this chaotic dream, she felt in her gut that she could trust this man. Yet, nothing about him was familiar to her.

"I won't hurt you."

Kenna's gaze momentarily dipped before meeting his eyes again. "I know."

"I'm Ben." He held his right palm out in front of himself, facing up.

It was an awkward angle for a handshake, and she stared at it, wondering what she should do. She wanted to slide her hand into his and feel the warmth of his touch, but at the same time she refused to let her guard down. "Nice to meet you, Ben. I'm—"

"Kenna! Behind you!" Ulissa shouted.

Kenna turned, just in time to see a lone Obard rushing toward her. Startled, she gasped and quickly spun to grab Ben, but he was gone. Vanished like the woman under the tree.

She ran like hell. Behind her, the Obard's breathing was fierce and predatorial.

It's only a dream. It's only a dream, she repeated as she tried to hold up her dress and run. She stumbled and tripped on the flowing folds of her dress, landing face down in the grass. Quickly, she rolled over and tried to scramble up, but her legs were tangled in the fabric.

When the Obard reached her, it towered over her, and she saw her reflection, eyes wide with fear, in the monster's faceplate. The thing lifted its sword high above its head and, without hesitating, brought the long black blade down on Kenna.

Her screams were the last thing she heard at what she hoped was the end of a dream.

16

The next morning, Kenna's mind was cloudy, and she couldn't tell if she was awake or still dreaming.

Ulissa? Ben? she called out in her mind, but there was no response.

Satisfied that last night's escapade had been nothing more than a chaotic dream, she relaxed in the safety of her bed. That was, until she yawned. A strangled gasp wheezed from deep in her lungs. She tried to lift her head, but her temples throbbed with an intense ache.

Pain.

Where's the arcstone?

She dragged a heavy hand to her chest and felt the outline of the crystal—no, Ulissa had said it was a stone—beneath her shirt. It took all her strength to push herself up into a sitting position. Childlike whimpers escaped as she forced her eyes open. The undersides of her eyelids felt like sandpaper. The sun was shining directly in her face, and she silently swore at herself for not closing her curtains last night.

Damn it, I can't think straight! It's too bright! Whether she wanted to or not, it meant getting out of bed and closing those damn curtains.

Again, Kenna pushed through the torturous agony of moving, and she slid her legs out from under the sheets. She concentrated on her goal of getting to the window and inched closer to the edge of the bed. Breathing had become more laborious, and dark splotches crept on the outskirts of her vision.

Okay, Ulissa. Now I'm dying. What do you say to that?

Soon, the pain in her arms and legs was replaced with a tingling sensation of pins and needles. She sucked in her bottom lip and wiggled her fingers and toes, hoping to wake up the nerves, but the motions only increased her nausea. Her dark hair hung low over her face, and between heavy breaths, she told herself, "Two—steps—to the window." There wasn't anything that didn't hurt right now. Her ears rang, her tongue felt swollen, and even her hair follicles stung like millions of sharp incisions all over her body.

Screw the curtains! I need help. If she could just get to her bedroom door and open it, then someone would see her.

She leaned forward and the moment her feet touched the large area rug, an intense, sharp pain struck her in the center of her chest. Ignoring the tingling sensation in her hands, she pressed one palm to her chest and yelped. After that, it wasn't long before her legs gave out, and she fell hard onto her hands and knees.

I'm not going to make it. I can't reach the door. Help! Someone please help!

Something warm ignited inside her chest. First it eased the agonizing pain in her core, and then it spread out into her limbs. When the pain finally subsided, there was a glimmer of hope that the worst was over. But it wasn't long before her hopes died, and the warmth turned to heat.

The inside of her chest burned as if someone had stuck a hot coal down her throat and left it between her lungs. She was a hundred percent positive she was about to become the next unexplained case of spontaneous human combustion, leaving only a pile of ash on the expensive rug Ally had given her.

The searing pain was too much. Sweat beaded along her skin. Defeated, she fell over and curled up on her side. She focused on her raspy breaths until eventually she welcomed the haven of unconsciousness.

17

A loud *thud* came from Kenna's bedroom, jolting Meegan awake. She presumed it was a random noise and snuggled deeper into the couch pillow, but after the second *thud*, she became concerned. She tossed off the knitted blanket and instantly saw something strange clamped to her right wrist.

What's this thing?

She twisted her elbow to see the underside of the extra-wide metal cuff secured to her wrist. Though, unlike a normal cuff, there was no opening or latch on the underside. It was solid all the way around. The metal was tarnished, like aged copper but darker. There were strange markings engraved along the center around a large oval white stone embedded in the top center.

It wasn't until her fingers grazed the smooth surface of the stone that she felt the hum of its power.

"Whoa! Is this what I think it is?"

It's a transessent stone. How the hell—no, better yet, who the hell has Anumen stones? First the arcstone and now a transessent stone?

She was about to cast an amula to test the transessent stone's power when another *thud* came from Kenna's bedroom. Meegan got up and went to Kenna's door. When she peered inside, she immediately spotted her friend lying on the floor.

"Shit! Kenna!" She hurried over and rolled her onto her back. The large metal bracer on Kenna's right wrist was hard to miss.

Another transessent stone?

"Oh man, you're burning up!" She grabbed Kenna's shoulders and tried to shake her awake. But all she got was a few mumbled words about some guy named Ben.

"Who the hell is Ben?"

Meegan looked up at the time on the alarm clock and did the math to determine how much time was left for the arcstone bond to complete itself. *Twenty-six hours for a bond to fully form, and the amula took effect yesterday around eleven thirty. Okay, so that means she's got three hours left.*

Transessent stones were natural amplifiers, and she suspected this was the reason for Kenna's fever. Having that much power course through one person, especially a human, was dangerous. On Anuminis, if an Anumen bonded with an arcstone, they were restricted from using transessent stones. They didn't need to. They had access to enough power within the arcstone.

There wasn't anything else she could do to help her friend besides separate the two stones, and as far as Meegan could tell, there was no way to remove the transessent stone from either of their wrists. Taking off the arcstone wasn't going to work either. Meegan could only hope that the Anumen in the arcstone was doing something to help alleviate any internal pain Kenna might be having.

The floor wasn't the ideal place to sleep. She slid her hands under Kenna's back and lifted her into a sitting position. Then she looped her arms under Kenna's armpits and, with a loud grunt, tried to hoist her into bed. The first attempt didn't go so well. Before she tried again, she borrowed a hair elastic from the bedpost and quickly twisted her black hair up and out of the way. She then reached under Kenna's arms again, but this time with a better grip and an amula on the tip of her tongue.

"*Olahar anau luhte*," she whispered. *Give me strength.*

The amula set into motion and converted the intake of air from her lungs into an energy that sought out and strengthened her muscles. Tiny white veins of light appeared on the surface of the transessent stone and boosted the amula effects tenfold. With the help of the amula, it took little effort to lift Kenna into bed.

She thought the word *stop* but whispered the command *déanta* to cease the amula. No use in wasting elemental powers.

Half-asleep, Kenna muttered, "Woman by the tree," and then rolled onto her side and hugged one of her pillows. "Mmm, Ben."

Meegan lifted the sheet over her and brushed a few strands of damp hair away from Kenna's face. "Can't wait for you to tell me about this dream. Especially who this Ben guy is."

The bedroom door opened, and Ally shuffled in. "What's going on in here? You guys woke me up." Loose brown spirals of hair sprang in every direction, a morning look Meegan wasn't used to seeing on Ally. Ally tightened the knot on her bathrobe, yawned, and then rubbed at her eyes. "What time is it?"

"Late for you. Almost ten thirty."

"What?" Her eyes widened and searched the room for Kenna's alarm clock. "I haven't slept this late in, like, forever." She pointed to Kenna and asked, "What's up with her? Doesn't she have class at eleven?"

"Yeah, but she's not feeling well. I'll email her teachers, but for now we should let her sleep." Meegan walked past Ally and left Kenna to rest.

"What the hell is this?" a shrieking voice erupted from behind her. Meegan hurried back in and shushed Ally. With the sleeve of her robe pulled up, Ally held out her wrist and showed Meegan the metal band clasped around her brown skin. "Who put this thing on me? And—and where—" That was when she noticed an identical one strapped to Meegan's wrist. "You too?"

The tall brunette turned and quickly lifted the bedsheet to inspect her roommate. "She's got one too! What the hell is going on?"

What do I say? What do I say?

"Ally, she needs to sleep. Can we talk out in the living room?"

Because I don't know what's going on. Oh, I wish I had one of my mother's old journals. Betcha there are some answers there.

Ally stomped out of the room, and Meegan quietly closed the bedroom door. She turned to face Ally, but Ally, who was now muttering to herself, marched off into the kitchen. Unsure about how to answer the questions Ally was sure to ask, Meegan settled on the couch and waited.

Someone had come in last night while they were sleeping. That much was obvious, but who, and why, were the million-dollar questions.

"I think we should call the police." Ally returned to the living room, surprisingly a bit calmer than Meegan had anticipated. She sat in the armchair with two cups of steaming tea and slid one across the coffee table to Meegan.

"Thank you," she said, accepting the tea. "Gunpowder Orange tea?"

Ally nodded.

Meegan cupped the mug and inhaled the sweet citrus aroma. "I don't think we should call the police."

"What? Why not? Someone broke in and"—she held up her right wrist—"attached these things to us." She froze. Her gaze darted to the corners of the room. In a hushed tone, she asked, "What if they're still here?"

Meegan held her tea close to her chin. "I think you'd be able to see if anyone were still here. There aren't too many places to hide in your apartment." The heat from the mug felt nice, soothing her anxious nerves.

Okay, how do I distract Ally from the situation? Get her thinking about something else.

"Hey, have you heard from Prue today?"

Ally sipped her tea and then shook her head. "No. Not yet. Why?"

"I think you should check on her. A quick call to make sure she's okay and let her know we'll be over as soon as Kenna wakes."

There was a long pause before Ally responded, "Yeah, I guess. But I'm going to call the police after I talk to her."

"Okay." Meegan sipped her tea.

Ally placed her tea on the coffee table and retreated to her room. A few minutes later she returned to the armchair with her phone. "Weird. Prue's not answering my calls or texts."

Meegan didn't want to bring up the police in case Ally had forgotten, but no such luck. Ally held the phone to her ear, and after a few seconds, she said, "Hello, yes, I'd like to report a break-in."

Shit, this should be interesting.

18

Darci sat with her knees tucked up to her chest in the corner of the locked room. A small vent in the floor gave little relief to the stuffy space, and a faint hum from the overhead fluorescent light had been her only company since she'd woken some time ago. Above her, in the corner of the ceiling, was a single surveillance camera. With no word from her captors, her mind was going crazy with questions of where she was, who was responsible, and what was going to happen to her.

The scrape on her hand had scabbed over. She could only hope that her captors hadn't noticed the color of her blood. Earlier, when she'd first woken up on the flimsy metal cot, she'd searched for clues to help figure out where she was. Out of the three doors in the room, all but one were locked. The unlocked door led to a sterile half-bathroom. There, in front of the mirror above the sink, she noticed three things.

The first was that someone had removed her clothes and dressed her in a gray T-shirt and matching sweatpants.

The second was the strange object around her neck. A snug, semitranslucent silicone device, like a fitted collar for an animal. Upon closer examination, there were several tiny blinking lights and what appeared to be black wiring beneath the pliable surface. Whatever it was, she assumed it was the reason her Linc had been unresponsive since she'd woken.

The last thing she noticed, which unnerved her the most, was that someone had removed her color contacts. Bright orange eyes stared back at her from her reflection in the small bathroom mirror.

Eventually, after there was nothing left to explore, she sat in the corner under the surveillance camera and waited. She debated calling out to whoever was watching behind the camera, but her fears got the best of her and she decided not to draw any unnecessary attention for now.

Other than the hum of the overhead light, the room was silent, which gave her time to think. Time to prepare for whoever would eventually walk through one of those locked doors. She had too many Sendarians depending on her. Breyah and the Aevo Compendium being one, but also Princess Emmalyn.

The princess had secretly tasked *her* with finding Gerard and relaying a message to him. Though the princess had expressed concern for Darci's novice status, because of the intel she'd acquired regarding Gerard's whereabouts on Earth, it just happened to fall under Darci's assigned region.

Darci had assured the princess she could manage both tasks. Even though inside she was nervous about her first Spiaire mission to an alien world.

At least one of my missions won't be a complete failure. Gerard has the plac with Princess Emmalyn's message. Now I've got to figure out how the hegah I'm going to get out of here in the next few hours before transport, or my essence may actually end up in Hegah if all goes wrong. I pray to Isoldesse that Kenna, Ally, and Meegan are at Prue's house for their scheduled transport.

Wait—what if I've been out longer than one night? What if the pickup was yesterday? Did I miss my ride home?

She got to her feet, stood in front of the camera, and yelled, "Hello! Hey! What day is it? I need to know what day it is! Hello! You can't keep me in here! Please! Just tell me what day it is?"

An overhead speaker clicked on and an audible static filled the room, followed by a woman's voice. "Hello, Darci."

They know my name.

"Where am I? I need to know the date."

"Your questions are irrelevant. My questions, though, are much, much more important."

"I'm not answering any of your questions until you tell me where I am, who you are, and what day it is!" From behind Darci, one of the locked doors made a clicking sound. The sound startled her, and she quickly raised both hands and moving her body into a defensive stance. The door popped ajar like an unspoken invitation. Applying what she learned during her Spiaire training on Priomh, Darci controlled her breathing and silently counted to twenty before cautiously approaching the door.

Slow and easy. No surprises. Stay alert. Be ready for anything.

Beyond the door was another enclosed space. This one was larger, with a lot more doors. She counted ten total and noted that above each handle was an electronic number pad. This room shared a similar emptiness to her previous holding cell. The walls and ceiling were white with the same cold gray cement floor. She eyed each of the four cameras positioned near the ceiling while assessing the room. A plastic patio table with four matching white chairs was situated in the center. A woman with long red hair sat with her back to Darci.

She swallowed the nervous lump in her throat and inched closer to the woman. "Hello?"

The woman turned, and Darci couldn't believe it—it was Eryn. She was wearing the same gray T-shirt and sweatpants, and like Darci, someone had removed her color contacts. Eryn jumped up, knocking over the chair, and hurried over.

"Darci!"

"Oh no, they got you too?" When Eryn nodded, Darci briefly glanced at the semitranslucent collar strapped to Eryn's neck and asked, "Are you okay? How long have you been here?"

"I'm okay. Not happy, but okay." Eryn picked up her chair and set it close to another chair. The two sat and leaned their heads together. "I don't know. I'd just gotten home from my da—" She hesitated before correcting herself. "—from hanging out with a friend. I didn't hear them come up from behind me."

"That's what happened to me too, except I was outside by my car."

"But I saw him. The Sendarian who attacked me. I'll never forget that face."

"Wait." Darci shot to her feet. "We were taken by Sendarians?"

Eryn grabbed Darci's hands, tugged her into her seat, and gestured to the cameras in the corners. "Shh! They'll hear you."

With this new knowledge, the newbie Spiaire didn't care who heard her. It hadn't been the humans who discovered their true identities, but their own people trying to sabotage the Aevo Compendium.

But who? And why?

Or were they here for another reason?

Gerard.

She'd left a voicemail with the banished Sendarian, but she had no idea if he'd gotten it or if they'd gotten to him first.

Darci pursed her lips and quietly asked, "Has anyone said anything to you? About why we're here? Or what day it is?"

"No. But I have to believe the transport is still in orbit. How else would these Sendarians get home?"

"The *Tarais*," Darci whispered. "Did you ever get to send that message to the *Tarais* about our concerns about Seph and Grace?"

Eryn shook her head. "No. I was taken right after we spoke." She scratched at her arm. Red streaks from her fingernails marked her freckled skin before slowly fading. "This is a disaster."

"We'll figure it out." Darci rested her elbows on her knees and chewed on her lip while she processed how and why Sendarians would be here. She glanced up at Eryn and said, "I think you're right. The *Tarais* must be their ride home, which means we still have a chance to get out of here and make sure the humans get to their assigned pickup location."

"Maybe. But I don't know where we are or what these things are." Eryn tugged at the top edge of her collar. With a heavy sigh, she then added, "Well, I'm glad you're okay. Have you seen or spoken to any other Sendarians besides Grace and Seph?"

"What? No." Darci shook her head to make her lie more convincing. "Only you, and Spiaires Seph and Grace." She'd sworn an oath of secrecy to the princess. She couldn't tell Eryn she'd been secretly meeting with—

Gerard. I called him and left him a message, telling him about...

"Wait! I did see another Sendarian. Before I was attacked. One of my human friends took a picture of her on her cell phone."

"A picture? Really? Of who?"

"Gemma."

Eryn leaned back in her seat and glanced at one of the cameras. She sat there, silent, for some time before shaking her head. Darci could see the tears welling along the edges of her fellow Spiaire's eyes. Barely above a whisper, Eryn said, "I can't believe it. Of course it would be her."

"I'm sorry."

"She was like a sister to me. One of the best Spiaires Priomh ever had. When Breyah finds out, she'll be destroyed." Eryn dropped her head into her hands and sniffled. Darci let her friend have a moment to process. When Eryn lifted her head, her freckled skin was damp and flushed from tears she couldn't hold back.

"Were Leadess Ganecht and Gemma close?"

Eryn wiped under her eyes with the bottom of her gray T-shirt. "They were childhood friends, and Breyah always called Gemma by her childhood nickname, Geevi. The two of them were inseparable. When the Queen of Sendara handpicked Breyah to be Priomh's new Leadess and to oversee the Aevo Compendium project, Breyah agreed with one condition. That her longtime friend Geevi be granted the open Spiaire position. The queen agreed to Breyah's terms, and both women left their families on Sendara and moved to Priomh. That was a long time ago, when the old research facility was still being used on Priomh. Breyah and Gemma designed and built the new Priomh compound to incorporate families. To better the morale of the researchers."

After a long pause, Darci bit her lip and hesitantly shifted the conversation. "Eryn, do you think what's happened to us is why we haven't heard from Seph in over a week? Or Grace in the last few days?"

Eryn wiped her cheeks. "I bet it is. Though, I pray to Isoldesse that they haven't been taken too, and that they are somewhere safe with their humans. I find it hard to believe that Gemma would act alone in kidnapping us and sabotaging the Aevo Compendium."

Darci abruptly stood, the plastic legs of her chair scraping against the hard floor, and faced the closest camera. "Gemma! Gemma of the Vaudd family, get your ass down here and explain yourself! Gemma!"

"What are you doing?" Eryn tensed, her gaze darting from one camera to the next.

Darci stared straight into one of the cameras and between gritted teeth, she said, "I'm getting us some damn answers!"

19

Darci continued to shout demands at the camera until one of the nearby doors clicked and popped open. Eryn, the senior-ranking Spiaire, who was at least four inches shorter than Darci, shot to her feet and positioned herself in front of her.

"Stay behind me."

Darci obeyed, even though she was fired up and ready to pounce on whoever came through that door. She needed answers, but right now the priority was escaping and getting to Prue's house.

What she didn't expect was a tall, broad-shouldered man wearing a baseball hat and holding a plac to walk into the room. He briefly looked up from his plac, and from beneath the rim of his hat, Darci glimpsed orange eyes.

"He's Sendarian," she whispered in Eryn's ear.

"Who are you? And why have you taken us?" Eryn straightened her shoulders and pointed to the man while asking in an authoritative tone, "Are Seph and Grace here as well? What's your purpose on

Earth? Did you arrive on the *Tarais*? And where's Gemma? I want to speak to Gemma!"

The man ignored the questions being thrown at him and concentrated on his plac. He glanced up a few times, but his gaze appeared to be directed more toward their neck restraints.

Eventually he spoke with a smug grin. "Sorry, but this may hurt."

Darci stepped away from Eryn and gripped the top edge of the collar. The silicone exterior felt smooth and pliable, but only for a second before it began to transition into a hard, solid surface. Whilst the collar altered its composition, it also got tighter.

"Eryn—" She struggled to form words. "I-I can't... breathe." A tight pressure, as if someone had their hands wrapped around her throat, pressed against the muscles in her neck.

"You can breathe fine," the man remarked and continued tapping his plac.

Eryn momentarily tugged at her device before her hands dropped to her sides. She went to reach for Darci, but her arm didn't move, and when she tried taking a step forward, her foot remained planted on the cement floor.

"What... did you... do?" Eryn croaked, her voice barely above a whisper.

Darci couldn't close her eyes, so instead she focused on trying to control her breathing. With each inhale and exhale she slowly counted to four. *I'm okay. This is bad, but I'm still able to breathe, hear, and talk. I'm sure it'll be over soon. He'll reverse the collars and we'll be fine again—I hope.*

The man circled the two Spiaires, glancing back and forth between them and his plac. "Twenty-two seconds for the paralytic restraints to complete the full transformation. I can confirm that both subjects' muscular systems have been incapacitated, while their vital organs, circulatory systems, and sensory nervous systems remain operational." From behind, he pinched Darci's arm.

"Ow!" She let out a strangled insult: "Stoo-pid *grón-tah!*"

Ignoring Darci's griping, he continued his report. "Collar readings show a ten percent decrease in airflow, and observation shows that the subjects have limited use of their vocals. Short-term auditory has no change. Though, I will continue to monitor their hearing under prolonged duress."

The Rhaltan Enforcers will banish him for creating such torturous devices.

Okay, stay calm—stay calm. I need to center my breathing.

Wait! Did he just say prolonged duress? *Oh, Isoldesse, I don't know how much longer I can breathe like this before I pass out.*

The man came around from behind, faced Darci, and stared into her eyes. "Do you like my paralytic restraints?" he asked with a wide grin. "They're still in the early development stage, but I'm already impressed with the results I'm seeing."

"Micah, there's no need to show off." A woman with bright red lipstick and silky red hair draped over one shoulder strutted into the room. The sleeveless pinstripe dress she wore hugged her curves and elongated her cream-colored legs. Darci recognized the defector from her public profile image listed within the Sendara Network.

Gemma.

From behind Micah and Gemma, another woman entered the room. She kept her distance and stayed close to the exit. She wore fitted black cargo pants and a cropped muscle tee that contradicted the elegance of her female counterpart. Her red hair was short, shaved on the sides and styled up and back like an overgrown faux-hawk. She was lean and muscular with a tattoo that peeked out from beneath her cropped shirt. There was also something off about the woman's gaze. She stared at Darci with eager eyes, like a child patiently waiting for permission to rip open a gift.

"Gem... ma," Eryn uttered.

Gemma turned and faced Eryn. "Beannaith to you, sister."

Darci could only imagine how those words burned Eryn.

"Not... my sis... ter."

"Once a Spiaire, always a Spiaire," Gemma sang before her gaze flicked to Darci. "Isn't that right, Darci?" Gemma's smug smile straightened as she barked, "Cahleen!" and then in a softer tone continued, "Be a dear and bring out those two guests I mentioned earlier."

Cahleen sneered before she pushed off the wall and walked over to one of the locked doors. It was hard for Darci to see anything that wasn't directly in front of her, but she could still hear. There was a set of six *beeps* followed by a clicking sound.

Meanwhile, Gemma instructed Micah to allow Darci, and only Darci, to speak. Micah pressed and held the screen of his plac until a section of the restraint, the inside front area that pressed up against her larynx, altered its composition and loosened to its original silicone state.

"Gemma? What the hell... are you doing... here?" Darci wanted air almost as much as she wanted answers. While she waited for the traitor to answer, she spotted the faux-hawk woman pushing a woman in a wheelchair into view. Whoever the woman was, sitting slumped forward with a pillowcase over her head, she seemed to still be in her pajamas. A knee-length cotton nightgown with V-neck lace detailing.

Cahleen once again vanished from Darci's field of vision. Another set of *beeps* sounded in the background while Gemma spoke.

"It's nice to officially meet you, Darci." The sarcasm in Gemma's voice matched her fake smile. "But anyway, let's get straight to the point. I'm curious, have you come across that Earth phrase *pish-posh* yet?" She crossed one arm and held her elbow while tapping one long shiny red nail to her chin. Before Darci could answer, she continued, "Well, it means *irrelevant* or *unimportant*. But let me tell you what *is* relevant and extremely important for you, Eryn, and our other guests." With a wide sweep of her hand, she gestured to the now two people in wheelchairs sitting side by side. The second unconscious person was also concealed under a pillowcase. Gemma turned and faced Darci. She crossed her arms and narrowed her eyes at the young Spiaire. "My questions are the only questions that are important."

"Okay, what do you want to know?" Silently, she was grateful that her breathing and speech had returned to normal, but also confused as to why Gemma's questions were directed at her and not Eryn. What could she possibly want to know from a young Sendarian with barely any Spiaire experience? Surely, any information she wanted regarding the Aevo Compendium Gemma would already know. Procedure hadn't changed. The sequential order of worlds they observed and visited hadn't changed. Nothing had changed since her departure.

"The two humans you occasionally met up with, who are they? And why are you meeting with them?"

Immediately, an intense guilt brewed. *This is happening because of me. Because of what Princess Emmalyn asked me to do. She must have noticed I was acting outside my Spiaire duties. Maybe she's here to find Gerard. Though, she hasn't mentioned his name. Surely, she would've recognized him if she'd actually seen him.*

"I've only had contact with my assigned humans. Fraternizing with humans outside my assignment is to be limited to unavoidable interactions necessary for gaining the trust needed for the Aevo Compendium selectors."

"Don't quote me lines from the protocol handbook!" Gemma snapped while spinning on the toes of her high heels. She then whipped off the first pillowcase revealing the identity of the woman in pajamas.

It didn't matter that the woman was unconscious and sporting a serious case of bedhead. Darci immediately recognized her human friend. *Prue.* "Oh, no, Gemma... Please tell me you didn't," she said, her voice half-pleading and half-surprised at what was unfolding in front of her.

Gemma continued to pull off the next pillowcase, revealing a man, but Darci's eyes were fixed on the brown-skinned woman.

"No!" Eryn tried to cry, but her restraint was still activated and constricted against her neck.

"Eryn! What's wrong? Do you know him?"

Gemma laced her fingers through the man's thick, wavy hair and yanked his head up. There was a faint bruise above his lip and a long cut scabbed over his right eyebrow.

Tiny whimpers from Eryn only added to Darci's guilt. "Is he one of the humans from your region? Eryn—Eryn, can you hear me? Oh, Isoldesse, I'm so sorry!"

Gemma cocked her head. "Why are you sorry? Have you done something wrong?" She toyed with Darci's words as if she already knew the answer. Gemma then held out her free hand and wiggled her fingers. On cue, Cahleen approached and handed over a long black dagger hollowed down the center. Assertively, Gemma said, "His life depends on your answer, because unlike you"—she paused for dramatic effect—"I have no use for this disgusting human. So, you see, Darci, you will answer my questions. Otherwise..." Gemma repositioned the blade and pressed it against the bronze skin of the unconscious man's neck.

"No! Plea— Gemma!" Eryn's voice cracked as she pleaded.

Darci blurted out the first thing that came to her mind. "Okay, okay—I'll tell you what you want to know, but first you must swear to Isoldesse that you'll return Prue to her house before transport comes, and you have to let that man go. After that, I'll tell you everything. I'll tell you who they are and why I was meeting with them."

Gemma released the man's hair, then used one of the pillowcases to wipe her hands as if she'd touched something filthy before stepping closer to Darci. "There's no need to worry about your little pickup today. It's still Monday, and besides, I personally made sure everything's in place." Her lips turned up in a wide, mischievous smile. "Oh, I wish I could see the look on Breyah's face when she sees the tweaks I've made to her precious project."

"What did you do? Please tell me you didn't disrupt the Aevo Compendium? It's blasphemous! Isoldesse will punish you and send your essence to be tortured in the pits of Hegah!"

Cahleen, now picking at her nails with a smaller, clawlike dagger, rolled her eyes and groaned. "You know, not everyone believes in your so-called goddess."

I can't believe she'd interfere with the Aevo Compendium. She must be lying. But what if she did? What if she did something to Kenna, Meegan, or Ally? I can't even imagine what the consequences will be! The transport is expecting to pick up four humans, yet Prue is here. And so is one of Eryn's humans, and—and neither are wearing their trackers on their wrists? They should've been equipped with their transessent bracers sometime last night.

"I'm waiting," Gemma said impatiently. "Why were you meeting with those two unauthorized humans?"

"Can you at least tell me one thing?" Darci asked with low hopes of getting a *yes*. But she needed to try and get some information out of all this confusion.

Gemma raised an eyebrow and nodded.

"Why do you care so much about what I'm doing? You're not a Spiaire anymore."

Gemma's mischievous, playful grin pursed, and her eyes narrowed at Darci. "I don't care. But you're obviously doing something outside your Spiaire orders, and whatever that something is might benefit the something we're doing."

"And what exactly are you doing?"

Gemma's roguish smile returned as she made a tsking sound. "Nice try."

"Fine. I was ordered to meet with humans outside my assigned Aevo Compendium group. I was provided a list of candidates to meet with, and..." Her lie needed to be believable. "And, well, nothing came of it."

"A list of candidates for what?"

"Gemma, it's not a big deal and has nothing to do with the Aevo Compendium."

"I don't give a shit about Priomh's research project! Whose orders were you following and why?" Gemma stepped closer, her face inches from Darci's.

"Breyah. It was Breyah." It stung to lie and blame her Leadess, but she couldn't betray the princess. Not to Gemma. "Breyah gave me a list of potential candidates I was to interview. I was to convince the best female option from the list to come on a trip with me. I followed a script Breyah wrote out."

"But what reason does Breyah need a human female for, if not for the Aevo Compendium?"

Darci swallowed hard. "For Matthew." Another innocent bystander thrown into her lie.

"Matthew?" When Darci confirmed with a slight nod, Gemma stared into Darci's eyes as if she was trying to decide if she believed her story. A few seconds later she erupted into laughter. "Oh, you've got to be kidding me! You're interviewing humans to bring back to Priomh for Matthew! Oh, this is priceless!"

"You know our laws. No Sendarian is to enter a committed and romantic relationship with an alien race. Matthew is human. He needs a human companion."

"Oh, the things Breyah will do to appease her human pet. What she should've done was send that loggie back to Earth. He should've never been allowed to stay on Priomh after the last Earth Aevo C." Gemma turned and waved a hand at Cahleen, who proceeded to unlock and push the man in the wheelchair from Darci's view. Gemma then faced Darci again. "Fine. I'll buy it for now. Though"—she lifted Prue's head and pressed the long dagger to Prue's neck—"if I discover you're lying to me, their blood is on you."

Gemma released the young woman's head and it flopped forward. Cahleen came into view, grabbed the wheelchair's handles, and pushed Prue from Darci's sight. Gemma strode toward the exit, and before she left, she turned and wiggled her fingers. "We'll talk more later. Ta-ta!"

After returning Prue and Eryn's friend to their secured rooms, Cahleen marched across the room and followed Gemma out the door. Micah stood from the patio chair he'd been sitting in and moved to leave too. He stopped in the doorway and explained, "I'll reverse the paralytic restraints once the door is locked. My best advice to you is to not make trouble. We'll be catching a transport ship back to the *Tarais* soon, and before you know it, we'll be home." He winked from under his baseball cap and then closed the door.

The restraints returned to their initial composition of soft silicone, and both Spiaires regained muscle control. Darci hurried over as Eryn collapsed to her knees.

"That was Brody," she said while gasping for air.

Darci pulled Eryn in for a hug, and asked, "One of your assigned humans?"

Eryn nodded. "But he's so much more than an assignment. Oh, Darci, there's something you should know."

"I have something to tell you too," Darci whispered. She glanced up at the cameras before leaning in closer to Eryn's ear, using one hand to shield her mouth as she quietly continued, "I lied to Gemma about Matthew. Oh, I pray to Isoldesse that the princess forgives me for breaking my oath, but I need to tell someone. There's no list of candidates or a search for a wife for Matthew. It was all I could think of in the moment."

"Okay, well, then who were you meeting with?"

"Prince Gerard."

20

Kenna reached her arm over her head to adjust her pillow when something hard struck her in the forehead.

"Ow! What the hell?"

The blow startled her, and she blinked a few times until her eyes adjusted to see the hard object. A strange bracelet, something that hadn't been there when she'd gone to bed, was strapped to her right wrist. A wide piece of tarnished metal like aged copper with a large white oval stone centered on the top. It was quite beautiful. A piece she could see her mom trying to acquire for the museum. But what was it doing there?

She sat up, cross-legged in her bed, and slid her glasses on. Her vision blurred.

She lowered the frames and glanced around her room. The dresser, the bed, even the books and notebooks sprawled out on the floor weren't blurry, but clear. Slowly, she pushed her glasses up the bridge of her nose and her vision turned hazy. There weren't any smudges or scratches on the lenses that would obstruct the clarity. *What is going on with my freaking eyes?*

Seeing no point to wearing her glasses, she set them on the nightstand and turned her attention to the strange metal cuff-looking bracelet. When her fingers touched the smooth white stone, she swore a hint of light glinted beneath the surface. After several minutes of failed attempts to find a latch or a release, she scooted out of bed.

A sudden recollection of last night's strange sighting flashed in her mind.

The windows.

She rushed to check the locks on both windows.

"Locked." She stared at the wide bracelet strapped to her wrist. "Oh, this can't be good."

A loud, vibrating *brrr* startled her and sent a burst of adrenaline across her shoulders and down her arms. With her phone in hand, she read the notification on her screen. She'd gotten a new text from Liam.

> Don't forget I'm going to call you later tonight, Stargirl.

It's kind of early for him to be texting me. But then she noticed the time in the upper right-hand corner. It was almost noon. "Shit! I missed my morning classes!"

Kenna tossed her phone onto her bed and scrambled to get dressed. Her mind was all over the place, bouncing between what she knew was real and the stuff she couldn't explain. Her eyes stung with the threat of a breakdown as she searched through the pile of scattered notebooks and toppled-over textbooks sprawled out over the area rug.

"Kenna," Ulissa's distant voice called out in the farthest part of her mind. "Kenna, I'm having trouble"—her voice faded in and out—"reaching you."

She shot up, holding an overstuffed binder, her evolution textbook, and a few loose pieces of paper, and called, "Ulissa?

Where are you?" She grabbed her backpack and began filling it with everything in her hands. "Hey, I can barely hear you."

"Must find an... Anumen..." Her voice wavered. "...the bond...you have to..."

"What about the bond?" Kenna slid her feet into her Birks and waited for the old woman to answer but got nothing. She grabbed her phone and slung her backpack over one shoulder. "Ulissa? You there? I have to go see my professors."

The moment she reached for the doorknob, the sunlight in her room receded as if an unexpected storm cloud hovered outside her window. Her small bedroom had become enveloped in a dim shadow, except for the space surrounding Kenna. She recalled how the same thing happened yesterday when she first met the mysterious old woman.

She spun to see Ulissa step out from the shadows in the same stunning gown, while reddish-orange smoke billowed from around her. Kenna noticed the soft golden aura had returned. She was both relieved to see the old woman and anxious to leave so she could speak to her professors.

"There you are. Okay, I've got like five minutes. We need to talk fast. So, what's happening to me?"

The woman began to speak, but without sound. Kenna waved for Ulissa to stop, then cupped a hand to her ear. "I can't hear what you're saying. Something's wrong." Ulissa pursed her lips and pointed to the white stone on Kenna's wrist. Kenna held out her arm. "You're talking about this thing? What the hell is it?"

Ulissa turned her palms upright and shook her head. She then held out one slender finger and gestured to the bracelet again.

"This is ridiculous. I don't have a lot of time, Ulissa. I need to go—"

Ulissa shook her hands. Her thin brows tightened, and the stern look in her eyes told Kenna she was trying to tell her something important.

"Okay, okay. Sorry. What is it?"

Ulissa pointed to the bracelet again and Kenna lifted her arm again. The woman pointed to the white stone and then to the arcstone beneath Kenna's shirt.

Kenna drew out the yellow stone and held it out for Ulissa to see. The old woman nodded and then pointed to the white stone and shook her head while waving her hands across one another.

"Uhm, no? You're saying *no* to this white stone on this bracelet thingy?"

The old woman nodded. Then she clapped her hands together and opened them wide while turning her palms outward. She did this a few more times before Kenna understood, or at least she hoped she understood.

"They need to be away from one another. The two stones... I need to separate them?" Kenna guessed.

Ulissa's shoulders dropped, and she nodded. For a brief second, the dark room, along with Ulissa, disappeared before quickly returning.

"What's happening? Why can't I hear you, and why are you fading like that?"

The woman pointed to the bracelet again. Kenna tugged at the edge of the metal, tight around her wrist. "I can't get this stupid thing off. I've tried."

Ulissa's body began to fade in and out again. She repeated the motion of her hands, clapping and then separating outward one last time before she completely faded away. In one blink, the mysterious storm cloud outside her windows vanished, and her room was once again filled with warm, natural sunlight.

"Ulissa?"

"*Anumen. Find... Anumen,*" were the last words Kenna heard in the back of her mind before Ulissa's voice trailed off.

"The witch group you belong to? How the hell am I supposed to do that?" Kenna adjusted her backpack over her shoulder and sighed. "Like I have so much free time to research some secret cult."

She decided to back-burner the Anumen search until after she talked to her professors about missing class. Oversleeping wasn't something she did, and she blamed her exhausted brain for sucking her into that stupid dream, forcing her to sleep like a rock. She could only hope that her professors hadn't thought she'd skipped their classes because she didn't get accepted into the summer intern program. That was the last thing she wanted. For them to think she was upset or resentful about their decision.

Meegan's voice of reason echoed in her mind: *Stop worrying so much.*

She reached for the door handle and thought, *If only I could.*

21

Out in the living room, Kenna came to an abrupt stop when she spotted Ally talking to a police officer. If it hadn't been for the uniform, Kenna would've assumed he was another one of Ally's many admirers. That girl could make friends with anyone anywhere. At one point, the offer cupped Ally's shoulder and assured her that everything was going to be okay.

Yeah, if only that were the case. Kenna crept to the sofa and sat next to Meegan, who was quietly watching Ally and the officer.

Meegan whispered, "I think he's almost done. But hey, how are you feeling?"

"I'm fine. What's he doing here?"

Meegan lifted her right wrist, then pointed to Ally's arm. "She called the police almost two and a half hours ago. The dispatcher said something about it not being an emergency, and they'd send an officer when they could. He's been here for twenty minutes taking our statements and a few pictures of the bracelets with his phone.

He just finished walking through the apartment with Ally. You know, to check for signs of a break-in."

"And?"

"Nothing. No busted locks or broken glass."

"That can't be right. How else would these things get on us? Did he talk to you?"

Meegan nodded. "Yup, and I have no idea what happened. I didn't hear anything. But you know me, I could sleep through a Fourth of July fireworks show." But Kenna could tell something was bothering Meeg because she was fidgeting with her mood ring.

I don't even want to imagine what else happened while we were sleeping. Meegan had every right to be unnerved.

"I'm sure these things are nothing. Some college prank or something?"

Truth be told, Kenna knew these bracelet things weren't some college prank. Especially if Ulissa knew to keep the white stone away from the arcstone. So, what were they? And why did Meegan and Ally have them on too?

Ugh... Doesn't look like I'm going to get to back-burner anything today. I guess I'm researching Anumen cults. How the hell am I going to find an Anumen?

They watched the young officer wrap up his speech before handing Ally his business card. He looked over her shoulder and noticed Kenna. "Excuse me, Miss?"

There was something intimidating about authority figures that Kenna could never get over. The feeling reminded her of the time she'd gotten in trouble in elementary school and been sent to the principal's office.

"Ah, yes, sir."

"I see you're wearing one of these bracelets too. Did you happen to see anything strange last night? Any suspicious people or activity in the neighborhood?"

Actually, I did, Mr. Officer. Last night while stargazing up on our roof, I happened to see a hovering aircraft about ten miles southwest of here. And then, get this... the damn thing spit out four smaller aircraft! I know, right? Crazy! Wait, there's more! After the smaller aircraft jetted off in different directions, I swear that mother-forking ship went straight up into space.

"Nope. I was sound asleep all night. Didn't see or hear a thing."

"Okay, then. I'll add your statement to my report, thank you." He then faced Ally again. "I'm sorry I couldn't be of more help. You have my business card in case you need to talk—I mean, call if there's another situation."

"Shouldn't we just call nine-one-one if there's another *situation*?" Ally emphasized her confusion.

The officer blushed and nodded. He turned to Meegan and Kenna, tipped his cap, and smiled at Ally before leaving. She slowly closed the door and stood there for a moment with one hand pressed to the wooden frame. Kenna could only imagine the paranoia racing through her roommate's head. Though, she had every right to be upset and afraid. Someone had come into their home, stood over them while they slept, and violated their space by attaching these bracelets, or whatever they were, to their bodies.

Ally eventually faced her friends and made her way to the armchair. A small smile began to spread on her face, but Kenna could see straight through her façade. Ally tugged the hem of her long-sleeve T-shirt over the bracelet and when she spoke, her voice hitched with the strain of holding back tears. "Hey! You're up. How are you feeling?"

"Feeling? I feel fine. I feel like I got a full night's sleep plus more. No drowsy, Walking Dead Kenna today. But more importantly, didn't you notice the tall, dark, and handsome cop flirting with you?"

"What? Oh, was he?" Ally rubbed her forehead and stared at her phone. "He was just being nice. Doing his job and all."

Kenna and Meegan side glanced one another. Kenna knew Meegan was thinking the same thing. It wasn't normal for Ally to pass on an opportunity to flirt with a hot guy.

Remembering she had places to be, Kenna slapped her thighs and stood. "I've got to run over to the university and see if I can catch up with my morning professors. I feel bad about oversleeping and missing classes."

"First of all, you didn't oversleep," Meegan said. "You were sick, and second, I already took care of it. I cc'd you on the emails. Both professors responded and hoped that you'd feel better soon." Meegan pointed to the cell phone in Kenna's hand. "Plus, I don't think we should be roaming around town right now. You know, in case *they* come back."

Kenna slowly sank onto the couch cushion. "You think whoever did this will be back?"

Meegan twisted her wrist and stared at the backside of the wide bracelet. "I do."

"And why did you say I was sick? I don't remember being sick this morning."

"Damn it!" Ally burst out.

Both Kenna and Meegan watched as Ally abruptly got up and stomped off to her bedroom. Unsure of the problem, they waited a few seconds before Kenna yelled, "Hey, you okay?"

From inside her room, she shouted, "It's Prue." She returned to the living room with her purse and phone in hand. "She's not answering her phone. With all this weird crap going on, I'm worried. I'm going over there now. You two can come with me now or follow in a bit."

"We can come—"

"We'll follow!" Meegan interjected before Kenna could finish. "I think Kenna should eat first and then we'll meet you at Prue's."

"You just said we should stick together."

"Ally's only going straight to Prue's, and we'll be right behind her. That's different from trekking all over campus."

"Well, I am kind of hungry." Kenna waved a go-ahead to her roommate. "We'll be fifteen minutes behind you."

"And if you see Darci, tell her to call us," Meegan shouted as Ally rushed into the kitchen and then back out with her car keys. "She's not answering my calls or texts."

Kenna picked up her phone from the coffee table and checked Darci's message thread. The last five texts were her own. "She hasn't answered any of my texts either."

"Okay, if I see her, I will," Ally said. "Don't dawdle, and I'll see you guys over there." Ally opened the front door and as she left, she added, "Be careful and call me if anything else happens."

"You too," Kenna shouted, but Ally was already out the door. She watched as the dead bolt turned into the locked position.

The two girls got up and made their way to the kitchen. Meegan sat at the counter while Kenna fixed herself a bowl of cereal. As Meegan twisted her mother's old ring, she asked, "Where are your glasses?"

"On my nightstand. I thought I'd try a glasses-free day?"

Meegan's eyes narrowed and her nose scrunched into her I'm-not-buying-that-bullshit face. "Is that the truth? Because I know for a fact that without them, you're borderline blind."

"Oh, we're doing the truth thing, are we?" Kenna held a spoonful of cereal inches from her mouth. "How about you tell me what really happened between you and Nick."

Meegan bit her lower lip and nervously patted the counter before giving her answer. "I'll tell you what happened between Nick and me if you answer one question—and before you ask, no, I'm not going to ask you about your glasses again. No trick questions. Just one thing I need to know before you can understand why I broke it off with Nick."

Okay. Well, at least that's clear. She broke it off, which means it wasn't mutual.

"Deal," Kenna said and pointed her elbow out toward her best friend.

Meegan did the same and bumped Kenna's elbow with hers. "Deal."

"Now, what's your one question?"

Meegan inhaled a deep breath before swallowing hard. "Okay, my parents are going to kill me but…" She exhaled and said, "I need to know the name of the Anumen in that arcstone."

22

*I*t was second period of my first day at a new high school, that I
met Meegan. The sweet, young-looking girl with straight black
hair sat in the back of the class, closest to the window, her nose deep
in a book. And not just any book, but one of my father's latest
releases.

I took it as a sign, seeing my father's book, that I should try and
talk to this girl. I remember being convinced that my high school
years were going to suck, mainly because Liam wasn't there, but
seeing this girl who was more interested in reading than trying to fit
in and be rowdy like the other kids had given me a bit of hope.
Maybe I'd be lucky and make a friend on my first day. As if she was
there waiting for me.

Maybe she was.

After a few stumbling introductions and some general
icebreakers, she eventually put her book away. We ended up talking
the entire class period, and by the end of the day it was as though
we'd been friends for years. Eventually, Meegan let down her guard,

allowing her humor and sarcasm to peek through the cracks of her so-called antisocial wall. I would've never guessed that the bookworm sitting alone in the back of my second-period class would grow to become one of my closest friends. Something more than a best friend. Meegan grew to become the sister I never had.

But now, years later, I'm not sure I know who the person standing in front of me is.

✻ ✧ ✻ ✧ ✻

"What did you just ask me?" Kenna's tone was a mixture of surprise and anger. "Tell me you're not the one who gave me this damn necklace? Or"—she lifted her wrist without breaking eye contact—"put these *things* on us?"

"No, I swear! I didn't—I mean, I don't know who did. Kenna, please—"

"Don't *please* me! Do you have any idea what kind of shit I've been going through? The pain and—and the hallucinations! I thought I was losing my mind!"

"You're not losing your mind, I promise. You're going to be fine," Meegan calmly said. Her reassurances only threw more logs onto Kenna's fury.

"You're kidding, right? Because none of this is *fine*! There's nothing normal, or *fine*, about what's happening to me!"

Meegan didn't flinch or shudder. Instead, her shoulders sagged forward and in one long breath, she pleaded, "I didn't give you that arcstone, Kenna. I swear, I'm trying to figure out who did because—well..." She paused and sighed. "An arcstone isn't supposed to be given to, or more importantly bonded to, someone like you."

"Oh, great! That makes me feel *so* much better! *Someone like me*, are you kidding me right now? I seriously don't even know who you are anymore." Kenna turned and headed into the living room.

Meegan was quick to follow. "Hey! We're not done talking!"

The overwhelming sense of emotions hummed beneath Kenna's skin and filled her tear ducts. But somewhere, deep in the back of her mind, a weak voice of reasoning pleaded with her to listen. To hear Meegan out and get some damn answers.

She stopped and faced Meegan. She crossed her arms tight over her chest and pursed her lips.

"I'm sorry I kept this from you. But I have my reasons." There was no hurt or betrayal in her voice, only flat honesty. As if it were none of Kenna's business. Except now it *was* her business. Meegan continued and Kenna let her. "I didn't want you anywhere near this and believe me when I say I'm doing everything I can to avoid my parents finding out. Though, they would know more about what's happening, but I'll tell you right now, if they found out…" She paused and shook her head. "Let's just say it wouldn't be good for either of us."

Kenna stared at her blankly, waiting for Meegan to say something that would help her believe that her best friend hadn't done this to her.

"I promise you I am trying to figure out who gave you that arcstone and who's responsible for putting these transessent stones on our wrists. But…" She sighed. "I'm not getting very far. And I'm really sorry your experience with the arcstone has been unpleasant."

"That's an understatement," she scoffed and shuffled over to the floral sofa. "Okay, let's say I believe you." Meegan followed and sat in the oversized armchair adjacent to the sofa as Kenna asked, "How long have you known about this kind of stuff?"

"My whole life."

"And you didn't trust me enough to clue me in?"

"Kenna, it's not my secret to tell. People here aren't ready to know the truth."

"Holy shit! Does Nick know?"

Meegan shook her head. "You would've known if he knew. He probably would've broken up with me the moment he found out who I really am."

"Why? Because you and your family are into witchcraft? That your little witch cult… what do you call yourselves, Anumens… are into *voodoo* spells and magic. You underestimate how much he loved you. Your secret life never interfered with our everyday friendship or your relationship. I'm sure he would've understood if you'd given him the chance. We both would've!"

Meegan stared at Kenna for two long seconds before she cracked a huge smile and burst out laughing. "Is that what you think is going on? That I'm part of some witch cult?" She rocked back into the armchair and between gasps of laughter and one loud snort, she said, "Oh, this is good! You think we cast spells into a black cauldron and dance naked in the woods during full moons! That we wear pointy black hats and fly around on brooms."

While her friend seemed amused at the situation, all Kenna wanted to do was cry and scream and throw things. She clenched her fists, waiting for Meegan to stop.

"Wow. Holy shit, I needed that laugh." Meegan wiped under her eyes and settled her giddy nerves. "Kenna, we're not witches. Though, we can do what you would call magic." Meegan seemed to be considering the similarities before continuing, "Anyway, is that what the Anumen in the arcstone told you? She told you we were witches?"

Well, not exactly, Kenna thought. *But what's the difference? Witches, religious cult, secret society, Anumen—whatever you want to call it. A cult is a cult.* Kenna kept her mouth shut, still unsure of what the hell was going on. Ulissa hadn't flat-out said the word *witches*, but she didn't want Meegan to know that. She wanted to hear Meegan's interpretation of what this Anumen cult was about.

When Kenna said nothing, Meegan's eyes widened, and all joking aside, she demanded, "Kenna! Now isn't the time to pull the stubborn-bitch card. Tell me who's in that stone. I promise, I'll answer whatever questions you have. Just give me her name."

"How did you know it's a *she*?"

"What?"

"You said *she*, and then you said *her name*."

A long sigh escaped her lips, and Meegan explained, "Only a female Anumen can transcend their essence into an arcstone, and before you ask what an essence is, think of it as your soul but a bit more involved. A living essence is constantly absorbing essences from the Eilimintachs around us. The elements are what fuel our existence. But anyway, after the physical body dies, a female Anumen has the option to ascend her essence into an arcstone, though there aren't many arcstones, so most continue on to what we call the Unforeseen World. Since Anumen men don't possess the biological ability to cast amulas—kind of like a spell, you might say—after their physical body dies their essence automatically ascends to the Unforeseen World, the realm in which we live our second life before final rest."

"That's a lot to digest."

"Yeah, it is. But it does seem like you have a basic understanding of the Anumen culture. That's good."

"No, not really! It all sounds crazy to me—and it's pissing me off! You're all casual like it's just another day, but it's not. Not for me!"

Meegan scooted closer over to the sofa and rested one hand on Kenna's arm. "Hey, you're not alone in this. I wasn't kidding when I said I'm trying to figure out what the hell's going on. Now that a huge weight has been lifted, you knowing my secret, we can solve this together. You have no idea how good it feels to be able to talk freely about this stuff with you."

She lifted Kenna's wrist and dragged two fingers over the white stone in Kenna's cuff—what Meegan had called a transessent stone. "First of all, you really shouldn't be wearing this and the arcstone at the same time. I do know that much."

"What is this thing?"

"I've never seen bracelets like these. But I also haven't been around transessent stones in, like, forever. What I remember from my lessons with my aunt is that a transessent stone has two purposes. One being an amplifier." She held out a hand and then whispered, *"Tarach bach sola."*

The air above her palm swirled until a marble-sized orb of light flickered to life. Kenna's eyes widened. She couldn't help but glance back and forth between the magical phenomenon and the Anumen casting it.

"Whoa. How are you doing that?" she asked softly.

"It's called an amula. Amulas are incantations, or a string of words that are encoded with instructions to manipulate the energy of the Eilimintachs. When a female Anumen recites an amula, the result is what you would call magic. *Tarach bach sola* means *come or bring soft, gentle light*," Meegan explained. "I convert nearby energy, or bits of essence, from the surrounding elements and alter their composition and purpose to whatever I want. Depends on the amula."

"Will it go away?" Kenna lifted a hand closer to the glowing orb and realized it was emitting heat, like a miniature sun.

Meegan nodded as the ball of light grew, doubling in size. She then lifted her arm and they both stared at the transessent stone on Meegan's wrist. The once-solid white surface now had thin, glowing veins marbling along the top.

What. The. Hell. Shit, this is so freaking cool!

"Normally, the amula would fade over time. Or you could say, '*Déanta*.'" The glowing ball of light, now the size of a softball, poofed into a cloud of yellow smoke, dispersing into the air. "*Déanta* means *stop*, a way to end the amula."

"So only females can cast magic—I mean, amulas?" When Meegan nodded, Kenna asked, "Well, why the hell was I able to bond with the arcstone? I'm not Anumen."

"I guess you don't have to be. I've never known anyone besides an Anumen to bond with an arcstone." She leaned back on the couch cushion and said, "Just another mystery for us to figure out. But I can tell you that the amula you read, *Banna idir dufiur et gohdeo*, means *the bond between sisters is forever*. Sisters meaning women." She bit her lower lip before she hesitantly added, "You know that I don't believe in coincidences. Which means—"

"—which means someone wanted me to bond with the arcstone."

"Exactly."

"But why?"

"I don't know. But we're going to find out... together."

Kenna rubbed the arcstone between her fingers and said, "Ulissa. Her name's Ulissa and I've only talked to her twice." Meegan's mouth dropped open as Kenna continued, "Well, three times if you count ten minutes ago in my bedroom. But the connection was spotty, so we didn't talk long."

Meegan licked her closed lips and pointed to the stone dangling from Kenna's neck. "Ulissa's in that arcstone?" Before Kenna could ask anything, Meegan shot to her feet and started pacing the length of the living room. She muttered curses under her breath. "Oh, shit! This is worse than I thought."

"What's wrong? Do you know Ulissa?" When Meegan half nodded, half shook her head and ended with a shrug, Kenna raised a finger and proclaimed, "I knew it! That old woman acted all sweet and friendly, but she's bad, isn't she? Like, one of your Anumen evil witches?"

Meegan stopped pacing and sighed. "I don't know her. I only know *of* her. And no, she's not bad or evil. From what I know, she's quiet, and sweet, and they say she's always been a private Anumen. It's not her I'm worried about. It's her sister, Isoldesse, that concerns me."

Kenna scrunched her nose. "She's never mentioned a sister."

"Why would she? She's probably just as confused as you and I are." Meegan looked at the transessent stone on Kenna's wrist again. "But you're not going to get any answers from Ulissa while wearing that transessent stone."

"Why?"

"Well, that's the second thing the transessent stone does. It overpowers the arcstone and puts the bond connection into a dormant state" Meegan began to pace again. "Which explains why your last encounter with Ulissa was pretty shoddy. You probably won't hear or see Ulissa again, or be able to harness the arcstone's power, until we get that transessent stone off your wrist."

"I don't understand. Why would someone give me the arcstone and the amula to activate the bond, and then go and put this blocker-stone bracelet thingy on me?"

Meegan shrugged. "I have no idea. Though, I'm betting my mother's ring that whoever put these transessent stones on us didn't know you had an arcstone. Or it could've been something else. Something much worse. An entirely different race. A race I hope you never have to meet."

"And by *different race*, you mean the Obard."

Meegan jerked to a stop and narrowed her eyes at Kenna. "You know about the Obard?"

How could she forget them? The scaly black armor of the soldiers with their dark mirrored faceplates. The ground-shaking steps as they advanced from behind the trees and out across the open field. The blue tendrils of hair draped from the tops of their helmets as they held their long black swords, ready to strike.

"Only from last night's dream," Kenna explained. "Nasty, scary-ass dudes. Thank God it was only a dream. Though, I swear I was going to have a heart attack when they started chasing me." Meegan's gaze dipped, her hands wringing as she stood there in silence. She'd never seen her friend so unraveled. "Meeg, it was just a dream. I'm fine. Besides, who are they? Some kind of witch hunters?"

"Kenna, you still think I'm part of some witch cult?"

"Well, duh. What else could it be? Witches, spells, magic—I can't see any other explanation. Two seconds ago, you said some magical words and poof! A mini sun floating in my living room!"

"But have you considered *where* I'm from?"

She swallowed hard and mentally kicked herself for not even considering *that* option. There was no way this was really happening. Stuff like this only happened in science-fiction movies or books. Not here in her living room. Not with her best friend.

She exhaled a deep breath before she said, "Okay. Tell me. Where are you from?"

Meegan slowly sat onto the floral sofa again. "My family and I are from a small planet called Anuminis. Three galaxies from Earth."

Kenna wriggled uncomfortably and inhaled deep breaths while her mind digested each word Meegan had just spoken. "Oh my God, this is really happening. My best friend is an alien."

Meegan chuckled. "Well, I'm happy to know that."

"Happy? Happy to know what?"

"That I'm still your best friend."

23

"**B**lessed Isoldesse, we could really use some help," Darci prayed into clasped hands.

Thwump, thwump, thwump, thwump.

"I'm trying to understand why—why this is happening. Why Gemma has kidnapped us. And what's she even doing here?"

Thwump, thwump, thwump, thwump.

The lights around the room were off, except for the one recessed light above the plastic patio set. Thus, leaving the edges of the room somewhat like Darci's dreary and defeated mood, dark and shadowed. She stood and tried to roll her neck, but because of the paralytic restraints and the limited range of motion, she couldn't stretch the tender muscles beneath the stupid device.

Thwump, thwump.

Darci crossed the room and crouched next to Eryn. "You have to stop. He's not going to wake up."

The weary Spiaire lifted her head. Her attempts over the last hour to wake Brody had gone from shouting and banging on the door to sitting and half slapping, half patting the door. Darci could see how drained her companion was and how much this human meant to her, but in the end it didn't matter. They were Sendarian, and he was not.

"We did this to him," Eryn muttered.

Darci brushed the loose strands of red hair away from Eryn's face. "I need you to get it together. Because—because I don't know what to do, and Prince Gerard is out there, and I have no idea if he got my message about Gemma. I have no clue where our humans are or—or what the hegah Gemma meant when she said she wishes she could see the look on Breyah's face when she sees *whatever surprise* Gemma left for Breyah! Seriously, Eryn, my head is about to explode!"

When Eryn said nothing, Darci tried to sympathize with the situation, but couldn't. There was nothing more to it. A relationship with an outside species was more than just frowned upon. It was forbidden. Regardless of what she felt about Eryn's predicament, she needed to snap some sense into her fellow Spiaire. "Look, I'm sorry this is happening. And I'm sorry we can't help Brody or Prue right now. But this is far from over, Eryn, and I can't do this on my own. I need your help to figure out what they have planned for us."

"I hope they leave us." Eryn leaned her head against the door. "Breyah can handle Gemma. I want to stay here... with him." She rested one hand on the door.

Okay, enough is enough!

Darci let out an exasperated sigh before grabbing Eryn's freckle-covered hands and yanking her to her feet. She yelled, "Stop it! We need to save *us* first before we can save them! Now get your shit together and help me figure out what the hegah we're going to do next. Because if we don't, Hegah's exactly where I'll end up once the queen discovers what I've done."

Eryn's head jerked up and her eyes narrowed. "What are you talking about? Why would the queen want to harm you? It's been over fifty years since the prince left Sendara. Maybe it was the queen who tasked the princess to commission you with your assignment.

You're being absurd. We must have faith in Isoldesse, who blessed the royal family to lead Sendara. They would never do you harm."

"Maybe." It was Darci's turn to wallow in her thoughts.

Oh, why did the prince have to live in my assigned region? Ugh, why couldn't Gerard have lived up north in Eryn's region?

Eryn squeezed Darci's hands. "Stop worrying. You did nothing wrong. Brody did nothing wrong! This is all that gróntah's fault. Gemma did this. She sabotaged the Aevo Compendium. It's her essence that's going to Hegah after death!"

Darci's shoulders dropped and her hands slipped from Eryn's. "But why? What made her turn her back on our goddess?"

Eryn started to look back at Brody's door, but before she could, Darci towed her farther from it. She needed to keep Eryn from drifting into her previous gloomy state. She also kept their proximity close to keep the cameras from seeing their lips while they talked. They still needed to come up with a plan, or at least figure out what their next move was. Their most obvious challenge was escaping while wearing these stupid paralytic restraints.

To keep Eryn's mind focused, Darci explained, "Princess Emmalyn never revealed what her message was. She said I was to deliver the encrypted plac to Gerard, and that was all."

"And you delivered the plac?"

"Yes. It was one of the first things I did after we arrived here. I contacted the prince and set up a meeting. Me, him, and his human wife."

Eryn's orange eyes grew wide. "Does his wife know who he *really* is?"

"Yes."

"She does? Well, that's interesting. Regardless"—Eryn leaned in closer—"we cannot let Gemma know he's here, or that you've been in contact with him." She paused and stared at the floor. When she looked up, her pale eyebrows pulled together, scrunching her freckled skin. "How did they not recognize him?"

"I have no idea." Darci shrugged and then casually added, "And, uh… I might have done some light reading in the Rhaltan files before we left Priomh."

"You hacked into the secured Rhaltan Network?"

"I was curious and—"

"You were snooping."

Darci nodded. "Yes."

"Now *that* I can see you getting into trouble for. Not even Breyah would be able to help you. Promise me you won't do that ever again or tell anyone else what you just told me." After Darci agreed, Eryn asked, "Okay, so what did you discover?"

Darci scratched at her shoulder beneath the sleeve of the gray T-shirt. "I found a file memo about increased activity with a small rebel group called the Athru, but they've always been more of a nuisance than a threat. But what really caught my attention was another memo, logged in a separate file, about how the Rhaltan Enforcers have upped the number of cadets being accepted into the upcoming training season."

"That is odd. Did the memo explain why?"

"Not exactly. Something about increased support for a new division being developed. Specifics were left out. Which also seemed a little odd. After reading that memo, I browsed the roster for the latest Rhaltan cadet class."

"And?"

Darci leaned in closer. "The number of graduating cadets was triple from previous years."

"Well, that is concerning. There's got to be a reason the queen's increasing her security. Maybe Princess Emmalyn knows, and she needs either Gerard's council or his help," Eryn said more to herself than to Darci. She then said, "It's out of our hands. Gerard has the message, and we can't do anything for him while we're stuck in here."

Both Spiaires tensed when they heard footsteps outside the exit door. Eryn used both hands to cover her mouth and whispered, "Stick to your story about Breyah searching for a human companion for Matthew. No matter who comes through that door. Don't say a word about Prince Gerard. It's the only way to keep us alive. To keep Prue and Brody alive."

Darci mentally prepared herself for another round of strangled pain from the paralytic restraints, but when the door opened, Darci gasped and muttered, "Where the hegah did you come from?"

24

W hen Darci saw the petite young woman with a plump figure and a round face walk in, her heart momentarily fluttered with excitement, though something in the woman's bright orange eyes warned Darci not to get too excited.

"Sabine!" Eryn exclaimed and rushed over to embrace Breyah's personal assistant. "Oh, thank Isoldesse!" She leaned back, still holding Sabine, and asked, "Is Breyah with you? Are you here because of Gemma? Are you here to rescue us?"

Darci stepped closer to the open door. This could be their opportunity. Their one chance to escape. But before Darci could plan out their next move, Sabine freed herself from Eryn's grasp, reached for the door, and slowly closed it. "Sorry, girls. I can't let you leave."

"What? Why?" The joy in Eryn's tone died. Her gaze flip-flopped between Sabine and Darci. "What's going on?"

Darci crossed her arms and cocked her head to one side. "Oh, for the love of Isoldesse, please tell me you're not helping Gemma sabotage the Aevo Compendium?"

"There's a lot more going on than sabotaging your goddess's ridiculous pet project," Sabine said with a loud scoff. "But what kind of Athru would I be if I divulged our entire plan?"

At the word *Athru*, Eryn covered her mouth and gasped. "No. You wouldn't!"

"I would and I did. Gemma was sent to watch you"—she pointed to Darci—"while I was sent to watch Eryn up north."

"You? But—but I was attacked by a man." Eryn blinked wet eyes.

"My companion for this mission. I'm sure you'll get the pleasure of meeting him again later."

"Hold on a second," Darci cut in. If this wasn't an opportunity to escape, then she'd take advantage of another opportunity and get some damn answers. "Why do the Athru want to sabotage the Aevo Compendium? I thought the Athru were a bunch of misguided *predults* running around Sendara blowing off adolescent steam. They've never been a real threat."

Sabine snickered. "That's what they want you to think. But in the past few years the Athru have had some leadership changes. Activists who have big plans for a new Sendara. The three leaders of the Athru are way past their predult years and believe in something other than what a false goddess had written in some book. For all we know, the Anumen Doctrine was written by the ancestors of the royal family."

"No!" Darci gasped under her breath. *Isoldesse is not a false goddess.*

Sabine continued, "Anora, Biryn, and Quaid will stop at nothing to bring down the queen and her bloodline."

Darci narrowed her eyes at Breyah's assistant. "Why are you here, Sabine?"

She hadn't thought the petite woman's smile could get any wider, but it did. "If you mean why did I join the Athru? Well, they recruited me—"

"No," Darci interrupted and stepped closer. She stood nearly a foot over the traitor. "I mean, why are you here... in this room? What do you want?"

Sabine sighed with a slight nod. Her bright smile sank, and she rolled her orange eyes at the two Spiaires. "Of course, you wouldn't want to know anything about *me*. No one wants to talk or get to know the girl always standing in Breyah's shadow. No one ever invites me to join them after hours to hang out or spar. No one except the Athru."

"It was you." Eryn's voice trembled, breaking the tension between Darci and Sabine. "You're the reason Brody's here."

Slowly, the corners of Sabine's lips curled up again. "Yes. Yes, I am."

Hand-to-hand combat was an essential part of Spiaire training, so when Darci saw the twitch of movement from Eryn, she lunged and grabbed her friend before she could attack Sabine.

"Let me go! Let me at her! I'm going to kill this gróntah for what she's done!" Eryn's hands clawed the air while Darci dragged her friend away.

"Eryn, stop!" She blocked Eryn from attacking again and faced Sabine. Between gritted teeth, Darci repeated her question. "Again, why are you here, Sabine?"

"Well, I only popped in to say hello and to let you know that I know you're lying."

Darci briefly glanced over her shoulder at Eryn, who asked, "What are you talking about?"

"Your lie about Matthew wanting a wife."

"I wasn't lying," Darci insisted. "He hasn't been around another human since the last Earth Aevo Compendium. It's either find him a wife or send him back to Earth, and he doesn't want to live in a place he's no longer familiar with."

The room fell silent, and eventually Sabine let out an exasperated sigh as she explained, "You forget. I know everything about what Breyah does, wants, sees, and has planned when it comes to life on that pathetic moon. Her pet human, Matthew, has never complained or spoken about wanting a wife." Before Darci or Eryn could say anything, Sabine leaned in and whispered, "If you ask me, I think he's messing around with a Sendarian up there. Someone who's okay with being banished if discovered."

"Matthew wouldn't do that," Darci said. "He wouldn't disrespect our laws like that. Besides, it was made clear, and he agreed to those conditions, when he requested to stay on Priomh after the last Earth Aevo Compendium." Darci couldn't help but shoot Eryn a quick side glance before continuing to Sabine. "No sexual relations or crossbreeding with other races. The Anumen Doctrine forbids it."

"Yeah, yeah—the Anumen Doctrine forbids it—blah, blah, blah." Sabine opened the door and stepped one foot out, her round figure still halfway in the room. "Listen, I won't say anything to Gemma, not yet at least. Mainly because I want to see how this ruse of yours plays out. Gemma's reaction will be priceless when she discovers the truth, because if you know her like I do, she always gets what she wants. Besides, you're not the only one she can get the truth from." Sabine stared at the two Spiaires with a closed-lip smile as she let that bit of information sink in.

"I'm not lying!" Darci clenched the top of a patio chair. "And— and what does that mean, *I'm not the only one you can get the truth from?*" Sabine was about to close the door when Darci cried out, "Wait, Sabine! I'm not lying! Who else has Gemma taken? Please, tell me!"

Sabine half stepped back into the room, cocked her head, and teasingly said, "Possibly one of the two people who also know your little secret. But again, I'm not at liberty to say."

Darci's shoulders slumped as she came around and sat in the plastic chair. "You don't know what you've done, Sabine."

"Don't go around blaming others. Their being here is no one's fault but yours," were the last words Sabine said before she left the room.

With wet eyes, Darci stared up at Eryn. "Oh no-no-no. This can't be happening." She cupped her hands over her mouth and explained, "They have Gerard's wife."

Eryn shook her head and sat in the plastic chair next to Darci. "Are you sure?"

Tears trickled down Darci's cheeks. "It has to be her. I don't know why Gemma or the others didn't recognize their banished prince, but I'm sure they would've realized who they'd taken once they got closer to him. Which means it has to be his wife, Honnah."

Eryn sighed. "It seems the Athru are more of a threat than expected. They've deceived us all. The queen, the Rhaltan Enforcers, and now us. We need to focus on that. We need to get a communication to the *Tarais*, who can then warn Breyah. She'll know what to do. She'll know how to warn the queen."

"Okay, but how? Our Lincs have been deactivated by these stupid things." Darci tugged at the paralytic band around her neck while staring into Eryn's orange eyes. "How do we get a message to the *Tarais* and help Prue, Brody, and now Gerard's wife?"

"We do nothing." Eryn rested one hand on Darci's. "You were right. We can't do anything for anyone while we're locked up in here. But we'll stay alert and be ready for when Isoldesse presents us an opportunity. We cannot lose our faith in our goddess."

"Never," Darci said and clasped Eryn's hands. This was the Eryn she needed. The Eryn with years of Spiaire experience and the ability to kick ass if needed.

In the back of her mind, she prayed to Isoldesse that Kenna, Meegan, and Ally were all at Prue's house and that the transport was still on schedule. No matter what, the Aevo Compendium must continue, even if that meant missing their ride home.

25

An alien.

Meegan is an alien.

My best friend—is an alien.

I've hung out, laughed, cried, hugged, vacationed, and spent most of my high school and college days with an alien!

She turned her blinker on and waited at the stoplight.

Oh God, Nick! They dated for two years.

Kenna watched Meegan flip through music stations and wondered if they'd had sex.

No way. She can't! I mean, it's not possible... or is it? Plus, that's something she would've told me. Alien or not.

But they'd kissed, and he'd most likely done *other things* with an alien.

She'd always wondered if intelligent life beyond their world would be similar, in humanoid form. Maybe Meegan wasn't technically an alien, just a different race of humans somehow off living on a different planet. Kenna could feel her excitement and curiosity swelling inside. Ever since she'd been a kid listening to her dad's bedtime stories about space travel and alien worlds, she'd desperately wanted it to be true, and more importantly, she'd wanted those discoveries to happen within her lifetime.

And now it was happening.

"Who's Ben?"

Kenna loosened her grip on the steering wheel and simmered her excited curiosity. "Ben?"

"Yeah, you were muttering his name this morning while you were curled up pretty much passed out on your bedroom floor. I thought you were into that guy, Liam?"

"I think you're exaggerating about the whole sick thing this morning, because I don't remember a thing. And I definitely don't remember talking about Ben." The tall, dreamy guy she'd encountered in her dream last night was just that, a figment of her imagination. And of course, he would be hot and heroic and chase away the bad, bad Obard. That's what all knights in shining armor would do and look like. Strong and handsome. A physique programmed into little girls' heads early in life from all those princess stories.

Kenna laughed at the irony of how the two main characters from her father's space adventure series were quite the opposite of the stereotypical role. The princess in his stories possessed all the magic and power and was the one always saving the day. While her love, a man from another world, and with no magical powers, always stood by her side during the ending battle scenes of the book.

Meegan swapping out a new song on the radio drew Kenna back to their conversation. "Seriously, you know me well enough to know I don't have time for that kind of drama. Ben was the name of the guy in my dream last night. I promise, he's not real." She picked up her phone. No new messages. "And Liam, well, Liam's a good friend. And—"

"Ben is some guy you've been crushing on?"

"Uh, *no*." She shook her head and glared at Meegan. "Did you not just hear me? I don't have any time to date. I don't even have time for a one-nighter! Besides, he's just some imaginary guy I ran into while running away from the Obard." She saw her friend stiffen at the word *Obard*. Kenna apologized and explained, "Meeg, it was only a dream."

"I'm not sure it was *only a dream*."

Kenna slowed to a stop behind a pickup truck waiting at a stop sign. When the truck continued straight, Kenna turned left onto Meegan's street. The homes in this part of town were nothing like the homes in her parents' neighborhood. The curb appeal alone screamed money. She always felt out of place whenever she drove her little old Corolla through this neighborhood. She brushed off her insecurities and said, "It sure as hell felt like a dream."

"Things are different now that you're bonded with that arcstone. But Ulissa showing up in your so-called dream isn't normal. I'll know more once I borrow—"

"You mean steal."

"No, I mean borrow, one of my mother's books. While we're at Prue's, I'll take pictures of the pages we need with my phone and then return it later tonight, or tomorrow. She'll never know we *borrowed* it."

"You have met your mother, right?"

"You worry too much."

"*Duh.* It's who I am. I can't help but worry." Kenna pulled into Meegan's driveway and parked behind a shiny black Lexus. After she turned off the engine of her decade-old car, she faced her friend. "She's home. I thought you said Monday afternoons she goes to her book club."

"I'm not sure why she's home. Probably has something to do with my aunt calling yesterday."

"Your aunt? The one up in North Carolina?"

Meegan nodded. "Yeah, well, my aunt is kind of special. She called yesterday to let my mom know she'd sensed a powerful amula and wanted to know if we were involved."

"Your aunt has Spidey-Senses that work three states away? That's freaking crazy, yet kind of cool."

"Like I said, she's special. One of the more powerful Anumens. Someone we call the Sëara. She can sense amulas, communicate with Anumens in the Unforeseen World, and occasionally get glimpses or premonitions through—"

"Through… what? Whoa, wait a second. What the hell is the Unforeseen World again? I feel like you've mentioned that before."

"You know what? Let me go get the book and then we can talk more after." Meegan hurried out of Kenna's beat-up sedan and across her parents' pristine grass. If her mother was home, Kenna knew Meegan would get an earful for running across the lawn and not using the walkway.

With the millions of questions compiling in her brain, Kenna hadn't once thought about what their lives must be like—for all the Anumens living on Earth. Them being discovered here would lead to being taken away, locked up, and most likely cut open and studied. The thought of Meegan lying on a stainless-steel surgical table with sections of her body pried open sickened her.

Makes me want to go in there and give Mrs. Prinor a big ole hug and swear some kind of Anumen oath that I'd never tell anyone their secret.

The sound of a basketball hitting pavement snapped her from her thoughts. Next door, a young boy, maybe seven or eight years old, dribbled a basketball in his driveway. A moment later, another boy, a little older, ran out from inside the open garage and the two began playing a game of one-on-one.

There was nothing out of the ordinary until she noticed the silhouette of a man standing inside the boys' garage. *Must be their dad.* But when the figure emerged, she gasped. An Obard soldier, dressed in the same scaly black armor, with the same dark reflective faceplate covering the front of the helmet, stood there. White smoke from beneath the helmet wafted into the air while long icy-blue strands of hair sprouted from the top and swayed over the eight-foot giant's shoulders. It took two long strides toward the young boys. Wide eyed and mouth gaped, Kenna slapped one hand to the window while her other hand fumbled the door handle. But before she could get out and warn the boys, the lone Obard raised its long black blade over one shoulder and positioned itself close enough to strike. Inches before the tip of the blade reached the boys' necks, she squeezed her eyes shut and screamed.

The whole thing was over in less than six seconds. She screamed again when Meegan opened the passenger-side door and hopped in.

"What's wrong?" Meegan asked, her eyes wide in concern. "I heard you screaming from my front door."

"I—I," Kenna stammered and wiped her eyes. She slowly forced herself to look at the neighbor's house. The two boys were there, laughing and playing basketball. No Obard in sight. "I thought I saw— It came out from inside the garage"—she faced Meegan, cheeks flushed and hands trembling—"and it killed them!"

"Who did? And killed who?" Meegan asked and scanned the area until she spotted her neighbors. "Scott and Henry?" The boys' basketball game had turned into a wrestling match on the grass. "They look okay. See?" she said and pointed to the two boys rolling about.

"No!" Kenna yelled. "It was an Obard soldier. He came out from inside their garage and then drew back his sword and— Oh my God, it all happened so fast."

"The Obard?" Meegan whispered and immediately dropped the book she was holding and lifted her hand with the mood ring.

"What's with that ring? You're always messing with it and looking at it whenever you get nervous. It's kind of your tell when something's bothering you." Meegan tucked a strand of black hair behind her ear and stared at the front of her house. Softly, Kenna asked, "It's not a mood ring, is it?"

Her friend sat quiet in the passenger seat for a long moment before answering. "No. Well, yes, it is, but my mother cast an amula on it so that it would change color if any Obard were near. She got the idea back in the mid-seventies when mood rings were first created. If the stone changes to a bright turquoise color, then you know we're in trouble."

"Obard." Kenna's voice trembled at the thought of the Obard being real and not something her mind had created as a nightmare. "How close do you have to be for it to work?"

"The distance isn't a guarantee. A little more than a hundred yards is what my mother told me. But, technically, we haven't run into any Obard to officially test it," she said with a soft chuckle. When Kenna didn't react to Meegan's attempt to lighten the mood, she continued, "Okay, so promise me you won't get grossed out, but we know the ring works because my mother severed a hand from a dead Obard during their escape from Anuminis. She knew she might need the bones for an amula one day. For something like this." She held up her hand with the mood ring on it. "It's still violet, which means no Obard. So, whatever you think you saw, it wasn't real."

"But—but it looked so real."

"Meegan!" Mrs. Prinor shouted from the front doorway.

Meegan picked up the small hardcover book with worn edges and tea-colored pages and pulled it into her lap. "I got what we need. Now quick, start the car before she comes over here."

Kenna started her car and shifted into Reverse. "Maybe we should clue your mom in, you know, for help?"

Meegan shook her head. "Not going to happen. I promise you she won't help you. But she will shove me in that car"—she pointed to her mother's Lexus—"and haul my ass up to my aunt's house."

"She wouldn't help me?"

"No. She'd probably lock you in our guest bedroom and let my father deal with you."

Kenna's nose crinkled at the words *deal with you*. She backed out of the cobblestone driveway and shifted into Drive. "What exactly does that mean?"

Meegan shrugged. "I don't know, and I don't want to find out. My parents are paranoid and will do whatever to keep me from…" She rubbed the top of the mood ring. "…from getting hurt."

Meegan opened her mother's book and flipped through the pages while Kenna drove. Prue's house was farther inland from the ocean, out of the city, and after a few minutes, Kenna asked, "Does the government know about you? I mean, like, do you have some secret agreement to live here?"

Meegan shook her head and continued flipping through the journal. "No one knows. Besides the Obard, humans are our only other threat. Hence my parents' extreme paranoia around you, Nick, and anyone else I invite over. They believe anyone could be bought off for the right price."

"You know I would never say anything, right?"

Meegan snickered. "I know. And there were a thousand times I wanted to tell you, but you get why I couldn't, yeah?"

Kenna nodded. They had some time before they'd get to Prue's and she had a million questions. "How many of you are there? You know, living on Earth."

"Not many. Less than a few hundred."

"Holy shit! There are that many aliens living on Earth?" Kenna blurted.

"Well, it's a guesstimate. But yes, that we know of because… uh, well, they're supposed to report to my—" She paused and shook her head. "Never mind. There's a lot to know about the history of our people and the rules we follow here on Earth. A conversation we can have later. Okay?"

"Yeah, okay. Later." Kenna sped up the car as they got onto the highway. Instinctively she reached to adjust her glasses, but then she remembered she didn't need them anymore, and she was still unsure which of the alien stones was responsible for her newly improved vision. Something else she'd have to get used to. "Okay, well, how come you look so *human*?"

"I think the better question is why do humans look so much like *Anumens*? Our existence dates well before your creation."

"Seriously?"

"Seriously."

"How long have you been living on Earth?"

"I've been here for over a hundred years, and—"

The car swerved to the right, mimicking Kenna's head whipping in that direction. Dirt wafted up from under the tires as they slid along the breakdown lane.

Meegan screamed, "Kenna!"

"Sorry, sorry!" She quickly straightened the wheel and tapped the brakes until the car was back on the highway and under control. "Shit, I'm sorry."

"What the hell was that? Do you need me to drive?"

"No, no! I just wasn't expecting you to say you've been here for over a hundred years! You barely look twenty-two."

"Thanks." She smiled and returned to reading the pages of the old journal. "Anumens age slower. Much, much slower."

"So, you're over a hundred?" Kenna asked shakily while getting her bearings again on the road.

"Don't freak out, but I'm more like three hundred and eighteen. Believe it or not, Earth's time is similar to what we had on Anuminis. I'm assuming it's because our planets are similar in size and have a relatively similar position around the sun. But I can't say for sure."

Three hundred and f'ing eighteen. Holy shit! Breathe, Kenna, breathe. Don't freak out. This is really happening!

Meegan jabbed her finger at one of the pages and cheered, "I found it! I knew I'd seen this amula in here."

"What does it do?"

"It'll allow me to communicate with the Anumen inside a bonded arcstone."

"Will it work while I'm wearing this transessent stone?"

Meegan shrugged. "I don't know, but we have to try." She continued to read until something caused her to sigh.

"What is it? What does it say? Shit, it says we need some weird ingredient that's only found on your world, doesn't it?"

"No, we should be able to find what we need at Prue's house, but it does say only Anumens who can handle the drain should cast the amula." Meegan grabbed a hair elastic from around the shifter and used it as a bookmark.

"What does that mean? Drain?"

"This amula uses the essence of the Anumen casting it rather than drawing from the essences of surrounding elements, or what we call the *Eilimintachs*."

"Wait, so you're going to barter part of your essence? I don't think I like the sound of you losing part of your soul for this." Kenna eased on the brakes as they exited the highway. Out here away from the city, things were spread out more, and much less convenient. Things like going shopping or even going to the doctor were more difficult out here. But it was where Prue wanted to live. She liked her privacy.

"No. Don't think of an essence as a soul. Think of it as energy that fuels the soul, your physical body, and how you interact with other essences. An individual's consciousness is embodied within an essence, and for us, when an Anumen's physical body dies and we ascend to our second life in the Unforeseen World, we do so as that energy. I believe, yet it's not really proven, that all forms of life, not just Anumen, ascend to a second life before final rest. But that's just me. My parents... not so much. They hold little regard for humans and their ability to ascend to the Unforeseen World."

Kenna wasn't sure if she was more offended or intrigued. Instead, she let that new piece of information soak in as she turned down Prue's road. Houses in this area were miles apart and often hidden by the brush or tall trees.

When Kenna's phone vibrated in her purse, she asked Meegan to check it.

"It's Ally. She's freaking out. Prue isn't home."

"Text her and tell her we'll be there in like two seconds."

Meegan did at the same moment Kenna pulled onto Prue's long driveway, a dirt road that stretched out almost a half mile before Prue's house came into sight. The quaint two-story craftsman-style home was something Prue's father had built for Prue and Ally to live in and to run their catering business out of. But since Ally had no interest in living so far from the city and the beach, it was now just Prue's home. Kenna, Meegan, and Darci would come out once or twice a month to swim in the pool, hang out by the firepit, and just relax. The open view of the stars at night was an added perk.

Kenna parked beside Ally's SUV and Meegan quickly unbuckled. With her car door open, she told Kenna, "Listen, we're not done talking about your so-called dream yet. It's something I want to ask Ulissa about too if this amula works."

"Okay." She held the keys in her lap and asked, "So, do we tell Ally?"

"Tell Ally what? That I'm not human? Kenna, we can't. You're an exception, and you know exactly why you're an exception. If it weren't for that arcstone, you'd still be in the dark about who I am."

"But what about these transessent stones? She's got one on too."

Meegan sighed. "Let's wait, okay? Until it's absolutely necessary. The less she knows, the safer she'll be."

"Yeah, I guess." Kenna opened her driver-side door. "Now, we have to help Ally figure out where the hell Prue is before she calls the police again."

"One problem at a time," Meegan said and closed the car door.

One problem at a time. That was something Kenna could never wrap her mind around. It was normal for her to have a list of things she was worried about. A list that constantly weighed heavy on her mind. But now, none of that seemed important. All that time and energy spent worrying about pleasing others, getting accepted into schools, programs, and internships, all of it meant nothing. In a matter of hours, her eyes had been opened to new possibilities. Yet she still couldn't help but feel that things were going to get worse before they got better. That seeing the Obard not once, but twice shouldn't be ignored.

One problem at a time.

Meegan was right. Kenna needed to focus on the problems they could see, and not worry so much about the unforeseen problems. *Besides*, she thought, *how much more could possibly happen by the end of the day?*

26

Meegan didn't want to think about her mother's last words from when she'd stormed out of the house, but they rang loud in her head, over and over again. *You have an obligation to your people! Don't put your trust in these humans!*

No. She was done with the constant goading of *don't let it be your fault we're discovered*, which had often bested Meegan's plans to spend time with Kenna, Nick, or any other friends. It had been her mother who convinced her to end things with Nick. She missed him terribly and regretted giving in to her mother's persuasions. But now wasn't the time to think about Nick. He was safe and living a normal life in Boston. Far, far away from the shitstorm they were in.

Kenna nudged Meegan's arm. "Hey, the front door is open." The two climbed the front porch steps and while Kenna pushed the door open farther, Meegan turned and scanned the yard. Prue's house sat on a plot of land in a secluded wooded area. She stared intently at the wooded area, trying to spot anything suspicious between the slender trunks of the tall longleaf pine trees. The sky was clear and the cluster of feathery pine needles bunched at the treetops blocked the afternoon sun from Meegan's eyes.

Meegan turned and headed inside after hearing Ally's voice echoing from inside the house. "Prue? Is that you?"

"No, Ally! It's just us." The two stood in the small foyer area until Ally emerged from the side hallway. Kenna tucked her phone into her back pocket and asked, "Prue's still not home?"

Small patches of brown fuzz lined Ally's hairline, and smudges of mascara smeared the mocha skin under her wet eyes. Ally huffed and rubbed the corner of one eye. "No," she whimpered. "I don't know where the hell she is. She's not answering my calls or texts, and I can't locate her on the tracking app we use."

"Her phone could be dead." Meegan closed the front door and followed her friends into the living room.

"Maybe." Ally sniffled while making her way toward the kitchen.

Out of all the homes Meegan had lived in during her time on Earth, she adored Prue's home the most. Not only for the lack of neighbors, but also for the open floor plan and the cozy farmhouse decor. It was the opposite of a fancy home yet had the same level of luxury. Meegan's mother would never consider a home that looked country chic. She'd insisted these types of homes reminded her of the inside of a barn. But Meegan liked the openness and vaulted ceilings, and all the whitewash furniture mixed in with dark stain pieces.

Normally, this place was tidier than Ally's apartment, but right now it was a disaster. The couch was covered in blankets, pillows, and what appeared to be crumbs of some sort. The oversized square coffee table was littered with empty cookie or cracker sleeves, candy wrappers, balled-up tissues, two bottles of opened wine, and one glass with maybe a sip or two left in it. Across the room, books, magazines, and DVDs were piled up on top of the TV console and along the floor.

"It looks like she's been binge-watching some movies," Meegan noted while browsing through of the DVD titles. Along the bookshelf were several picture frames filled with photos of Ally and Prue. Similar in physical features with their healthy brown skin and dark, soft spirals, yet so unbelievably different in their personalities.

"Who knows what the hell she's been doing," Ally snapped and continued into the kitchen.

Meegan returned the movies to their pile. She sidestepped Kenna, who was collecting the garbage from off the coffee table, and followed Ally into the kitchen. "Holy shit! What the hell happened here?" Meegan closed one of the open cabinet doors to get a better look at the disaster in the kitchen. Besides cabinet doors being left ajar, there were dishes stacked next to the sink that looked like a bad game of Jenga and a buffet of empty cookies containers, cracker boxes, and chip bags all over the beautiful granite countertops. Crumbs littered the hardwood floor while a variety of dirty pots sat on the stovetop filled with— "Is that soup?"

Kenna tossed the garbage into the trash can and then moved closer to the stove. She lifted the ladle in one of the pots. Reddish goo trickled with a *plop, plop, plop* sound back into the pot. "Yup. Smells like tomato soup."

"Who in their right mind would be eating soup in this heat?"

"She's not in her right mind," Ally said after getting herself a glass of water and sitting at one of the counter stools, careful not to touch the mess on the countertop. "She was upset about that asshole, Xander, remember?"

Kenna began to clean up the pots on the stove, moving dishes out of the sink so she could dump the stinky old soup down the garbage disposal. "I didn't realize she was this upset."

"Me neither," Ally said. "I guess we should've come over sooner. I shouldn't have trusted her *I'm fine* text messages."

When the doorbell rang and the sound echoed up into the vaulted ceilings, all three women flinched. They stared at one another until Meegan rolled her eyes. "Geez, it's just someone at the door." She made her way toward the front door and opened the speakeasy hatch and looked out the head-height little window. Outside, on the front porch, was a young man holding a small bouquet of wildflowers. His dark brown eyes, which stood out against his pale skin beneath the brim of his baseball cap, were eye level with the speakeasy grille.

"Can I help you?"

He removed his baseball hat, leaving an indentation along his reddish-blond hair, and held it over his chest. "Hello, I was wondering if Prue was home?"

"I'm sorry, she's not home at the moment."

A hard shoulder slammed into Meegan's side and shoved her out of the way. Ally stuck her face into the small opening and, with a little more haste in her voice, asked, "You know Prue? Have you seen her today?" Meegan couldn't hear his reply, but it must have satisfied Ally's curiosity because she slammed the speakeasy hatch shut and opened the front door. "When was the last time you did see her?"

The man was about to answer when Meegan pulled the door open wider and stood next to Ally. "Hey, I'm sorry, I didn't catch your name?"

The man, taller than both Meegan and Ally, smiled and took a step closer. "Oh, right, I'm Micah." He held out his hand, which Ally was quick to shake.

After, he held his hand out to Meegan, but she ignored it. "So, Micah, Prue's never mentioned you before?"

He retracted his hand and stuffed it into the front pocket of his jeans. "Oh, well, we just met yesterday at the grocery store. She seemed to be stocking up on soup. Which I couldn't help but think was odd."

Ally leaned in closer and, behind one hand, whispered, "She *was* eating a lot of soup."

"Mm-hmm. I know." Meegan narrowed her eyes at the young man. His height and broad shoulders alone were enough to overpower both her and Ally if he really wanted to get inside, but she also saw a sweet expression in his smile and eyes that threw her. He was either a professional bullshitter or being sincere in knowing Prue. "What's with the flowers?"

"After Prue and I talked for a bit in the soup aisle, we ended up going for a walk, which then turned into talking over dinner." He wrinkled his nose and leaned in as if he were telling them a secret. "I think she needed an ear to vent to."

"Oh, see, Meeg!" Ally's voice carried the weight of her guilt. "She did need me!"

"And what exactly did she vent about?" Meegan didn't trust this guy. Not with the transessent stones showing up on their wrists this morning and Prue being MIA. Ally was about to say something when Meegan shushed her. "I was asking Micah."

"She was upset about some guy named Xander and how stupid she was for falling for such an ass."

The two women glanced at each other before looking back at the man on Prue's front porch. *He knows about the soup and the breakup with Xander.*

"Anyway, last night before we said our goodbyes, I asked Prue if she wanted to meet up for breakfast, but she said she couldn't and that she had some errands to run. Something about dropping off some brochures to a few clients. I don't remember the details, but I asked if I could stop by after lunch and she said yes. I hadn't heard from her yet, and it's almost three, so here I am."

When Micah stepped closer, Meegan reacted and pressed one hand against the doorframe, blocking Micah from entering. "Well, like I said, Prue's not here. And I was raised not to let strangers in the house." She cocked her head and narrowed her eyes at the quarterback-looking young man. "And you, Micah, are a stranger. Until we hear from Prue, you can call her or stop by later."

"Right," Micah said with an apologetic look as he put some distance between himself and the front door. He stretched one hand out, offering up the small bouquet.

Ally thanked him for the flowers while Meegan led Ally farther back inside. Meegan watched the twenty-something-year-old walk away as she closed the door. Meanwhile, Ally hurried over to the window and swept the curtain open. Meegan stepped closer and pulled the curtain open farther so she too could watch Micah climb into the driver side of a black SUV.

"Who was it?" Kenna called from the kitchen.

When they headed back into the kitchen, Meegan was surprised to see how much Kenna had cleaned in the short time they were at the front door. Ally headed straight to the wine rack in the dining room and pulled out a bottle of red. "I think I need a glass or two of this."

"You're not worried about Prue anymore?" Kenna asked while loading the dishwasher.

"I forgot all about this morning's meeting with the two hotels up in Jacksonville. She's gotta be up there. She always turns her phone off when she's in a meeting with clients."

"But why isn't her location showing up on your locator app?" Kenna asked.

"It won't pin her location if her phone is off." Ally popped open the bottle of wine. "Cabernet Sauvignon, anyone?"

"Yeah, I'll have some," Meegan said while scanning the main living space. The double doors to the office, off to the left of the front door, were open. Inside, she spotted Prue's laptop. It was open but not on. She went over and carefully picked it up, then brought it to the now-clear kitchen counter. "Hey, by any chance do you know Prue's password to her laptop?"

"Bolognese, with zeros for the O's," Ally replied and handed Meegan a glass of wine. "It's her favorite sauce."

After she typed the password and hit Enter, the laptop came to life and Prue's Google Calendar was front and center. *Shit. It's all right here, plus the soup on the stove.* She watched Kenna add the dishwasher detergent. *If he were in here, he could've somehow seen the calendar and the soup on the stove.* She closed the laptop and muttered, "I don't like that guy."

"What's not to like?" Ally filled her wineglass to the brim so high she had to lean in to take a sip before picking it up. "I sure as hell liked what I saw, so I'm pretty sure Prue would too." She downed a big gulp of her wine and added, "It's called a rebound.

Maybe you should get one." Ally pivoted on her toes and walked over to the sliding glass door. She opened the backdoor and stepped out onto the large deck. From outside she yelled, "Let's sit out here and wait for Prue. I'll make us something to eat in a bit."

Kenna whispered, "That was a low blow. Ignore her. The girl weighs a hundred and twenty pounds soaking wet. One sip and she's buzzed. Besides, you don't need a rebound."

"I know."

"But maybe you could call—"

Meegan shot a hand up. "Do not finish that sentence. You now know why we can't be together. So, don't go there. He deserves to live a normal life."

Kenna seemed to understand and said no more. She poured herself a glass of wine and came around from inside the kitchen. "So, where the hell do you think Darci is? Shouldn't she be here by now too?"

Meegan shook her head. "I'm telling you, something's not right. Prue's missing, and my gut is telling me that guy Micah is somehow involved."

"But Prue's not missing."

"We don't know that for sure." Meegan sipped her wine and nodded. "Text Darci again and let's hope she's just being Darci. Lost in social media or diving into more articles about celebrity gossip or odd facts on the internet."

"Yeah. I've never met someone who loves to read anything and everything as much as she does." Kenna pulled out her phone and tried texting Darci again.

"In the meantime, we should try and cast that amula. We need to talk to Ulissa." Meegan set her wine down and checked the time. "I think we're good on time. I'm gonna run out to the car and grab my mom's journal. I'll be two minutes. Do you think you can get a pitcher of water, grab some sea salt, and start to cut up some lemon wedges? Oh, and we'll need that copper mug and a few of those candlesticks from the mantle."

"You're sure we should do this amula now?"

Meegan was halfway through the living room when she replied loud enough for Kenna to hear. "Yes! And besides, who better to ask about all this than the sister of the Anumen who probably started this whole mess?"

Outside, clusters of gray clouds had started to roll in. One of Florida's typical afternoon thunderstorms. Not the worst of their problems, but still, she'd never been a fan of thunderstorms. The booming thunder often reminded her of the Obard invasion day on Anuminis.

Now that Prue's situation was somewhat under control, she could focus on contacting Ulissa. Hopefully, Ulissa would have some answers about who put these transessent stones on them and why, because the uneasiness swirling in her gut was only growing fiercer. And over the centuries, she'd learned to trust her gut as much as she trusted the violet stone in her mother's mood ring.

27

From the front passenger seat of the black Expedition, Gemma watched Micah through the dark tinted windows as he stood on the porch talking to two of Darci's humans. When he handed over the small bouquet of flowers, Gemma exhaled a deep, satisfied breath and said, "I think they're buying it."

In the second row of the SUV, Logan sat next to Cahleen. He and Sabine had arrived earlier that morning along with their captives, Eryn and one of Eryn's humans from her Aevo Compendium group. Gemma had only met Logan a few times and didn't know much about him except that Anora trusted him. He looked like the average Sendarian man, well over six feet with a healthy physique, a full head of reddish-blond hair, and vibrant orange eyes. She'd noticed a long fading scar rounding the right side of his lower neck when he'd first arrived, and she couldn't help but wonder what the story was behind that scar.

"Are you sure they can't see us?" the newcomer asked.

She ignored Logan's concerns and watched her brother approach the driver-side door. "Shh, he's coming!"

"Why are we here?" the man asked and then continued to protest. "We've got orders not to interact."

Gemma heard Cahleen reply in a mocking tone, "Side project."

The man shifted in his seat and cursed while Micah climbed into the SUV. Gemma lowered her oversized sunglasses and insisted on knowing every word that was said, and Micah obliged.

"The dark-skinned woman was eager to know more about Prue's whereabouts, and probably would've let anyone in."

"And what about that other one? The one with the straight black hair? She's the one who was staring daggers at me at the outlets yesterday."

Micah shook his head and shrugged. "She's smart. Like, protective smart. But still, they're only human. I wouldn't put too much faith in their ability to figure out what's happening until the shit hits the floor."

"You mean until the shit hits the *fan*, ya loggie," Cahleen snickered from the back seat.

Before Micah could respond, Logan muttered, "This is a bad idea. We shouldn't be this close to the humans."

"Oh, shut it! All of you! Especially you, Logan. I don't even know why you came with us. This doesn't concern you." Gemma slid her sunglasses up and snapped her fingers and pointed to the keys in the ignition. "Now, if you would please get us out of here," she insisted. "Park somewhere close on the main road, but not too close. We need to be able to see Xander when he pulls into the driveway."

She then opened the large designer tote sitting on her lap and pulled out her cell phone and a small black plastic tube. She uncapped the tube, twisted the bottom shaft, and applied a fresh coat of red lipstick. When she was done, she blotted her lips together and told Cahleen, "Get ready. You're up next."

28

Cahleen sat and stared at Logan. His jeans were snug and the short-sleeved shirt he wore hugged his biceps nicely. Maybe on their journey home, she could convince the Sendarian to spar with her and then seduce him into bed.

Sabine had mentioned that Logan used to be one of Quaid's Scouts. *Used to be.* She wondered what had changed between Quaid and Logan for him to secretly pledge his loyalty to Anora. This game Anora was playing, spying on her brother Quaid, was a dangerous game. She wasn't sure if it would help or hurt the Athru's cause in the end. Either way, the Athru were bound for bloodshed, and hopefully she'd be there to get a piece of the action.

From the front seat, Gemma was on a call with Xander. The pathetic human's voice whined through the SUV's speakers as he insisted he was there, parked in the driveway, and ready to go up there to officially break things off with his ex-girlfriend. Per Gemma's instructions, Micah had parked down the street, out of sight for any approaching cars, giving them a clear view to keep watch.

"He's not there," Cahleen whispered between the two front seats.

Gemma covered the mouthpiece with her hand and snapped, "I can see that!"

Micah sighed and pressed the Activate button on his plac. The soft exterior morphed into a hard black glass surface. Unlike her younger brother, Cahleen preferred to occupy her free time with pointier and sharper toys. She drew out her black claw dagger and stabbed the bench seat between her and Logan. He didn't budge, but instead rolled his eyes and turned his attention to look out his window. She rocked the blade back and forth and asked, "So, Logan, what's the story with you and Sabine? You two lovers?"

He drew in a long breath through his nose while opening and closing one hand. As he released the air from his lungs, he said, "Anora asked me to accompany Sabine on this mission. That's all you need to know."

"Ah. You're doing Anora then?" From the tick in his jaw, she could tell she was getting under his skin. Cahleen weighed the benefits of pushing her luck but opted to leave him be. More because she heard Gemma wrapping up her conversation with Xander. From the front window, she could see Xander's blue two-door convertible car turn and park in the dirt driveway, nowhere near the house.

"This is ridiculous, Gemma. Prue's a smart girl. She can take a hint."

"Xander, sweetie. I need to be sure. I want to trust you but—but you know my heart's been broken before, and—and I need reassurance that it's over between you two." When in reality, they knew Xander had to be at this location with the other humans for when the transport came to collect the humans for the Aevo Compendium.

"And my word isn't good enough?"

Cahleen had to admit, hearing an agitated Xander—a new side she hadn't seen—made the human more amusing. Maybe he wasn't such a pushover, a weak loggie after all. Her curiosity flared. Would he stand his ground and leave or abide Gemma and hand over his manhood?

His rear brake lights flickered off and the white reverse lights lit up as he put the car in park and shut it off. *He's totally going to try and wiggle his way out of this.* Cahleen pulled the curved dagger free from the leather seat and stared intensely out the front window.

"I'm not going up there," Xander said.

"Well, then we're through."

"Gemma, no! Wait!"

And there it is. Ball sac number one.

Xander sighed into the phone, a mixture of nervousness and fluster resonating with each breath. One of Cahleen's many talents was sensing a person's intentions, regardless of how many observations she could take in. This skill was something Anora had picked up on early in their acquaintance, and it had eventually led Anora to ask Cahleen to pledge her loyalty to the Athru as one of Anora's personal Scouts.

She could tell that on the other end of this call, Xander was shitting his pants while he contemplated what to do. Cahleen leaned between the front seats and moved her finger in a rolling motion as if to say, *He's about to break. Keep going.*

"Gemma, please. There's no reason for this."

"And I'm telling you if you don't drive up that driveway, go into that house, sit her down, and have a heart-to-heart, then we're through. Do I make myself clear?" When he didn't answer, Gemma yelled into the phone, "Oh, for heaven's sake, just go in there and get it done." Then she lightened her tone when she added, "Call me when you're done. I have something special planned for you later tonight."

"Really? And then we can move past all this?"

And here's the other sac. Pathetic loggie.

"Yes, my sweet. Kiss, kiss, and see you later tonight, as long as you start that damn car and get up there!"

"Wait? How did you know? Oh, for fuck's sake! You're here? How long—"

Gemma disconnected the call, cutting Xander off. Everyone stared out the front window, watching the blue convertible, and for a moment, Cahleen thought her part in all of this was good and done. Xander put the car into Drive and started up the driveway, but then moments later, they spotted his reverse lights as he backed down the driveway.

"Shit! Cahleen!"

"Yeah, yeah," she said while sliding on her sunglasses, already halfway out the door. *Stupid gróntah!*

Cahleen reached the end of the driveway before Xander. When he finally stopped, inches from her knees, she walked to the passenger-side door and tapped on the window.

He cracked the window and freezing air-conditioned air wafted toward her. "I can't believe you're here. What the hell do you want, Cahleen?"

Through her Oakley sunglasses she glared at him. "Hey, dipshit. Open the door."

It took a few seconds, but he eventually unlocked the door. Cahleen slid into the cool, soft leather seat, much softer than the SUV's seats, and smiled at the loggie. "It kinda looks like you were about to leave." She made a disapproving tsking sound. "Now, how do you think Gemma will react to you leaving?"

"This is ridiculous, and frankly I don't give a shit if Gemma gets pissed at me. I'm not going in there. Now, get the hell out of my car and go do what you do best. Tattle on me like we're in the fucking second grade."

She smirked at him as if she could smell the anger and frustration fuming from his skin. "I'm impressed, Xander. I didn't think you had it in you."

He blinked and cocked his head slightly. "Had what in me?"

"The balls to tell Gemma no."

"What? You wanted me to say no?"

Cahleen laughed and said, "Hells yeah, I wanted you to say no, but regardless, you still have to get up there and stay in that house."

"Stay? No one said anything about staying." His eyes narrowed and Cahleen could tell he was serious. "I don't know what's going on, but I'm done."

Cahleen adjusted her sunglasses and slid her tongue across her front teeth before swiping the keys out of the ignition. Xander barely flinched and only noticed after the fact. "Xander, let me explain something. You're not even close to being *done*." She rested her forearm on the center console and leaned in closer. "You think you... a pathetic, simple-minded human... can break me with petty words." She let out a low, wicked snicker. "Let me tell you something, *human*." She pointed to the metal cuff wrapped around his wrist. "Do you see that pretty little transessent bracer you're wearing?"

He dropped his hand from the steering wheel and looked down at the piece of metal attached to his right wrist. "I don't know what it is. I woke up with it on this morning."

"I know."

His head twisted up and he gaped at her. "What do you mean, *you know*?"

"Because I took it off the intended human and put it on you, shithead. Because *you* have a role to play."

"*You* put this thing on me? Why?"

"You'll see."

"Okay, I've had enough. Get the fuck out of my car, Cahleen!"

At the mention of her name, Cahleen drew out her favorite clawlike blade.

Xander flinched, eyes wide and locked on the blade. "*Ah*—what are you planning to do with that?"

"Oh, this little thing?" With one finger looped through a hole in the handle, she playfully spun the black blade as if it were a harmless toy. "This is motivation." He gripped the door with one hand and braced the other firmly against the center console. "Calm down, you big baby. I'm not going to hurt you. Didn't I just say you have a role to play?" She pointed the tip at him. "Geez, Xander, you gotta learn to pay attention."

He swallowed hard. "What do you want from me?"

She pressed the tip of the blade against her own pointer finger, pricking it. "Listen, I'm not supposed to get into the details of what's been planned. All you need to know right now"—she wiped the tip of the blade down the front of her black shorts before tapping it on the front window—"is that you need to go into that house and wait. That's it! Drive up there. Knock on the door. Go inside. And wait for Gemma's call."

Cahleen rubbed her thumb and pointer finger together, right over the spot she'd pierced, until shimmery yellow blood started to trickle down her finger. His lips parted and he gasped. She then tipped her sunglasses down the bridge of her nose, revealing her bright orange eyes. When he finally made eye contact, he jerked hard against the driver-side door. His gaze toggled between the blood and her eyes.

"What the fuck?"

"Ah, there it is!" She sucked on the end of her bleeding finger and smiled. "I think you're starting to get the bigger picture here, yes?"

He gaped at her and his whole body trembled. Cahleen was hoping he'd give her a nod or something, but nope. Nothing. Just a look of shock.

She snapped her fingers and yelled, "Hey! Do we have an understanding?"

Xander twisted in his seat and scrambled to open the door, trying to escape. Cahleen rolled her eyes while she quickly switched out her blade for a syringe. Right as he opened the door, she uncapped the needle, stuck it deep into his neck, and depressed the plunger until the syringe was empty. Instantly, his limp body fell against the partially opened door. Cahleen sat there and watched their pawn drop to the dirt driveway, his feet and legs still propped awkwardly inside the car.

"Oh, you stupid loggie," she mumbled while recapping the needle. "If it were up to me, I would've chosen a smarter puppet. But shit ain't up to me, now is it?" She got out of the vehicle about to make her way over to a knocked out Xander when Logan slammed the door of the SUV and walked over.

"What the hegah are we doing, Cahleen?"

"Just help me."

Logan shook his head in defeat and lifted Xander over his shoulder while Cahleen moved the sports car out of the way. Once Xander was secured in the back seat of the SUV between Logan and Cahleen, Micah drove them halfway up the driveway; far enough, but still out of view of the house.

"He needs to be near the house," Gemma instructed, "specifically toward the backyard. That'll be in range for when the barrier comes down."

"You're sure?" Cahleen asked.

"Trust me," Gemma confirmed, facing the back seat, one corner of her mouth raised in a smirk. "Standard Aevo Compendium pickup."

Logan offered to help, and Cahleen accepted. He followed her up the driveway with Xander over his shoulder. When they reached the house, they waited, and when they agreed it was safe, they crossed the front yard to the side of the house. Logan carefully dropped Xander's body inside a row of shrubs next to a large shed.

"He's good there," Cahleen noted and walked away without waiting for Logan. Concern for his well-being was something he'd have to earn. And he wasn't there yet.

Whenever her mind was uneasy, Cahleen did the one thing that gave her solace. She gripped the hilt of her holstered blade. The security of a weapon pressed against her palm, ready to be drawn at her will, gave her the reassurance she needed to squash out those brief moments of weakness.

Storm clouds began to roll in as they climbed into the SUV. An indicator, according to Gemma, that the transport would be taking place soon. Another Spiaire privy piece of information Gemma had shared with them about how the *Tarais* had the ability to manipulate certain weather conditions for most of the observed planets. A high-level storm helped disguise and hide any transport ships entering the planet's atmosphere. If the Athru had access to tech like that, there would be no stopping them from a direct attack on the queen or the Rhaltan Enforcers.

But as it was, they didn't have access to Rhaltan tech. They had Anora and her cunning plan. She'd assured the Athru that her plan required time. It wasn't going to be a quick victory, and Cahleen trusted Anora enough to believe they'd succeed. Though, that would also depend on Anora keeping her two brothers, Quaid and Biryn, in line. Quaid was a monster, no question about that, but Biryn had kept to the shadows. No one had ever seen him besides a few select Athru. Cahleen wondered what his reasoning was for keeping his identity a secret. Something to ask Anora after they left Earth and met up with her on Priomh.

No sooner did Cahleen slam her door shut than Gemma asked in a sarcastic, lively tone, "So, how did it go?"

"Can we just get out of here?" Cahleen snapped. "We have everything we need. I don't want to be late in meeting Quaid."

Micah started the SUV and shifted into Drive. "Our contact on the *Tarais* will be picking us up in one hour."

One hour. One more hour on this miserable planet.

29

Seven years of bad luck was the least of their problems after Kenna and Meegan cracked the corner of the large mirror while carrying it from the foyer to the guest bedroom. During their not-so-steady endeavor, Meegan mentally prepared a list of questions for Ulissa.

If the amula worked, she could finally get some answers about the attack on Anuminis. About what the hell Isoldesse had been doing off world and what exactly she'd done to piss the Obard off.

But would knowing change anything or help Kenna right now? As they set the mirror down onto the carpet, Meegan decided those questions about the destruction of her home world would have to wait. Kenna was the priority. They needed answers about where the arcstone came from. Then, if there was time, she'd bring up Isoldesse.

If all goes well, and we get the answers we need, I can tell my parents. They'll be ecstatic to know Ulissa's essence is alive and well. All those years of not knowing the truth about the attack on

Anuminis. I bet they'll be so excited that they won't even be mad at me for lying and keeping the arcstone a secret.

"What does the wax do?" Kenna asked, scooching closer to the oversized rectangular mirror.

Meegan blinked and refocused her pensive gaze. The flame from the lighter she was holding flickered inches from the wick. "The wax," she said and touched the flame to the tip of the candle. "Well, it'll act as a barrier to the window I need to create on the surface of the mirror."

"And what's with the lemony saltwater?" she asked while holding up the copper mug filled with lemon wedges, coarse salt, and tap water.

"Electrolytes. To power and hold the connection." Meegan sat back on her knees. "Before we get started, you remember what you're supposed to do, right? Because I won't be able to stop and explain once I recite the amula."

Kenna set the Moscow mule mug on the mirror and took off the arcstone necklace. Carefully, she held the stone while picking up the copper mug again. "Okay, now I'm ready."

The flame on the end of the candle flickered, providing a soft glow over the mirror. Even with the blinds open, the bedroom had a bleak ambience from the late-afternoon storm clouds rolling in. Meegan nodded and lowered the tip of the tapered candle. Once the first drop of wax hit the glass surface, she recited the amula, "*Olahar radhac et banna nausc*," over and over again.

Give me sight into the bond connection.

Kenna pressed the arcstone against the first drops of wax, the tip of the stone pointing to the center of the mirror. While Kenna firmly held the yellow stone in place, Meegan carefully dripped more wax over the top, then moved the candle clockwise in an oval around the mirror, making a wax frame. Finally, with the arcstone bound within the wax frame, the window was complete.

Now to activate it.

Positive the wax edges were solid and impermeable, Meegan gestured to the Moscow mule mug. With her free hand, Kenna gently poured the solution into the center of the oval wax frame. The cloudy water took to the edges, searching for a break or a weak spot in the barrier. She stopped pouring when the entire reflective surface within their wax frame was covered. After setting the mug off to the side, she joined Meegan by watching her friend's lips and reciting the amula, "*Olahar radhac et banna nausc.*"

White veins of light gradually materialized along the tops of both girls' transessent stones. They continued to chant until the liquid on the mirror casted a vibrant light up onto the ceiling. A woman called out from within the light. "Kenna? Kenna, is that you?"

"Yes! Ulissa, it's me! Are you okay?"

The illumination faded, and Ulissa's image appeared on the liquid's surface. At first the connection rippled and Meegan worried she wouldn't be strong enough to hold the channel open, but the ripples eventually subsided into a smooth plane. The golden aura that surrounded Ulissa was barely noticeable, but it was there.

"It's working!" Kenna leaned closer to the mirror. "Can you see us, Ulissa?"

The old woman nodded while Meegan inhaled a deep breath and cringed. A faint headache threatened her temples, and fatigue began to settle into her arms. The journal's warning hadn't been kidding when it noted her essence would feel the drain. The sense of being overly tired and weak hit her faster than she'd expected. After a few calming breaths, Meegan introduced herself. "Ulissa, my name is Meegan. My family, and many other surviving Anumen, are living here on Earth as refugees."

A tense smile of acknowledgment appeared on Ulissa's face. "Kenna is blessed to have you there with her. To guide her when I cannot. Tell me, how is it someone gave Kenna a transessent stone during the initial arcstone bonding? That was reckless and dangerous."

"I was hoping you'd know more about that," Meegan countered. "You, out of all the Anumens, who could've prevented—" She stopped herself from unleashing decades of bottled-up anger and confusion. This wasn't the time. She swallowed hard and started over. "My name is Meegan Prinor. I need to know who your Guard was."

"Prinor?" Ulissa repeated. "A Fawness, I assume." Meegan said nothing. Ulissa narrowed her stare at the young Anumen, then briefly shifted her gaze to Kenna. Then she nodded at Meegan, as if she understood that Meegan didn't want to discuss her title or position with Kenna in the room. "That makes sense. It takes a special Anumen to cast a sight amula into an arcstone bond. I'm impressed."

"Who was your Guard?" she demanded a second time.

"What's a Guard?" Kenna whispered, leaning over the mirror's edge.

"I'll explain later," Meegan whispered back.

"Last I knew, it was my sister, Isoldesse. And before you ask— no, I don't know her whereabouts. I only saw her one other time after she forced my essence into this arcstone."

"But you know what Isoldesse was doing off world, yes?"

The old woman lifted her chin and straightened her shoulders before confirming Meegan's suspicions. "I don't know the specific details of her *project*, but yes. Please know that I am not proud of our family connection, of what she did, but she's family. She'll always be my sister. She and our mother believed what they were doing was in everyone's best interests. To share our good fortune, the ways of Anuminis, with other worlds."

Other worlds? How many other worlds? Oh, Isoldesse. What did you do?

"And the Obard? What do you know of them?" Meegan asked before briefly closing her eyes and centering her balance. A low wave of nausea crawled through her stomach. Their time was limited, and she was getting off track, but she needed to know.

It wasn't until a warm hand pressed against her skin, just above the metal bracelet, that the nausea subsided. Meegan opened her eyes and saw her best friend smiling at her and mouthing reassuring cheers like *you got this* and *you're doing great*. Kenna seemed unaware of the energy pulsing from her own essence into Meegan's. A boost of some sort to help strengthen the amula connection.

That's amazing. How is she—

"Is everything okay?" Ulissa called as the wavering liquid smoothed out.

Now feeling less of the amula drain, Meegan knelt forward and said, "We don't have a lot of time. What can you tell us? I highly doubt Isoldesse left your arcstone outside Kenna's front door. Especially since Kenna's human."

Ulissa nodded. "It wasn't until our second encounter that I realized she wasn't Anumen. I'm just as confused as you are." There was a pause before she softly continued, "I don't know how long it's been since I last saw Isoldesse. Time works differently inside the arcstone. But I can tell you the last time I saw her was right before I ascended into the arcstone. I was living on Anuminis and she surprised with a late-night visit. It had been years since I'd seen Isoldesse. So long that my children had had children of their own since her last visit. She wanted me to do something for her. A favor from *defiur et defiur*."

"Sister to sister," Meegan translated for Kenna.

"She asked me to ascend into an arcstone rather than face what was coming. I begged for an explanation, but she wouldn't give me one. I told her I wasn't ready to leave the physical world. But before I knew it, she took it upon herself to ascend my essence into the arcstone."

"How?" Kenna softly asked.

Meegan was also curious, but deep down inside she knew what had to be done to ascend into an arcstone.

The older woman's head dipped, and without looking up she said, "I didn't see it coming. The blade that pierced my side. The pressure of her hand pushing the hilt harder against my dress. She pleaded with me to forgive her as her tears and my blood spilled. She shoved the arcstone into my hand and held my palm closed over it while she recited the ascension amula. My thoughts raced with everything I hadn't finished. The family and friends I would never see again. Isoldesse took that from me. She took everything from me and left me in solitude. Yet—I cannot hate her."

Kenna's fingers dug into Meegan's skin, but Meegan didn't complain because she needed the boost of energy Kenna was channeling. "She killed you and stuck your essence into a rock! A fucking rock! How could you not hate her for that? You've been alone for God knows how long!"

"Shh, let her finish." Meegan shook her head at her friend before addressing Ulissa. "Listen, I'm sorry about what happened to you. And I'm sorry to be the one to tell you about the Obard."

"I know about the Obard." The old woman's features seemed to age within mere seconds. Knowledge weighed on her soft skin, creasing it into fine wrinkles. Her eyes glossed over as she explained. "Isoldesse used an amula, similar to the one you are using now, to visit me here in the arcstone." Ulissa cracked a small smirk. "My sister's power was beyond anything like other Anumens'. Almost as strong as the—"

"Just tell us what happened," Meegan cut in before Ulissa could say the word she dreaded to hear. The title she refused to accept. "What did Isoldesse show you?"

There was a long moment of silence before Ulissa continued. "While visiting me in the arcstone, she showed me the day our world fell. A dimensional projection of the past." The water rippled, and Ulissa disappeared. In her place, Anuminis appeared as if they were watching a scene from a movie. A simple single-story home set on a shallow cliffside came into view. Not too far below, settled in the valley at the base of a mountain, was a large village surrounded by a thick forest.

"Isoldesse showed me my home on the mountainside and what I would've succumbed to if I hadn't ascended into the arcstone." From within the clouds, an enormous black sphere cut through the sky. It centered itself over the village.

Meegan recalled seeing the black sphere from her own home on Anuminis. She had been a youthen, a young child, and terrified of the gigantic black ball floating over the nearby local village.

"When the floating object transformed, it morphed into an expansive flat disc that hovered over the entire village. Isoldesse and I watched from my balcony as a bright red light sparked to life along the edge of the floating disc. Everything happened so fast after that. A narrow ring from the outer edge and underside of the ship dropped to the ground with a deafening *boom*. When the dust settled, we saw the dark metal ring surrounding the entire village."

"I remember seeing it too," Meegan whispered. "Those who first saw it, and survived, said at first glance there was no reason to be alarmed. Something an Anumen could easily jump over. They didn't deserve what happened to them."

"No. No they didn't," Ulissa quietly agreed, and then continued, "Isoldesse refreshed the dimensional projection and took me in for a closer look. At first, like you said, it was just a metal ring that stretched out throughout the forest, enclosing the village within. Broken trees lay in its wake, homes destroyed if too close, and many, *many* roads blocked. Isoldesse brought me to a section of the ring that a few Anumen men were inspecting."

The girls watched in the mirror as Anumen men gathered near the black metal tubing of the ring.

"Hey, you two!" Ally jiggled the guest bedroom door handle. "What's going on in there?"

"We'll be out in a few minutes! Meeg's on the phone with her mom!" Kenna shouted.

Ally released the door handle. Her voice trailed down the hall as she said, "Okay, but I'll be done with dinner in a snippety-snap. So, get your butts out here when you're done."

"Yeah, we'll be out soon!" Kenna shouted in response.

Meegan's gaze remained glued to the scene unfolding in the mirror on the floor. Her eyes trembled and stung with the threat of losing it. She didn't have to ask, but she did anyway. "What happened next?"

"The red light from along the edge of the spacecraft shot down and connected with the ring surrounding the village. Those closest to the ring died instantly. The red beam had formed an impenetrable energy barrier and destroyed anything it touched." Ulissa stood among the chaos as the projection showed Anumens screaming and crying and running in every direction. Many tried to flee, but when they collided with the red barrier, their bodies disintegrated into ash.

"It was a horrific thing to watch." Ulissa's voice trembled between sentences. "I never knew such evil could exist."

At the time of the invasion, Meegan had been too young to grasp the intensity of the situation, but she remembered seeing the red lights from a distance. Ulissa's village hadn't been the only community attacked that day. There was an ache in her heart as she watched the end of Anuminis come about, but something else too that sparked inside her. Seeing the Obard invade her world boiled her blood with a fuming, vengeful anger.

The scene in the mirror shifted to a group of Obard soldiers marching through the village. White smoke seeped from beneath the black scales of their armor as they swatted innocent Anumens like flies with their long black swords. Some Anumen women formed a defensive line and tried to cast protective amulas, but the Obard were too many and too strong. The line of Anumen women were taken, dragged off to what Meegan could only imagine was their deaths.

The water rippled, and the scene of the village disappeared. Ulissa returned to the mirror's surface with nothing more than the soft orange glow surrounding her. "My sister is the only one who knows the truth about why the Obard invaded. I don't know what happened off world to anger them or draw their attention to Anuminis. She never told me."

"All those innocent people," Kenna whispered.

Kenna's voice jolted Meegan from her memories. "Can you tell us anything about who Isoldesse might have entrusted your arcstone to? A relative maybe? Did you have children?"

Ulissa nodded. "Though, I hadn't spoken to any of my children in over a hundred years before my death. The only other person on Anuminis Isoldesse trusted was our mother, and she passed away before the invasion."

Meegan wiped a tear from her face and with a sniffle, she asked, "You said she wanted to share the ways of Anuminis with other worlds. Did she share arcstones and transessent stones with any of those worlds?"

The old woman shrugged. "It's possible. Though, a supply that large would need approval from the"—she paused and seemed to consider her next words—"the overseeing family."

"What? No!" Meegan gasped. "That can't be. They wouldn't allow it!"

They knew. How could they know and not say anything?

"Hey, uh, Ulissa," Kenna cut in. "I'm not sure we'll be able to take these transessent stones off anytime soon. Will you be okay in the meantime?"

Before Ulissa could answer Kenna's question, Meegan sharply said, "I know where to start asking questions, and they better have some damn good answers."

"Fawness, please remember that every decision made has a consequence. Good or bad. You need time to reflect and fully understand the decisions that were made. Rash judgments will only end with regret. Please remember that when you speak to—"

"I know," Meegan interrupted before her elder could finish.

Kenna mouthed the word *Fawness*, but Meegan ignored her friend's inquiry.

"Before you go, let me show you one more thing," Ulissa said. "It may help you understand where the transessent stones came from." Ulissa closed her eyes, and the girls watched the water ripple as another scene unfolded. A pale woman with short red hair appeared, dressed in a dark uniform that had a bunch of weird symbols and red patches sewn into the jacket. She stood over Kenna, who was asleep in her bed.

"Hey, that's my bedroom," Kenna said and leaned in closer. "What's that lady doing to me?"

"I think Ulissa's showing us what happened last night." Meegan leaned forward and cocked her head. "Do you see that guy? The one standing behind her?"

The woman's bright orange eyes were mere inches from Kenna's. The intruder forced one of Kenna's eyelids open before inspecting the rest of her vitals. A few moments later, the man handed the woman one of the metal bracelets, minus the white transessent stone embedded in the top. He was wearing the same black uniform except he wasn't as decorated with patches.

The woman worked quickly to attach the metal bracelet to Kenna's wrist before stepping aside and allowing the man to come closer. Carefully, he set the white transessent stone in an indented space perfectly shaped for the stone. He then pressed and held his fingers against it until glowing veins appeared. The veins of light faded when he stepped away. The redheaded woman lifted Kenna's wrist and inspected the stone. Appearing satisfied, she said something to her companion before the two orange-eyed beings turned and headed for the door. The man exited first, carrying a large case, and the woman closed the door behind them.

The water on the mirror rippled again, and the image shifted back to Ulissa. Winded, she said, "I need rest."

They weren't Obard, and they didn't acknowledge the arcstone. Nothing makes sense! What the hell is going on?

"Do you know who they are?" Kenna asked Ulissa. "Or what they want?"

"Like I said, my sister never told me anything about what she was doing off world. But if I had to guess, I'd say they're probably from one of the worlds Isoldesse intervened with."

"There've got to be journals or documentation somewhere. This is so fucked up," Meegan snapped while looking out the window.

Kenna waved both hands in the air. "Okay, what do we do now? Are they going to come back for us? Are they friendly or are they like the Obard?"

Meegan felt the drain of energy again the moment Kenna's hand slipped from her skin.

"Meegan," Ulissa called out, "the next time you cast the sight amula into the arcstone bond, use *dyreac* instead of *radhac*, and skip all the reflective surfaces and binding agents. Just be sure to have contact with the arcstone. It'll bring your essence straight to me."

Meegan nodded. "Thank you. Until next time, *iya*."

"*Iya* to you as well."

Meegan released the amula with a single word. "*Déanta*." The connection broke, and the girls were left with a big wet mess in the middle of Prue's guest bedroom. Meegan swept her legs out from under herself and lay back on the carpet. "Damn, that took a lot out of me."

Kenna slipped the arcstone over her head. "You okay? Can I get you anything?"

"I'm okay. I just need rest, and maybe something to eat."

"Kenna! Meegan! Where are you guys?" Ally shouted from the kitchen. "Dinner's about done!"

"Perfect timing!" Kenna chuckled and then helped Meegan to her feet. "You know you'll have to explain to me most of what just happened, right?"

Meegan smiled. "Come on, let's go eat and try to figure this shit out."

Whatever Ally had cooked for dinner smelled amazing. Hints of lime and freshly chopped onion filled the air. They were about to head out into the living room when Kenna grabbed Meegan's arm and dragged her down the hall again.

"What? What's wrong?"

"Ben!"

"The guy from your dream?"

"Yeah, the guy from my dream! He had orange eyes. I mean, they were more like a deep brownish-orange, but I'm positive he's one of them! The woman under the white tree! Her too! That can't be a coincidence."

"Shit!" Meegan dropped her head into her hands and shook it. "I was so wrapped up in knowing the truth about Isoldesse and the invasion that I forgot to ask Ulissa about your weird dream."

"Well, good thing Ulissa told us an easier way to contact her. We can ask her later, after dinner." Kenna tucked her pendant necklace under her shirt. "You do remember the word she told us to use? So we don't have to use the mirror."

"I do."

"Good! Now, let's get some food into you. No more worrying."

No more worrying? What happened to her best friend who was constantly overthinking and overanalyzing everything?

And what the hell was up with that boost of energy after she touched my arm? Ah, the questions keep piling up faster than I can handle. Though, I know two Anumens who owe me answers. But before I make that call, I need a glass of wine.

30

Kenna watched as Ally poured herself another glass of wine. Her third, maybe fourth glass. On the plus side, the spread Ally prepared and set out on the patio was impressive. Grilled chicken seasoned with lime and salt, grilled zucchini and squash, her signature spicy red rice, and a side of tortilla chips with Kenna's favorite, Ally's homemade pico.

Her interest shifted from Ally's glass of red blend to Meegan, who sat quietly, sifting through the last of her grilled vegetables. She'd barely said two words since Kenna mentioned Ben and the mystery woman from last night's dream and how they both had *orange eyes*.

Ally was more than happy to provide conversation for all three of them. "Who is she to turn her fugging phone off?"

Kenna contemplated taking away the wine but abandoned the thought of intervention after a *boom* of thunder erupted from the sky. She shuddered and twisted in her seat. The clouds had grown darker and were inching closer to the fence lining the far end of Prue's property.

"Guys, maybe we should head inside."

"And—and why didn't she call me"—Ally waved her cell phone in the air, ignoring the thunder and Kenna—"when she got home from her date with Mr. Melt-My-Soul-With-Those-Gorgeous-Brown-Eyes? And oh my God, did you see those arms? Oh, the things I betcha he can do with those arms."

This was one of those moments Kenna was happy the nearest neighbor was over a mile away, because Ally plus alcohol always equaled loud. "Who are you talking about?" Kenna asked while moving the empty wine bottle to the other side of the table.

"Oh my God! That's right!" her roommate shrieked and slapped her hand on the table. Meegan flinched and briefly looked up before rolling her eyes and pushing her plate forward. "You didn't see 'em! *Mm-mmm-mmm.* You missed out on some ser-ee-ous—"

"Ally! I get it. He was hot," Kenna said loud enough to stop her roommate's drunken ramble. "It's not the first or last hot guy you'll be pining over."

"Oh, stop. I can tell there's somethin' special 'bout that one." Her words were barely understandable from all her giggling. Ally tilted her head up to the gray sky and leaned into the patio chair. When the chair almost tipped over, she yelped, "Whoa!" and, without missing a beat, continued her admiration. "Oh man, let me tell ya. I'd like to know what that man can do with those arms. I betcha those arms would have no problem lifting me up and—"

"Okay, okay! We get your point," Kenna shouted in a pleading *that's enough* tone.

"Oh geez, I can't remember! His name... What was his name?" Ally snapped her fingers and cursed into the evening air. "I think it was Mike or Mark? Yes! Mark! It was Mark. *Mark, Mark, Mark.* Where did you go, Mark?"

"It was Micah—his name was Micah," Meegan snapped with an annoyed glare. "Now, can you please stop yelling? Or at least take it inside."

"Yes! Micah! *Micah, Micah, Micah,*" she sang. Her dark curls rustled from the increasing winds. "Come back to me, Micah! Come back!"

Kenna turned in her seat to assess the distance of the storm because it should've hit by now, yet strangely it lingered south. Even though she wasn't sure when the storm was going to hit, she did know that they'd be sitting in the dark soon enough.

"Have you heard from Darci?" Meegan asked. "Because I haven't."

Kenna picked up her phone. "Nope. But it looks like I missed a call from my dad." She stood from her chair and pointed toward the stone firepit out by the back fence. "There's a mug out by the firepit. I'm gonna go grab it and call my dad back." Two steps off the deck, she stopped, cocked her head toward Ally, and told Meegan, "Watch her."

"What? I don't need watching! But I'll tell you what I do need. I need to be singing!"

She ignored her roommate and walked out into the yard, past the large lemon tree and in-ground pool, and over to the firepit. One of Prue's favorite mugs sat on the arm of an Adirondack chair. Full to the brim. *Huh, I wonder why she didn't drink her coffee? Or why she left it out here.* She dumped the cold coffee into the grass before calling her dad.

"Kenna? Where are you?" Her dad's voice sounded miles away.

"We're hanging out at Prue's. Sorry I missed your call, and I'm sorry I didn't stop by today. How about tomorrow?" A gust of strong wind blew in from over the fence, causing Kenna's hair to blow in her face.

"Hey, hold on a sec. I have to fix my hair." She set the phone on the arm of the Adirondack chair and gathered her hair into a low ponytail. Dark strands flew in every direction. "Sorry about that. So, we're good for tomorrow?"

"Yeah, yeah, that's fine. Have you talked to your mother today?"

"Talk louder! The wind's picking up." Kenna plugged her finger into her free ear. "Hey, can I call you back in like five minutes? After we're done cleaning up and go inside. This storm is getting crazy."

"Never mind the storm, Kenna. Your mom. Have you talked to her today?" This time he shouted.

Walking across the yard, empty mug in one hand, she told him, "No, not today. I saw her Saturday afternoon, at the museum. I brought her lunch and forced her to take a break from the new exhibit. Why? What's going on?"

"Oh, I forgot all about the new exhibit. And you're sure that was the last time you saw or spoke to her?"

"Yeah, why?" Halfway across the yard, the deck lights turned on and the backyard lit up. Kenna shuffled closer to the lemon tree, hoping to use the trunk as a shield from the wind. "What's going on? I can tell when you're worried." He began muttering something, but with the wind she couldn't make out his words. "Dad! You're freaking me out! What's wrong?"

"Oh, I'm sorry. You know how I get worried when you girls don't check in with me. I forgot about her new project. She left for work this morning and hasn't come home yet."

On the deck, Meegan cleared the table while Ally leaned over the railing and sang Micah's name. Kenna rolled her eyes before telling her dad, "I bet Mom has no idea what time it is. You should go to the museum and surprise her with some takeout."

"That sounds like a good idea. Hey, sweetie?"

"Yeah?" Kenna said while watching Meegan clear the last of their dinner spread.

"Where do the stars and ocean meet?"

Her response was automatic and always carried a smile with the words. "They meet at the edge of the world near *Darg Shoal*." The phrase was something he'd said to her every night before bed when she was a child. A phrase he'd ended up using in his debut novel. "Okay, Dad. I'll stop by the house tomorrow after classes. Give Mom hugs for me when you see her."

"Will do," were his last words before he hung up. It comforted her to know that she and her father shared the same you-worry-too-much gene. Up on the deck, Ally was MIA while Meegan sat with her knees pulled to her chest on one of the lounge chairs.

"How come you're not inside? The storm's about to hit."

Meegan lifted her head to the sky, closed her eyes, and smiled. Her olive skin appeared a shade darker from the gloom. "It's not here yet. I'd say we've got twenty or thirty minutes before it passes over us."

"You can tell that?"

Meegan nodded. "Air is one of the strongest forms of Eilimintachs, and I can sense the patterns and shifts."

The dark clouds, with their billowy front, rolled closer and closer now at a determined pace. "Well, I think your alien radar is wrong. That storm's going to hit in a lot sooner than twenty minutes." The phone in Kenna's hand rang. She lifted it and saw a picture of a young guy with dark brown hair and blue eyes beneath to-die-for thick eyelashes. Above his photo read, *Liam*. Wide eyed, she showed Meegan the screen. "Oh my God! What do I do?"

It'd only been a few weeks since they'd reconnected on Instagram. A distraction she would've never allowed herself with anyone else, but this was Liam. Her childhood friend who was now a *very* attractive grown adult. She often wondered, if he weren't living up in Boston but somewhere closer, what would come of their online friendship.

"Go talk to him," Meegan said with a favorable grin. "I've got to go call my mom. There's something I need to ask her. Plus, I want to clean up our mess we left in the guest bedroom." When Kenna took a step closer to the sliding glass door, Meegan grabbed her arm. "Don't go in there. Ally said something about listening to a new song she heard the other day." Then, as if on cue, music blared from inside the house.

Great. Just great. "Is she really that drunk?"

Meegan nodded. "Yup."

The phone stopped ringing. "Crap. I missed it."

"You can call him back. Just do it over there." Meegan pointed off the deck toward the shed. "You've probably got about ten minutes until the storm really hits."

Kenna nodded, hit the Call button under Liam's name, and jogged over to the side of the shed out of the wind.

It rang twice before he answered. "Hey, I was about to leave you an awkward message."

"Well, if you want, I could hang up and let you call back."

"Let's not."

The shed was angled so the front faced the deck. Kenna huddled on the right side, away from the incoming wind. She debated going inside and asking Ally to turn down the music, but she knew there was no point in trying to ask her anything in her condition.

"So, the weather's crazy where you are too?" Liam asked loudly.

"Yeah. Normally our afternoon thunderstorms are short and wet, but not this one."

"Us too. We got hit at our campsite about fifteen minutes ago. I swear it came out of nowhere."

"Oh, that's right," Kenna shouted into the phone. "I forgot you posted that you and your friends were going camping this weekend. How's everyone? How's Nick?"

She shot an annoyed glance at the house, where the bass was now booming louder than the approaching thunder. It was then that she noticed something small and white sticking out from under the bushes. The deck lights weren't any help since they were pointing out into the yard rather than over here on the side of the house.

"Nick's good," Liam answered. "Though I can't say the same for Brody. That jackass pulled a no-show. But I'm not too surprised. He and his girlfriend, Eryn, have been spending almost every free minute they have hiding in Eryn's apartment, you know, doing… stuff." There was a moment of silence over the line before he continued, "Anyway, you know what I'm talking about. And now I'm stuck here with Jules and her girlfriend, Devaney, and they're fighting worse than this freak storm."

"I'm sorry, Liam. But at least you have Nick there with you, right?"

"I guess. He is a cool guy. But still, Eryn was the one who set this whole thing up and then bailed without telling us. And she knows how much I hate camping!"

Kenna squatted low and tried to get a better look at whatever was sticking out of the bushes without having to move away from the shed. No luck though. Without better lighting she couldn't make out what it was. All she could tell was that it was small and white. *A bunny, maybe?*

Liam continued to vent. "Listening to a catfight and sleeping out here when I could be home in my warm bed isn't even the worst part. The worst part is how we all woke up this morning with these strange bracelets on. I don't know where—"

Kenna shot to her feet and faced the shed wall again. One finger plugged into her free ear, she yelled into the phone, "What did you just say about bracelets?"

"What? Oh, I don't know what they are or who put them on us. They look old—well, the metal does at least."

They've got them on too. What the hell is going on? Why us? Why them?

Her heart rate kicked up a notch, and any nervous knots she'd had about talking to her middle school crush were carried off by the wind. Now, she was solely concerned with how he'd gotten mixed up in the same alien drama they were facing.

"I hate to cut our conversation short, because you've no idea how nice it is to hear your voice again, but I've gotta go help Nick with the tent."

Nick. Oh my God, Meegan's going to lose her mind when she hears this.

"Liam, wait! Is there an oval white stone in the top of the bracelet?"

"Yeah, why?"

"And who else woke up with one on?"

"Uh, me, Jules, Devaney, and Nick. Why?"

"Oh, you've gotta be shitting me!" Then she yelled into the phone over the wind, "What about a necklace? Or anything with a yellow stone in it? It'll look like a crystal but it's a stone, if that helps."

"Nah, nothing like that. Only bracelets. But hey, I really gotta go help Nick. Our tent collapsed and—and I don't see the girls anywhere. But once we get settled, and the storm dies down," he shouted into the phone, "I'll call you back, okay? To catch up. Because I miss my Stargirl."

And then, without her brain's approval, the words just slipped from her lips as she told him, "I miss you too, Liam."

"Good. I like hearing that. But I gotta go. Talk to you soon."

"Bye," she whispered, not knowing if he heard her or not. She stood there, loose strands of hair whipping against her face. The threat of the storm faded as she mulled over his words.

Because I miss my Stargirl. He said my *Stargirl.*

She rested her forehead against the wood siding of the shed. *Maybe I could invite him down for a week, or I could go up there and visit. We could hang out and... and what? Jesus, Kenna. Stop fantasizing about something that's not going to happen.*

A tree branch snapped from the lemon tree out in the yard. The storm clouds were now over Prue's house. The wind had picked up even more, making it difficult to see straight ahead. This storm was getting out of control and she needed to get inside. About halfway to the deck, she remembered the white bunny. Curiosity got the best of her and she returned to the row of bushes. She shielded her eyes with one arm, attempting to hold her long hair back with the other. When she reached the shrub, she turned on her phone's flashlight and pulled aside the branches at the base to see a pair of white sneakers.

"What the hell?"

She leaned farther into the bush, ignoring the pain of the branches poking and scraping her skin until a familiar face came into view.

"Xander?"

With her phone in the grass, she grabbed Xander's ankles, dragged him out, and knelt next to his unconscious body. "What the hell are you doing out here?" With one hand on his chest, she felt the subtle rise and fall of his breathing. She grabbed her phone and was about to head inside when she noticed the bracelet strapped to his right wrist.

"Oh, you've got to be kidding me. Douchebag has one too!"

31

The evening thunderstorm had become a mini hurricane. Kenna left Xander by the shrubs and ran to the deck. The wind lashed against her arms and face, making it difficult but not impossible to get inside. In the house, the bass to the music boomed through the living room's surround sound. Kenna's roommate might have been perfect at a lot of things but singing and dancing weren't among them. Especially after a few drinks.

"Ally! Where's Meegan?"

Ally shrugged in between shimmying and spouting out the wrong lyrics, then spun around and returned to her solo performance.

Oh, shit. I totally forgot she's checking in with her mom.

Kenna hurried toward the guest bedroom. Slowly, she opened the door and saw Meegan sitting on the bed and yelling into her cell phone. Not wanting to let the loud music overpower their conversation, she stepped inside and quickly shut the door.

"You should've told me!" There was a pause before Meegan erupted again, "It doesn't matter how I found out—I found out!"

Kenna tried to wave a hand in front of Meegan's face, but she twisted and shushed Kenna away. "Uh, no! You don't get to turn this around on me. You're the one who's been keeping secrets, and now you need to tell me the truth."

"Meeg—uh, I really need your help," Kenna insisted, fully aware that this wasn't the best time to interrupt. "We have a bit of a problem."

Meegan lowered the phone, holding her hand over the mouthpiece. "Can't it wait? She hasn't told me anything useful other than they had their assumptions about what Isoldesse was doing."

"No, not really. It's about Xander. He's outside."

"Well, you don't need me for that. Tell that asshole Prue's not here."

She raised the phone and was about to continue her tirade when Kenna shouted, "I found Xander passed out by the shed. Someone stuffed him under the bushes and—and he's wearing one of these." She held up her wrist. The one with the metal bracelet.

Slowly, Meegan lowered her phone. "You're kidding, right?" Kenna shook her head and Meegan raised the phone to her ear. "Mom, I'll call you back." She disconnected the call and surveyed the storm out the window. "Is he still out there? In the storm?"

"Yup. And I'm thinking we're going to need Tipsy out there to help us carry him in."

When Meegan's phone rang, she sent her mom's call to voicemail. "I'll call her after, and we don't need Ally. I can cast an amula to lift him."

She'd completely forgotten about Meegan's magical abilities. Having an alien friend who could cast magic would take some getting used to.

Out in the living room, Ally muted the music and asked, "Whatcha guys doing?"

Oh, shit. She is so drunk.

Without thinking, Kenna blurted, "Xander's outside." And the second the words left her mouth, Meegan shot Kenna a glare that translated to, *Great! Now I can't use magic to pick up that dumbass!* Kenna cringed and mouthed an apologetic *sorry*. Silently, she prayed that Ally's train of thought was set to delay and hadn't processed Kenna's words, but nope. Her roommate placed her wine on the coffee table and fell in line behind Kenna and Meegan, bumping into them as they stopped at the sliding glass door.

"What's Xander doing out there?" Ally asked with a drunken slur while standing on her tippy toes surveying the backyard. "Didn't someone tell him there's a storm out there?"

Ignoring her roommate, Kenna focused on what they were about to face. It wasn't as if they'd get blown off the deck, but they would have to be careful and stay close. Out in the yard, the lemon tree swayed in the deck spotlight as if to warn them to stay inside, but they couldn't leave Xander out in this. No matter how much they hated him.

Meegan ran out first, followed by Kenna and then Ally. When they reached Xander, Kenna tapped Ally's shoulder and pointed at his feet. She nodded with one arm over her eyes and then positioned herself by his feet. Meegan's black hair thrashed in the wind, making it hard to talk. Kenna barely heard her friend's voice instructing her to lift his left shoulder. It took a few attempts, but eventually they picked him up. Their steps were slow and out of sync, but at least they were moving.

When they were halfway to the deck steps, a flash of lightning lit up the sky, immediately followed by a deafening boom of thunder. Ally was the first to let go, dropping Xander's feet. Kenna's hands slipped from under his shoulder, forcing him to fall hard onto the grass. Kenna crouched and wrapped one arm over Ally's shoulders. Meegan shouted for Kenna, and when Kenna glanced up, she pointed two fingers to them and then to the sliding door. Kenna nodded and nudged Ally to follow her, leaving Meegan to take care of Xander. Ally didn't argue and let Kenna lead her to the deck.

Kenna had one hand on the deck railing when an ear-piercing metal grinding sound emitted from the clouds above. Instinctively, she squeezed her eyes closed and clasped her hands over her ears. As she crouched down, one of her knees scraped the edge of the wooden steps. The stabbing pain in her knee threw her off balance and she fell out into the yard. A quick glance up and she saw Ally crawling up the deck steps.

She was about to roll over and make her way to the deck when the ground beneath her shook. A few lemons fell. One even hit Kenna on the head. Then the lemons in the grass started jolting, bouncing like chattering teeth.

Eventually, the ground stopped shaking, and the screeching fell silent. Slowly, all three women uncovered their ears and got to their feet.

Through the strong winds, Kenna shouted, "What the hell was that?"

Meegan brushed off dirt and grass from her legs. "Not sure, but we've got to get him inside before anything else happens."

Kenna was about to ask if she needed help with Xander when Ally shouted, "Screw this," and took off toward the sliding door.

Seconds later, a bright light so massive it consumed the entire backyard and momentarily blinded Kenna. When her vision returned, she saw Meegan blinking and rubbing her eyes. "Hey, you okay?"

"Yeah."

The violent winds had finally stopped. Everything had stopped. The only sound Kenna heard was someone whimpering. Both Kenna and Meegan hurried up the deck. There, a few feet from the back door, they saw Ally on her butt, rubbing her nose.

"What happened?" Kenna asked while helping her roommate up.

"I don't know. I ran into something," she whined, one hand on her nose and the other outstretched, feeling for whatever she'd run into.

Ally moved past them and with her palm stretched out, she pressed her hand flat against something invisible. A faint blue outline of energy appeared along the edges of her fingers and hand. Looking through the barrier, Kenna could see the sliding door, merely a few steps away, blurred behind the trailing blue energy created by Ally's moving hand.

Without turning around, Ally asked, "Hey, are you guys seeing this? What the hell is it?"

Kenna inched closer and reached out to test the invisible barrier, but before her fingers made contact, Meegan's voice cut through the air with a loud cry. A tense shudder shot through Kenna, and she quickly drew her hand away from the invisible wall before spinning to face her friend.

Wide eyed, Meegan stumbled away from the barrier, frantically shaking her head while yelling, "Don't touch it! It's them! The Obard! They're going to kill us—they're going to kill everyone!"

Kenna glanced between her best friend, whose olive skin had turned a ghastly pale, and the invisible wall. Ally was now dragging both of her hands across it, creating fleeting trails of blue light. "Hey!" Kenna shouted and grabbed Meegan's arms. "It's not them! Look," she said and pointed to Ally's hands. "It's not the Obard. The wall, or whatever it is, isn't red, and she's fine. Her hands aren't disintegrating. It's just a weird invisible wall."

Meegan's body trembled, and she stood frozen, staring, as Ally slid her hands across the barrier's surface. "Okay, okay," she mumbled, followed by a couple of deep breaths. She twisted her mother's mood ring until the stone was facing up. Still violet. "Not the Obard."

"Not the Obard," Kenna reassured. "I'm guessing this has something to do with the orange-eyed beings Ulissa showed us."

"That can't be any better."

"No, it can't."

"How are we supposed to get inside?" Ally asked while leaning against the barrier, facing them. "I left my wine on the coffee table."

She wiggled, and the blue outline along the barrier mirrored her movements.

Kenna wasn't sure how they were supposed to get inside. Relieved the wind had stopped, she redid her windswept ponytail, finally getting it out of her face. She stepped off the deck and out into the grass, past the lemon tree and over to the pool. Curious, she surveyed the wooded area out beyond the other side of the pool.

Everything was quiet, yet somehow on the other side of the yard the high winds continued to rush over the line of trees, forcing their slender trunks to bow like servants. It was the same behind the shed and toward the far end of the yard behind the firepit. It was like any other peaceful night, but only inside the barrier. Beyond the wall, the storm raged on.

Looking up, Kenna couldn't see the night sky or the stars. There were only dark gray clouds, furiously swirling. Occasionally, random blue surges of energy spider-webbed along the sides and top of the barrier.

"It's a dome," she whispered. When Meegan's shoulder bumped hers, she pointed up and said, "We're under a dome."

"Fantastic," Meegan grumbled while holding her cell phone up high and circling the area. A few moments later, she threw it out into the yard, where it landed in the grass by the firepit. "*Ughhh*. There's no reception under this stupid thing."

"Maybe we should try to wake Xander," Kenna suggested. "He might know more about what's going on." Meegan didn't agree, but she didn't disagree either. She followed behind Kenna to the side of the house where they'd left Xander's body.

Kenna knelt in the grass next to Xander and gently slapped his cheeks. Nothing. She leaned her weight back and sat in the grass. From the deck, Ally came bouncing off the steps and sauntered over to them. She wrapped her arms around Meegan from behind and asked, "What the heck is going on? Are we being pranked or something?" When Meegan freed herself from Ally's embrace, Ally sank to the ground and pressed her fingers to her temples. "Whoa, I don't feel good."

"So," Kenna stood and asked Meegan, "does this count as *absolutely necessary?*"

Meegan rolled her eyes in defeat. "I guess. But—" she quickly added before Kenna rambled off everything that'd happened to them over the past twenty-four hours to Ally, "let's hold off on telling her the truth about me. We can clue her in about the bracelets and the orange-eyed people."

"Who's got orange eyes?" Ally asked while lying in the grass next to Xander, poking at his arm, shoulder, and face. "And why is this poopy-head here?"

"On second thought," Meegan added, "let's wait until she sobers up a bit."

"Agreed."

Meegan crouched next to Xander on the grass. She inspected his head and then, with two fingers, rubbed the back of his head. When she drew her fingers away, they were covered in blood.

"Why is he bleeding?" Kenna asked, glancing back at the shrubs she'd found him in.

Meegan shrugged. "Who knows? But I need some blood for a concealing amula. I took a guess that someone knocked him out, and look"—she held up her fingers covered in blood—"I was right. Turns out, Dumbass is somewhat useful."

"A concealing amula?"

"Yeah, don't worry about it. I'll explain later. I'm going to grab my phone while you hang out here and watch these two." The second Kenna nodded, Meegan took off running out into the yard.

With everything she'd learned in the past few hours, Kenna wasn't sure if she was terrified or excited for whatever was coming for them.

I don't know how to fight or defend myself. What if the orange-eyed people are dangerous? What if they're working for the Obard? Or worse, what if Meeg was right to freak out, and the Obard are the ones who trapped us here? I mean, it's possible they may have more than one type of energy wall. Oh shit, this is bad.

Out by the firepit, her friend retrieved her phone. She was holding it up, looking for service again, but eventually tucked it into the pocket of her shorts. Guilt swarmed Kenna's gut. She knew she should've told Meegan about Nick and the others also having these bracelets on, but she thought it was best for her friend to cool off first. Besides, there wasn't anything they could do to help Liam and the others. Right now, their main concern was their own safety and to prepare for the worst.

We need weapons.

Kenna left Xander and Ally, who was now snoring next to Xander, and headed over to the shed. "There's got to be something in here that we can use." With one tug on the string, the overhead lights turned on and Kenna smiled. "I can work with this."

32

What have we gotten ourselves into?

Meegan walked the entire perimeter of the dome and found no openings or weak points. She even tried to cast an opening amula to break through, but her efforts proved useless against the barrier. They were stuck until whoever trapped them came to get them.

She glanced over her shoulder. Kenna had wandered off into the shed while Ally lay in the grass next to Dumbass.

Time to protect my identity.

With her hands held over the firepit, she whispered, *"Tarach amach et tiin."* A gust of air appeared, carrying a thin stream of fire, and circled the inside of the stone pit. She leaned closer and gently blew on the logs, fueling the flames from her amula, until the fire was stable on its own.

She allowed the fire to grow. When the tops of the flames reached her height, she held out her two fingers, covered in Xander's blood, and prayed to the Eilimintachs that they would strengthen the amula she was about to cast. The fire flicked its flames against her fingertips, absorbing the essence from the dried blood. When the flames turned blue, she smiled at their blessing and wasted no time in chanting, *"Ganea mise Eilimintach. Ganea mise Eilimintach. Ganea mise Eilimintach."*

The fire sank, releasing a blue vapor of smoke that snaked upward. Meegan inhaled the blue tendril of smoke—the concealment amula—through her nose with one long, deep breath. At first the amula burned as it coated her insides with a masking layer of human genetics.

Meegan hunched forward, her hands pressed to her knees. After a few minutes, the burning sensation stopped, and her heated skin returned to normal.

"I did it!" she said while gasping. "Oh, thank the Eilimintachs, it worked! Now whoever is coming for us will think I'm human."

With a new confidence, Meegan crossed the lawn to where she'd left the others. She walked by Ally, curled up with her head nuzzled into Xander's shoulder, and over toward the shed. A bright yellow light streamed out onto the grass from between the shed doors. Inside, she found Kenna rifling through Prue's gardening tools.

"What are you doing in here?"

"Oh, hey!" Kenna stood, hands on her hips, staring at the tools meticulously hanging on the painted teal pegboard lining the wall.

Meegan stepped inside. The side walls of the shed had custom wooden shelves built in and were painted a bright white. An array of outdoor supplies like tarps, terra-cotta pots, water cans, bags of planting soil, and pool supplies lined the narrow shelves.

Meegan shimmied in beside the riding mower. "Are we doing some gardening?"

"No. I thought we could use some weapons. But go figure." She sighed and pressed one hand to the invisible barrier blocking them from reaching the pegboard.

Meegan lifted a hand and hesitantly pressed it to the barrier. The second the blue outline appeared, she pulled her hand away. "Not the Obard," she whispered.

"Not the Obard," Kenna repeated. "Though, we can't know for sure that these orange-eyed beings aren't working with the Obard."

Meegan followed Kenna out of the shed, shutting the doors behind herself. "I doubt it. I can't imagine the Obard being the type to stop and form an alliance or negotiate with anyone. They invade, destroy, enslave, torture, kill, and then move on to the next world."

Kenna stopped Meegan and said, "Listen, there's something I need to tell you, and you're not gonna be happy to hear it."

"We're stuck in an alien bubble. I'm already not happy. So, what is it?"

Kenna chewed her lip and after a few hesitant moments, she stuttered out, "Okay, so Liam told me that—uh, that he and his friends all woke up wearing these bracelets."

"Liam?" *Oh, shit.* "And…?" Kenna's eyes looked everywhere but at Meegan. "Kenna, just tell me! Does Nick have one on too?"

Her friend's subtle nod confirmed that the man she loved had somehow been dragged into this shit show. Nick was somewhere up in Boston, probably trapped under an alien energy dome too. She should have never let her parents split them up. The possibility that she'd never see or talk to him ever again tore her up inside.

The moment she opened her mouth to ask what else Liam had told Kenna, they heard Xander groaning in the grass. With one hand pressed to his head, he slowly got to his feet. Both girls hurried to help him.

"Xander, you okay?" Kenna helped him balance and only stepped away when he was able to stand on his own.

"Where the hell am I?" he asked, dragging his fingers over a cut on the side of his head.

"What do you remember?" Meegan asked while inspecting his injury. It wasn't bleeding anymore, which was good because they didn't have access to any medical supplies.

He surveyed the area. "Are we at Prue's house? How did I—? Oh damn, that stupid bitch." Under his breath, he cursed, "Fucking Cahleen."

Meegan leaned on one hip and rested a hand on the other. "What are you talking about? Who's Cahleen?"

Xander brushed his fingers through his disheveled hair, pulling out leaves and twigs, and then winced when his fingers grazed the cut again. "She's no one. Just some crazy chick who roofied me."

"Roofied you?" Meegan asked. "Why would anyone drug you and then dump you in Prue's bushes? Why don't you tell us what's really going on? And besides"—Meegan held up her wrist—"you've got one of these on too. So, talk."

Kenna crossed her arms and glared at the sun-kissed man. "How did *you* get mixed up in all this?"

He glanced at his right wrist. "I don't remember…" he drawled. "I think Cahleen put this thing on me. I mean, I'm pretty sure that's what she told me right before she shoved a needle in my neck. I don't know what she's up to. That chick is crazy! I've been see—" He paused and stared at the ground before scowling at them. "Never mind. All you need to know is that it was Cahleen. She's the one to blame for these bracelet things."

No one said anything. He threw his arms open and yelled, "I don't know why she does what she does! The girl's not normal! She's crazy! You know, like *angry* crazy. Always talking about how she's gonna save the world."

Kenna discreetly shot Meegan a side glance before she asked, "Did she have orange eyes?"

Xander's shoulders dropped and his lips tightened. He blinked a few times while looking off into the yard, and then he licked his lips. Meegan thought they were about to get some real answers, but instead he shook his head and turned away from them. "This shit is getting too weird for me. I'm outta here."

"Xander, I wouldn't—" Kenna warned as he stomped toward the wooden arbor nestled between the bushes and the side of the house. From the corner of her eye, Meegan caught Kenna trying to adjust her glasses. The glasses she didn't need anymore.

Kenna chuckled and said, "Oops, I forgot."

"A side effect of the arcstone," Meegan said and then returned to watching Xander. For a millisecond, she believed he was going to walk right through the barrier. But he didn't, and she couldn't help the giggles that escaped when he smacked right into it.

"I tried to tell you," Kenna shouted. "We're trapped under some sort of energy dome."

While Xander cursed and examined the barrier, Meegan heard a faint hum of electricity. She glanced up to see a bright ring of blue light circling the top of the dome. When the humming got louder, she tugged at Kenna and gestured up. "Guys, I think something's happening!"

Three slim blue strobe lights illuminated the center of the yard.

"Shit! Quick, get Ally!" Meegan shoved Kenna forward while calling to Xander, "Run!"

Kenna and Meegan hurried to wake Ally. Knowing they didn't have much time, they looped her arms over their necks and dragged her along.

"To the shed?" Kenna asked.

"Yeah. We can hide in there!" Meegan swallowed the lump of fear clogged in her throat. With Ally's arm over her neck, she turned to see the strobe lights out in the yard expand to the size of a Hula-Hoop.

"Meeg!" Kenna screamed. "The lights, they're moving!"

"We've got to hurry!" Meegan looked at the lights. Kenna was right. The strobe lights began to scour the yard, as if they were searching for something—or someone.

"Xander, come on!" Kenna yelled while half dragging, half leading her roommate away from the lights.

Ally's head bobbled during their rush to the shed. Still groggy, she asked, "What's going on? Why did you wake me?"

When a fourth strobe light shot down in their path to the shed, all three women screamed. The urgency of their situation set in and Ally jerked upright. "What the hell is that?"

"To the deck!" Meegan shouted. "Stay close!"

"Is that Xander?" Ally yelled.

Meegan slid to a stop. Xander was where they'd left him, in front of the arbor. He'd been caught under one of the strobe lights. His mouth gaped and his eyes were wide. Both hands were up as if to shield him from something from above, while one foot had frozen behind him, midair in retreat.

"Oh my God!" Ally's voice trembled. "Is he—*ahh!*"

"Ally!" Kenna ran past Meegan, but Meegan grabbed her friend's waist and dragged her back.

Ally had tripped and fallen, caught under the light. She lay frozen, face up in the grass, arms crossed over her eyes.

"Let me go, Meeg! We have to help her!" Kenna yelled.

"We can't help her! There's something going on with the light, like it's freezing them or capturing them somehow! I don't know, but we can't risk letting it shine on us!" Meegan pleaded. She held Kenna's arms tight while dragging her toward the deck. "We can only hope that we'll find each other after…" She didn't want to think about the *after* part right now.

"After?" Kenna's voice trembled. "This can't be happening! We're seriously about to be abducted by aliens! I need to graduate college! I need to see my parents! Meegan, what do we do?"

I don't know what to do, and—and I want to see my parents again too.

"Meeg, can't you transport us out of here or cast an amula to stop this?"

Meegan shook her head. "No, I already tried to use an amula to break through the barrier. And…" She looked over the deck railing at Xander and Ally. "I've never seen technology like this." Lights that could immobilize a person.

Up on the deck, they stood against the invisible wall. Kenna leaned into Meegan's shoulder, and Meegan embraced her friend, knowing that their outcome was inevitable.

"Listen," Meegan leaned away and said, "I need you to do something for me."

Kenna wiped her tears. "Of course. Anything."

"Whatever's coming for us, I need your help to keep my identity secret. Please," Meegan pleaded, grasping Kenna's shoulders. "I already cast an amula to mirage my body to mimic a human one."

"You can do that?"

"It wasn't easy, and I needed the help of the Eilimintachs to strengthen the amula. Plus, there's no guarantee that it'll work." Her shoulders tensed when one of the last two beams advanced over the deck railing next to the steps. "I don't know what to expect, but we need to look out for one another—and our friends."

"I can do that." Kenna's tears returned and she slid her hand into Meegan's. "I'm scared."

"Me too." But the moment she turned to tell her friend they'd make it through this together, one of the strobe lights snuck up from behind. "Kenna! Watch out!" But it was too late. Before she could save her friend, the light took ahold of her. The blue illumination shone down and paralyzed Kenna where she stood. Meegan stumbled back, almost tripping over one of the patio chairs. There was no helping her now.

I need more time. I gotta get a message to my parents. Shit! Think, Meegan! Think!

Meegan dodged the next incoming strobe light, bolted off the deck, and ran out into the yard, taking cover under the lemon tree. Between heavy breaths, she watched as four new strobe lights descended from the center of the dome. Out in the grass, the large blue circles of light hastily scanned the area... searching... hunting for her.

She hugged the trunk and said, "*Teacht iima mahl.*" The lemons on the branch above her shriveled and wilted as their essences fueled her amula. When the amula took effect, she watched the strobe lights slow their advances until they stopped moving. She knew she only had minutes before time resumed, so she quickly picked up one of the fallen leaves, pressed it to her lips, and whispered, "*Ompar et focah doa* Prinor."

When she felt the leaf quiver between her fingers, she spoke her message: "Where to begin. I don't know how I got mixed up in all of this, but this morning we woke up—me, Kenna, Ally, and who knows who else—with these metal cuffs on our wrists, and—and they had transessent stones in them, and now—now we're under some kind of energy dome, and I think they're going to take us. The ring is still violet, but I don't know who *they* are. I'm scared..." She stopped, realizing she was rambling. "But I'll be okay. I need to be strong and protect my friends. Our paths will cross again, I promise. *Iya* and I love you both."

When the leaf stilled, she carefully placed it on a nearby branch where the limb connected to the trunk. A slight shimmer glistened through its green veins. "You'll be safe here, and when the barrier comes down, you'll be free to deliver my message."

Seconds later, an intense ringing resonated from out in the yard. Meegan cringed and stepped out from under the lemon tree. The strobes of light were now violently vibrating as they fought to break free from the amula. With no reason to hide, she swept her black hair over one shoulder and marched out to the closest beam of light.

"I'm right behind you, and we'll face whatever this is together," she said and glanced over at Kenna, trapped up on the deck. She barely finished her thought before her body grew stiff, as if a layer of cement had been poured over her. A blue film draped over her vision and an eerie silence filled the space between her ears. Her heartbeat and breathing slowed, and she felt drowsy. The weight of their problems drifted from her consciousness, and for a moment, she swore she saw the glittery outline of a leaf from behind the blue haze as a gust of wind carried it off.

There wasn't anything she could do now but sleep. Sleep and pray to the Eilimintachs that she and her friends would come out of this together and unharmed.

PART

II

PRIOMH

33

"We keep meeting like this."

The man's voice tickled her ears. His closeness triggered Kenna's dormant senses to full alert. Her eyes were open, but she only saw a vast white vacuum of space. A pressure squeezed inside her ears whenever she swallowed, as if she were swimming underwater. Her heartbeat and anxious nerves hummed beneath her skin, yet there was no skin. There was nothing physical about her, just a conscious mind.

Oh man. Is this another weird dream?

"It's been a while since we last saw one another," he said. "I imagine Isoldesse is pleased with me."

Isoldesse? Ulissa's sister. Okay, seriously, what the hell is going on?

"You don't remember me? You ran straight into me out by the forest."

"Ben?"

"You do remember," he said.

An image of Ben formed in her mind. The chunky dark blond layers of his hair and that boyish cowlick above his eyes—above his *orange* eyes.

Ben is one of them.

"Ben, where am I?"

"I'm not exactly sure, but come here. Come sit on the bed with me."

A bed? How is he able to see our surroundings and I can't?

"Ben, why am I here?"

"You are a gift from my goddess. She often sends me gifts while I sleep in the form of adventures, memories, and occasionally intimate encounters."

Dreams. He's talking about his dreams.

"I especially look forward to the pleasurable moments, like now… with you."

"Hold on, cowboy. Let's figure this out first."

"What's to figure out? She's obviously pleased with me for the discovery I made regarding the rebels." He hummed an erotic groan that sounded way too close. "But I don't want to talk about Sendarian politics or the Athru right now. Please, come sit."

"Ben, please don't come any closer. I need you to tell me about these *Sendarian* people first."

He ignored her attempts to talk, and instead he prayed, "Blessed be Isoldesse—you saved Sendara and you saved me. My life is your life and I honor your glory with every breath of every day. I'm humbled by your gifts that you bestow upon me, and I'm more than pleased with the young woman you've sent to me while I sleep. She will do well to alleviate my heartache and stress."

Heartache? Alleviate his stress? What the…

"*Uh*, excuse me! I am not here to *alleviate* anything for anyone!" Whatever this place was, she needed to wake up, and fast. "Ben, please, stop! I can't see anything. I can't see you—or me!"

"Ah, but I can see you. Now, come here and let me hold you. Let me—"

"Oh my God! Just stop! Stop talking!"

I need to wake up. How do I wake up? Come on, come on, think!

"Ben, you do realize I'm a real person and not some imaginary person your mind... or goddess, whatever... thought up?"

Wait? Why is he calling Isoldesse a goddess?

Two hands caressed her invisible shoulders and she jerked, or at least in her mind she shook herself free from his grasp.

"Ben! Seriously, don't you have someone you can talk to? A friend... with benefits, maybe? I don't know, just not me and not here! There's got to be someone in the real world you can do this with. A real companion. Someone special to you. I don't know, anything but this."

She waited. When he didn't respond or make another advance, she called, "Ben? Are you still out there?" There was nothing but a somber chill that swept through her conscious mind. An aching for something lost.

Shit! Where did he go? I need answers and—and why the hell do I suddenly feel like crying?

An overwhelming sense of abandonment and loneliness flooded her thoughts. She wanted to focus on figuring out where she was, but a thick layer of heartache enveloped her entire being, yearning for something... or someone.

What the hell is wrong with me?

Seconds from a ghostly cryfest, Kenna felt the familiar warmth of the arcstone energy float through her mind. She immediately tried to call out to her bonded companion, "Ulissa! Is that you? Can you hear me? Are you okay?"

But the only response Kenna received was a heated energy that countered the onslaught of sorrow like white blood cells devouring bacteria.

After the last of the sorrow had seeped from her existence, she returned her attention to the vast, empty white space. *Now to figure out where the hell I am.* But the mystery was short lived. The pressure of the arcstone's energy inflated against the boundaries of her subconscious.

"Okay, okay! That's enough!" The heat of the energy grew hotter and fiercer. "Stop! Please, *stop!*"

From the corners of her vision, a reddish-yellow glow crept inward, consuming the vast white space. When the pain grew to be too much, she screamed.

The abrupt silence and soft fabrics surrounding her told her she was awake. Or at least she hoped she was awake. She pried her weary eyes open and saw white again, but not vacuum-space white. Something was physically blocking her view. A white object with a chalky scent.

Her arm muscles felt heavy, as though she'd slept for too long, as she reached up to her face. Whatever was covering her face, it was smooth and had some flexibility to it. Her fingers continued up into her hair, where she felt something like one of those wide plastic headbands little kids wear. Nervous adrenaline hummed beneath her skin when she realized the ends of the headband didn't go behind her ears, but rather plugged into her ear canals.

We were taken. By the orange-eyed beings. Ben had orange eyes, the woman crying under the tree had orange eyes, and I think—I think that girl who roofied Xander had orange eyes!

After prodding the headband loose, she carefully, and somewhat painfully, pulled out what felt like super-long earplugs wedged deep in her ears. Fresh air filled the canals, along with a new sense of silence. Slowly, she sat up, careful not to pull or strain any of her sore muscles. The face shield dropped to the floor with a soft *thud*. A sweet scent drifted in the air. Whatever it was, she liked it.

Daylight filled the room from a glass wall ten feet in front of her that doubled as an exterior wall. The scene outside the window was breathtaking. A lone snowcapped mountain sat under a perfect blue sky. A lush green forest surrounded the base of the rocky mountain.

A quick glance at herself, and she was happy to see she was still wearing her own clothes, except for her sandals. When her fingers found the arcstone pendant beneath her shirt, she noticed the transessent bracer still around her wrist.

Damn thing. How do I get you off? First things first, though.
Figure out where the hell I am.

Moving one stiff leg in front of the other along the hardwood warm beneath her bare feet, she reached the glass wall. When she pressed one hand to the sunbaked glass, a display screen activated on the window's surface. She flinched away, and it instantly disappeared.

"What the...?" She slowly pressed her palm flat to the clear surface again. The semiopaque screen reappeared along the glass. She removed her hand, and the screen disappeared. She pressed her hand to the window, and it returned. She surveyed the length of the entire window. It was like a giant tablet. She then glanced to the grounds below.

"Holy shit! Are those people down there?"

A few stories below her, a small crowd of people was standing around and talking. There were a few off to the side, sitting on benches reading their tablets. Wherever she was, the vibrant gardens and stone walkways of the courtyard below were impressive and meticulously well kept.

Kenna returned her attention to the screen displayed on the glass. She shuddered when a large red symbol flashed in the center of the screen.

Red plus flashing never equals good.

"Time to leave."

She turned to make her escape through a nearby side door, but then she saw the other beds, behind the one she'd woken in, all lined up in a long row down the center of the room. She counted sixteen platform beds. Every bed like the next, with its simple lines and dark wood. A slab of clear glass stuck out of each headboard and extended up into one of the wooden beams stretched across the white ceiling. Lights blinked and symbols scrolled on the glass screens.

Curious, she tiptoed closer to one bed while taking in the rest of the room. Besides the beds, there was a long upholstered bench against the wall behind the headboards while the wall facing the footboards had random-sized rectangles etched into it.

Out of the sixteen beds, seven were occupied, and all seven occupants were wearing those face shields and headbands. Kenna didn't need to see who was under the mask in the bed she approached to know who it was.

Meegan.

Hunched over her best friend, Kenna whispered, "I have no idea what to do or how to get us out of this, so how about you wake up and work some of your magic to get us the hell out of here." She tried to pry out the ends of the headband plugged into Meegan's ears, but they weren't budging. Not wanting to cause any permanent damage, she stopped fidgeting with the headband and sidestepped to the back of the headboard. Large red symbols scrolled across the glass screen. She glanced down the row of beds. Red symbols flashed above the headboards of two other beds.

Oh, that can't be good.

She recalled her promise to Meegan to do whatever she could to help keep Meegan's identity a secret.

Okay, Meegan first, and then I'll help whoever's in those beds.

The glass console displayed a multitude of semiopaque mini screens.

Ohhh, what do I do? She tried to interpret the symbols and graphs displayed. *Dad would know what to do. Or at least one of the characters from his books would know what to do.*

Through the transparent glass headboard, she could still see Meegan lying in bed, but the moment she tapped one of the mini screens, the glass's opacity increased until she couldn't see through it. Not sure what the hell she was doing, she began tapping symbols, moving sliders up and down, and anything else to mess with the system. There was one symbol that erased everything in that mini screen when tapped. Pleased with her discovery, she tapped her new favorite button as many times as she could until all of the mini screens were blank and flashing red.

Error... error... shit's been deleted... Ha! She couldn't help but laugh at the dialogue her dad would've narrated for her if he saw her now.

Voices grew loud outside the doors at the other end of the room. She quickly squeezed Meegan's hand and whispered, "I gotta go, but I'll be back." Then, a set of *clicks* followed by the door opening made her heart leap into her throat just as Kenna slipped out the side door.

Outside the room stretched a long corridor. White plaster walls with glass panels every few feet, about an arm's length wide, extended up from the floor to the ceiling. She started to think these orange-eyed people had taken smart-glass technology to a whole new level.

She needed to hide and make a plan. With each door she passed she hoped no one would walk out and find her. But no one did. As she got closer to the double doors at the end of the corridor, she heard voices from the other side and stopped. They were getting louder, which meant she needed to get the hell out of there, and quick.

She backtracked, trying to open any of the side doors until one opened. She ducked inside and cracked the door just enough to hear what they were saying as they walked by, but they weren't speaking English. She wasn't sure what language they were speaking.

Softly, she closed the door and looked around the room. A thin window ran across the far wall, letting in enough daylight for her to see she was in a storage room. Tall shelves lined the walls. To her left, tucked in the corner, was a long wooden table.

Perfect!

The best thing she could do right now was hide. That was one of the tips she'd picked up from watching all those science-fiction and action movies. Plus, she'd have better luck after hours, in the dark, to sneak in and rescue her friends.

But for now, the plan was to hide under this table.

I can't believe this is happening, she thought as she ducked under the table and scooted close to the wall. *What if we never get home?*

Her fingers traced the outer edge of the white transessent stone.

What if I never see my parents again?

Tears began to stream down her cheeks.

What if the Obard are involved?

She rested the side of her head against the wall and squeezed her eyes shut.

What if I can't save my friends? What if Meegan's secret gets out?

She slumped her curled-up body into the corner of the wall and cried. She buried her mouth into her arm to quiet her sobs.

I don't know if I can do this.

From the back of her mind, she swore she heard Ulissa say, "*Yes you can, Kenna,*" before her emotionally drained mind drifted off to sleep.

34

Breyah closed the doors to her office, her fingers trailing the lines of the ornate design carved into the wooden panels of both doors. She shuffled farther into her office, never taking her gaze from the iron door handles.

But the handles never moved.

The barrage of questions and concerns she'd been addressing since the *Tarais* had docked earlier that day had begun to take its toll. She needed a moment to process and think about the mess they were in without interruptions.

Finally, alone. She relaxed her confident posture and the optimistic expression she'd been parading all day. If the words *everything will be fine* or *it's not as bad as it seems* left her mouth one more time, she might have shown the Sendarians of Priomh another side to their Leadess.

She poured a glass of water from a carafe before crossing the room. Her office was a long, narrow room with a solid glass pane stretching the full length of the exterior wall. Geevi's old home may have the best view of Mount Nocholus, but it was the view of the center courtyard below that Breyah favored. To watch the many Sendarians go about their day walking and talking, sitting and reading, and enjoying the nearby gardens. She especially loved those moments at the end of the day when a fellow Sendarian would sit and wait for their loved one. Then to see them walk home together, hand in hand, toward the community of homes was exactly what she and Geevi had wanted for this place. To be more than just research. They'd wanted this to be a community, and the Sendarians here in their little community meant *everything* to her.

Yet, somehow, she'd let them down.

The *Tarais* had returned from Earth without their Spiaires. The torment of not knowing where Eryn, Seph, Grace, and Darci were scared her, especially Darci. It'd been the young Spiaire's first mission. And now she was out there, hopefully not alone.

She finished her water and decided to refill her glass with a stronger tonic. The clear liquid burned her throat, momentarily distracting her from her chaotic day before her thoughts returned to trying to understand what had gone wrong. Where were her Spiaires?

Breyah set her empty glass on the wooden table that doubled as her desk and faced the window behind her. She pressed one hand to the clear glass, activating a large display screen.

A three-dimensional portrait of Darci wearing her black sparring attire appeared in the top right corner. Her fair red hair was tied back into a sleek, long tail, and her freckled cheeks were plump from her beaming smile. That girl had nothing but pure enthusiasm and an eagerness to help, which always brought a smile to Breyah's face.

She wiped her eyes and closed out the file.

We will find you. I swear to Isoldesse that we will figure out what happened.

She reopened the Commander's official report and read through the part when the *Tarais* first lost contact with Seph's signal, and then Grace's tracker a week later. Both of the Spiaires' Lincs had somehow been deactivated. The Commander's final conclusion in her report was that the Spiaires had defected.

Deactivated? Why would they deactivate their Lincs? Unless they were deactivated by force. I don't believe for one second that this young Sendarian, or any of the Spiaires, would defect.

She continued reading. The Commander then stated that it wasn't until transport day that Eryn's and Darci's Lincs went off-line. She'd made the executive decision to continue forward with only Eryn's and Darci's human groups. She didn't want to return to Priomh empty handed and run the risk of a failed Aevo Compendium. Something was better than nothing, even if that meant leaving the Spiaires behind.

Something being eight humans instead of sixteen. It wasn't the ideal situation, but one they could still work with.

Knock, knock, knock.

She couldn't help but wonder if their goddess had a hand in what was happening. *Did they do something to upset or anger Isoldesse?* She stared at the courtyard below and realized there wasn't anyone else who could have done something to upset Isoldesse... *but me.*

Knock, knock, knock.

It had been Breyah who pushed for the new Priomh compound, something bigger and more like home. A place where Sendarians didn't have to live in isolation and could do both—research and enjoy the company of their families. Though, the more she thought about it, who was she to change the original design created and built by Isoldesse? It was Breyah's fault because she'd encouraged others to abandon the original facility for her ambitions of what Priomh could be.

KNOCK, KNOCK, KNOCK!

"Yes, yes, come in!" With her chin raised and her shoulders squeezed together, she once again slipped into her Leadess role. When one of the double doors opened, a short, round man waddled into the room. His orange gaze darted everywhere but at Breyah.

"Beannaith, my Leadess, I wanted to remind you that Sabine is due to return from her trip to Sendara tomorrow."

Sabine. A pleasantry among all this chaos.

How she missed her assistant's friendly smile, not to forget her amazing organizational skills. Sabine's absence had not gone unnoticed, and Breyah longed for her assistant to return. "Thank you, yes. I've arranged for a few baked treats and some sweet-brew to be delivered to her home in the morning."

"Oh, she loves sweet-brew!" The man's gaze met Breyah's, and the corners of his lips pushed his cheeks high. "Sabine will be ecstatic to see such a wonderful welcome home. You're too kind, Leadess."

"Beannaith," she said with a bow of her head.

"Oh, yes, yes, Beannaith, my Leadess. I'll see you at first light."

After he was gone, Breyah continued reading over the Commander's notes until her Linc notified her of an incoming transmission. "It's Captain Ganecht of the Rhaltan Enforcers."

Breyah stepped to the side to open a new display screen on the window. "Accept transmission." The call opened to a headshot of a man covered in soot and dried mud and wearing a black Rhaltan uniform. Behind the man, black smoke billowed from a nearby building. The ash hadn't covered the six red ribbons sewn down the jacket over his left shoulder. She hated those ribbons.

"Bennach, I hardly recognize you," she said. "You could've at least washed your face before calling me."

"Beannaith, sister." He rustled his fingers through the mud caked in his hair, releasing a small dust cloud. "I have news and wanted to notify you that I'm leaving here—"

His words trailed to a distant murmur as an incoming urgent message in large red letters scrolled across a new screen, above the two other open screens.

EMERGENCY COMMUNICATION: BREYAH YOU'RE NEEDED IN MEDICAL. ONE OF THE HUMANS HAS WOKEN AND IS MISSING.

Bennach's lips were moving, but she heard nothing. She just kept reading the looped messages over and over again.

Has woken—and is missing? From deep-space sedation? How can that be?

"Breyah?"

Bennach's sharp voice calling her name snapped her from the urgent distraction. "Yes. You were saying?"

"I know it's sudden, but I've made a big discovery regarding the rebel threat here on Sendara. I've been granted some time off while Diagnostics maps out our next move."

"That's wonderful," Breyah commended while she nervously rubbed the yellow stone set in her arm cuff.

He narrowed his dark orange eyes and asked, "So, you're not upset?"

"Upset? Why would I be upset? That sounds wonderful. I'm proud of you and what you've done for the Rhaltan." He opened his mouth, but Breyah cut him off. "Bennach, can we talk more tomorrow? There's an urgent matter I need to attend to." It was wonderful to hear from her younger brother, and she could use some good news after everything that had happened today, but it seemed the day wasn't over.

"Of course. We'll talk more tomorrow."

"Yes, tomorrow. Beannaith, brother."

Her Linc closed out the transmission video and the other open screens. Breyah stood there in silence and prayed to her goddess for forgiveness... forgiveness she wasn't sure she deserved, before heading to Medical.

Breyah hurried out of her office and down the spiral ramp from within the annex building. The Lead Building consisted of five smaller annex buildings with the Centrum hub in the center. Her office was in the Operations and Administration building, and she needed to meet Rian at the Medical skywalk located across the Centrum.

From within the glass-enclosed skywalk that connected the Ops and Admin building to the Centrum, Breyah instructed her Linc to send for Matthew. "We'll need him if Medical hasn't activated the EarLincs yet."

She exited the skywalk and entered the Centrum. There were no walls along the front of the Centrum and the ceiling was open to the sky, in which Breyah noted the flickers of blue energy crackling against the evening clouds.

The barrier dome over the entire compound had been activated.

"*Leadess,*" her Linc spoke in her ear. "*It took a few attempts, but Matthew's on his way.*"

"Thank you, Linc."

The Centrum consisted of white plaster walls and network-infused glass that complemented the simple yet modern design she and Geevi had been going for. Perched in the center of the Centrum, held up by a series of thick stone pillars, was a cylindrical stone structure covered with glass windows. A wide stone ramp with a glass railing spiraled around the cluster of stone pillars, leading up to the first of three levels of living quarters. Each level housed two residential quarters for the Leads of Priomh.

At some point, she'd be making that trek up the ramp to the third level, where her private quarters were located. A feat she knew wouldn't be happening anytime soon.

Without revealing her urgency, Breyah walked, smiled, and greeted the few lingering Sendarians who passed by, all heading home for the day. The Sendarians in the Archives annex were usually the last to leave, except for Medical. Holt always kept a few staff members on through the night, especially when there was an active Aevo Compendium in progress. Not that the trial subjects could do much during their deep-space sedation. Having one wake was almost impossible, yet here she was, rushing toward Medical to find out what happened.

It wasn't hard to spot Rian with her porcelain skin and icy-blue hair. She always stood out among the many shades of red and blond hair.

Rian turned and matched Breyah's brisk pace down the Medical skywalk. "I was with Holt when his medics reported the incident. They estimated she's—"

"It's a female?"

"Yes. Subject fifteen."

"That's one of Darci's." When Rian nodded, Breyah asked, "How does one wake from deep-space sedation and then just *wander off*? Why hasn't anyone tracked her location through her transessent bracer?"

"We've tried, but for some reason, her transessent stone isn't showing on our tracking system."

"Are all the other subjects' bracers working correctly?"

Rian nodded.

"Do transessent stones' power supplies ever expire?"

"Not that I know of."

Well, fantastic.

"So, you're telling me that this human girl woke... all on her own... and somehow *turned off* the tracking bracer. Making it impossible for us to locate her." Breyah pursed her lips and mumbled, "Can this Aevo C get any worse?"

They approached a set of tall double doors with medical symbols etched into the wood. Rian pressed her hand to the door. "Actually, before we go in, there's something else you need to know."

"I was kidding! Please... please tell me you're kidding." She inhaled and swallowed the lump that had formed in her throat. This Aevo Compendium was pissing her off, and for one fleeting breath all she wanted to do was send the humans home and focus on finding her Spiaires.

But then she remembered: the mission comes first.

No matter what.

Abandoning the Aevo Compendium because of a few drawbacks, regardless of their severity, could possibly anger Isoldesse even more. *Whatever Rian says, we'll figure it out—we always do.* She told herself the same lie she'd been telling her staff all day.

"Okay," Breyah said with a long, exasperated breath, "what is it?"

Her Lead of Security, and closest friend since Geevi had disappeared, dipped her head and stared Breyah in the eyes. "I can tell when you're stressed out. You tend to stand taller and smile more. We'll fig—"

"Don't! Just... tell me. Holt's waiting for us."

Rian blinked her unique sapphire eyes several times before dropping her hand from the door and crossing her arms. "You don't have to snap at me. I'm only trying to help."

"I know, I know, I'm sorry. Please, continue."

"Well, you should know that during check-in, Holt discovered a few unknown humans among the group."

The laughter that broke out inside Breyah's mind almost escaped her lips. "Enlighten me. How is that possible? The *Tarais* mission logs show all eight preselected subjects from both Eryn's and Darci's groups were tagged with transessent bracers."

"I don't know," Rian said with a shrug. "Right now, there are two unidentified humans wearing transessent bracers assigned to subject ten and subject sixteen."

Subject number ten is from Eryn's group. I think his name was Brody. And subject sixteen is from Darci's group. Her name was Prudence, if I recall correctly.

Rian handed Breyah a plac. "And there's more."

This time, the bubble of laughter escaped as she rolled her eyes and took the plac from Rian. "Of course there's more."

"Subject fourteen's data was deleted."

Breyah scrolled through subject fourteen's profile. Nothing. The only remaining detail was her profile image, which showed a young human with long straight black hair, dark eyes, and slender features beneath her sand-colored skin. And that was it. Even the data collected prior to the Spiaires' arrival on Earth had been erased.

"Holt can tell us more."

"Thank you." Breyah handed Rian the sleek piece of glass. Her gaze fixed on the black latches of the doors. Her thoughts kept drifting to the idea that something bigger, more divine, might have had a hand in what was happening.

Rian was about to open the door when she paused and cocked her head. "You normally enjoy a good challenge. What's wrong?"

Breyah shifted and glanced up at her second-in-command. "What if I brought this on us? What if Isoldesse is punishing me for taking on Her project as my own? Geevi and I should've never redesigned and relocated the Priomh facility. Isoldesse built the original facility, and we threw it away. Nothing more than a mere memory. What was I thinking? How could I've thought I knew better than our goddess?" The pressure of guilt grew inside, and her glossy eyes trembled with the threat of losing it right then and there.

"Right, so that's what you think is going on? Easy fix. I'll make the official announcement come first light that we're packing up and moving the entire community... and the humans... to the original facility. Done. Problem solved. Isoldesse will be pleased and fix this mess we're in, yeah?"

"No!" Breyah's brows furrowed. "We can't all fit in that facility, and besides, it's probably overgrown with roots and vines from the forest. No one should venture out there. It could be dangerous!"

Rian raised a pale blue eyebrow at Breyah.

"You're not funny, and I'm not in the mood to be patronized." Breyah turned toward the door but stopped and faced her friend again. "I get it. What's done is done. But I still think making things right with Isoldesse will help. Otherwise, who knows what could happen during the next Aevo C."

Rian opened the door and let Breyah continue through. "What's happening has nothing to do with Isoldesse. If I had to guess, I'd say something happened on Earth that complicated the Spiaires' position. They made a judgment call that resulted in them being left behind. We may need to consider sending a rescue ship."

"I'd love to send a rescue ship, but we don't have the resources. It may just have to wait until the *Tarais* leaves to bring the humans home once the Aevo C is finished." Breyah stopped midway down the corridor toward Medical Observation One and asked, "Do you think there's foul play at hand? Sabotage?"

"I do, and I've already taken extra security measures and activated the energy barrier around Priomh."

"I saw that."

"Also, I requested logs and video feeds from the *Tarais* commander. My security team is sorting through *every* mission log and *every* video recording from *every* glass surface on that ship. If there were unauthorized personnel aboard the *Tarais*, we'll have their identity by morning."

Breyah nodded. "Thank you. I don't know how I could manage all of this without you," she said with a sincere smile.

"It's my keen sixth sense you love. It's never wrong. Now, wipe that look of dread from your face and let's go talk to Holt."

35

Medical Observation Room-One smelled of Hiccum flowers. The small yellow flower wasn't one of Breyah's favorites, too potent for her liking, but from previous assessments the sweet floral aroma had proven to create a calm, welcoming environment for the trial subjects after waking. Plus, they were found all over Sendara and the Priomh moon.

Breyah stared out the exterior glass wall at the end of the room. The silhouette of Mount Nocholus against a sunset sky reminded her of the view from Geevi's home. Her gaze dipped to the lush treetops of the Endless Forest huddled along the base of the western side of the mountain where the original Priomh research facility had been located.

An older woman with graying red hair pulled tight into a large bun hurried by them. The medic offered a brief greeting smile to Breyah and Rian before squeezing herself into the small group talking at the other end of the room.

Normally, all sixteen beds would be occupied. But this Aevo Compendium was anything but *normal*. This assessment would go on record with many firsts. The first time not all subjects were picked up, the first time subjects had somehow gotten mixed up, and the first time they'd lost their Spiaires.

Why would Isoldesse swap out two transessent ID bracers after our Sendarians attached them to the correct subjects? That doesn't seem like something a divine being would do. Maybe Rian's right. Maybe there is something or someone purposefully intervening. But who would do such a thing? To defy our goddess...

"Holt!" Rian waved when the older man talking to three Sendarian medics and two security officials glanced their way.

"Ah good, you're here." Holt dismissed the group and approached his fellow Leads. He scratched at the hint of gray blending in with his red beard. "We've got quite the mess here. Subjects swapped out, missing profile data, and the best, a subject who wakes up and strolls off."

"Yes, well, let's focus on what's in front of us." Breyah nodded toward the seven full beds. "Are the trial subjects that are here well and healthy? No medical complications?"

"Vitals are stable for all seven humans. They'll all be ready for the Waking come tomorrow." Holt turned and gestured to the glass panel embedded in the white plaster wall next to the door. "But here, I want to show you video footage of the girl who woke. She's the one who deleted subject fourteen's data. Whether it was deliberate or accidental, I can't say."

The video began and Breyah watched the girl with long, wavy dark brown hair sit up in the last bed. Slowly, she made her way to the exterior window. They watched the human press her hand to the glass and experiment with the display screen before sidestepping to the second bed in the long line of beds.

How terrible. She woke up alone in a strange place with no explanation of where she is.

Rian stepped closer. "What's she doing?"

"This is where she messes with subject fourteen's file," Holt explained. They watched her tap and drag her fingers along the glass above the headboard. "We're assuming she was trying to wake her friend." Holt pointed to the door next to Rian. "She ran out that door. Breyah, you should know that I've ordered subject fourteen's vitals and samples to be recollected."

"Good. What about the girl who woke? Subject fifteen. Show me her file."

Holt pulled out a plac tucked under his arm and tapped the screen. When he handed the device to Breyah, she blinked and lifted the screen closer. "I've seen this girl," she whispered.

"We all have. We've been studying her profile, along with those of the other fifteen subjects, since before we sent the Spiaires to Earth."

"No, that's not what I mean. I've seen this girl before."

"Before today?" Holt asked.

Breyah nodded and explained. "Only one time, but I swear this girl was in my dream last night."

"Oh." Holt blew out an exasperated sigh. "It was just a dream. Breyah, I dream about our subjects all the time."

True. She did often picture a few of the subjects, from whatever Aevo Compendium they were preparing for, in her dreams. But seeing subject number fifteen from this Earth Aevo C in her dream felt different. It had only been a brief encounter, but it felt so real. The human girl had approached Breyah beneath the Phantom Tree, a mystical tree located in the sacred gardens of the Elemental Council's sanctuary on Sendara. She often dreamed of the Phantom Tree, but never the horrific scene of armored soldiers massacring the Sendarians of their peaceful Priomh.

Why would anyone want to attack us? What a horrible nightmare.

"Breyah," Rian said, jolting Breyah from her reverie.

"I'm fine." She moved past Holt and stood at the footboard of one of the occupied beds. "Have you activated their EarLincs yet?"

Holt shook his head. "We attached the implant bands and inserted the canal plugs. Only the bio-electrode coupling coils have been activated. The coils take time to fuse accurately to the host's central and peripheral nervous systems."

While Holt continued to update Rian with the status of the translator pods, Breyah moved over one bed and stood at the footboard. A male with bronzed skin lay sleeping beneath the white blanket. His black hair feathered out from the top of the implant band and the monitoring shield that covered his face. The glass headboard that extended up to the ceiling listed his status as *unauthorized* in bold red letters. A woman in the next bed had the same *unauthorized* alert displayed across her glass medic board.

He's from Darci's group and she's from Eryn's group. How did this happen?

Breyah faced her Lead Medic and second-in-command. "I've asked Matthew to join us in finding the human girl."

"Oh, please say you didn't." Rian dropped her head into her hands. Thick blue strands of hair fell forward as she shook her head.

Holt had the opposite reaction. "That's a good idea!" He then waved and beckoned one of his medics over. "He is human, after all, and can communicate with the girl. I'll inform my team to upgrade Matthew's clearance level."

"Temporary upgrade," Rian stressed while lifting her head from her hand. "Don't give that loggie too much access."

"Leave him be." Breyah opened the door to leave. "He's the only one right now who can talk to the girl." She turned back to Holt and said, "Keep me posted on your progress, and if you figure out why subject fifteen's transessent bracer isn't working properly."

"Yes, yes, something else we're looking into."

"And come to my office when you've finished here. We can talk more in private about how to proceed."

"Will do," Holt said and turned to the medics patiently waiting behind him.

After leaving Medical, out in the corridor, Rian asked Breyah, "Really? Matthew?"

"Yes, he may be useful."

"Matthew is anything but useful." The tall woman rolled her icy-blue eyes. "He's more like entertainment."

"You're not wrong, but he has a good heart, and you have to admit, he has matured over the years. I don't regret my decision to allow him to stay."

Rian laughed. "Uh, you didn't *allow* him to stay. We both know who allowed him to stay."

"We agreed not to question or assume the real reason behind Matthew's request to stay on Priomh, remember?"

"Yeah, yeah. Keep my mouth shut and play nice with the human."

From the other end of the corridor, they heard a man arguing with someone on the opposite side of the doors. When one of the double doors opened, a stocky man with wide shoulders strode in, cursing at the security guard behind him. "I told you I've got clearance, dumbass."

When the man saw Breyah and Rian, his frown brightened, and he opened his arms wide. "Beannaith. You called, and I came!" His green eyes stood out against his tanned skin. After his request to remain on Priomh, he'd chosen to live out beyond the borders of the Priomh compound, but not too far, and he came and went as he pleased. He'd built a cabin in the Endless Forest and preferred to spend most of his days exploring and mapping the moon's terrain. Breyah recalled the quiet young man he'd been when he'd first arrived for Earth's last Aevo Compendium. Now, fifty years later, not much had changed except his confidence.

Rian pursed her pale blue lips and crossed her arms as the man approached, a slight bounce in his step. Breyah knew that behind that annoyed expression Rian had a soft spot for Matthew. He was different, like she was, and though Rian would never say, Breyah knew she considered him family.

Matthew scratched the top of his head. His blond hair had been trimmed slightly longer than the scruff along his chin. He smiled at

Breyah, then winked at Rian. "Hey, Blue-bee! You been avoiding me?"

"Always," she groaned.

"Beannaith, Matthew," Breyah greeted him.

He jerked to a stop a few feet from them and narrowed his eyes. "Wait a sec. You aren't planning to send me home, are you? Back to Earth and all?"

"Wouldn't that be a dream come true?" Rian joked.

Breyah approached her friend and looped one arm through his, then led him closer to Rian. "Not unless you want to go. Otherwise, no. Your home is here on Priomh with us."

His smile returned. "Phew, good. That wouldn't have gone over too well with—" He paused before clearing his throat. "Ah, never mind. What can I do for you ladies?"

The two women exchanged looks before Breyah explained, "One of the female humans from the Earth Aevo Compendium has woken and wandered off."

Matthew's nose wrinkled and Breyah thought he was about to say something, but instead he made a few groaning sounds while scratching the scruff along his jawline. "The transessent bracer not working?" Breyah shook her head. He then asked, "How long ago did the girl wake?"

"Not too long ago," Breyah answered, and then thought about how she was glad Matthew had stayed while everyone else in his Aevo C trial had returned to Earth all those years ago. He was kind and caring. Though, deep down inside, she also hoped the truth behind his request to stay on Priomh remained a secret.

"I assume you and Holt have your teams scouring the place?" he asked Rian. When she nodded, he added, "So, what? We just wait here until they find her?"

"Yes," Rian answered before Breyah. "You're here for a secondary option. I doubt you'll even be needed."

Matthew's smile spread wider. Breyah knew that Rian poking him only fueled his need to prove her wrong. It was an ongoing rivalry between the two of them. Both competitive. Both headstrong. Both also two of Breyah's closest friends.

"Did you check in here?" Matthew asked while shimmying between the two Sendarians and pointing to a storage room door behind them.

"Why would she be in there? And besides, Holt would've had these rooms checked first," Rian protested, but he'd already opened the door and stepped inside. Rian shot Breyah an annoyed look. "We really don't need him."

"It's not a question of whether we need him or not. The point is we have him here in case we do need him. Besides, I think this is a good opportunity for him to catch up with his own kind."

"Ah…" Rian said with a grin. "I see what you're doing. You're trying to get him to want to go back to Earth on his own. To see what he's been missing."

"No, but wouldn't you want to talk with your own kind if you'd been separated from them?"

Rian looked away, and Breyah instantly wished she could take back her words. "I didn't mean you. You have to stop thinking you don't belong. You're Sendarian. Like me, Holt, and everyone else here. Isoldesse just blessed you a little different. She blessed us all with something special. You just happen to have a little more *special* in you."

Rian sighed. "I wish I could believe that."

Breyah was about to console her friend when Matthew walked out from inside the storage room. Rian straightened and snickered. "I told you she's not in there."

"*Ah*, but she is," Matthew said with a wide grin. He tucked his hands into his pants pockets and leaned back on his heels, pleased by the surprised look on Rian's face. "You owe me a drink."

"Nice try, loggie, but we never made a wager."

"Okay, okay, you two. Cut it out. Thank you, Matthew." Breyah told Rian to go get Holt, which she did, leaving Matthew and Breyah alone in the hall. "Is she hurt?"

"Nah, but she did fall asleep under the table."

Asleep? That seemed odd. "Can I ask another favor, Matthew?"

He nodded. "Of course."

"Can you stay with the human girl in her quarters until Holt activates her EarLincs?"

"Yeah, sure. Anything for my Leadess."

Breyah felt warm blood rising in her cheeks. "Thank you."

Holt and his team rushed through the door behind them, Rian on their heels. Matthew pointed to the storage room. Holt entered alone while everyone else waited out in the corridor. When he emerged, he informed his team that the girl had been sedated again and was ready to be moved to the Aevo C accommodations wing.

Matthew followed Holt and his team while Breyah and Rian headed toward the Centrum. With Matthew staying with the human girl, and Rian's security team investigating the logs and ship recordings for unauthorized personnel, Breyah felt a little more at ease. Hopefully tomorrow they'd have some answers and be back on track to move this Aevo C forward.

"Let's head to my office. Holt will meet us there shortly."

"Sounds good." Rian scrolled through her plac as they walked. "Sabine comes back tomorrow, yes?"

Breyah nodded. "It'll be nice to see her after such a long break."

Halfway over the skywalk to the Admin building, Rian said, "I still can't believe you approved her request for time off this close to an Aevo C."

"Her mother was sick. How could I say no?"

"I guess."

In Breyah's office, Rian went straight to the cabinet that housed Breyah's secret stash of spirits.

Outside, the courtyard lights flickered along the stone pathways as the night grew darker. The evening was coming to an end. Finally. Rian joined her at the window and handed her a flute filled with one of Rian's specialty cocktails. "Thank you. I think enough has happened today for us to relax and finally enjoy a drink."

"I can only stay for one, so Holt better hurry and get here. I'm meeting up with the Commander for a late-night meeting. I have a few more questions to ask her."

"Must be nice," Breyah said playfully and nudged Rian's elbow. A cold chill ran through Breyah the moment their skin touched.

"It's not like that. She's a friend, and besides, you know who I have my eye on."

"I do, and after all this is over, you'll have to give me an update on how that's progressing. But for now, let's enjoy the downtime with a drink, and then I'm heading to bed."

36

With her eyes closed, Gemma visualized her old home and the picturesque view of Mount Nocholus from her sitting room. But it was hard to trick her mind into thinking she was somewhere comfortable or warm when the stone floor she'd been sitting on felt like a sheet of ice. The *pitter-patter* of tiny feet scurrying across the docking station storage room ceiling joists wasn't helping her nerves either.

Gemma eventually lost track of how long they'd been sitting and waiting for Quaid to return with an escape vehicle.

There was something broken in that man. His confidence and righteousness stemmed from an unnatural rotting essence. Whatever his intentions were, he still hadn't shared anything with her or the others. But it was clear to Gemma that his idea of a new Sendara wasn't the same as what Anora had promised.

He was supposed to be the Lead on this Earth mission, yet their fellow Athru, Abastian, was missing, and only two of the four Spiaires were in their custody. Gemma worried that Quaid had killed his Spiaire. If he had, it sickened her to think that Seph had been left on such a vile planet and would never receive a proper Sendarian burial.

Let's just hope that two Spiaires and three humans are enough to bargain an exchange for a princess.

A tussle of violent squeaks erupted from somewhere inside the storage room they were hiding in, sending Gemma's nerves into a frenzy. She scooted away from the wall and tugged the hood of her sweatshirt farther over her face—as if that would protect her from the vermin. She hated not knowing where the little shits were scampering about, and she hated not knowing how much longer they were going to be stuck in this tiny closet. She also hated not having a clue as to what was going to happen next. She wanted answers and it boiled her blood to know she wasn't going to get them.

She reeled in her frustration and reminded herself that she still needed to figure out what Quaid was planning. He'd kept his distance during the journey home, locked away in the main sleeping chamber of the quarters they'd stowed away in on the *Tarais*. Not even Cahleen had been able to uncover what he was hiding from the rest of them. The most popular assumption among their little group was that he was hiding a plac with his master plan.

The pesky squabbling continued from above where the dimly lit overhead lights dangled from wooden beams, casting shadows over the wooden crates lining the storage room. Sabine was asleep on one of the crates while Cahleen lay curled up on the floor next to Gemma, her arm tucked under her head. She had no idea how either could sleep in such a disgusting place that reeked of stale air, old wood, and feces.

Someone needs to tell Breyah to take better care of these storage rooms.

"It looks like they're finishing up out there." Micah stood guard at the door. His broad body took up much of the door while he watched the activity out in the docking station. After they'd snuck off the *Tarais* and into the docking bay storage room, Micah had used his talents to hack into Priomh's network and disable the translucency commands and recording capabilities for this storage room window and the adjacent one. It would've been a tight squeeze with everyone in one room, so Logan volunteered to babysit the captives one room over.

As annoying as her brother was, his technical abilities did come in handy. She peeked out from under her hood and asked, "Any sign of Quaid?"

Micah didn't turn from the door's window. "No."

"Where is that gróntah…?" Gemma's words trailed off as she rubbed her neck, just under her chin. She needed to be smarter. More careful with her words if she was going to survive. Watching her tongue had become a chore these past few weeks while they traveled home, but it worked. Quaid had paid her less attention and even joked with her sometimes. But they were both playing a dangerous game of pretend. It had been Cahleen's idea to play nice until they could figure out where Anora was and how to begin phase two of bargaining their captives for the princess.

It killed her not to be able to send word to Anora, but Micah felt it was in Gemma's best interests to deactivate her Linc. At least until he could figure out a way to permanently deal with the search query Breyah had initiated. Otherwise, their location would be compromised and transmitted to the Rhaltan within a day.

"Hey," Cahleen groaned, rolling onto her backside. The sides of her shaved pixie-style haircut had grown out during their journey home.

"I don't know how you can sleep in here," Gemma whispered with a hint of disgust as she watched her sister pat her hip. Quaid had confiscated all but one of Cahleen's sharp toys. A small arrowhead-like dagger with a T-shaped hilt that she'd strategically placed beneath her clothes. Gemma should've picked up on the red flags the moment Quaid took Cahleen's blades, but she hadn't been thinking straight then. She'd been too worried about their missing Athru companion, Abastian, and the other Spiaires.

Gemma's hand grazed the front of her neck as she remembered the day they'd left Earth on the transport shuttle. She couldn't stop thinking about the Beast's thick fingers squeezing her throat. How he thought he should be the one to decide if she deserved air after she'd asked too many questions about Abastian and where their Spiaires were. He'd pinned her to the hull wall with one hand while using the other to ward off Cahleen.

She could still feel his scruff along her cheek and his guttural voice seeping into her ear. "You only speak when spoken to. Take this as your last warning, little bug." All she could do was nod while pleading to Isoldesse for the strength to stay alive, because it wasn't her time. He wasn't going to be the one to end her life.

Gemma had almost lost herself to a darkness that reduced her confidence to a pebble, but it had been her sister who'd lifted her essence during those first days on the *Tarais*. She'd reminded Gemma of who she was and the power she held within. The power of intelligence and manipulation. Cahleen was stealthy with her knives, but she was nothing without Gemma's lead. It was then that they, with Micah, Sabine, and Logan, devised a plan to play nice and treat Quaid as the Athru leader he thought himself to be.

For now.

At the rear of the room, Sabine woke. The round woman hopped off the crate, brushed her hands along the front of her knee-length dress, and slid her flats on. "Can I leave yet?"

"Not yet," Micah said from the door.

"Well." Her plump cheeks protruded with gleeful anticipation. "I cannot wait to see Breyah's face come first light after she learns of the mess we've created. It's going to be hard to hide my giddiness."

"Well, try," Cahleen snapped.

"I was just kidding." Sabine's smile twisted into a frown. "You don't have to be so villainous."

"But I am a villain." Cahleen glared at the older woman.

Sabine huffed and hugged her arms while looking away. She mumbled something, but Gemma paid no attention. She was more concerned with getting out of this storage room and finding Anora.

Gemma got to her feet. She glanced down at the skinny jeans, sweatshirt, and black sneakers she'd been wearing these past weeks, which oddly, she'd grown accustomed to the comfort of. The boring clear nail polish and trimmed nails were going to take some getting used to after her stint on Earth, but if all went as planned, Anora's promise of a new Sendara would allow some of those luxuries she'd had on Earth.

She approached Sabine, but when the woman looked away, Gemma snapped her fingers and instructed her to investigate Darci's story about Matthew wanting a companion. "I'm not sure I believe Darci, but who knows. Breyah's pet human may actually be ready to settle down, start a family… blah, blah, blah."

Sabine chewed on the bottom corner of her lip and made a soft humming sound. Gemma couldn't tell if she was about to protest or dive into one of her long speeches about her responsibilities as Breyah's assistant. Gemma's patience was wearing thin and she opened her mouth to yell, but Sabine was quick to assure Gemma, "Yes, yes. I'll look into it."

"Good. Now, Micah, what does it look like out there?"

Micah faced Gemma and summarized the activity he'd been watching out in the docking station. "I'm pretty sure I just spotted the Commander leaving the ship. She'd most likely be the last one off, so I'd suspect Quaid will be returning shortly with a transport vehicle."

"Yes, most likely," Gemma whispered.

Micah turned to stand guard again, but instead he stumbled back and fell against a stack of wooden crates. There in the window of the door stood Quaid.

The Beast's partially shaved head was lined with deep scars over his left ear, and the rest of his long, bright red hair was twisted into a bun toward the back of his head. Most of his scars were concealed by the freckles splashed across his pale skin, but Gemma always stared at the one across the bridge of his nose. Or at least she used to. Now she only looked at his feet. She wanted nothing more than to be done with the Athru. To be done with Quaid.

Another reason she wished she could send a message to Anora and tell her that the Beast needed to go.

It's either him or me.

Micah opened the door. "You scared the shit out of me."

"You scare too easily. Now, let's go," Quaid commanded with a deep, disturbing laugh.

Micah walked out past Quaid without another word and proceeded to the adjacent storage room, where he let Logan and the captives out. Cahleen followed next, with Gemma right behind. As Gemma walked past, Quaid grabbed her arm. "I want you to drive."

"I didn't sleep much and would probably crash that oversized tank," she said without looking up.

"You'll do fine. You know the roads better than anyone else." His breath was hot and smelled as if the man had never brushed his teeth a day in his life.

Slowly, she lifted her gaze and stared into his dull orange eyes. "Wouldn't you rather Logan or Micah drive?"

"No. They've activated an energy barrier over the entire compound, so you'll have to get us out through one of those secret tunnels." Gemma was about to protest again when he continued, "I need you to make room for one more too. My little friend here is coming with us." He stepped to the side, turned his towering body, and pointed to the petite figure slumped on the floor by the rear tire of the stolen transport vehicle.

A thin woman sat curled up against the back tire, her short red hair clumped together with dirt and grease. When she bobbed her head up, a mix of purple and yellow outlined one of her eyes, and she had dark bruises running down both arms. Scabs covered her knuckles on both hands.

It took everything inside of Gemma not to cry out. It was Grace. Quaid must have had the Spiaire hidden in his room on the *Tarais* the entire trip home. A familiar heat rose in her gut. She wanted answers and she wanted them now, but the protective part of her brain reacted first, shutting away any explosive comments threatening to escape.

Calmly, Gemma asked, "Where did *she* come from?"

A tsking sound slipped through his lips. A warning. "Put her in the cargo hold with the others. We need to get going." Gemma swallowed her anger and was about to agree to all his demands, until he added, "Oh, and leave the red bloods."

Gemma spun and faced the Beast. He was one of the leaders of the Athru but so was Anora, and they needed the Spiaires *and the humans* for phase two, the exchange. Especially because they were short two Spiaires.

"Anora gave specific instructions to bring back the Spiaires *and* the human subjects we switched out. What am I supposed to tell Anora if I don't complete my mission?"

A thin, wide grin spread across Quaid's elongated face, and he dipped his head so his face was inches from Gemma's. "You, little bug, don't need to worry 'bout Anora. No more Anora, understand?"

"What the hegah does that mean, Quaid?"

Micah stepped aside, allowing Quaid to pass. Gemma widened her eyes at her brother and silently pleaded for him to do something. Micah cleared his throat and said, "Quaid, we don't have an extra paralytic band for this Spiaire."

With one swift motion, Quaid unlatched a dagger from his belt and sent it whirling through the air until it landed with a wet *thud*. None of the captives reacted, since they were all still under the control of Micah's paralytic restraints, except for one. Gemma watched as one of the female captives crumbled to the stone floor of the docking station. Gemma's gaze locked with Darci's and she could see the tears trickling down the Spiaire's cheeks regardless of the paralytic restraints wrapped around her neck.

"Quaid!" Gemma cried out. "What have you done?"

The Beast cocked his head and pointed a finger at Gemma before making his way over to the fallen body.

"The boy needed one of his neck toys, so I gave him one. You're welcome!" Everyone stood in silence as Quaid retrieve the bloody knife. "See, I'm a problem solver!"

He then raised the bloody blade to the neck of the human male.

He's going to kill him.

"Okay, okay!" Gemma yelled. "You've made your point. Now can we get out of here?"

Without facing Gemma, Quaid drew his hand from the man's neck. "Fine, bring them. I may get bored later." He laughed and pulled out a dirty rag from his pants pocket to wipe the blood from his blade.

"Well, go on. Load them in," he told Logan with a wide sweep of his arm toward the transport vehicle.

While Quaid trudged to the passenger side, Gemma saw Sabine hurrying away, toward the side entrance of the docking station. A moment of envy swelled inside Gemma as the door slowly close.

Gemma turned her attention to Micah, who was kneeling besides Prue's crumbled body. He unlatched the paralytic band from the fallen human before attaching it to Grace's beaten neck. He and Logan lifted the Spiaire and carried her to the back of the vehicle.

Cahleen whispered, "You do realize what this means now, right? Breyah and the others had no idea we were even here on Priomh."

Gemma stared at the pool of red blood inching farther out from beneath Prue's lifeless body. "Well, they'll know now."

37

Every so often, a web of blue energy crackled along the protective dome above, drawing Breyah's attention to the night sky. Strong winds were not uncommon during Priomh's windy season. A minor inconvenience if anything.

The window off to her right reflected Rian and Holt over in the sitting area of Breyah's office. Their late-night debate about what to do going forward had grown heated. Rian, who towered over the Lead Medic, looked fierce in her fitted white dress. The high neck collar and sleeveless design were her own. Fashion wasn't considered an essential resource on Sendara, so those with the talents to refashion their garments often did.

"We have an obligation to find our people," Rian said with a commanding tone. "Security comes first." Holt tried to interject, but Rian raised her voice over his attempts. "We don't know what happened on Earth, and that puts us at risk! Enabling the protective shield may not be enough."

Breyah's gaze followed the outline of the barrier against the starry sky. It was faint, but she could see it, especially on a night with strong winds. Rian wasn't wrong—the Sendarians of Priomh were her responsibility, and as their Leadess, it was Breyah's decision.

"I understand that, and I'm not saying I don't agree. But we also have an obligation to Isoldesse, one that cannot go unfulfilled." Holt's reflection showed him stepping closer to Rian. "We cannot send the subjects home, not yet. We have to finish."

A chill wafted through the room and across the nape of Breyah's neck. She hugged her arms as the temperature in the room dropped dramatically. Breyah didn't have to turn and look to know what was happening.

Oh, please, Isoldesse. Not now.

She faced her second-in-command and watched the pigment of Rian's skin transition from stark white to pale blue, blending in with her hair, eyes, fingernails, and lips. The corners of the plac Rian clutched turned white as ice crystals formed beneath her fingertips and sprawled out along the black surface.

"Rian! No! Please, you need to calm yourself." Breyah slowly stepped from behind her desk and over to the sitting area while trying to remember how long it had been since Rian's last episode.

"There's no need to overreact," Holt pleaded gently, one hand held out while the other searched his jacket pockets. "Take slow, deep breaths and remember that you're in control."

White fog rolled off Rian's skin.

That's new.

Breyah eyed Holt, silently directing him to move away, and he did. "We're going to find our friends, I promise. I have a plan, but first you need to calm down, okay?" Hands out, inches from Rian's hands, she anticipated the cold bite she was about to endure that would surely leave an icy burn for days.

Rian closed her eyes and shied away. Breyah relaxed and Holt came around with a thin metal canister. He shook it before removing the cap and holding it out to Rian. "Here, take an extra dose. You know I always carry one, just in case."

"No, I don't need it," Rian reassured them. "I'm fine. Really, I am." She faced them and slowly opened her eyes. Her blue skin gradually returned to its natural porcelain white. "With everything going on, I'm just a bit overwhelmed and—and, well, to be honest, something feels off. I don't know what it is, but there's something nagging at my insides."

"I can run some tests in the morning, if you like." Holt recapped the canister and offered it to Rian one last time. When she declined it again, he slipped it into his pocket. "Come see me before the Waking. It won't take long."

"Yeah, I think that's a good idea." Rian slowly sat on one of the upholstered benches and leaned against the arm. "So, you have a plan? Or were you just lying so I didn't kill you both?"

"You wouldn't have killed us." Breyah hoped Rian couldn't hear the doubt in her voice. "And I do have a plan."

She wasn't worried about Rian going along with her idea. It would be Holt she'd need to convince. Breyah stared at the marital token around his neck, resting against the gray fabric of his tunic. A coin-sized piece of wood that he'd cut and carved out from a fallen tree in the Endless Forest. Though unlike most Sendarian couples, he only needed one betrothal token. There was no partner or special someone. He'd carved the name of their goddess on it. Holt was committed to his work and solely devoted to Isoldesse.

"I suggest an amendment to this Aevo C," Breyah said.

"An amendment?" Rian repeated. "What sort of changes were you thinking to make?"

"To the story we tell the humans. Right now, they know nothing of why they're here, but they may know more about what happened to our Spiaires on Earth. I say we alter our damsel-in-distress story to include our Spiaires."

"You mean reveal to the humans the Spiaires' true identity?" Holt crossed his arms and shook his head. "No, we can't do that."

Rian stood from the upholstered bench and paced the room. "That might actually work *and* still fall under the guidelines of our expected research."

"That is exactly what the Anumen Doctrine guidelines say not to do," Holt said. "We cannot reveal any information about the inner workings of the Aevo Compendium to the subjects."

"There needs to be an exception, Holt." Breyah faced her Lead Medic. He rubbed the token hanging from around his neck. Breyah reached for his arm, hoping he'd come to understand. "This is one of those exceptions."

"I don't know," Holt whispered. "But you're the Leadess, so it's your decision."

Breyah offered a compromise. "How about tomorrow I sit and casually ask subject fifteen, Kenna, what information she has about Darci? We can reconvene after I meet with her and make our final decision then."

"I can work with that," he conceded. "You're not telling the Kenna girl that Darci is one of us, so we wouldn't be going against any protocols or guidelines."

Breyah allowed herself to smile. "Excellent! We can continue with the compendium *and* search for our friends."

"Oh, thank Isoldesse." Rian raised her hands to the ceiling. "I never thought we'd agree on something."

From within Breyah's ear, her Linc notified her of an urgent incoming communication. *"The Lead Medic of the Tarais would like to speak with you."*

"Understood," Breyah responded while holding one finger up. Her Leads ceased their conversation. "Display incoming message." A wide display screen opened on the exterior glass pane behind Breyah's desk. A woman appeared holding an ice pack to the side of her head. Dried yellow blood was caked in her light-red hair and smeared along her freckled cheek.

"Maura, is everything okay?"

"Beannaith, and I'm sorry to bother you at such a late hour, but no, everything is not okay, my Leadess."

Rian approached the screen. "What happened to your head?"

"I was leaving for the night when I heard voices arguing by the line of transport vehicles." Maura licked her dry lips and continued, "I went to check on the commotion, and that's when I swear I saw Grace."

"Grace?" Breyah repeated. "As in our missing Spiaire Grace?"

"I believe so. She looked awful, beaten and weak, but when we locked eyes, I swear to Isoldesse it was Grace. Someone snuck up from behind me and knocked my head against one of the station pillars." Maura lifted the pack from her head, inspected it, and winced when she carefully pressed it to her head again. "Anyway, when I came to, whoever I saw was gone along with one of our transport vehicles."

"I can meet you in Medical," Holt said to Maura. "We need to examine your injuries."

"Yes, but first there's something else you should see." Maura stepped aside and turned her plac to show a woman lying on the ground in the docking station.

Breyah's eyes went wide, and she clasped a hand to her mouth while Holt turned away and immediately called his emergency medical team to meet him in the docking station.

Rian pointed to the screen, head cocked. "Is that blood *red*?"

Maura returned to the screen. "Yes. Human blood. It appears she was stabbed. Her pulse is weak, and I've lined her wound with a temporary healing gel-plate, but it won't hold for long. There's internal bleeding and she won't survive if we don't get her into surgery."

Holt moved to the side of Maura's video call and opened another display screen. He entered his Lead security code and began sending out response unit instructions. "Surgery bay one is being prepped as we speak."

"We've underestimated the severity of the situation." Rian narrowed her icy-blue eyes at Breyah.

"I believe you may be right." Breyah silently prayed to Isoldesse for some help. "If that was Grace, then those involved with sabotaging the Aevo Compendium could still be here on Priomh. If Grace is here, then maybe the other Spiaires are here too."

"I've got to go," Holt said. "I'll keep you updated." He rushed out of Breyah's office without waiting for a response.

"The human's wound is fairly fresh," Maura commented. "I'll keep watch over her."

"Thank you, and Beannaith to you, Maura." Breyah closed out the video display and turned to Rian. "The energy barrier is up. Whoever did this must still be close by."

"Unless they know about the escape tunnels," Rian offered.

Breyah's eyes closed and her shoulders slumped. "This can't be happening."

"It is, and I have to go."

"We should notify the princess and have her—"

"Already done," Rian said. "There's an automatic message sent to her guard whenever the barrier is activated."

"Yes, I'd forgotten. It's been so long since we've had any sort of emergency."

Much of this moon was covered in a thick forest with a few clearings and one beautiful snowcapped mountain. Breyah assumed that if there were transgressors on Priomh, and they had escaped through the tunnels, they'd most likely be hiding somewhere out in the Endless Forest.

Maura's words, *beaten and weak*, haunted her mind. Who would bestow such cruelty, and why? Poor, poor Grace. She prayed to Isoldesse to watch over her Spiaire along with any others who were under duress.

"I need to go," Rian said.

"Are you okay to go?"

"I'll do better to control my emotions. But yes, I'm fine." Rian reached for Breyah's arms. "Plus, Holt will be nearby with his special sedative if I become a threat."

"You're not a threat," Breyah reassured. She held steady, knowing that her friend's episode had passed, and her touch was no longer harmful. Cold, but not lethal.

With a gentle squeeze, Rian pleaded with her Leadess. "I can't worry about you and focus on the threat. Promise me you'll go straight to your quarters and stay there until morning."

Breyah rubbed her shoulders, her fingers grazing the metal prongs of her arm cuff before meeting Rian's fingers. "I promise."

"Good." She gave Breyah a weary grin before striding out of the office in pursuit of Holt.

Halfway up the spiral ramp in the center of the Centrum, Breyah was lost in thought about climbing into her bed and putting this day behind her when Matthew appeared, jogging down the ramp. He wasn't paying attention and almost ran Breyah over.

"Whoa! Hey, you!"

"Matthew? I thought you were watching the human girl over in the Aevo C subject wing. What were you doing up there?" she asked, gesturing toward the top floor of the Lead residential quarters. There were only two quarters up there, and one of them was Breyah's.

"Uhm, yeah. I was—I mean, I am watching her, but, ah… she's asleep and I thought I would, uh… I mean, I'd, ah… You know what, it's late and I gotta get back before she wakes up." Matthew's smile was ear to ear. "Are you planning to stop by in the morning?" He continued past Breyah, walking backward down the stone ramp, dragging one hand along the glass railing.

Breyah looked up the spiral ramp and then back at Matthew. "What's going on, Matthew?"

But he didn't stop and continued to jog down the spiral ramp before reaching the main floor. He hurried across the empty Centrum, his voice echoing up into the grand space. "Great! We'll see you in the morning." Once he reached the entrance to the skywalk leading to the Aevo C subject wing, he disappeared from view.

That was odd.

"*Breyah*," her Linc announced in her ear, "*you have an incoming call from Lead Rian.*"

She continued up the ramp toward her quarters. "Patch her through."

"Holt and Maura have stabilized the human. We've identified the human as subject sixteen."

She's from Darci's group. "Prudence, I believe was her name."

"Yes," Rian confirmed.

"But how did she end up in the docking station?" Breyah asked, her hand hovering over the black latch of the front door to her quarters.

"I'm not sure, but I'm going to stay a bit longer and try to piece a few things together. We've identified which transport vehicle was taken and we're working to track its location. You get some rest, and we'll update you come first light."

"Beannaith." Breyah's Linc disconnected the call, and when she opened the door to her quarters, she was greeted by another surprise.

"B!" a slender, petite woman exclaimed, her thick red hair loosely braided and twisted into an intricate updo.

Another woman stood to Breyah's right, tall and husky, wearing a burgundy cloak. Her red hair was brushed flat and tied beneath the fabric of the cloak.

"Beannaith, Shea," Breyah said to the royal guard as she stepped farther inside.

The Sendarian guard gave Breyah a curt nod before stepping outside the quarters.

"Emmalyn, what are you doing here?"

Breyah's home was an open living space. Across the room was a narrow ramp that followed the curve of the exterior glass window up to a small sleeping chamber and washroom. It was up there, in her bed, that she longed to be.

The princess swept one arm open. The flowing white fabric of her tunic billowed down her arm and cinched along the cuff of her sleeve, which was embroidered with golden thread. She wiggled her fingers, layered with golden rings, and gestured for the Leadess to come sit.

Breyah gracefully obliged the princess and sat next to her on the plush cream-colored sofa. It was late, and she wasn't in the mood to argue with the princess who'd become more like a younger sibling than her superior over the years.

The surrounding space of her quarters was dark, except for the faint moonlight shining in through the expansive glass wall and the soft illumination coming from the underside of the low table in the center of the seating area.

Emmalyn crossed one leg over the other, the heavy white fabric of her wide trousers hiding her slender frame. Her cheeks were rosy and plump under her bright orange eyes. Breyah had never seen Emmalyn not smiling, but tonight there was something more behind her elated expression.

"Shea told me about Priomh's shield going up and insisted we come and stay here until whatever drama you've gotten yourself into settles."

"This was not my fault—" She paused. *Unless it is my fault. Whether I angered Isoldesse or provoked another, maybe I am to blame.* "You know you're always welcome here."

"I know that!" Emmalyn said with a giggle. "I've already had Shea unpack my bags in the royal guest quarters across the way. Look, I know you're wanting to get to bed, but I needed to see you. I promise I'll leave you to your own private space soon enough."

"It has been a long day."

The princess's story about why she lived on Priomh and so far from the royal home on Sendara was a long one. One that Breyah still didn't quite understand. But after her brother, Prince Gerard, had been banished from Sendara by their mother the queen, Emmalyn left Sendara. Against her mother's order, she'd commissioned a home for herself just west of the Priomh community. Breyah never questioned or pried any more than Emmalyn offered, but maybe, with everything going on, it was time for Emmalyn to return home.

"I think it would be wise if you would consider traveling to Sendara until we've sorted things here. For your own safety."

The burst of high-pitched laughter that erupted from the princess was unexpected. "B! I'm not going anywhere. You know how I feel about my mother's laws. She needs to agree to make certain changes before I even consider going home. I'm a patient Sendarian. I can stay up here and wait my turn to be queen. Oh, it's going to be so much fun when I'm crowned queen!"

This was what Breyah was afraid of. The thing she and Rian agreed not to speak of. "If this has anything to do with—"

"It has everything to do with Matthew."

Breyah closed her eyelids and willed the world to disappear. *No sexual relations or crossbreeding with other races.* The Anumen Doctrine forbade it. Something drilled into every Sendarian's head when they came to live and work on Priomh. The princess must have missed that memo.

"I'm not going to lecture you about right versus wrong, but your brother was banished for falling in love with a human. And here you are, doing the same thing!"

"B, don't be so naïve. That's the story they told you. Besides, you can't tell the heart who to love and who to not love. You should know that better than anyone." Emmalyn playfully shook Breyah's arm. "There's a freedom there that Sendarians deserve to have. We need to lift the ban and allow our people to explore the stars."

Oh, it's too late at night for this conversation.

"It's been a long day, Princess. Can we talk more about your political aspirations tomorrow? I hate to be rude, but my head will literally explode if I focus too much on you and Matthew and the downward spiral that'll come of it if the queen gets word."

The princess smiled, stood, and kissed the top of Breyah's head. "Beannaith, my friend. I'll come and find you tomorrow." As she sauntered out the front door, off to the guest quarters across the landing, she excitedly shouted, "Don't worry, B! I have a plan to fix everything!"

Before Breyah could ask or stop Emmalyn, the princess was out the door, leaving Breyah alone with her thoughts.

Do I go after her and demand an explanation? Or... She stared at the ramp leading up toward her bed. Bed won. Seriously, how much damage could one princess do over the next six to eight hours while Breyah slept?

I guess I'll find out come first light.

38

Out in the living room of their apartment, Ally sat with her legs tucked under herself on the couch, reading a *Magnolia* magazine. Kenna closed the front door, her mind foggy. She couldn't recall where she was coming from or where she was supposed to be going.

I need to find my day planner. I'm supposed to be somewhere.

She crossed the living room and headed for her bedroom. Warm Florida sun shone on the hardwood in bright rectangles from the windows.

"Don't forget to take care of your friends," Ally said from behind her magazine.

Kenna stopped and turned, but the apartment was empty. The familiar magazine lay open on the couch. "Ally?"

From behind her bedroom door, there was a strangled, low *hur... hur...* grunting sound.

What the hell?

She turned the doorknob and instead of walking into her bedroom, she stepped out into a dimly lit black space filled with a smoky white fog. As Kenna moved farther into the space, the grunting got louder.

"Hello?"

The fog parted and revealed a shirtless man. He stood, arms curled close to his chest, fists clenched, ready to strike. His loose pants tied around his waist while the hem of each pant leg cinched above his calf muscles. His feet were spaced apart with one foot slightly forward. When he jabbed his right fist into the invisible punching bag, an explosion of chalk billowed in the air. Punch after punch, he slammed his fists into the bag. With his last punch, he screamed a loud, primordial cry that reverberated deep in her mind.

"Ben?"

Bare chest heaving, he faced her. "Kenna? What are you doing here?"

Okay, so she'd seen plenty of hot, half-naked guys around campus, at the gym, and of course at the beach. But they never talked or paid any attention to her... unless Ally was around, and then only sometimes. But Ally wasn't here, and Ben was talking to her. A shirtless and *very* sweaty Ben.

"I wasn't expecting to ever see you again," he said. He must've noticed her staring, because he glanced down at himself and grinned.

Her head tipped up and she tried to look anywhere but straight. "I don't know. I—I was just in my apartment and—and then I ended up here."

He stepped closer, and she felt his presence in every part of her body. She lowered her gaze and by the time he reached her, his sweaty appearance had changed. Now, he stood in front of her wearing a fitted dark gray T-shirt and pressed black slacks. His dark blond hair was neatly brushed, in a disheveled kind of way, with that cute rebellious cowlick sticking up.

"How?" Kenna's brows knitted together. "How did you change so quickly?"

"Prefer the other view?" The corner of his lip curled up. "We never got around to—"

Kenna pressed one hand to his chest. His firm, firm chest. "Do not finish that sentence."

He leaned away, crossing his arms. "Fine, but why do you insist on talking all the time? That's not what we're here for."

"Ben, where exactly is *here*?"

"I only see you when I'm sleeping."

Okay. So, I'm dreaming... again... I think? Oh, these can't be dreams. They're too real. He's too real.

"You do realize I'm a real person out in the real world, right?"

"Maybe." He brushed a long strand of dark hair from her forehead. "Whether you're real or not, there's something about you that intrigues me. And"—he stepped closer—"I like our little encounters."

How about the fact that I'm human and you're an alien? Or at least I think you're an alien. Oh, what if this arcstone thing is poisoning me and I'm slowly dying... and hallucinating. Oh my God... am I dying?

"If you're going to be here with me, then be here with me." His orange eyes were intense and reminded her of the glow that surrounded the sun as it set behind the ocean horizon. She desperately wanted to give in to the seductive trance of those eyes. If only for a moment.

But then Ally's words, *Don't forget to take care of your friends*, shook her from his gaze. This was nice, something she hadn't felt in years, but she needed answers and she needed to find her friends.

"Ben, I need to ask you—" But then a loud, drawn-out snore echoed from within the air above them, as if blaring through giant invisible speakers. Kenna's shoulders tensed, and she circled for the source. It didn't sound like the Obard, but she couldn't be sure. The last thing she wanted was to be chased down again by those medieval-looking space soldiers.

"What the hell is that?" She turned to Ben, but he was gone.

Oh! I hate these stupid dreams!

The white fog rolled in against her legs, becoming denser and colder. She hugged her arms and squeezed her eyes shut.

Wake up, Kenna! Wake up!

The snoring sound was so loud, it woke her like an alarm clock. Once she felt the comforts of her bed, she knew she was no longer dreaming. But oddly, the ceiling above didn't seem right. No constellation stickers or science-fiction novel posters tacked over her bed. Just a plain, boring ceiling covered in silver moonlight.

This isn't my bedroom.

She sat up and searched for her glasses, but then remembered she didn't need them. A few feet from the end of her bed, a solid glass wall stretched the length of the narrow room. The glass muted the moonlight, giving the room a grayscale appearance.

The moment she leaned out of bed and touched one toe to the floor, the snoring started up again.

Someone's in here with me.

She tiptoed toward a small seating area, every so often the bottom of her foot skimming an open knot in the hardwood floor. From behind the two-seater sofa, she saw a man. He was lying on his back sound asleep, one arm draped over his face, the other strewn across his chest. One foot was tucked under a knee that hung over the side.

God, that looks so uncomfortable.

Whoever this guy was, he was out cold, breathing heavily and snoring through his open mouth. Not wanting to wake him, she crept around the sofa and over to a wide, shallow hall with two doors. The room grew darker the farther she tiptoed away from the window.

What do I do, and where do I go after I get out of this room? I don't even have shoes on! What if I get caught? Maybe I should stay? Oh, I wish Meegan were here.

She wiggled her toes and worried about how her feet would hold up if she had to run for her life. But beggars couldn't be choosers and there was no time to stop and ask for a pair of sneakers while evading aliens.

First, she checked the door along the wall to her right. It was unlocked. Inside, a thin strip of light lined the edge of the ceiling and illuminated an empty space with walls covered in what looked like plastic shiplap. She closed the door and tried the one at the end of the hall, but it was locked.

"Where you off to?"

Kenna shrieked and spun, then darted past the man and over to the far window. A surge of adrenaline exploded and tingled along her arms, shoulders, and chest. When she reached the window, she gripped the sofa's armrest and positioned herself so the two-seater was between her and the stranger.

"Don't touch me!"

"Not gonna," the man said with a smirk. He had a familiar accent, but then again how was she to know what an alien sounded like? "Linc, lights to fifty percent."

Similar to the lighting inside the small closet, a thin trail of lights gradually illuminated along the ceiling's edge. The room had a modern-day hotel vibe mixed with a cozy farmhouse feel. The walls were covered with a subtle white plaster, except for the accent wall that had been lined with reclaimed wood panels along the left side of the room.

She paid close attention to the man's movements, watching to see if he'd try to attack or trick her in some way. But he didn't. He dragged his feet over to the accent wall and pressed a finger to the corner of one of the wooden panels. "Linc, lower the energy shroud and extend counter surface."

Who and where is this Linc person, or device, he keeps talking to?

A counter extended out from within one of the seams between two long planks lining the wall. Then, a section of the plank wall flickered before disappearing to reveal a hidden nook. They were using holographic technology as cabinet doors.

The man rubbed an eye with the heel of his palm. "You want coffee?"

"Ah, okay," she said, noting their use of the technology.

She couldn't quite see inside the nook or watch what he was doing to make the coffee, but she did notice he was using something that resembled a French press. After a few minutes, he walked over and handed her a glazed ceramic mug filled with a dark steaming liquid. She hesitantly took it and smelled it before taking a sip, her gaze still watching his every move. The coffee had a rich, sweet flavor, as if the beans had been infused with vanilla, sugar, and pure happiness.

Coffee never failed to bring out a smile in her, and that smile made her think of someone else who loved coffee. The always happy and bubbly Darci popped into her mind. Even though she missed her friend, she was glad that Darci hadn't gone to Prue's house that day. Otherwise, she'd be lying in one of those beds with Meegan, Ally, and whoever else was down there with one of those alien face-shield thingies on.

Then, because of the freight train that was her mind, one thought leading into another, she couldn't help but wonder, *Who else is down there?* She hadn't had time to look at the other beds, concentrating on keeping Meegan's identity safe before she was almost discovered. But they had clearly found her hiding in the storage room anyway.

Liam said he was wearing a transessent bracer too. He could've been lying in one of those beds! And Nick! Oh, please, please don't let Liam or Nick be down there.

She needed a plan. To figure out how to help her friends and get everyone out of wherever the hell it was they were. Across from her, the man got comfortable in one of the armchairs. He was mumbling something about how stiff and uncomfortable the cushions were.

If I act cooperative, then maybe this dude will tell me what's going on.

Kenna raised her mug in a cordial manner and put her plan to win him over with kindness into play. After a long sip, she said, "Pretty good coffee for an alien."

The man laughed. "I'm not an alien."

She studied his eyes. They didn't appear to be orange. And his accent did seem familiar.

"My name is Matthew and I'm actually from Boston."

"I thought I recognized your accent." She lowered the mug and narrowed her gaze. "Okay, Matthew from Boston, what the hell is going on? Why am I here? And I'm going to assume *here* isn't anywhere near the New England area."

"You assume right. We are not anywhere near there." He leaned into the chair and crossed a foot over his knee. "Ah, man, I haven't seen home in over, well… fifty years. That was the last time." His eyebrows shot up and he chuckled. "Damn, time does fly."

"You don't look older than thirty. There's no way you can be over fifty."

"It's this place." He waved a hand in the air. "Aging works differently." He paused and then in a lighter tone continued, "You know, I'm not usually the one giving the welcome speeches. That's my friend Breyah's job. I mean Leadess, sorry. She's in charge around here and will be stopping by in the morning to explain everything to you."

"Okay, so what can *you* tell me?" She dragged her hair forward over one shoulder and cocked her head. "I'm worried about my friends. Do you know when I can see them? Are the orange-eyed people going to hurt me or my friends? Will they let us go—"

"Whoa! I just told you you'll get your answers in the morning." Matthew shook his head over his steaming mug, accentuating his Boston accent as he raised a hand to stop Kenna from continuing. "Geez, it's good to know that humans are still the same stubborn, impatient beings I once knew."

"Put yourself in my shoes." Kenna tried to restrain her flustered tone.

"I *was* once in your shoes."

"Then you understand—"

But she was cut off by his "wait a sec" raised finger as he tilted his head and stared off to the side. "Okay, let me hear it."

"Uh, all right. I was just going to say—"

He quickly shushed her. "Not you."

With a scowl, she tipped her mug and finished her coffee, and then got up to check out the fancy counter area where Matthew had made their drinks. She carried her empty cup to the cubby area above the counter and refilled her coffee. It *was* a French press. The inside of the nook was lined with white walls, and against the back section was the same strange etching she'd seen in the room she'd woken in. Except this time, the rectangle sections were smaller and had a small glass tile embedded in the bottom right corner. She touched one tile and a compartment door popped open. Swinging the door open, she saw the inside was lined with drawers. She pulled out a drawer and removed a thin metal rod with two sharp prongs at the end.

A fork?

There were also things that resembled spoons and butter knives.

"It's custom to stock stuff familiar to the guests."

Kenna looked at Matthew while returning the fork to the drawer. "Guests as in other races from other worlds?"

His brows knitted together, and instead of responding, he returned to the armchair. "I just got a message from our Lead Medical guy, Holt. He said your ear implants are good to go and ready for when Breyah… ah, sorry, for when the Leadess comes to talk with you."

Kenna sat on the love seat again, coffee mug in hand. Her fingers trailed over her ear. "Someone stuck *implants* in my ears?"

"Yeah, but don't get your panties in a bunch. It's temporary. They'll take them out when you go home."

So, we will be going home. Good to know. Not crazy about having alien tech jammed into my head, but I'll worry about that later. Right now, keep him talking.

"So, Matthew, can you at least tell me what these implant things do?"

"Oh, they're so you can understand what everyone's saying. Not everyone in the galaxy speaks English, you know." He scratched the peach fuzz on his head. "My turn to ask a question. I'm curious, how'd you wake up?"

She resisted the urge to touch the arcstone beneath her shirt. This guy seemed nice and all, but she was nowhere near trusting him. The only ones she trusted regarding the arcstone were Meegan and Ulissa.

"Listen, Matthew, there're a lot of things I don't understand. That being one of them," she said, hoping she sounded confident. She needed to shift the conversation quickly and hoped she could change the subject as smoothly as her best friend could. "I'm pretty hungry. So, how about we get something to eat and wait for your Leadess?"

His smirk returned. "I will never say no to a hot meal."

39

First light had yet to rise when Cahleen stepped outside the abandoned building. Overgrown vines and wild plants from the Endless Forest had been allowed to claim most of the exterior of the original Priomh facility. Not the ideal way to show respect for something built by a so-called goddess. Not that Cahleen believed in Isoldesse. She had her own theories about Sendara's beloved goddess.

She'd snuck out and left Micah to watch the captives while she ventured to Quaid's piece-of-shit ship. Quaid's clunker of a decommissioned transport ship was parked out on the landing pad. She used the remnants of the night's darkness to her advantage and moved quickly along the front of the building. When she reached the edge of the east wall, she peeked around the corner and spotted a lone guard sitting on a crate next to the ship's loading ramp. Eyes open, but barely. His head propped up with one hand on his knee.

Lazy loggie.

Normally, she'd have no problem coming and going from the ship. Everyone there was Athru, except for the captives. But Cahleen wanted evidence proving that Quaid's interests were no longer aligned with the Athru cause.

When they'd arrived late in the night after their escape from the Priomh compound, Quaid had given two instructions. The first was to keep the prisoners off his ship, and the second was to stay out of the ship's command decks. Locking them out of the bridge and comms room was Quaid's mistake. It gave Cahleen a starting point to see what she could uncover about what that gróntah was up to. So, here she was sneaking aboard Quaid's ship to snoop in those restricted areas. Specifically, the comms room.

She glanced up at the treetops surrounding the old building. Daybreak had started to lighten the sky.

Ticktock, ticktock. Let's see. Distract, run, and board. Wind... none. Good.

With one quick throw, a high-pitched whizzing sound casted through the air followed by a *thwump*. She watched as the guard's eyes shot open. He drew his blade and made his way to the edge of the landing pad, toward the forest where Cahleen's throwing knife had vanished through the thick brush. Even before he'd lifted his butt from the crate, she was running. She circled the opposite side of the landing pad with light, swift steps. Her eyes focused on the ramp while staying alert to movements made in her peripheral vision.

Once on the ship, she crossed the cargo bay and entered the code Micah had given her. It was a skeleton-key code for if the crew ever locked themselves out of the command deck. During his hack to access the key code, Micah had rambled on about how the newer transport ships' skeleton-key codes were a bit hard to crack, but not the ones for these older decommissioned models. Information Cahleen filed away for another day.

Inside, she climbed two flights of stairs up to the bridge corridor. The rusty grated floor clanked every few steps, but not loud enough to raise suspicion. When she reached the comms room, she was about to enter the skeleton-key code again when she heard a subtle intake of air, as if someone nearby was trying to hold their breath. With one swift motion, she swung her arm out. The arrowhead blade of the push-dagger pointed out between two knuckles, ready to slice open a neck, shoulder, or face… whatever was closest.

Logan dodged her strike. He grabbed her wrist with his right hand while his left pressed hard into her shoulder, redirecting her body away from his.

"What are you doing, Cahleen? If Quaid finds you…"

"He won't." She lowered her arm and tucked the blade into its sheath beneath the waistband of her pants, next to her hip. "You following me?"

"Maybe."

"I can take care of myself."

"I know. I was on my way over to the old building. I wanted Micah to run a scan on this old plac I found." He opened his jacket, revealing a scuffed-up old plac in the inside pocket. "I was hoping he could set up a secure line so we can contact Sabine, or maybe even Anora."

Cahleen crossed her arms and smiled at him. "And that's the only reason you were going into that old building? To get Micah to fix that outdated paperweight?" She flicked his jacket, hitting the plac under it. His breath hitched. His gaze latched on to her. She could see his mind working… remembering the countless hours they'd spent together aboard the *Tarais* during the journey home.

She traced her finger along the scar that rounded the right side of his neck. When the crude pink line disappeared beneath his collar, she tugged at his shirt and said, "I think you're lying to me."

His eyes grew hungry and his gaze shifted from her eyes to her lips. His lips parted and for a moment she thought he was going to kiss her right there in the corridor, but instead he said, "You don't need to hack into the comms room. I can get you in."

"Oh, is that right? The Beast has entrusted *you* with all ship access?"

Logan nodded and leaned in closer to the keypad, pressing his chest to hers as he entered the comms access code. The door slid into the wall pocket, and Logan gestured for Cahleen to go first.

The second the door closed behind them, he shoved Cahleen against the bulkhead and seized the few moments they had. She reached under his shirt and explored the lines of his back muscles. Her fingers swept along the top of his pants while he kissed her neck, ears, and lips. When his head dipped to her chest, Cahleen spotted a communications monitor behind him. It was active, showing two parallel audio lines. The top line was flat while the bottom displayed a fluctuation of sound waves.

"Wait... Logan, stop!" Cahleen pushed him aside and moved in closer to the display screen.

Breathless, Logan said, "What? What is it?"

She activated the audio and heard Quaid's voice. "You promised me Sendara."

There was a long pause before a deep, almost mechanical voice spoke, with elongated words. "You will have Sendara, but only once we have what is ours. Be forewarned that if you come between us and what is ours, we will take everything from you and your world."

Logan stepped around from behind Cahleen. All the lust had vanished from the room. They glared at one another before moving in closer to hear Quaid's response.

Quaid's voice was lighter than usual, not as threatening. An agreeable tone unfamiliar to Cahleen. Quaid continued, "I don't know what it was that was taken, and if you say it's here on this moon, then by all means come and get it. I don't care. I just want Sendara. Do what you want with Priomh and the Sendarians here."

"We will send word of our arrival. Do what you must and then leave."

"Aye. I'll be done and out of your way within days."

The breathing on the other line was fierce and disturbing. "One more thing, Quaid of Sendara."

"Aye?"

"What of Isoldesse?"

Isoldesse? What does she have to do with any of this?

Quaid's answer over the comm sounded just as confused as Cahleen's thoughts. "What of her? She's a myth, a fabrication, a figure for the Sendarians to put their faith into. She's just a name. Not real, never was."

Well, at least she could agree with him on that. But still, whoever Quaid was talking to seemed to believe otherwise.

Cahleen closed out the audio and moved past Logan. "We need to go."

"But they're not done talking. We need to hear more—"

"We've heard enough. If we wait until he's done, we risk being discovered. Trust me." She opened the comm-room door, then checked to see if the corridor was clear before leaving. She heard the door shut behind her and her lover's feet move in step with hers. "Stay quiet until we get to Gemma."

Quaid was up to something, and from the sound of it, Priomh was going to be under attack in days to come. They needed to find Anora and find out what happened to their plans of using the captives to exchange for the princess. Anora had left Priomh for a reason, and Cahleen was starting to think it had something to do with whoever Quaid was talking to.

The Beast had new plans—that much she could tell from the conversation. What those plans entailed and what goal he was trying to achieve were yet to be uncovered. All she knew was they needed to get off Priomh, and soon.

40

"**G**emma, wake up!" Cahleen deactivated the tint of the slim window next to the bunk Gemma was sleeping in.

Gemma could hear her sister but chose to ignore her. What she couldn't ignore was the horrid smell of old potatoes and rust. She drew the thin green blanket over her nose and groaned. "What is that horrid smell?"

Half-asleep, the former Spiaire rolled over and smacked her hand against the cold metal wall lined with bolts. She muttered a few curses before she remembered where she was. No more California King bed with soft sateen sheets. She lifted the bandana from over her eyes and winced at the bright stream of light.

"Go away!" she grumbled and lowered the bandana while folding the pathetic, lifeless pillow in half for better support. "I want to be left alone."

"Gemma, we need to talk."

Slowly, she remembered what had happened last night in the docking station. Who knew if the human girl they'd left lying in her own blood was dead or alive? All she could think about was how it was her fault. How she could've prevented the Beast from attacking the girl, if she'd only said yes to his stupid request to drive the transport vehicle.

This game of obedience was wearing thin, and she hoped they could get word to Anora soon. Cahleen and Micah stayed out in the old research facility with the captives while she and Logan had been escorted onto Quaid's ship. She longed to be on Anora's newer transport ship—granted, Anora's ship was also *borrowed*, but at least Gemma knew that the hull would hold up during space travel. This piece of junk was held together with rickety spare parts and luck.

"Get your lazy ass up!" Cahleen kicked the wall beneath the bunk.

"All right, all right!" Gemma ripped the bandana from over her eyes and tossed the blanket aside before ducking her head out from within the bunk hole. Her life, clothes, and luxuries from her time on Earth were memories, left at the beach house for someone else to claim. Now, everything she owned was neatly packed into one pitiful duffel.

She grabbed her bag from the top bunk and pulled out some clean, or semi-clean, clothes. Standing there in just wool socks, black underwear, and a thin black tank top, she asked, "So, what is it?"

"Not here."

Gemma slipped on her skinny jeans from yesterday. "Have you seen Anora? Is she here? We need to talk to her about—"

"What you *need* to do is finish getting dressed and then come with us."

"Us?"

"Yes, us." Cahleen pounded on the wall next to the cabin door. When Gemma poked her head through her oversized sweatshirt, she heard a familiar voice cough out in the hall.

Logan.

Gemma tucked her untamed red hair into a slouchy beanie she'd brought from Earth, and before she could holler a good morning to him, he called, "Do you want tea with your breakfast?"

Cahleen pressed one finger to her lips. Within seconds, two Athru women walked by the open doorway. Their clothes were a mishmash of browns and greens. One girl with a shaved head locked eyes with Gemma. A wicked grin crossed her face before she disappeared out of view.

"I hate this place. I hate this rusty piece-of-shit excuse for a ship," Gemma seethed. "We need to find Anora!"

"You need to keep your voice down. You heard Quaid last night," Cahleen whispered and gestured for Gemma to do the same. "He said we don't need to worry about Anora. *No more Anora.* Remember?"

Gemma could feel the scream bubbling inside her, pleading to escape. She was so done with this shit. If there was no Anora, then what the hegah were they doing there?

"Let's go check on the captives. Micah wants to show you something." Cahleen tapped her ear with her finger, pointed it up, and then circled it in the air.

Of course that gróntah would be spying on us. Gemma rolled her eyes. "Fine, let's go see Micah."

The metal grate flooring clanked with each stomp. Pieces of missing grate left large holes here and there. The newer transport ships had replaced the industrial walkways with sleeker, solid plated floors. Even Anora's *borrowed* ship had the newer model floors and wall panels.

They passed the common area of the ship, where a few Athru had gathered and were eating their morning meals. When they reached the cargo hold, they encountered a few more men and women who were standing around talking, none paying them any attention as they passed.

Out on the landing pad, farther from the transport ship, Gemma got a whiff of the fragrant Hiccums that bloomed in the trees throughout the forest. The wooded scent of the Endless Forest dredged up memories of her time before the Athru. The walkway along the front of the old facility was filled with cracks sprouting weeds. A thick wall of vines, with thorns longer than her finger, scaled the outer wall, twisting and covering the front windows.

The late-morning sun began its rise above the surrounding treetops. There used to be a road leading out to the new Priomh compound, but it was now blocked with several fallen trees and a wide variety of overgrowth.

Cahleen pushed open the front door of the old facility and led the way, though Gemma didn't need a guide. She knew these halls blindfolded. The inside was no better than the outside. A layer of dry dirt coated the white walls. But Gemma looked past the ruin and remembered the beauty of this place. The first time she and Breyah had walked these halls. The excitement she'd felt in her new role as a Spiaire, and the plans she and Breyah had had to improve the Aevo Compendium project.

How could I be so stupid? All those years I thought it was Priomh that needed changing when it was Sendara that needed to evolve. Isoldesse is all about watching her worlds evolve... grow to their fullest potential. Yet the Elemental Council and the royal family have prevented Sendara from evolving.

That's how we'll prove ourselves to Isoldesse. We'll show her that Sendara can evolve better than any other world... given the chance. And thanks to the Athru, Sendara will get that chance.

But how was she to do that now without Anora? They needed to find Anora.

Inside the facility, Gemma grabbed Cahleen's arm and stopped her halfway across the foyer. There were two hall entrances, each one on opposite sides of the large space, and to her surprise the glass ceiling was fairly clean except for a few clouded spots. The foyer was filled with bright morning light and old memories.

"What?" Cahleen groaned, shaking her arm free from her sister's grasp. "Micah's waiting."

"Micah can wait. What did you and Logan need to tell me?" Gemma ignored the tall Sendarian as he walked by them and disappeared down the west hall toward the subject holding cells.

"Fine. Logan and I came across a transmission between Quaid and… and honestly, I have no idea who or what he was talking to. But they weren't from Sendara. They said they were coming to Priomh to get what's theirs."

Gemma's nose wrinkled. "What the hegah does that mean?"

"I don't know, but they said, 'We will take everything from you and your world,' if they don't get whatever they're looking for. Gemma, I'm not even kidding when I tell you I got a chill from listening to that deep, evil-sounding voice."

She didn't mean to crack a smile, but hearing Cahleen say she feared something caught her off guard.

Cahleen rolled her eyes at Gemma's reaction and turned to follow Logan. "You're a fucking taut you know that!" she yelled with her back to Gemma.

"Wait! I've never seen you scared of anything." Gemma caught up to her sister, and they walked side by side down the hall. "Okay, so how long do we have until this creeper being you heard gets here?"

"A few days, maybe a week? It was unclear," Cahleen answered. "I highly recommend that we not be here when whoever the hegah that was gets here."

"Agreed. First, let's hear what Micah needs and then we can figure out our escape plan."

At the end of the hall, Cahleen punched the code into the keypad. The dirt on the keypad had been swiped clean, yet there was still a fogginess to the screen that Gemma assumed would never come clean. Everything about this place was meant to be left in the past.

There was a loud clicking sound as the bulky metal pins across the door retracted from within the wall. Cahleen opened the large metal door and proceeded inside.

The subject holding cells were small rooms with a single bed and a relief station. Not much privacy, yet still more room than the sleeping cabin she'd been assigned on Quaid's busted-up ship.

It had been Breyah's idea to redesign the holding cells and give the subjects a cozier and more welcoming feel in the new Priomh compound. To have the trial subjects feel more like guests rather than captives. Breyah was always trying to make everyone happy, a quirk Gemma planned to use against her old friend.

They entered the long hall lined with doors. This section of the building seemed to have held up better than the main common areas. The white walls were still white, and the keypads on the cells were dust free. She recalled how the original research team were overly paranoid and made sure to take extra precautions to make this wing airtight. Something about not wanting the subjects to get loose and attack the researchers.

"One of the first things Micah did last night after we arrived was restore full power to this sector," Cahleen said, opening the door to the first holding cell. Micah had brought in a small table and a few chairs. He was sitting, nose deep in his plac. Logan stood against the back wall, arms crossed, and head tilted toward the ceiling.

"Any word from Anora?" Gemma's oversized sweatshirt slipped off one shoulder.

"Nothing. But Quaid's got receiving modules posted in the forest, surrounding the area. He's tracking any incoming comms, so even if Anora replied to any messages I sent out, he'd know about it."

"Great. How about you figure out a way to bypass that problem? She's out there somewhere. Anora wouldn't leave us here."

"Unless she's dead," Cahleen pointed out.

Gemma ignored her sister and left Micah to his plac. She went back out into the corridor and moved to look at the next cell. Through the window in the door, Gemma could see Grace lying on a mattress on the floor, her head resting in Darci's lap. Eryn was pacing the room.

"Micah!" Gemma called.

Micah walked out of the first cell, turned his baseball hat backward, and looked into the cell. "What's the problem?"

"Where are their paralytic restraints?"

He gently nudged the full duffel on the floor next to him with his foot. "I took them off. No way was I going to give that piece of shit another reason to kill someone."

He does have a point.

"They're not going anywhere." Logan stepped closer. "Besides, we've got bigger problems. I assume Cahleen clued you in to what we heard?" When Gemma nodded, he turned his attention to Micah, waving him over. "I need you to look at something for me."

Logan held up an old plac at Micah. The edges were faded and it looked as if it'd seen some better days. Gemma quickly lost interest in their conversation and after one more glance into the Spiaire's cell, she sidestepped to the next cell over. There, sitting against the far wall, were their two human captives. The young man with his wavy brown hair and bruised temple sat with his head tilted back, staring at the ceiling. He'd originally been intended as one of Breyah's Aevo Compendium subjects, but thanks to Sabine and Logan switching him out with someone else, he'd missed out on that adventure. The middle-aged woman was still a mystery. She was one of the humans Darci had been meeting with outside her assigned subjects. It'd been Cahleen's idea to separate the humans from the Spiaires. She'd told Gemma she enjoyed seeing Eryn upset and whining about her pet human.

She fell in love with a human. How disgusting. But then thoughts of Xander and his words, *Ti amo*, popped into her mind, and she cringed at the feelings brewing inside.

Gemma threw open the cell door and stepped inside. Neither human stood, and the only reaction she got was a smirk from the woman. Her dark brown eyes stared up at Gemma.

"He needs water," she said, gesturing to the young man at her side.

Gemma cocked her head before drifting her gaze to the ceiling. "I can see that he gets some water, if…"

"If I tell you why my husband and I were meeting with Darci."

Gemma froze and then narrowed her eyes at the woman. She was older, but not too old. The few lines visible on her face weren't deep or creased with age. She had a healthy glow to her olive skin and her straight black hair might have fine strands, but it was thick and lustrous.

Curious, Gemma started with the most obvious question. "How do you know Darci?"

"She's a friend of a friend. But it was you, Gemma, who surprised me. Has it been that long? Tell me, how is it you didn't recognize your own prince?"

Prince? Prince Gerard?

"Explain." She briefly glanced over her shoulder at Cahleen, who was now standing in the doorway listening.

"Darci was simply delivering a message. That's all."

Gemma spun on the balls of her feet and pushed Cahleen out of the cell. She jabbed a finger into Cahleen's chest. "You said nothing about Gerard being the other person meeting with Darci."

Cahleen slapped her sister's hand away and then barked, "How the hegah am I supposed to know what the banished prince looks like after fifty years on Earth? Gem, I was a fucking predult and didn't give two shits about the royal family when the prince was still on Sendara. So back the fuck off."

The tension in the room was getting heated, and Gemma didn't want Cahleen to lose her temper. Bad things happened when her sister got angry. Gemma cursed and rubbed her forehead beneath her beanie. "I'm sorry. It's just… Well, I don't know what's going on or what to do. I wish Anora were here. This is her mess."

"No, this is *your* mess. You brought that woman here," Cahleen snapped, pointing to the cell door.

The guys made their way out of the first cell, where Micah had been working on Logan's old plac. Micah looked between his two sisters and asked, "Oh, shit. What happened?"

Gemma ignored her brother and marched into the cell again. She crouched low, eye to eye with the woman. "How do you know Gerard?"

She scoffed a chuckle. "I told you. He's my husband."

Gemma's lids closed over her eyes, and with a sigh she slowly stood. *Oh, you've got to be kidding me.*

After a few turns of the small space, she crossed her arms and said, "His wife? You expect me to believe that you're the human he fell in love with during the last Earth trial? Over fifty years ago. You don't look older than a human in her forties."

"You're focused on the wrong question. I know you and your little group mean well, but there are better ways to remove a warden from a prison. You think your queen will hand over her throne just because you've taken her daughter?" The smile that crossed the woman's face mocked everything Gemma thought the Athru could accomplish.

How does she know what Anora had planned?

It was her turn to bark out a laugh. "Says the woman married to a coward. You're the reason Sendara lost its prince. He left us here when he should've fought for what he believed in."

The woman tucked her black hair behind her ears and stood before her captors. "You know, you're not wrong." She steadied herself before taking a few steps closer to Gemma. "But that was a long time ago. We were foolish to think we could escape the laws of the Anumen Doctrine. Gerard and I had a plan to bring about change to Sendara, but the plan changed, and things got complicated. But that's a story for another day. Right now, you should know that what you're doing is not what Isoldesse would want. But if you want to make Sendara a free world, then yes, you must remove the overseeing powers Isoldesse established."

Oh, I hate riddles. Gemma stepped closer, inches from the woman's face. She stared into the woman's dark brown eyes. "How do you know about Isoldesse?"

The woman's lips stretched into a smile. "I've tried many times to convince Gerard to return and set things straight, but he wasn't ready to leave his life on Earth. Now, you've forced his hand and change will come."

Cahleen walked in and whispered in Gemma's ear. "Leave her. We have bigger problems than this crazy lady."

Gemma shuffled a few steps back and nodded while holding her stare on the woman.

"I'm not crazy," the woman said, holding Gemma's gaze. "Let me help you make your world into whatever it is you want. Not what Isoldesse wants."

"Seriously, how do you know about—" But then she remembered. Gerard. He would've told this human everything about their people and their ways, their culture, and even their faith.

Gemma didn't respond. She only turned and walked out of the cell, then locked the door behind herself. The woman approached the door and stared out through the large window.

"She can't see us. It's one way," Cahleen explained, grabbing Gemma's shoulders and turning her sister to face her. "We need to come up with a plan to get the hegah out of here."

"I think I can get this old plac to work," Micah interrupted. "I'm thinking it's outdated enough to slip through Quaid's comm trackers." He turned and headed back into the first cell. Gemma followed, leaving Logan and Cahleen out in the corridor. Inside, disassembled parts from both Logan's outdated device and Micah's plac were sprawled out on the table. "I'll make it work, and then I'll find Anora."

"Make it happen, and keep it hidden once you're done. I don't want that thing to be traced back to us if Quaid gets word," Gemma instructed and then exited, waving for her sister to follow. The two of them headed out of the holding wing and into the large foyer. "Once Micah gets word to Anora, we'll need to be ready to move. There's a clearing in the forest, south of here. The road is overgrown, so you'll have to make your way on foot, but I need you to scout the clearing. Make sure it's safe for us."

"Got it." Cahleen didn't wait for Gemma to say anything else and took off.

Gemma slowly made her way toward the main entrance of the building. How much trust should she put into this human and her promise for a new Sendara? What could a measly human do to crumble a queen? Was this woman trying to beat Gemma at her own game? Or had Isoldesse presented Gemma with an opportunity?

"All right, Isoldesse. Let's see what you've got planned," she said under her breath, swinging open the main entry doors and walking out into the bright, promising daylight.

41

Breyah picked up her mother's arm cuff from her dressing table and slid it up her arm. The metal band, made from the same ore as the transessent bracers, fit snugly above her elbow. Affixed in the center of the cuff was a yellow stone, and unlike the transessent stones with their natural source of energy, her mother's stone was purely decorative.

"You have an incoming call from Lead Medic Holt," Breyah's Linc announced softly in her ear.

"I've been awake for fifteen minutes."

"I'll inform Lead Medic Holt to leave a message."

"No! No, it's fine. Put him through."

A video display within the mirror above her dressing station expanded open. Holt appeared while Breyah slid an elegant cuff, a mesh of golden wire, over the outer part of each ear.

She greeted her Lead Medic, "Beannaith. How's our injured guest doing?"

"Stable. Surgery went well and we've induced her into a sedated sleep. Only time will tell if she'll recover."

"Yes, well, keep me posted on her health. In the meantime, are we on schedule for the Waking?"

"Yes." A tinge of concern weighed on his expression. "But…" He paused and rubbed the bridge of his nose. She noticed he was wearing the same long-sleeve gray tunic from yesterday, except the top two buttons were unfastened. His beard seemed to have grown thicker in the hours they'd been apart.

"Did you sleep?"

"Barely," he said while blinking several times. "Breyah, we need to discuss last night's incident."

"You said she was stable."

"Not that incident."

He's talking about Rian.

"What about it?"

"I think we need to consider the threat she poses." Before Breyah could interject, he waved his hands as if to rephrase. "What I mean is, I think you should consider asking Rian to refrain from entering the subject building. We don't need her to have an episode in front of the humans."

He wasn't wrong. Rian's episodes posed a certain risk. Having an emotional breakdown around her and Holt was one thing, but in front of the humans… Well, that could end badly. Breyah considered Holt's advice. "Let's wait to make any final decisions on her involvement with the subjects. At least until after you run some tests. We owe her that."

"Fine, fine. It's your call, but I wanted to voice my concerns."

"Your concerns are just, and I'll take them into consideration. But after."

Holt nodded in defeat. "I'll see you for the Waking, yes?"

"Yes. We can continue this discussion then. Beannaith."

"Beannaith."

The video screen minimized and then vanished, leaving Breyah staring at her reflection. Not in any rush, she took her time brushing her long red hair. She then intertwined some golden string into a loose braid along the top of her head before wrapping it with the rest of her hair in a delicate knot high on her head.

Pleased with her handiwork, she finished applying a fresh layer of powder to her freckled cheeks, nose, and forehead before heading down the ramp to the main living room. She stopped midway when she heard dishes clanking.

"Beannaith?"

From behind a partitioned wall, Emmalyn emerged with her hands on her hips. Her fair ginger hair was loose and flowed past her knees. "B! I'm so glad you're finally up! Come on… come on! I've got so much to talk to you about!"

Finally up?

Breyah glanced at the sky outside the glass wall.

The sun's barely up.

"You have no idea how long it took me to find your plates, but no worries. I found them!" Emmalyn raised a stack of plates. "It's not usually my thing to find stuff, but here I am… finding stuff!"

"Emmalyn, what are you doing here?" Breyah descended the ramp and walked over to the dining table.

"I hope you're hungry," Emmalyn said while setting the plates on the table. "I love this table. It's wood from the forest, right? Have I ever told you that before? That I love this table?"

"Yes, you have." Breyah sank into the cushioned seat of the low-back dining chair. "Princess, this is kind of you, but I can't stay long. I'm meeting with Rian before the Waking."

"I know, I know. But before you go," she said while placing a large platter in front of Breyah, almost wider than her arms could hold, full of fruits, breads, and aged cheeses, "I wanted to let you know that I sent my trusted guard, Shea, to Earth."

Breyah dropped the glazed bread-curl she'd reached for. It fell awkwardly on the pile of cheese. "You did what? And without discussing it with me first? Why?"

"Oh, you're too cute!" The princess scrunched her nose at the Leadess. "Ask first—ha! When do I ever ask? Besides, the only

Sendarian I ask permission from is my crazy mother, and that's only if I know there's a high risk of getting caught! But even then"—she slouched forward and tapped Breyah's nose—"I don't always wait for my mother's blessing." The princess shot upright and turned to the provision alcove. "Maybe that's because I know she won't—"

"Emmalyn, please... focus. Where is Shea now?"

Emmalyn held a large decanter full of iced coffee. Breyah then noticed three more glass decanters full of coffee sitting on the counter inside the alcove.

How many people was she expecting?

"Oh, Shea's probably orbiting Earth by now, or close to it."

"What? How's that possible? It takes weeks for the *Tarais* to travel to Earth."

"Ahh," the princess said with a wink, "Shea's using my *special* transport ship. I call it my Starzoom ship, but it's really one of the Rhaltan's *secret* pinships. No one outside the royal family and a few high-ranking Rhaltan officers knows about it. And, hey! I guess you know now too! Whoopsies!"

Breyah didn't have time to sit here and talk in circles with Her Highness. Rian was most likely waiting for her in the Centrum, and she was eager to get to her meeting with subject fifteen.

"But why did you send Shea? She's your counsel, and more importantly, your protector."

"Aww, B! I love that you care so much, but don't fret. I'm perfectly safe up here with you and my dearest—"

"Nope! Do not say his name." Breyah glanced up at the wooden beams supporting the ceiling while waving one hand. "I don't want to know the details."

"Okay, okay." The princess shied away. "But he is the most wonderful, gentle, and loving man."

"He's human, Emmalyn. End of story."

The princess sat and rested her hands on Breyah's. "Listen, it's not too often I can help. And I want to help. *Starzoom* is a special pinship that uses space-pinch technology. I don't know the specifics, but the blueprints for design of the transport ship were left by

Isoldesse specifically for the royal fam in case of an emergency. You know, for a speedy getaway… if ever needed. It's supersecret tech." Emmalyn closed her mouth and ran a finger over the seam between her lips. "But you know my mom, she's always wanting the best of the best and needed, like, a fleet of secret transport ships."

What the hegah is space-pinch technology? And why does the queen need a secret fleet of transport ships? If anyone had inside information on this new supersecret tech, it'd be her brother. She'd have to make time later to call Bennach to find out if what the princess was saying was true or if she had finally lost her mind.

"I just wanted to help you, B. Plus"—she crossed her hands over her heart—"I promise on my royal lineage that I will not leave your quarters or mine. I know how important I am. So, safety first, right? Good! Now eat. You must be hungry."

Breyah picked up the bread-curl and nibbled on the end. "And what exactly is Shea going to do when she gets to Earth?"

"Oh, I've specifically instructed Shea on what to do. We… by that I mean the Rhaltan Enforcers… have ways to track our people. More supersecret tech! But shh, they don't know I have access to their toys." She giggled while biting into a piece of cheese. "I uploaded their tracking program onto *Starzoom*. Shea knows what to do from there. She'll make contact and be back before you know it!"

"I wish you would've told me last night. If Rhaltan Enforcers get word that you've *borrowed* some of their tech, that could look bad for us. Especially since you're using it to find our Spiaires."

"Find the Spiaires? Oh, that's right, they're missing! Shea will for sure find them in no time. Given they're all still on Earth."

Oh my goddess. I cannot believe this is our future queen.

Breyah thought back to Maura and how she swore she'd seen Grace, a beaten and tormented Grace, in the docking station. She could only hope that Rian's security team had uncovered some truth about who was behind all the chaos.

She stood and thanked the princess. "Stay here. And as a thank-you, I'll have… well, you-know-who come by and check on you."

At least I can trust Matthew to watch her.

Princess Emmalyn jumped up from her chair and hugged Breyah. "Really?! Oh, B, I knew I could trust you. Yes, please send him up. I'm dying to see him again."

"Okay, okay. I really must get going. Rian is waiting for me."

Meeting Rian in the Centrum and walking the main courtyard before beginning their day had sort of become a morning ritual over the years. Though, today they weren't walking the courtyard. Today they were meeting with subject fifteen.

"Stay here," Breyah pleaded to the princess, hoping her words sank in. "Please."

"I will, I will. Now go! I'll clean up and put all this food away for later. Or for midday meal. Yes, come back and—"

"I'll call if I can make it up. The Waking is today, and I may be detained for most of the day." She headed for the door and, before exiting, shouted, "Please, Princess... stay here!" and then shut the door behind herself. Sometimes talking to that woman was like talking to a predult who refused to grow up.

"Beannaith," Breyah greeted one Sendarian after the next as she made her way through the morning crowd inside the Centrum toward the Medical annex building. Rian was there talking with a group of Sendarians assigned to the Archives division in front of the Medical skywalk. When she spotted Breyah approaching, she gestured in Breyah's direction and the three Sendarian women from Archives turned and smiled, each one pleased to see Breyah. She greeted them all by name and asked how their days had been during this windy season. It was policy not to discuss the ongoing Aevo Compendium with any Archive personnel, so Breyah was happy that they wouldn't be bombarding her with the onslaught of questions everyone else had been asking.

When they were finally alone, Rian said, "I'm sorry I can't go with you to meet subject fifteen. Holt keeps pestering me and requesting a location status every two minutes." Rian opened the deep side-pocket on her black sparring pants and pulled out a rolled-up plac. She unrolled it and pressed the On button. The pliable surface hardened into black glass and she scrolled through her notifications. "See, he just sent me another one."

"He only cares for your safety."

"I know. And once he's done scanning my insides and running whatever tests he's planning on running, I'm going to head over to Security for an update on our docking station incident. I'll check in with you after that." She rolled up the inactive plac and returned it to her pocket. "But anyway…" She pointed a blue fingernail at Breyah's head. "…I like how you did your hair today. Getting all fancied up for the Waking. Nice."

Breyah wasn't one to indulge in the finer things, even though her status and family connections permitted her certain luxuries. It was important to be approachable, and she wanted every Sendarian on Priomh to feel comfortable around her, which meant dressing and living like everyone else. But today was special. She pressed her hands to her midsection and dragged them over the silky fabric of her blouse. "Yes, well, I want to present a good first impression to number fifteen. To Kenna."

"Good luck with that, and I'll catch up with you after. That's if Holt lets me leave. He may end up locking me in one of his observation rooms and burning the access code from his brain."

"Stop it," Breyah said with a chuckle. Rian parted ways with her and strode off toward Medical. When Breyah spun to make her way to the Aevo C building skywalk, she bumped into someone.

"My apologies, my Leadess," a woman, much shorter and rounder in the midsection, said.

"Sabine! You startled me." It had been over two seasons since Breyah had seen her assistant. "I'm so happy you're home from Sendara."

"Beannaith and thank you for the sweet-brew and the many delicious pastries you had delivered to my home this morning. I brought them up to share with the others in the Ops and Admin building."

"That was nice, and you're welcome." Breyah began walking toward the Aevo C annex building at the rear of the Centrum. "Would you like to accompany me to meet subject fifteen?"

Sabine scrolled through her plac while walking with her Leadess. "Subject fifteen? Did we move up the Waking timetable? Did I miss something?"

It was early, and Breyah guessed Sabine hadn't had time to review the Aevo C reports from everything that had happened yesterday. "No, the Waking is still scheduled for later today. But subject fifteen woke on her own. I recommend you read through yesterday's reports from both the *Tarais* and Medical."

"I guess I should've done that. My apologies." Sabine stopped and asked, "But how did she wake from deep-space sedation?"

Breyah faced Sabine and shrugged. "It's unknown. Matthew is with her now. I was on my way to introduce myself and check on her status."

"Any other surprises I should know of?"

"Yes, there are two unexpected humans among the two groups we retrieved. Darci's and Eryn's groups. And the other two groups we were unable to retrieve at all. We're still investigating the whereabouts of all four Spiaires, but I'm hoping subject fifteen will have some answers. Oh, and the Lead Medic from the *Tarais*, Maura, found a human girl bleeding out on the docking station. She was one of the original subjects. It's all a mess, this whole Aevo Compendium."

"Oh, I already knew that... I mean, I saw, read it on this morning's memo from Holt." Sabine's skin flushed behind the splash of freckles along her cheeks and nose.

"You did?"

"Is her body in stasis aboard the *Tarais*? I assume she'll be returned to Earth so her family can properly bury her."

"No. She's in Medical. They were able to get her into surgery last night. Holt reported this morning that her vitals are stable."

Sabine's body swayed, one hand out for balance while she gripped the edge of the plac with the other. When Breyah leaned in to touch her and ask if she was okay, her assistant jerked away. "Oh, I'm so sorry. I-I'm not feeling too well. It usually takes me a day or two to shake off the lag of space travel, but I'll be fine. I just need to go sit, maybe get some fresh air."

"Okay, we can meet up after. If you need to go see Holt, please do."

Sabine nodded and Breyah watched her assistant skitter away, toward the front entrance of the Centrum and out to the main courtyard.

I hope she's okay.

Resuming her route, Breyah continued toward the Aevo C annex. The skywalk was empty, as no one was permitted to enter the Aevo C building except those with Lead access, and Matthew with his temporary access.

She could only hope that subject fifteen, Kenna, had some answers about where Darci was. Because if she didn't, Breyah's hopes of finding answers would fall into the lap of one eccentric princess.

42

Kenna's so-called shower wasn't a typical shower. It was more like a car wash with tiny spigots misting her with what Matthew called a cleansing solution. What that meant, Kenna had no idea, but the hot mist felt amazing against her skin and smelled even better. Whatever fresh, outdoorsy scent the cleansing solution had been infused with, she wanted to bottle it up and bring it home.

It was weird, standing naked in a room that was nothing more than a large shower stall. Caught off guard, she almost slipped and fell when the misting switched over and warm air blew against her wet skin. Now, she definitely felt as if she were standing naked in a miniature-sized car wash.

Once the air automatically turned off and her hair and body were dry, she moved to the opposite side of the shower-closet where Matthew had extended out a shelf from between the "shiplap" panels. Prior to her shower, he'd shown her another holographic section along the paneled wall that stored clothes, bathroom essentials, a pair of canvas shoes, and extra blankets. She'd made a mental note to come back later when she was alone to see what aliens considered bathroom essentials.

All the clothes, including the strappy-style yoga bra and boy-short undies, were black. After putting on a semi-loose V-neck, she slid on the softest pair of skinny pants she'd ever felt. The shirt's sleeves were three-quarter length, rolled and stitched at the ends, leaving plenty of room for her transessent bracer.

Before heading back out to find Matthew, she pinched the arcstone between her fingers and whispered, "Ulissa? If you can hear me, I'll try and get this transessent stone off today. Hopefully."

Out in her room, Matthew was over by the window, talking to someone through that invisible earpiece again. She grazed her own ears while walking over to him and wondered what exactly they had stuck in her head. The exterior wall was a solid piece of glass from one side of the room to the other, and from floor to ceiling. The lower half was frosted while the top half of the glass, from Matthew's shoulders up, was crystal clear. The sun shone in and the room looked even more luxurious than before.

He smiled at her and then continued talking, which was fine. She wanted to see what lay outside the window. It was another beautiful, sunny day. The snowcapped mountain she'd seen when she'd first woken was off to her left, but barely in view. Below, along the ground, wildflowers butted up against a massive stone wall. Behind the wall, a thick forest continued out into the horizon.

"Hey, all clean! Good, because Breyah's on her way to see you." During her shower, Matthew had changed out of the gray shirt he'd been wearing earlier and into a fresh, clean white one. Though, he was still wearing the same weathered jeans from last night.

"Remind me," Kenna said while running her fingers through her long tousled hair, trying to tame the teased eighties-look from the bombardment of air being blown on her after her shower. "Who is this Breyah lady?"

Matthew crossed the room and opened a drawer from inside the nook with the bathroom essentials. Kenna couldn't help but wonder how many other hidden alcoves were concealed within the walls.

"Here," Matthew said and handed Kenna a brush that had a smooth wooden spindle for a handle. Everything here seemed to be made of wood, stone, or glass.

She thanked him as he set a pair of canvas shoes by the bed.

Knock, knock, knock.

"She's here."

Kenna laid the brush on the bed, and Matthew disappeared behind the corner. Kenna peeked around the wall. There in the doorway stood the woman... the woman from Kenna's dream. The one crying under the white tree. Unlike in her dream, the woman's dark ginger hair wasn't down, but rather braided up with loose strands framing her face, and her eyes were a dark orange and strangely familiar. She appeared a little older than Kenna. More like Ally and Prue's age range of mid-to-late twenties.

"Hello, Kenna."

The words flowed from Breyah's lips as if she'd spoken English her whole life. Kenna stuck one finger into her ear and rubbed. She'd been expecting some kind of second voice with a slight delay as it translated the foreign language. But no.

Holy shit! How cool is this tech! Not cool that they jammed something into my ear, but holy shit... it works!

"Uh, hello."

"May I come in?"

Kenna nodded. They moved to the sitting area, and Kenna got comfortable in an armchair while Breyah sat across from her on the two-seater sofa. Kenna noticed the yellow stone affixed to the center of the woman's arm cuff. Now, seeing it up close, she was positive it was an arcstone.

How the hell did I see this woman in my dream? And where did she get an arcstone?

Kenna noticed Matthew still over by the door, looking for something. Before closing it, he asked, "Where's your tail?"

Breyah smiled at Matthew, the kind of smile Meegan's mom, Mrs. Prinor, often gave Kenna. "She's not coming." Then to Kenna,

291

"You'll get to meet Rian a bit later. I'm afraid she's needed in Medical."

"Medical? What happened?" Matthew sat next to Breyah and joked, "Did you guys lose another sub—" but he stopped mid-sentence after acknowledging the don't-push-me glare Breyah was giving him.

She smiled as she turned her attention to Kenna. "I'm sorry you had to wake alone yesterday. How are you doing today?"

"I'm okay. Confused and worried about my friends."

"There's no need to worry. They'll be waking shortly." Breyah leaned against the end of the sofa, her elbow resting on the arm. "Do you recall how you woke?"

Kenna shook her head. "No, but I'd like to know why you abducted me and my friends? And I say *abduct* because you're aliens, right?"

"Not an alien," Matthew chimed in.

Breyah smiled at him and then said to Kenna, "We are not from Earth, so yes, we are aliens to you. We brought you and your friends here without your permission, but only because we're desperate for your help. There are these aliens…"

Oh God, please don't say the Obard.

"…and they've threatened to hurt us if we don't hand over certain technology."

"Technology?"

I can't imagine the Obard being the type to stop and ask for anything.

"Who are these aliens?" Kenna asked, emphasizing each word.

Breyah scooted to the edge of the sofa, her hands pressed to her knees, and then as if they were in a crowded room, sharing secrets, she whispered, "Pirates."

Kenna scoffed and scrunched her nose before clarifying that she'd heard correctly. "Pirates?"

"I believe that's what you call them on Earth. They steal technology, weapons, anything of value."

Kenna lifted her right wrist. "Do they want these?" She didn't want to use the arcstone, so she went with the transessent stone. If these pirates did want the transessent stones, then maybe they were Obard. Ulissa had said the Obard wanted the power inside the arcstones, so maybe they wanted transessent stones too.

The woman's orange gaze flitted to the white stone embedded in the metal cuff. "No, they want our technology."

Why do I get the sense that she's telling me a bullshit story? But sure, let's go with pirates for now.

"And exactly how are a bunch of twenty-something-year-old humans supposed to help you?"

"The selection was purely random. We weren't sure who would arrive to help us."

Random? How random could their selection have been if my best friend and roommate are here too?

"I need to ask a favor," Kenna said, veering the conversation. "This metal cuff thing is itchy and hurts my wrist. Can you take it off?"

"It shouldn't be hurting you, but I can see about getting it removed."

"Thank you." She lowered her arm and glanced out the window. "So, where exactly are we? Matthew wouldn't say."

"You are on a moon called Priomh."

"A moon?"

"Yes, we're an isolated community on the smallest of our three moons. We call it Priomh. We also call our community here Priomh."

She'd never imagined a moon could have a forest, gardens, and breathable air. Suddenly, the amount of information she knew... any human knew... about life beyond Earth seemed minuscule. There was so much to learn, and her curiosity took the driver's seat.

"Matthew is human, like you, but the rest of us are from a nearby planet called Sendara."

"Sendara. And everyone there has orange eyes, like you?"

Breyah nodded. "Though there are always the exceptions."

"Blue-bee." Matthew rubbed his nose. "She's definitely an exception and a pain in my—"

"Kenna," Breyah said, interrupting him, "I was wondering if I could ask you about someone we were expecting to be here with your group. Her name is Darci."

Random, my ass. The word expecting *implies you knew who was coming. Thank God this woman doesn't have a wooden nose that grows whenever she lies.*

"Darci wasn't with us when you brought the energy dome over me and my friends. Well, minus Xander. That guy is not my friend."

"Xander, the man with the bushy black hair? He's not your friend?"

Kenna's bare toes curled against the bottom of the armchair. "Supposedly, someone drugged him and then stuck him in Prue's shrubs. He was wearing one of these"—she lifted her wrist with the transessent bracer on it—"and he wasn't too happy about it either."

"But no Darci?"

Dang, she really wants to know about Darci.

"No Darci."

"Did she say or do anything odd that day?"

Kenna sucked in her lower lip. "We didn't see or hear from her that day. We'd been trying to call her, but she never answered."

The woman's gaze dropped to the hardwood. Her fingers tensed. "Thank you," she finally said with a concerned smile.

"She was going to head out to California to see a friend. Told us her friend was in trouble. Maybe that's why she wasn't at Prue's. She might've caught an earlier flight, and they don't allow cell phone use in the air."

"Yes, maybe." Breyah stood, brushing her hands down the front of her charcoal-gray one-piece romper. The high neck elongated her features while the sleeveless cut of the top showcased her slender arms and vintage-looking arm cuff. "We'll be waking your friends soon. Would you like to join us? I can see about having Holt remove the transessent bracer while you're there."

A burst of excitement erupted inside of Kenna. "Oh, yes! I'd love to be there when Meegan and Ally wake!"

"Good, I'm sure they'd love to see you too," Breyah said as someone knocked at the door.

"I'll get it." Matthew jumped up from his seat.

"I have to attend to a few things first. I'll have Matthew escort you to Medical and introduce you to our Lead Medic. His name is Holt. Ignore the stern look. He doesn't smile much, but he's very friendly and kind."

"Good to know."

"Breyah, it's for you," Matthew called out.

Breyah excused herself while Kenna shot to her feet. She hurried and grabbed her canvas shoes and turned to follow Matthew and Breyah. When Kenna rounded the corner, she jerked to a stop. The shoes slipped from her fingers and fell to the floor. She gasped and stared at the man standing in the doorway.

Ben.

He was here, in the flesh. Tall and handsome. Even with the look of utter surprise sketched on his face, he looked exactly as he had during their dreamlike encounters. In the doorway, he stood wearing a waist-length gray jacket with a black shirt and dark pants. He looked as if he'd just left a Banana Republic photo shoot. So well put together, even with that rebellious cowlick above his left eye.

His orange gaze locked onto her. Kenna counted her breaths. One... two... three seconds before he broke away from their stare-down.

"Beannaith, Breyah." His voice was shaky. His gaze fluttered to Kenna's once more before he muttered, "I'm sorry," and then darted from the doorway.

"Bennach!" Breyah glanced at Kenna. Her expression was a mixture of joy and confusion. "My apologies, I have to go. Matthew will escort you to Medical. I'll be there shortly. And please, if you remember anything else regarding Darci, you'll let me know?"

What is this lady's obsession with Darci?

Kenna reached for the shoes and slowly slipped one on, and then the other. They had a similar feel to her old pair of Toms.

Ben is here, she kept repeating in her mind. *And he recognized me. How is that possible? I was dreaming. He was dreaming. Oh man, what is happening to me?*

I need Meeg... or Ulissa. They'll know. They'll explain to me that it's a common side effect of the arcstone. To share dreams with a stranger. Who's an alien, and who could easily pose for the cover of a GQ magazine.

Kenna stared at the empty doorway, not sure what to think.

"You okay?" Matthew asked, coming up from behind her.

She jumped, having forgotten he was still in the room. "Oh, yeah. Sorry. Who was that guy?"

Matthew activated the holographic panels concealing both the mini-kitchen and clothing nooks. "Oh, him. That's Captain Ganecht of the Rhaltan Enforcers," he said in a manly-hero voice, and then in his normal voice added, "Breyah's little brother."

"Brother?"

"Yup. Now come on. We've got to get to Medical and talk to Holt about getting that bracer off you. He gets grumpy when things don't go smoothly."

"Things aren't going smoothly?"

"I'm guessing no, but then again they don't tell me much," Matthew said, holding the door, ready to close it. "Come on, let's go see your friends."

43

"**B**ennach, wait!" The legs of Breyah's pants swished as she hurried after her brother. He was almost to the end of the Aevo C wing skywalk when she finally caught up.

"Hey, what was that about? And—and what are you doing here?" Not wanting to make a scene out in the Centrum, she blocked him from leaving the glass-enclosed tunnel.

"Nothing. I've never seen one of your subjects before. She's not what I expected. That's all." His jaw tensed, and she watched his eyes. Not blinking was his tell.

"You're lying." She pointed at his eyes.

"I'm not lying," he said while pushing past her.

"Okay, so what are you doing here?"

Out in the Centrum, they walked arm in arm, hopefully not drawing too much attention. If she was late to Medical, she knew Holt would have a conniption fit, but it had been years since she'd last seen her brother. Her strides led them along the Centrum wall, toward the skywalk leading to Medical.

"Breyah"—he stopped and faced her—"I told you yesterday in our video call that I was coming to Priomh. I thought you understood that?"

She tried to remember, but with everything that had happened yesterday their call was a blur.

He's not wearing his uniform, so it must not be Rhaltan related. Oh, I can't recall him saying he was coming or why.

"My apologies. I was distracted during our call. We've had some complications with the current assessment." Then, as a test, she added, "You can assure your superiors that everything is under control."

He led her away from the many passing Sendarians, off to the side of the Centrum. Once they had some privacy, he said, "I'm not here as a Rhaltan officer. I'm here to visit my older sister. You haven't been home in years, and I've never been to Priomh. I made some progress with an ongoing threat from a rebel group on Sendara and was given some time off while our intelligence officers decipher the intel."

"What rebel group? I wasn't aware there was a situation going on."

"It's not really Breyah's thing," Rian explained, coming up from behind them, "to read the Network feed and keep up with current events on Sendara. But ask her how Trace, one of our medics' sons, is doing on his genetics project in school, and she'll give you a full update." Rian held her plac to her chest. "Besides, we're too far from Sendara to worry about annoying predults who are bored and acting out against their parents."

"Bennach, this is Rian. My second-in-command and Lead of Security."

The Rhaltan officer studied the tall woman, eyeing her like an anomaly to be solved. "Yes, I've heard your name once or twice before."

Breyah looped her arm through her brother's again and continued the introductions. "Rian, this is my brother, Bennach."

Rian, still wearing her sparring clothes, held out her palm. "Beannaith. It's nice to officially meet you."

Bennach stared at the open pale hand and then up to her sapphire eyes before sliding his hand along the top of hers. "Beannaith, Rian." He narrowed his eyes and asked while still in her grasp, "Where did you say you were from?"

"She's Sendarian," Breyah corrected him.

Rian slid her hand from his. "Supposedly, I have a rare condition. Something to do with the pigment of my skin, eyes, and hair follicles. A medical mystery, I think that's what they eventually labelled me. But you're not wrong about having other beings here on Priomh. We do have one human who lives among us. His name is Matthew, and he's from the previous Earth assessment." Rian turned and they slowly continued over the skywalk toward Medical. "He's more like a mascot, if you ask me."

"Rian," Breyah interjected. "Never mind about Matthew. Right now, we need to get to the Waking." The three were almost to the double doors when Breyah asked Rian, "Were you coming from Medical? Is Holt preparing for the Waking?"

"He is. Subject fifteen and our beloved mascot just showed up as I was leaving. I'll catch up with you later. I need to check in with my security team and see what progress they've made with the *Tarais* video logs."

"Keep me posted," Breyah said as Rian smiled at Bennach before walking away. Breyah continued toward Medical and was about to enter when she noticed Bennach was no longer with her. She retraced their path and found him standing in the skywalk, watching the grounds below.

"What are you doing?" she asked. "Don't you want to see your first Waking? I promise, the humans we're assessing are harmless. They're from one of the less hostile worlds and still classified as primitively intelligent. They're nowhere near the advancements needed for space travel."

"Rian mentioned subject fifteen was there." He watched the grounds below through the glass enclosing the skywalk tunnel. "What did you say her name was?"

"Kenna," Breyah answered, her head tilted to get a better look at his face. "And yes, she's there now. Shall I ask her to leave?"

"No, it's fine."

"Good," Breyah said and beckoned him to come. Bennach sighed and, after a moment, continued with Breyah toward Medical. Breyah looped her arm through his again. "Now that you're here, I can't wait to catch up. I want to hear all about our parents and how life's been treating you on Sendara. Are you still involved with that wonderful woman you're always talking about? What was her name? Eana? No, wait, I think it was Nora?"

"Close. Her name was Anora, and no, we're no longer together."

44

"I s there water?"

"Here." Darci lowered a small metal cup to Grace's lips. Her friend sipped from the edge, coughing and wincing but determined to drink. "Good, that's good. You need to stay hydrated."

Eryn had dwindled to a gangly, petite thing in the weeks since they'd been taken. Darci watched her senior Spiaire refuse to eat and throw tantrum after tantrum demanding to see Brody. This infatuation Eryn had with the human was becoming unhealthy, yet Darci had no idea how to sever it.

When Eryn grew tired of yelling at the door, she slumped to the floor, head resting against the wall. Darci didn't dare say anything for fear she might reignite her friend's persistence. She savored the few moments of silence and used the time to try and think without distractions.

"Are you cold?" When Grace nodded, Darci reached behind from where she sat and spread open another blanket for a second layer of warmth. "There. Let me know if you need another one."

"Thank you, Darci." Grace's lips barely moved. Her condition hadn't improved, and Darci began to worry the beaten Spiaire might have internal damage. *What did that man do to you? Hold on, please hold on.* She brushed loose strands of red hair from Grace's eyes. She needed to convince Micah to reconsider letting them go, or to at least let Grace go.

Eryn began muttering and slapping the door again.

"Hey, why don't you come sit with us?" Darci said. "We need to think of our next move. We need to get Grace out of here."

"There is no next move. You don't get it, do you? We're not getting out of here," Eryn grumbled, both hands now nervously rubbing her sides. "We're going to die in here."

"That's not going to happen. Have faith in Isoldesse. Now please, come sit."

The second Eryn got to her feet, a man's muffled voice sounded from outside their cell. One after the other, Eryn's fists pounded the window in the door as she screamed demands and yelled for help. When the door clicked open, Eryn charged at Micah. Darci was about to stand and help Eryn fight Micah, now that they weren't wearing his paralytic neck bands, but he had constructed a new way to restrain them. Some sort of metal wand with a small ball at the end. Darci yelled to warn Eryn, but it was too late. Micah jabbed the end of the rod into Eryn's shoulder. Eryn dropped to the concrete floor, screaming in pain while her body twitched.

"That's the lowest setting, so stay down or I'll crank up the electricity."

Eryn scooted on her side over to Darci. Darci got to her feet and stepped closer, hands raised to draw his attention away from Eryn. "Easy there. What do you want, Micah?"

Over the past few weeks, Darci had made it a point to learn her captors' names. Cahleen, Logan, Quaid, and someone named Anora—whom she had yet to see or meet. It was mainly Micah who watched over them. Occasionally, the man with the scar along his neck, Logan, would show his face.

"How is she?" Micah pointed the taser at Grace.

"Not good." Darci glanced at her shivering friend and then up at her captor. "Don't you think it's about time you tell us what's going on? Why we're here?"

"Actually, I don't." Micah faced her and crossed his arms over his broad chest.

"You know, I read an article while on Earth describing all the different forms of government in all the different countries, past and present. Actually, I spent quite a bit of time researching how humans rule over one another." When Micah didn't protest her story, she continued. "Anyway, it got me thinking about how people on Earth are constantly trying new ways to govern and how on Sendara we've been using the same method for over two thousand years. Why are you guys trying to change what isn't broken? Isoldesse established the Elemental Council and royal family for a reason. Are you trying to turn Sendara into another Earth? That planet probably only has a few more centuries—if that—of natural resources!" She didn't mean to raise her voice, but with Eryn's constant whining, Grace's failing health, and her own teetering emotions, she couldn't help but yell.

Micah raised one eyebrow beneath the brim of his baseball hat. "You do make a valid point, but regardless, it's time for a change."

"There's no reason for change. The laws and systems written in the Anumen Doctrine have worked for generations."

"But what if the Elemental Council and your beloved queen aren't following the Anumen Doctrine?" Micah countered. "What if the queen was already making changes outside of the laws and systems written within the Anumen Doctrine? Small changes over the years. Things no one would even notice or question."

Darci wasn't sure how to answer. Why would the Queen of Sendara not follow the Anumen Doctrine? Why would she take it upon herself to alter the laws and systems set in place by their goddess?

"Explain," was all the response she could muster.

"I don't have to. Just believe me when I tell you that the Anumen Doctrine you've read isn't the same one Isoldesse wrote."

"Lies." *No one would dare. That would be the ultimate act of disrespect.*

"Not everyone believes Isoldesse will return. Not even your queen."

No. He's lying.

"And the Athru are going to prove it. Then we're going to set Sendara free from both the Elemental Council and the royal family. Sendarians should be allowed the freedom for *more*."

"To be like Earth. Did you not see the results of their freedom? Their planet is dying because of prosperity and greed."

"We'll see. Sendarians aren't humans."

Darci shuffled closer. "Micah, what does all of that have to do with us being here now? What part do we play in your new Sendara?" She swung her hand out, gesturing to Grace and Eryn on the floor.

"No more questions. I only came in here to ask if she's—"

His words were cut off by the *creak* of the cell door being pushed open. Logan walked in, closed the door halfway behind himself, and waved Micah over. They huddled in the corner. Logan's hands moved with his words, and by the looks of it, he was agitated, concerned, or both. She couldn't see Micah's face, but he shook his head as he listened.

Darci tilted her head and leaned closer. When Logan's gaze flicked to her, Micah raised his homemade weapon, warning her. But she didn't need to get closer, because what these two idiots didn't know was that Darci had exceptional hearing. Occasionally, she even heard a man's voice in the next cell over, but there was no way she was telling Eryn that.

She stood perfectly still while they talked. The few phrases she overheard sounded like *we need to get ready to move* and *they're coming with us*, and finally, before they parted from their conversation, Darci heard Logan ask Micah if he'd gotten the old plac working so they could send the message.

Micah nodded.

What old plac? And a message to whom?

Darci bit her lower lip, hesitating to interrupt their conversation. But after Micah dropped his head into one hand, obviously frustrated, she wanted to offer some form of truce. "Micah, whatever's going on, let us help."

"You need to mind your business." Logan moved passed Micha, pointing a bottle of water at her before tossing it to her. Darci fumbled with the bottle, almost dropping it before twisting the cap off and taking a sip.

From behind Logan, Micah added, "If you want to stay alive, you'll keep your mouth shut and do as we say. Otherwise, no promises."

My business? This is my business, you stupid gróntah!

But now wasn't the time to push buttons. Instead, with her palm slightly raised, she dipped her head and asked, "Can you at least tell us if the humans are okay?"

Logan let out an annoyed huff and stormed out of the cell, while Micah lowered the taser and answered Darci. "They're fine. Tired and confused, but fine. Now, please just sit and do as you're told. Logan's right, I can't promise you you'll make it out of this if you draw too much attention to yourselves." He shot Eryn a pointed look.

Darci understood and nodded.

Halfway out the cell door, he turned and said, "We live in a world of constant deception. Remember that."

After Micah left, Darci returned to her spot above Grace's head and handed the bottle of water to Eryn. "Do you get what he's saying? You're going to get us killed if you keep running your mouth and acting out like an immature predult. Brody's fine, and it sounds like this will all be over soon."

She then thought about Gerard's wife, Honnah, in the next cell with Brody, and wished she could speak with her for only a moment. To reassure her that everything would be okay. Honnah knew about Gerard and where he was from, but to be taken and dragged out to an alien world was a whole different story. She just hoped the human woman was doing okay.

This is all my fault. I should've been more discreet in our meetings. I've let both the princess and prince down. I vow to Isoldesse that I will get Honnah home to Gerard. Somehow.

She needed to get word to Priomh, to Breyah. But how? Whatever Micah and Logan had been whispering about sounded as though it was going to happen soon. And here she was, stuck in a cell with two broken Spiaires.

But then she spotted it.

Across the cell, lying on the floor, was a plac.

Did he...? Micah's warning streamed through her thoughts. *We live in a world of constant deception.*

She lifted Grace's head, carefully set it on the mattress pad, and then crawled over to the handheld device. It was an older model, the screen scratched and faded.

Had one of them left it by accident? Was this a test? When she activated it, she saw the power cell had eight percent and a full frequency signal. She browsed the storage files and recent activity. Both blank.

The power dropped to seven percent.

Shit!

Whoever left the plac had blocked the Sendara Network. It appeared the only way to get a message out was through an internal file request through Priomh's Archive department.

"Oh, you've got to be kidding me." She took a deep breath and opened the link into the archives. She clicked on the Request File icon and filled out the requester information before carefully considering her message. Once the message was sent, she tucked the old plac under the mattress pad and prayed to her goddess that someone in Archives would find it and pass it on to Breyah, Rian, or Holt. She'd even take help from Matthew. Anyone to get them out of there, and soon.

45

Bright daylight poured in from the glass wall at the opposite end of the medical room. Kenna noted the left-side door at the other end, the one that led to the storage closet she'd hidden in after waking up. The line of beds ran down the center of the narrow room. A floor-to-ceiling glass wall at the far end of the room revealed blue skies hugging a lone snowcapped mountain. The same mountain she'd seen when she'd first woken. Off to the right of the row of beds, against the wall, was a long white upholstered bench stretching the length of the room. Most of the Sendarians were clustered on the other side of the room. There along that wall, numerous alcoves within the wall were open, revealing various cabinets, drawers, and workstations. Kenna recalled how the wall had looked when she'd first woken, with various-sized rectangles etched in the wall. Well, now she knew what was behind all those rectangles.

Matthew gently tapped Kenna's arm. "I see Holt. Come on."

Her steps were slow as she followed Matthew. One after another, the beds were empty until they weren't, and she noticed the face-shield thingies had been removed. When she reached the first occupied bed, she stopped and moved closer. Her hands gripped the beveled edge of the footboard—it was Liam.

He's here. I can't believe he's here. A transessent bracer hugged his right wrist. *There's no way we were randomly picked. Why me? Why Liam? Why any of us?*

He looked so peaceful sleeping under the white sheet, hands out and resting at his sides. The boy she'd grown up with now in a man's body. She'd seen plenty of pictures of him on his Instagram, so seeing him as an adult wasn't too much of a surprise, but still. Here he was. No longer that scrawny kid with shabby hair and clothes full of holes and dirt from playing outside all day.

She was about to move closer, to Liam's side, when a man called out to Matthew. She twisted and pressed her butt against the wood of the footboard.

"Kenna, this is Holt," Matthew said. "He's our Lead Medic here on Priomh."

Holt held his hand out, palm faceup. She stared at it and remembered when she'd first met Ben and how he'd held out his hand to her in the same manner. She glanced up at the Lead Medic, unsure what to do. Thank goodness for Matthew, who reached out, placed his hand on Holt's, and dragged it across the open palm. Holt held his hand out to Kenna again, and this time she smiled and mimicked Matthew's movements.

The woman in charge, Breyah, had been right about this guy and his fixed expression. His thin, linear lips were overshadowed by a graying beard. He didn't appear old enough to have gray peeking through, but who was she to say when these aliens reached maturity? He continued his introductions, and Kenna noticed an eager gleam to Holt's orange eyes—bright and inviting, like a kid about to pour vinegar into his school volcano project.

"Yes, well, I have a few questions for you, but later. We have much to do to wake your friends." He was about to walk away when Kenna held out her wrist, the one with the transessent bracer on it.

"Ah, yes. Breyah did mention you've requested to have your bracer removed."

Kenna nodded. "It's a bit tight."

Holt raised a reddish-blond eyebrow. "Normally, I'd say no, but it seems the biotracker in your bracer isn't working properly." He flipped her wrist over, his fingers inspecting the metal surface.

"What does it do?" Kenna chewed on her lip. Her curiosity was begging to take over. For her to learn more about their world, their star system, and their customs, but the worrywart part of her brain refused to give up control. *Focus on getting this damn thing off and waking everyone up.*

Holt released her wrist and explained, "The bracer is a tracker. It also monitors your vitals. A precaution for you and the others during space travel and throughout your duration here, on Priomh. Not all worlds have the same atmospheric composition. If that makes sense to you."

"It does," she said, nodding.

He waved over a medic and instructed her to remove the device. "And do it fast. We're on a schedule. As soon as the Leadess shows up, we'll begin."

The medic beckoned Kenna to follow and, without waiting for Kenna, scurried over to one of the nooks. Kenna inched closer to Matthew, unsure of what to do. Stay with Liam, or go with the medic alien-lady?

With his hands tucked into the front pockets of his tunic, Holt faced Matthew and said, "Breyah wants you to report to the Leadess's quarters. I don't know what for"—he drew his hands out of his pockets and held them up while shaking his head—"but you're needed there."

Kenna could see her new friend's eyelids open to their fullest. His chest puffed out, and she swore if he were a bird, his feathers would've ruffled. Matthew turned to Kenna and cupped her shoulders. "Are you okay if I leave you here? There's, uh, someone I need to see. I'll check on you later, or tomorrow."

His excitement radiated, and she couldn't help but smile. "I'll be fine."

"Good!" he said and darted toward the side door. The same door she'd snuck out of yesterday.

"Over here, please," the medic woman with light-red hair called to Kenna. A mass of brownish-red freckles covered her face, neck, arms, and hands.

Holt returned to the line of aliens, who all wore the same navy-blue tunic and pants. They were assembling behind each one of the headboards. In a million years, she'd never have thought she'd be here standing in a room with a bunch of aliens.

Sendarians. I think that's what that Leadess lady called them.

All with shades of red hair. Some men were more blond, but all the women were redheads.

They look so human. How is it that Anumens, humans, and now these Sendarians all have similar anatomy? There's got to be a connection—an origin that we all share.

From within the nook, the medic opened a drawer and pulled out a clear pencil-like tool. Kenna held out her wrist while the woman gently pressed the tip under the edge of the bracer, against Kenna's skin. It was warm. She wasn't sure how the medic activated the glass stick, but when she did, the end morphed into something fluid-like that moved in an oscillating motion as if it were alive. Kenna shuffled backward, her mouth agape.

"Don't move," the medic ordered, her free hand holding Kenna's forearm. "It won't hurt, but you need to be still. The release latch is underneath the bracer."

The gelatin-tipped tool slithered beneath the bracer. She could feel the warm, slick movements roll over her veins. Within seconds, a seam appeared in the metal like magic, and the bracer popped apart just enough for Kenna to slide her wrist out. The woman held the glass stick as it reverted to its original solid state.

The medic turned away with the bracer, and Kenna faced the line of beds again. Her wrist was slightly flushed from the bracer, but it was off, and the effects were immediate.

A familiar overcast engulfed the room, and everyone slowed until they were locked in the moment. The light that surrounded her was as if a glowing orb hovered above. An orangish-red cloud appeared at the edge of her circle of light. When Ulissa stepped through with her golden aura, Kenna rushed to the old woman.

"Oh, I'm so glad to see you!"

"*Iya*, Kenna. I missed you too." When Kenna released Ulissa, the old woman turned to take in their surroundings. She swiped her hand across the air, and the darkness that surrounded them swished away as if she were swiping through pictures on a cell phone. Sunlight filled the room again, and the Sendarians stood posed like figures in a wax museum.

"How did you do that?"

The corners of her mouth lifted, and tiny creases formed along her upper lip. "*We* did that. Now that our bond is complete, and you're no longer wearing that ridiculous transessent stone, there's so much I can teach you. The power of the arcstone is vast, depending on you."

"Sounds great, but it'll have to wait. There's too much going on right now for me to play apprentice." Kenna pointed to the line of beds. "They're about to wake everyone up."

Ulissa moved closer to one of the beds while surveying the room. "Where are we?"

"Well, we're not on Earth anymore." Ulissa narrowed her chocolate-brown eyes, and Kenna continued, "Remember those orange-eyed beings? Well, they took us. They call themselves Sendarians, and we're on a moon called Priomh. Why we're here is still a bit of a mystery. I'm not buying the bullshit story they told me, but I'll have to get back to you on that one." She moved to the end of Liam's bed and added, "And I don't think the Obard are involved."

"Hmm, maybe. Regardless, don't let your guard down." Ulissa cocked her head and stared at the glass panels stretching up from the headboards. "Those words... that language... there's something in the angles of their symbols that shares similarities with—"

"Ulissa, I hate to cut this short, but I'm excited to see my friends. We can talk more later, but first I need to let the Sendarians do their thing and wake everyone up. I'm hoping once Meegan's awake she can help me figure out what's really going on here."

"Your Anumen friend, Fawness?"

"What does that mean, *Fawness*? She gets mad whenever her mom calls her that."

"A discussion for you to have with your young Anumen friend."

"Fine." Kenna grazed her hand down Ulissa's arm. The golden beads of her gown were smooth and knitted tightly together. "I'm glad you're okay, and that we can talk again."

"Me too. We'll talk more later." Ulissa's body faded, and the bustle of the room resumed. Kenna was about to head over to the bench when Ulissa spoke inside her head. *"Something's not right. I sense one or two weak essences. They're preparing to make the journey into the Unforeseen World."*

"What does that mean?"

"What does what mean?" the nice medic with all the freckles asked.

Kenna blinked, ignoring the Sendarian, and stared at the wooden beams along the ceiling. "Hello? What does that mean?" she muttered to Ulissa but received no reply.

"Kenna?" Breyah stepped in front of Kenna, startling her.

"Oh, hey." She quickly pointed to the ceiling. "Just admiring the wooden beams… up there. I like the whole rustic vibe you've got going on in here."

Breyah gestured for them to move toward the upholstered bench. Once seated, Breyah said to Kenna, "Holt has asked that you remain here with the others so he can run some tests. To make sure your body is adjusting to our environment. Then you and the others will be escorted to the guest accommodations."

"Yes, Holt did mention he wanted to speak with me after."

Breyah was about to say something when her attention was drawn to the main door. Kenna followed Breyah's gaze. Ben had entered and was talking to one of the medics. A burst of adrenaline exploded in Kenna's muscles, numbing her senses and ability to think straight. They'd almost shared an intimate moment, and would have if she'd allowed him to have his way with her. She touched the arcstone from the outside of her shirt. By his reaction earlier, he'd recognized her, which told her what they were experiencing couldn't have been a dream. More like a mental connection of some kind. Of course, that was only a guess and something she'd have to ask Ulissa or Meegan about.

Watching him, she recalled how intense his emotions had been in their last encounter. As he approached, Kenna wondered who had left him with such sorrow. She also wondered if *real* Ben looked as good without a shirt on as *dream* Ben did. The minute he sat next to Breyah, she snapped back to reality.

"Kenna, this is my brother, Bennach. He's visiting from our home world, Sendara."

Bennach?

Kenna glanced and waited for him to look, but he never did. He ignored her and stared ahead at the busy medics.

Uh, okay. What's his problem? One minute he's trying to alleviate his stress with me and the next he won't acknowledge my existence!

Holt greeted both Breyah and Ben, and then quickly went over the Waking process, occasionally glancing at Kenna. He seemed to be wrapping up his report when a high-pitched alarm sounded from one of the beds. Holt spun, and without another word, he and a team of medics rushed to the bed with the glass pane illuminated in red.

Breyah excused herself and moved closer to the outer edge of the medical huddle. Kenna was about to sneak a glance at Ben when another alarm sounded. Three beds to the left, the display glass went from looking like all the others to flashing an alarming red.

It was Liam's bed.

Kenna jumped up and hurried over to her friend. From the corner of her eye, she saw Ben spring to his feet. She even swore he tried to reach for her, but she didn't stop or turn to see what his intentions were. She focused on the rapid pinging sound, in rhythm with the first alarm.

Not caring, she squeezed between two Sendarian medics to get to Liam's side. With his hand in hers, she turned and scanned the line of beds. The first alarm belonged to a young woman. Someone she'd never met and whose picture she couldn't recall seeing on any of Liam's Instagram posts. She was fair skinned with bleached hair that spread out in short, tousled layers, blending in with the white pillow. A team of medics surrounded her, a few of them breaking away and rushing over to Liam's bed.

Kenna glanced up at the glass above Liam's headboard. A dot moved along a red vertical line, zigzagging out every few seconds as it trailed down from the ceiling.

"What is that red line?" Kenna asked one of the medical ladies.

"His heartbeats."

"Why are his and the other girl's heartbeats in red?" Kenna locked eyes with the woman and thought how at any moment someone would grab her and escort her out of the way like in the movies, but no one did.

"Their bodies aren't acclimating to our environment," Holt explained as he came up from behind. He stepped closer to examine the data displayed on Liam's screen. "The goal during the Waking process is to achieve homeostasis, but it looks like his glucose levels are too high. The same thing is happening with subject ten."

Subject? Did he just say subject? *What. The. Fuck?*

Kenna pinned that piece of information to her mental corkboard and focused on how to help Liam. She recalled reading about hyperglycemia in diabetics, but Liam wasn't diabetic, or at least he hadn't been when they were kids.

"Insulin! He needs insulin!"

"I don't know what that is. Can you describe its chemical makeup?" Holt stared at her, waiting for an answer. Her blank stare told Holt his answer. She didn't know. He continued to bark out orders at Sendarians running in every direction.

"*You can save him,*" Ulissa said inside Kenna's mind.

"*How?*" she silently replied. "*What can I do?*"

"*Look beyond the surface of the living. You can access the overlap between the two worlds when an essence travels to the Unforeseen World.*"

"*I don't see anything!*"

"*Concentrate on his essence. On what makes him... him.*"

Kenna inhaled a deep breath and squeezed his hand. She closed her eyes and thought about their time together in Kansas. Running through fields and catching frogs in the creek and lightning bugs at night. His empathy and courage whenever Kenna had been scared or hurt. They'd been inseparable at school, after school, during the summers—any time they could spend time together, they had.

When Kenna opened her eyes, the daylight had grown dim. Time had slowed to a snail's pace. One of the medics worked to cut Liam's shirt up the center with something that looked like a flossing pick. The thread sliced through the fabric at a super-slow speed.

"*Do you see his essence?*"

"*How do you see an essence?*" But then she saw it. It was beautiful. A faint glow of white shimmered beneath Liam's skin. The light grew brighter and eventually lifted from his body. It was him, but in a glowing form, hovering inches above his physical body. The gleaming lines of his features flattened as the edges pulled inward until a sphere the size of a grapefruit formed. The sphere hovered over his physical body, still glowing.

She looked to see the reactions of the Sendarians, but it was as if they couldn't see what she could see. *Good thing because I don't even know how to explain all this alien magic.*

"*Ulissa!*" Kenna shouted as she watched the ball of light slowly rise. "*What's happening?*"

"*His physical body is dying, and his essence is preparing to leave this world. But we can stop it. You can heal the infliction and return his essence to his body.*"

"*How the heck am I supposed to do that? His sugar levels are too high. He's having a stroke!*" Kenna could feel the palms of her hands sweating. She pulled one hand free and reached toward the floating ball of light—toward Liam's essence.

The light began to shrink, and Kenna knew she needed to act fast. Inside her mind, she asked, *"What's he doing? Where's he going?"*

"His light is bright, which means he'll be welcomed into the Unforeseen World with openness."

"No, no, no! I need him here!" Kenna thrust her hand inside Liam's essence. It was like opening a memory box. Images, emotions, hopes and dreams, routines, and common behaviors... everything and anything that made Liam... Liam. All of it flooded her mind.

"This is amazing!" Connected, she heard his concerned thoughts about how he'd forgotten to feed his fish.

Then, as if he felt her presence, he asked, *"Hello? Who's there?"*

"Liam? Can you hear me? It's Kenna!"

"Stargirl?"

An old memory appeared in her mind. She closed her eyes and embraced the vision as if she were really there. They were maybe nine or ten years old, playing a board game on his parents' wraparound deck in Kansas. The child version of Liam looked up at her and held his hand out. "Here, I know you like being the car."

With her hand out to accept the tiny metal figurine, she thanked him. "I do, or I did. I haven't played this game in years." She took the figurine and placed it on Start. "Liam, I don't want you to go."

"It's okay. I don't mind going first."

She drifted into the air, away from the memory, watching him play alone on the porch. When she opened her eyes, she was back in the medical room, time still slowed. Liam's essence was now the size of a grape. She curled her fingers over the ball of light and pulled. At first there was resistance, but then his essence relinquished its hold and allowed Kenna control.

The medics were still busy trying to save Liam and the other girl, three beds down. Kenna focused on Liam's essence. *"Ulissa, now what?"* Ulissa didn't respond. Instead, an orange light pulsed from under the skin of her hand.

Liam's weary voice trailed through her mind with a yawn. *"Kenna, I'm so tired. Can we talk later? I think I need to sleep for a bit."*

"Damn it, Liam, stay awake! Hold on, do you hear me! Stay. Awake!"

Then Ulissa spoke again. *"Kenna, we're going to call upon the Eilimintachs to come and heal his affliction. Now, repeat these words,"* she instructed. *"Teacht Eilimintach hiigas et fhada."*

She repeated the phrase softly, barely above a whisper. The words were foreign yet the power they evoked felt amazing. Heat flowed from her body into Liam's essence. Her mind focused on healing him and lowering his glucose levels. Within seconds, she felt his strength return and knew she'd done it. Now she needed to get his essence back into his body before his light shrank any more. She lowered his essence over his torso and pushed her fist hard against his chest, opening her fingers and returning his essence into his body.

The moment his heartbeat monitor changed from red to white, time returned to normal.

Holt scratched his beard while he and his medics tried to decipher how Liam's vitals had suddenly stabilized. But it was a fleeting moment of relief, because three beds down, the alarm of Liam's friend flatlined. The prolonged note rang through the air, proving the sound of death was the same for both their worlds.

Kenna glanced toward the woman. Her lifeless body appeared as if she were still sleeping. Kenna had managed to save Liam, but not his friend. A sadness ached inside her, and she wished she could've done more.

Her guilt was disrupted by a loud, piercing scream. At the end of the room, Meegan was awake and trying to console a panicked Ally. Kenna released Liam's hand and wove through the Sendarians closing in on them.

"It's okay! Ally, I'm here!" Kenna shouted and hugged her roommate. With both hands she secured Ally's face, forcing the girl to meet her gaze. "They're not going to hurt us. Hey, look at me!"

Ally's eyes trembled and her body shook. Meegan came up next to them and whispered while watching the Sendarians, "You sure we're good?"

Kenna nodded. "Yes. They're not going to hurt us. But we do have a lot to talk about."

Liam was out for most of the day while Kenna sat with Meegan and Ally during the medical tests. The body of the girl had been removed before anyone could notice, and Breyah asked Kenna not to mention the incident to the others, which she agreed to only because she didn't want to upset the alien woman.

Ben kept his distance, and Kenna caught him glancing her way more than a few times. Eventually, Breyah and her brother left, and Holt and his medics continued their evaluations of everyone after their waking. Of how the *subjects* were acclimating—a term that didn't settle well with Kenna. A minor slip on their part, but more evidence for Kenna to prove Breyah was telling a bullshit story.

46

*H*e hates me. I'd hate me if I were him. But he's here... Nick's here. Five feet behind me, and I'm dying to run into his arms and beg him for his forgiveness.

"You'll be staying in our guest building," the man from Medical explained. The hall they were walking through had no windows except for the illuminated frosted glass ceiling. Meegan took the lead, wanting to put some distance between her and Nick. However much she wanted him, letting him into her life again meant opening up and possibly revealing certain truths about herself. Something she wasn't ready to do.

"The Leadess will come by shortly to check on you." Their escort continued talking about some Leadess lady and their accommodations, but all Meegan could think about was Nick.

Kenna and Ally followed behind with arms linked as their group of six followed the Sendarian man. They would've been seven, but Liam had been asked to stay behind for a few extra tests.

Ally hadn't taken the news well after learning where they were—more specifically, where they weren't—and had Velcroed herself to Kenna. More than once, they'd both tried to reassure Ally they weren't in danger, even though Meegan had her doubts. She found it hard to believe that Kenna was okay with all this, because whenever they'd been in iffy situations in the past, she'd always found something to worry about.

Meegan glanced over her shoulder to check on her friends. What she wasn't expecting was Nick to be walking right behind Kenna and Ally. His eyes found hers. His lips parted, and he slowed his pace. She quickly faced forward, mentally kicking herself for making eye contact.

From behind, she heard Xander urge Nick to move. "Dude! Why are you stopping? Go!"

She needed to be smart. It was great and all that he was there, but the fact of the matter was they'd been taken by aliens. Aliens who had yet to reveal the truth about why they had brought them here. She needed to keep her head straight, even if her heart felt there was an opportunity here for her to fix things between her and Nick.

She could almost hear her mother's voice trying to reason with her heart. *"Let the boy be. You're not meant to be together. He is human, and you are not. Anumens live ten times longer and you'll only cause yourself more pain by watching him grow old and weak, and eventually die."*

No. She wasn't going to let her mother win. Not this time.

Maybe tomorrow, after a good night's sleep and after Kenna and I talk to Ulissa. Then I can think about how to fix things with Nick.

One good thing going for her was they hadn't flagged her or approached her about her vitals or anatomy being different from the others'. The concealment amula she'd cast at Prue's was working, but for how long? She had no idea how long they'd be here or if they'd ever return to Earth.

Their escort stopped at the end of a long hall. He punched in a long passcode next to a set of tall double doors stained the color of dark-roasted coffee beans. He then grabbed one of the black iron handles, twisted it, and using two hands, pushed open the heavy door. The iron hinges creaked, and they were led inside to an open space with a high ceiling.

The open space was softly lit by a thin strip of light embedded within the grout lines of the oversized stone tiles. The walls were white, like most of the walls she'd seen, except for the rear wall, which was solid glass and curved around to the left side of the room. The sun was setting, and Meegan could see the silhouette of treetops through the window wall. Behind two semicircular sofas facing one another, glass doors within the expansive glass wall opened onto a balcony. Toward the back of the open room, where their guide was currently pointing, were two farmhouse-style dining tables. One of the tables appeared to be filled with food and drinks.

The man from Medical waited until everyone was inside before another Sendarian entered and explained, "Your meal is set, and the Leadess will speak with you shortly."

Without waiting for a thank-you or asking if anyone had questions, both Sendarian men turned and exited the room, then locked the doors behind themselves.

"Now what?" Ally squeezed Kenna's arm. Meegan noticed Ally's brown spirals lacked their usual bounce.

"I guess we eat." Kenna steered her roommate toward the tables. Xander and another girl, someone she didn't know, followed. Meegan stayed close to Kenna and Ally, not wanting to be left with Nick.

There was a massive spread with a variety of cheeses, breads, some sort of pastry-like things, and other foods Meegan couldn't classify. Everything smelled and looked delicious.

"Is it safe?" the girl, now standing between Xander and Nick, asked. Meegan recalled overhearing someone calling her Julianna. Julianna scrunched her nose while holding up and inspecting a glazed roll that twisted into a stick. She was a tiny thing with modest curves and a set of meticulously groomed full eyebrows that matched her long, silky sable hair. Combine that with her warm skin tone, and Meegan could see her being Nick's type and wonder if there was something between them.

Julianna tossed the roll onto the table and crossed her arms. "I don't trust these *extranjeros*." Her words struck with a distinct Latina accent.

Xander slid onto the long bench, grabbed one of the white ceramic plates, and began filling it with food. "They didn't bring us all the way out here to kill us," the douchebag snapped and then, with an eye roll, added, "So sit down and relax, muchacha."

"Call me *muchacha* again and see what happens." Julianna narrowed her eyes.

"Ignore him," Ally sneered. "He's an ass."

Xander ignored the two women and picked up the roll Julianna had tossed. He bit into it with a wink. Meegan was fine with letting him be the taste tester, even though he was right. It was unlikely that they'd bring them all this way to poison them during their first meal.

"I guess we eat." Nick shrugged and sat across from Xander.

One by one, everyone sat and picked at the assortment, except for Julianna. She nibbled on a plain roll—the closest thing that resembled human food. The variety of new food had piqued Ally's culinary interests as she smelled, examined, and tore into one of almost everything on the table. Meegan selected a few pieces of fruit... or vegetables, she wasn't sure.

The conversation was mainly kept up by Xander, Julianna, and Nick throwing out questions that no one had answers to. Well, maybe Kenna. But her friend's lips were sealed shut, so they'd have to wait until someone came to talk to them.

"How come you're not wearing one of these bracelet things?" Xander asked Kenna with a mouthful of food.

"They told me it was broken, so they took it off."

Nick, who sat on the same bench as Meegan, but on the other side of Julianna, held out his wrist. "If it breaks, then that means it does something." Meegan noticed he needed a trim. His dark hair brushed low on his forehead.

Kenna nodded. "The medical people—"

"You mean aliens," Julianna corrected.

"Right. Well, they told me that it's a monitor to track our vitals in case our bodies have a reaction to the environment. I don't know, you'll have to ask one of them for specifics."

"I guess that's a good thing." Julianna finally ventured out of her comfort zone and picked up a cookie-looking thing topped with red jelly.

Meegan scanned the row of doors along the side wall from where they'd entered. She counted eight doors on the first floor, eight on the second, and a spiral ramp with a glass railing that connected the two floors in the far back corner.

Sixteen beds in Medical, now sixteen rooms. Huh, I wonder if we're missing some people?

"So, how do you know each other?" Xander pointed a sugary pastry from Nick to Julianna.

"We only recently met through a friend," Nick said. "We were out camping when a storm hit."

"Yeah, shit got weird after that. Some energy bubble trapped us." Julianna lowered her foot from where she had propped it on the bench. Her nose scrunched as if she'd remembered something. "Hey, speaking of camping. Wasn't Devaney with us? Where do you think she's at?"

Nick shrugged. "Maybe with Liam? I don't know."

Kenna shot Meegan a worrisome stare.

"Hey, Xander," Meegan chimed in and veered the conversation. "Didn't you say your new girlfriend knocked you out and dumped you in Prue's backyard? And didn't you say she had orange eyes like these aliens?"

"No. It was her sister, Cahleen. That bitch."

"Wait, you knew about them beforehand?" Julianna raised a dark eyebrow.

"Ah, no. That crazy psycho showed me her eyes two seconds before sticking a needle in my arm and knocking me out." Xander pushed his empty plate away and crossed his tan arms on the table.

"I woke up in the grass with these three, under the same stupid bubble."

Across the room, the double doors swung open and two Sendarian men dressed in black uniforms stepped inside. Everyone at the table stopped talking and stared. Two women walked in and made their way toward them. The elegant redheaded woman with orange eyes fit in with all the other orange-eyed beings they'd met, but not the woman by her side. That woman was tall, like professional basketball player tall, and her skin was paler than that of the other Sendarians. But what really stood out were her blue lips, eyes, and hair.

"Beannaith and welcome. My name is Breyah," the redheaded woman announced, "and this is my second-in-command and Lead of Security, Rian."

A reply of quiet hellos circled the table. Breyah was continuing her welcome when someone kicked Meegan in the shin. "Ow!"

Breyah paused mid-sentence.

"Sorry, banged my knee," Meegan said and then waited a few seconds, to avoid making it too obvious, before glancing at Kenna across the table.

Kenna's eyes were wide, and behind a hidden hand, she pointed down. Meegan lifted her hands and looked at the table to see what the problem was. Her plate was half-full. Not sure, she mouthed a subtle, "What's wrong?" Kenna reached across the table and rapidly tapped Meegan's finger. Meegan followed Kenna's finger to her mother's mood ring. It was a vibrant turquoise.

Obard.

She turned and looked at the pale woman with blue hair and blue eyes standing slightly behind Breyah.

No. It can't be.

There was no fight reaction, only flight. Meegan shot to her feet and scrambled from the bench, her plate crashing and shattering on the stone floor. "Get away from me!" She half skipped, half stumbled from the table until her back hit the glass wall. With her hands raised, she yelled, "She'll kill us all!"

The room fell silent, and everyone's attention was on Meegan, even Nick's. Kenna quickly grabbed Ally's arm and dragged her roommate over to Meegan, putting herself and Ally in front of their friend.

"Who is she?" Kenna demanded, pointing to the tall blue-haired woman.

Breyah's brows furrowed, and she gestured to the woman by her side. "This is Rian, I just explained that. Do you not remember Matthew mentioning her this morning? He asked where my tail was."

"Tail?" Rian snapped. "That gróntah called me your *tail*?"

"Shh, not now." Breyah moved closer but stopped when Meegan released another frantic scream. Breyah eased away and motioned toward the double doors. "We just wanted to see how you were all settling, and to bring up your friend."

Meegan, still cowering behind her friends, saw over Kenna's shoulder a man standing between the two Sendarian guards.

"Liam!" Kenna exclaimed under her breath but didn't budge from Meegan's side. Julianna, on the other hand, didn't hesitate. She jumped up from her seat and rushed over to him.

Meegan's gaze darted between the reunited friends and the Obard woman standing less than ten feet from her.

This can't be happening. Is she looking for me? For my family? I can't stay here.

"I'm not sure who you think I am," Rian tried to rationalize.

But Meegan was quick to cut her off. "You're the Obard. Hunters and—"

"Stop!" Kenna spun, grabbed Meegan's shoulders, and quietly warned, "You need to watch what you say."

Kenna was right. She needed to shut up and calm down. Acting out and talking like this would only raise questions. And explaining herself wasn't something she wanted to do, not now... not in front of Nick.

"What the hell is going on with you two?" Ally shuffled in closer. "I'm scared enough as it is. I don't need you two freaking out on me like this!"

Kenna straightened and faced Breyah. "I think she needs to rest. We all need to rest. Can the welcome speech wait until morning?"

Breyah nodded and addressed the group. "We're quite excited to have you all here with us. You're our guests, and we look forward to getting to know you all a bit better during your stay."

"So, we'll be going home?" Julianna asked.

"Of course. It's not our intention to keep you here against your will, but we'll talk more in the morning." Breyah glanced over to Meegan, Kenna, and Ally. "Beannaith," she said with a bow before turning to leave.

When they were gone, all eyes were on Meegan again. All except for Nick's. He sat staring at his plate, elbows resting on the table, hands clenched. Meegan could only imagine the embarrassment he must be feeling. She whispered to Kenna, "Get me the hell out of here."

"Ah, everything's okay. We'll be right back," Kenna explained while leading Meegan to the first room. Kenna was about to close the door when Ally appeared.

"We'll be right out," Kenna told her. "We just need a moment."

"I can't come in?"

"It's okay. She might as well know the truth," Meegan said from farther inside the room as she slumped into an armchair. "If the Obard are here, then none of us are safe."

Kenna swung the door open and let Ally in. Meegan caught a glimpse of Liam out in the common room and felt bad that Kenna hadn't had a chance to say hi. "You know, we can talk later if you want to go say hi to Liam. You haven't seen each other in forever. I bet he'd—"

"No." Kenna stopped Meegan from finishing and closed the door. "I can say hi after. Right now, we need to figure out what we're going to tell the others and what we're not going to tell them."

"Uh? What are you guys talking about?" Ally leaned against the arm of the two-seater sofa. "Why wouldn't we tell the others everything?"

"Ally, there's something you need to know about me, and that woman with the blue hair." Meegan inhaled a deep breath and tucked her legs up under herself in the armchair. "That woman, the one with the blue hair, her people hunted and almost wiped out my people."

"Your people?" Ally blinked several times before swallowing and sliding from the sofa's arm into the seat next to Kenna.

And here we go again. My parents are definitely going to ground me and send me to Aunt Bea's house for a very, very long time.

47

After showing Ally how to work the shower, Kenna sat on the edge of the bed and brushed Meegan's hair from her face. Their talk with Ally had gone better than expected. Though, she'd overreacted a bit when they told her about the hostile aliens hunting Meegan, her family, and others like them.

Kenna lifted the blanket up and over Meegan's shoulders and whispered, "We'll figure this out... together."

"I know," Meegan mumbled and reached for Kenna's hand. "Love you."

"Love you too. Now, get some rest. Ally will be out in a minute. She's going to sleep in here with you tonight."

"What about you?" Her voice was a mixture of exhaustion, concern, and gratefulness.

"I'll sleep in the next room over. No point in overcrowding the bed and sleeping like shit."

"Not going to argue with that, but stay close, please." Meegan closed her eyes, slid her hand free from Kenna's, and rolled over. "I bet you wish your geriatric recliner was here."

Kenna laughed. "Hells yeah, I do. I miss my chair."

"Tell Liam I say hi."

"And Nick? Should I tell him you say hi too?" Kenna sat there for a long moment, waiting for Meegan to answer, but she didn't.

Following Matthew's example, Kenna deactivated the holographic panel over the nook stocked with clothes, bathroom stuff, and extra linens. She pulled out one of the extra blankets before heading back out to the common room.

The lights in the grout between the stone tiles were set to a low glow. Kenna made her way over to the sitting area, where Xander and Nick were spaced out on one of the semicircular sofas while Julianna and Liam sat thigh to thigh on the other. Kenna wrapped the blanket over her shoulders, scooted past Xander, and slid into the seat next to Nick. He welcomed her with a hug and then stretched one arm along the top of the sofa.

She smiled at her old friend. "Hey, Liam."

"Hey, Stargirl. Your friend okay?"

"She's fine. Just tired. And confused. And frustrated."

"Aren't we all?" Julianna ran her fingers through the top of her hair. She flipped a section of it from one side to the other, creating a dark wave of hair across her head. "They haven't exactly told us why we're here."

"We're here because they selected us. They see value in us." Xander sipped the drink he was holding, smacked his lips after, and then rested it on his knee. "They could've taken anyone, but no. They picked us."

"Picked us for what?" Liam's gaze flicked to Kenna before coasting to Xander. "Don't you think it's odd that they picked people that know each other? It's always strangers that get thrown together."

"What the hell are you talking about? How do you know?" Xander scowled.

"Because that's what they do in the movies." Liam shrugged, and Julianna agreed.

Short hair looks good on him. I remember I used to joke with him about cutting his long girly hair. Makes it so I can see his blue eyes. Damn, his eyes are sexy. What the hell am I thinking? Now is not the time to be drooling or testing the waters.

Okay, so Breyah said they randomly picked us. Yet we're all somehow acquainted? How does us knowing each other play into her pirate story? Random, my ass.

"I don't know you... or you," Xander said while pointing to Liam and Julianna. "And I vaguely recall meeting you with this twirp's other half." He pointed at Nick, then nodded at Kenna.

"Meegan's my girlfriend, and yeah, we've met. Unfortunately."

Xander laughed, and before he took another sip, he asked, "Did anyone tell her she's your girlfriend?"

Nick jumped to his feet. The blanket sagged from Kenna's shoulders as she grabbed Nick to keep him from lunging.

Xander held his hands up in surrender. "Dude, you need to calm the fuck down." He set his glass on the coffee table, or makeshift coffee table. It was three sections of a tree trunk, cut and set close to one another. A coat of clear varnish had been poured over it to preserve its natural beauty.

"I'm going to bed," Xander said. "No point in sitting around and playing *guess why we're here* with you nubs." He pushed up from his seat, careful to avoid Nick, and sauntered off to the last door on the first floor.

"That guy's an ass," Julianna said.

"I never understood what Prue saw in him. He's got major ego problems." Nick slowly sat again, his eyes focused on the coffee table.

"You have no idea how right you are." Kenna readjusted the blanket and shivered. She hadn't realized the balcony doors were open until a cool breeze had swept in. "Have you guys gone out there yet?"

"Yeah, not much to see but trees, trees, and more trees." Julianna stood and slapped Liam lightly on his leg. "I'm going to head to bed too." She scanned the row of doors. "Which room should I take?"

Kenna pointed to the first two doors. "Ally and Meeg are in the first one, and I'm going to stay close and sleep in the second room if that's okay?"

"Fine by me." Julianna leaned over and whispered something in Liam's ear, after which he smiled and then briefly glanced in Kenna's direction.

"Night, Jules." Liam settled in his seat before resting one arm along the back of the cushion. "So, what should we talk about now?"

The chill in the air was flushed out by the warmth Kenna felt whenever he looked her way. Yet why did she feel so awkward? Maybe because she'd assumed if they ever saw one another again, they'd fall back into their old ways. But the more she thought about it, their *old ways* would've had them acting as if they were twelve. She felt stupid for assuming they were still close. Now, they were merely social media friends.

"Does your friend prefer Julianna or Jules?"

"Depends on if she likes you or not."

Over her shoulder, Kenna watched Liam's friend enter the third room and decided to stick with Julianna for now. "How long have you known her?"

"Since sophomore year of college. We've got the same taste in... uh, well"—one side of his lip curled into a blushing half-smile—"dating preferences."

Not competition. Noted.

"Well, she seems nice."

"She is." Liam's long lashes barely blinked during their brief exchange. She wished the arcstone allowed her to read minds, because it was killing her not knowing what he was thinking.

"Kenna." Nick leaned forward, elbows resting on his knees and fingers interlocked. "I heard what that woman, Breyah, said to you.

About how you two talked earlier in the day. How long were you awake before the rest of us?"

"Oh, you picked up on that?" She rolled in her bottom lip and grazed her teeth along the skin. How much should she tell them? If she didn't know them, she might not have told them, but she trusted these two guys with her life. "I actually woke up yesterday."

They both narrowed their eyes and immediately began throwing questions at her.

"Shush! I didn't want to get into it, especially around Xander. I don't trust him. But yeah, I woke up... don't ask how, I just did... and they put me in that room"—she pointed to the room Meegan and Ally were sleeping in—"with some guy named Matthew, who is also human. He's been living here with them for years. I don't know much more than that. Breyah promised me she'd explain everything once you guys were awake." That last part was a white lie, but there was no need to get into the pirate discussion when they'd only ask more questions Kenna didn't have answers to.

"We were camping with Devaney. Did they say if she was here?"

"No. I mean, yes." Kenna wasn't sure what to say. The truth, or at least a piece of the truth. "I saw her, but I guess there were some complications. Her body wasn't adjusting to the environment here. I..." She could see Liam's eyes glossing over. "I don't think she made it, but I'm not sure. They put her in stasis, back on the ship, until we go home."

Liam scooted closer to the edge of the sofa, elbows resting on his knees. "Oh man. I guess I didn't think about any of us dying out here." He swallowed, his Adam's Apple bobbing as he stared up at the glass ceiling, one hand dragging down his face. After a long pause, he looked at Kenna and Nick, eyes glossed over. "I didn't know her very well. She and Jules were only dating for like a month or two. I think. I can't remember."

"I didn't want to say anything earlier." Kenna glanced at Nick, and then out to the night sky. "This is already a lot to take in, being on an alien world and all. Plus, Breyah had asked me not to bring it up. It wasn't their fault. It was an accident, and they tried to save her."

Liam leaned into the sofa and exhaled a grieving sigh. "I'll tell Jules when the time is right. Their relationship might have been a recent thing, and possibly on the outs, but she wouldn't have wanted Devaney to die."

Nick rubbed one hand through his hair. "Oh man, that sucks. I'm sorry."

Liam squirmed in his seat and wiped under his eyes. "Thanks." He cleared his throat, and Kenna got the impression he wanted to talk about something else when he asked, "How's your friend? The one who freaked out earlier?"

"Meegan? Oh, well, she's not one to be away from her parents like this. And that blue-haired lady really spooked her. That's all."

"You sure?" Nick asked. "I can go and talk to her, even though she might not want to talk to me. I'm worried about her. Plus, we kind of need to clear the air. Find out where we stand."

"Nick, I know you mean well, but give her some time. Things are complicated, and besides, she already told me she plans on talking to you tomorrow." She patted his knee. "She's just being Meegan."

"I hope you're right." Nick pulled Kenna in for a hug and rested his head on top of hers. After a long moment, he released Kenna and got up. He yawned, then said, "I'm hitting the hay. See you two in the morning."

"Night, Nick." After the soft sound of a door shutting, Kenna glanced over at the open balcony doors. "Looks like a clear night."

"It does." Liam got to his feet and held his hand out to her. "Does Stargirl want to go take a closer look?"

At the stars or at him?

Oh, this is so not the time to be crushing. But then again, why not? We're on an alien planet... well, moon... and who knows if we'll ever get home to Earth.

She slid her hand into his and let him lead her out onto the balcony.

❀ ❁ ❀ ❁ ❀

After standing by the railing overlooking mounds of treetops blanketed with the moonlight for what seemed like an hour, they eventually moved to one of the double-seater lounge chairs on the balcony. The seats were cushioned with a white fabric that was almost too soft for the outdoors.

To the left of the full moon and three times bigger was a planet. It was beautiful and had a faint glow similar to moonlight. She recalled how Priomh was a moon and assumed the planet must've been Sendara. "I wonder how many moons Sendara has? You know, it's not uncommon for planets to have multiple moons."

Liam draped one arm over Kenna's shoulders. "I didn't know that."

The night air was crisp. She took off the blanket she'd been wearing like a cape and draped it over their legs while Liam squeezed her closer. The scene felt and looked like something straight out of a rom-com. They sat cozy under the blanket, beneath the stars, and laughed and reminisced about their childhood days. They talked about everything and anything except the fact that aliens had abducted them.

"I wrote God knows how many letters to you after you left," Liam said, "but I was too chickenshit to mail them. Figured you were enjoying your new life out in Florida. A new high school filled with guys who looked like they'd just walked off the set of Disney's latest teen-heartthrob movie."

She laughed at his assumptions, but in reality, she was sad he hadn't mailed those letters. "I wish you had. And I wish I could go back and write you a letter or two." The move and the anxiety she'd felt before her first day at her new school were a blur. "I guess I shut down and hid from the world. I was so angry and lost after we moved."

"But hey, here we are. Funny how things work out." His lips parted and she stared at his perfect white teeth.

The more they talked, the more she felt as if she'd been given a second chance. An opportunity to explore what could have been if she'd never left Kansas. She nuzzled in and he squeezed her tighter. For a moment, the conversation fell short and their focus shifted to the masterpiece splashed across the sky.

"I wish we lived closer. You know, back on Earth."

He wants us to be closer!

"Me too."

She tipped her head up to look at the unfamiliar cluster of stars.

"Kenna?" Liam asked softly.

"Yeah?" she answered, taking in the millions of twinkling stars above. When he didn't answer, she lowered her gaze and stared into his blue eyes. Normally, they were a light blue, but out here under the night sky they were darker and filled with mystery. She wanted nothing more than to dive in and rediscover everything about him.

He smiled and then licked his lower lip before leaning in. She didn't move but didn't resist either. She let him press his lips to hers and just as he was about to pull away, she lifted her chin and held the kiss a few seconds longer.

When they parted, she blinked several times, hoping their moment wasn't something she'd imagined. But he was looking down at her with the same hungry eyes.

That. Just. Happened!

"It's getting late, and we should probably get some sleep." He grinned and lifted his arm from behind her.

She wondered if he meant actual sleep or sleep as in together… in one bed… and not really sleeping.

"Uh-huh," she croaked. She cleared her throat and agreed. "It is getting late."

He was up and at the door, waiting, before Kenna could finish folding the blanket. He walked her to the second bedroom door and gave her a soft kiss on the cheek before saying goodnight. "I'll see you in the morning." His hands grazed her arms as he walked away. She slowly reached for the door latch and watched him enter the room three doors down.

Well, I guess he means actual sleep. He's probably just being a gentleman. He always was so sweet and respectful.

Inside her own room, while changing and getting ready for bed, she tried to convince herself that she was overthinking things again. In bed, she lay there and waited for a knock at the door, but no knock came.

Okay, well, now I'm confused. Why did he kiss me? Maybe it was just something he's been wanting to do since we were kids and now it's done. Or maybe he does want something more with me. Ugh... stop thinking about it and go to sleep.

She tried and tried, but that kiss was all she could think about until sleep finally overtook her. And when it did, Liam wasn't the one there waiting for her in her dreams.

Kenna got out of bed and tiptoed out into the common room. The lighting along the grout lines was off, and the sky outside the glass wall was pitch black. The only light came from a stone fireplace set off behind the semicircular sofas.

"I don't remember that being there?" She crept closer to the fire. "Hello?"

A man strode by her from behind. She yelped and jumped to the side. "Jesus, Ben, you scared the shit out of me."

He crouched in front of the fire and repositioned one of the engulfed logs with a long metal poker. Without turning, he asked, "What do you want?"

"What do I want? More like, why do we keep meeting like this?" She could feel his frustration as if it were her own. Her skin hummed with tension. She wasn't sure if it was him or her that felt like they wanted to throw or break something.

"I'm guessing it's the will of our goddess," Ben said, breaking the silence.

"Goddess?"

"Isoldesse."

"Ben, I don't think Isoldesse is—" But she stopped herself from saying something she might regret. Questioning the faith of others never went well on Earth, and probably wouldn't go well here either. "Okay, let's go with Isoldesse… for now." Kenna sat on one sofa, arms loosely crossed, one hand scratching her elbow. "Ben, are my friends and I safe here? Are your people going to hurt us?"

He twisted from his crouched position in front of the fire and faced her. "No. My sister is only continuing the work of our goddess. To check in and document the progress of the worlds Isoldesse mothered."

"Isoldesse *mothered* worlds? Worlds as in plural? What does that even mean?"

He rose, and she sensed his irritation growing like a forest fire. She couldn't read his thoughts, but the belittling emotions that emanated from his mood sank deep into her mind.

The fiery light outlined the line of his jaw. His fists clenched, arm muscles tense. "I shouldn't be here. Not with you."

"Ben, I don't understand." She got up, stepped closer, and shook her head. "Did I do something wrong? We need to talk about whatever this is. Why do we keep meeting in our dreams?"

He dropped the poker and it hit the stone floor with a loud *clang*. He marched in her direction, and she held her hands out, ready to stop him from leaving, but his body faded and vanished before he reached her.

None of this makes sense. He seemed so nice… so friendly.

In front of the glass wall, next to where the fireplace had been two seconds ago, she looked up at the stars. *The worlds Isoldesse mothered* looped in her mind. What did that mean? There were other worlds out there that Isoldesse visited? More questions for her and Meegan to ask Ulissa. They needed to find out exactly what Isoldesse had been doing on these worlds and why.

When her eyelids were too heavy to keep open, she trudged her way across the common room. She unlatched the handle for the second room in the long line of doors, eager to return to bed. The door swung open and there, standing on the other side of the door, pointing a long black sword at her head, was an Obard soldier.

Her body trembled, and she wanted to scream, but the shock of seeing an Obard soldier froze her. White smoke flowed from beneath its helmet. The smooth black glass of the faceplate hid the Obard's face. The Obard stepped out from under the doorway, and she mustered the strength to move her feet backward. But with every retreating shuffle, the Obard continued to close the space between them. The Obard lowered its arm, bringing the sword with it, while removing the helmet with its other hand. Kenna gasped when she saw Rian's face. Though, her skin wasn't her normal porcelain white but an icy blue that blended in with her hair, eyes, and lips. Small peaks of white smoke drifted from her skin.

"Are you going to kill me?"

Rian's blue lips curled up. "Fear this form but do not fear me. We're both questioning our purpose and should look to one another for answers. But you should know, I come to you now as a messenger. A leak from behind a locked door deep inside Rian's essence. She needs help to remember. Your help."

Kenna blinked and Rian no longer stood before her in the scaly black armor of the Obard soldiers, but instead she wore a fitted white dress. The black sword was replaced with a tablet-like device.

"We have both been lied to by those who love us. I've always wanted to know where I belong—do you not want to know where you belong?"

"I belong with my family, and my friends... on Earth," Kenna whispered but oddly, for the first time, she didn't fully believe herself or her words. Her head dipped, and she stared at the tile floor. *Where do I belong?* She'd always felt drawn to the stars. Was she meant to be here? Was that what the messenger was trying to tell her? The moment her thoughts cleared, and she went to ask, Rian was gone.

More riddles and more questions.

Fan-freaking-tastic.

48

"**I**'m heading to meet Rian in the Centrum," Breyah dictated. "Whenever you decide to crawl out of bed, meet us at Medical. Rian and Holt can update you on the docking station incident and about our two—well, now one—unexpected subjects. Thank you, brother. Your insight and expertise are appreciated. I know this is your time away from work, but when it comes to matters of our goddess, there's no time off."

"*Message sent to Captain Ganecht of the Rhaltan Enforcers.*"

"Thank you, Linc."

Breyah descended the center ramp that spiraled toward the main floor of the Centrum. The stone ramp spiraled like a piece of art with its glass railings. Her interneural assistant continued in her ear with new incoming messages and a summary of her daily agenda, but all Breyah could think about was how they'd lost one of the subjects yesterday.

Her death is on me. Even if she wasn't supposed to be here, the human girl's death is our fault. We should've taken more precautions before waking her.

The morning sun filled the grand Centrum from the open blue sky above, even with the energy barrier still active. She spotted Rian across the way, talking with Sabine by the skywalk entrance to the Aevo C building.

Hopefully Rian has found some answers.

"Linc, update on my search query for Geevi," she interrupted, causing Linc to pause and process her request. She continued to greet and wave to the many Sendarians going about their day, being sure to address each one by name.

"No progress to report. Your query to locate former Spiaire Gemma Vaudd will expire in ninety-eight hours. Would you like to submit a request for an extension?"

"No, but if I change my mind within those four days, I'll let you know."

"Understood."

As she got closer to her intended party, Breyah took a second to admire Rian's sense of fashion, something her second-in-command could pull off with little effort. Her skin was flawless, and the lines of her body were sculpted to a long and lean figure. Today, Rian wore wide-legged black pants with a fitted white halter top. Fabric, along with most manufactured goods, was limited when it came to pattern or color options. Though Rian enjoyed sparring and overseeing Priomh with Breyah, Breyah knew her friend's true passion was in the clothes she wore.

Thick silver bangles hugged Rian's neck and wrists. Her blue hair was twisted up, away from her face, while Sabine's hair was pulled into a tight, slick bun that sat low on her neck. Her assistant wore a plain tan dress that hit below her knees. Sabine's neck tilted up, as if she were looking for something high in the sky, while she talked to her fellow Sendarian.

"Beannaith," Breyah greeted them both.

"Beannaith," they said in unison—though Sabine added, "Leadess," to the end of her greeting.

"What has security discovered from the *Tarais*'s video recordings?" Breyah jumped straight to the point, hoping to start the day off with some good news.

"There was no unauthorized activity recorded on any of the glass surfaces throughout the ship," Rian reported. "The Commander has ordered a diagnostic team to do a manual scan of the ship's network. If someone did tamper with the network to redirect or loop video feed, they'll find the foreign code." Rian drew out a plac from under her arm. "So, for now, we have nothing."

Breyah's brows scrunched as she shook her head. "There has to be some evidence that someone was aboard the *Tarais* who shouldn't have been. We have proof—Prudence." Before either Rian or Sabine could respond, Breyah added, "Well, I'm happy to inform you that Bennach will be assisting you with your investigation." It was hard to sound happy, with the human's death still fresh in her mind, but she tried. "He's not officially on duty, but this is what he's trained for. Sniffing out clues."

"That is good news," Rian agreed, narrowing her blue eyes.

Oh, Isoldesse, she's giving me that look. How does she always know when something's bothering me?

"Y-yes," Sabine stuttered. Breyah and Rian both turned their attention to her. "His track record for uncovering certain truths precedes him." Her assistant's grin struggled to stay afloat while she shifted her weight from one hip to the other, a strange expression on her face.

"Are you still not feeling well, Sabine?" Breyah asked.

"I think I should go and see Holt." Sabine's shoulders dropped, and she pressed her plac flat to her chest. "If only for a quick checkup, and then I'll return to my duties."

"Oh, stop. Go see Holt and then if you need the remaining day to rest, take it. The Aevo C has resumed its normal proceedings, and with Bennach here to help Rian, we'll soon have that issue resolved as well."

Sabine nodded. "Thank you, my Leadess. Could I have your approval to silence my Linc so as not to be distracted?"

"What? No—" Rian began to object.

"It's fine. But please only silence, not deactivate. Then come first light tomorrow, report directly to Holt before heading up to Ops and Admin. I want to make sure you're feeling better before returning to work."

"I will. And thank you." Her plump cheeks flushed behind her faint freckles.

The moment she shuffled off, Rian turned to Breyah. "Something isn't right. There's no need to silence a Linc for a headache."

"Leave her be. She just lost her mother, and she doesn't travel through space well. It may take her a few days to ground her feet." They entered the Aevo C subject wing skywalk, Breyah's long dress brushing the stone floor. About halfway through the glass tunnel, Breyah whispered, "Now, I didn't want to say anything in front of Sabine, mainly because I don't know how much truth there is, but Princess Emmalyn has some kind of special transport ship. It's called a pinship and is supposedly en route back to Priomh from Earth."

"And?"

"And"—tears streamed down her cheeks—"she just informed me that Shea found one of the Spiaires. Seph's body."

"What?" Rian stopped and faced her Leadess. "What do you mean *his body?*"

Breyah swallowed the lump and wiped her eyes. "Shea was able to follow Seph's Linc tracker to his location." She shook her head. "I don't understand how or why, but he was dead."

Rian stomped away. Reaching the end of the skywalk, she slammed her fist into the wall. Without removing her fist, she pressed her forehead to the wall and cursed. "I'm going to kill whoever did this."

Breyah came up from behind and rested one hand on Rian's shoulder. "Are you good?"

Rian shook her head. "No, I'm not good, but if you're asking if I'm about to have an episode, then yes, I'm fine."

"Justice will be served, but we need to keep this quiet. We can mourn when he's back home. Emmalyn said Shea will have returned by day's end."

They continued the rest of the way in silence. Two of Rian's security guards stood watch outside the entrance to the subject holding wing. They were about to enter when Breyah asked, "Are you sure you want to go in there again? Subject fourteen might still be upset."

Rian held her chin high. "She can react however she wants. It's not the first or last time someone will react to how I look." Breyah's shoulders dropped and before she was able to comfort her friend, Rian added, "Besides, I'm hoping to find out more about who or what the Obard are. I put a request in with Archives to do a network search on the word *Obard*."

"And?" It was Breyah's turn to be anxious for some good news.

"They haven't gotten back to me yet. But I've instructed my Linc to prioritize anything coming in from Archives."

"Good, and let me know the minute you hear from them." Breyah nodded to the two security guards, who proceeded to open the double doors.

Breyah smiled, and before they entered the subject holding area, she said under her breath, "Well, let's hope this chat goes better than yesterday's."

49

U lissa's projection paced the foot of the bed while Kenna and Meegan sat on the side, both holding the arcstone. It was a good thing Ulissa had told them an alternative way to contact her, because Kenna hadn't seen one single mirror.

"So, what do you think these dreams mean? And why always with him?" Kenna asked.

"It is odd, but not unheard of." Ulissa faced her two young friends and explained, "I've heard stories of a pioras but have never witnessed one."

"*Pioras*, that sounds vaguely familiar," Meegan recalled like an attentive student. "It means *unexpected*, right? Like an accident?"

"Yes and no." Using two fingers, Ulissa raised Kenna's chin. The old woman might've been a projection, but Kenna could feel her touch. Tiny wrinkles creased in the outer corners of her brown eyes. "You may not be Anumen, but you are special."

Kenna cocked her head, pulling away from Ulissa. "Special isn't always a good thing."

"You have got to stop overthinking things!" Meegan jumped in. "Special means special. Everyone is special in one way or another." She faced Ulissa and gestured for her to continue.

"You are a wise and mysterious one, young Fawness." Ulissa narrowed her eyes at the young Anumen. With each graceful twist or shift, the beads of her gown glittered in the sunlight.

Meegan held up her hand not holding the arcstone. "Please, don't call me that."

"But you are—"

"No. We're not getting into that right now. Right now, you're going to explain this pioras."

Kenna stayed quiet, feeling bad that Ulissa was getting to know the don't-push-me side of her best friend. Something Kenna, Nick, and all their friends had to go through when getting acquainted with Meegan.

"There's not much to explain until I know more about Kenna's family or the person who sent her the arcstone. They'd have the answers to why Kenna's able to connect with others—specifically this Sendarian man. I'm guessing someone wove a little something extra into the amula that bound us."

"Extra?" Meegan locked eyes with Kenna. "Huh, interesting. Whoever wanted you to bond with the arcstone knew you weren't Anumen. They wanted a guarantee that you'd bond with the arcstone."

Ulissa nodded. "Risky, and not without consequences. Hence when side effects do happen, we call it *pioras*."

"But we don't know who sent this thing to me." Kenna glanced between Ulissa and Meegan. "Plus, it happened on Earth and now we're here."

Ulissa faced the glass wall and opened her arms to the warm sun. "The easiest way to find an answer is to retrace one's path."

"You mean to backtrack?" Kenna pursed her lips and recalled that morning. Her and Meegan sitting in the kitchen, then Darci showing up, and Darci giving—

No, it can't be. Not Darci.

And then Meegan, clearly thinking about that morning too, blurted out, "It was Darci. She's the one who gave you the package."

Kenna touched her temple, again trying to adjust the glasses she no longer needed. "But Darci said she found it."

"Well, let's play hypothetical," Meegan suggested. "What if she was lying?"

Why would she lie?

Then Breyah's repeated concern about Darci popped into Kenna's head. "You know, when I first met Breyah, before you woke up," she explained to Meegan, "she was asking me a lot of questions about Darci." She tried to imagine Darci fitting in here with her fair skin and strawberry-blonde hair. The only thing that didn't fit was her green eyes. "Is it possible Darci is one of them?"

"Anything's possible at this point." Meegan rubbed the top of the transessent stone still attached to her wrist.

"There's something else that happened in my dream last night. I saw—" Kenna was interrupted when the door opened. A commotion of voices from out in the common room filled the sleeping quarters.

"Hey, you two." Ally popped her head around the corner of the carwash-shower-room and came over to the two girls sitting on the bed.

Meegan released her grasp on the arcstone, and Kenna quickly draped the pendant stone around her neck. Meegan asked Ally, "What's up?" while Kenna turned to Ulissa. But the old woman had disappeared.

"We'll talk more later," Ulissa said in Kenna's mind.

Ally wore the same black V-neck shirt stocked in the clothing nook and the same style of tapered pants that both Kenna and Meegan had on.

"Those two women from last night are here, and they want to talk with everyone. One of them is that lady with the blue hair, so heads up, Meeg."

"I'm good, but if she comes near me, I can't make any promises."

"Just stay close to Kenna and me." Ally cupped Meegan's shoulder. "We won't let her anywhere near you."

"Neither will Nick," Kenna added with an elbow nudge. "But I don't think we have anything to worry about with that Rian lady out there."

"Really?" Meegan stopped short of the door. "Why's that?"

"She was in my dream last night too, or at least some version of her. She said she was a messenger. A leak from deep inside something hidden and locked up. She made it sound like we need to help…" Kenna paused, not sure how her friend would react. "…each other. Plus, I don't think she's dangerous."

"Well, we'll see about that." Meegan lifted her hand. The mood ring that'd been purple two minutes ago was now a bright turquoise. "If what Ben told you is true, and these Sendarians worship Isoldesse, then maybe there's a connection between whatever she was doing here and why there's an Obard here."

"Guys, hurry!" Ally waved them over.

"I'm sure between you, me, Ally, and Ulissa we can manage to figure out what the hell is going on." Kenna moved closer to the door, taking a quick second to see where Liam was.

"I hope so." Meegan followed Kenna and Ally out into the common room and over to the sitting area. The three girls lined up behind the sofa, Meegan between Ally and Kenna while Nick, Liam, and Julianna sat on the sofa.

Breyah and Rian walked into the room and everyone got quiet. Kenna quickly tapped Liam's shoulder and when he turned, she smiled and gave him a low-key wave. He mouthed a *hey* and mimicked her subtle wave before facing forward again.

Kenna then asked the trio, "Have you guys seen Xander?"

Nick shrugged and briefly shot Meegan a smile before looking away. Julianna also shrugged. It was Liam who answered, "Some short woman came and got him early this morning. He hasn't come back yet."

"He can stay gone for all I care," Julianna muttered.

"Maybe she was from Medical?" Meegan asked more as a thought out loud.

Julianna shook her head. "Nah, I don't think so. She was in a plain tan dress with shoes like these," she said and lifted her foot. Julianna was wearing the same Tom-like black canvas shoes that Kenna and everyone else had been given. "Except her shoes matched her dress color."

Kenna glanced at their group and noticed how they were all wearing the same black clothing. *Now we definitely look like subjects... or patients... or prisoners. God, I hope Ben was right and we're not in any danger.*

Breyah opened her arms and began her welcome speech... again. This time without Meegan's theatrics. The redheaded woman told her story about needing help to ward off the pirates, the same bullshit story she'd fed Kenna yesterday morning. When she finished, the frenzy of questions began.

Everyone but Kenna, Meegan, and Ally tossed out questions about *why them* and *what were they supposed to do to stop alien pirates* and *what if they didn't want to help* and *what would happen if the pirates couldn't be stopped.* Nick, Liam, and Julianna continued to talk over one another as if they were at a White House press meeting.

Kenna felt bad for the Sendarian woman, yet her composure and blank expression gave Kenna the impression she'd been here and done this before. Kenna was more interested in the Obard woman standing off to Breyah's side. She was staring intensely at her tablet.

"She's lying, right?" Meegan whispered while scratching her nose.

"Who? Breyah? I'm thinking yes, but I have no idea why. Maybe it's like a test to see how we'll react or what we'll do."

"Why bring a bunch of humans, who've barely lived an adult life, out here to see how we react to a story?" Ally whispered behind Meegan's back to Kenna. "What isn't she telling us?"

Kenna shrugged at the same time Breyah gestured for everyone to quiet down. "Please, I'll address your questions one at a time."

But before she could do anything of the sort, the Obard woman whispered in her ear. That was when Kenna noticed Ben, over in the doorway, next to one of the guards. Arms crossed against his waist-length dark gray jacket over a fitted black shirt. Orange eyes fixed on Kenna.

Kenna tugged Meegan's sleeve and tilted her head in his direction. Meegan casually looked to the doorway. "Jesus. That's Ben?" she whispered. "That's the guy you've been meeting up with in your dreams?"

"Uh-huh," Kenna nonchalantly affirmed while trying not to stare. But she couldn't help it. Not because he was movie-star material, but because she wanted to remind him that she was real and that he couldn't ignore or dismiss whatever was happening between them.

Breyah politely excused herself and followed the blue-haired woman over to Ben. Meegan stepped behind Kenna and pressed her forehead into Kenna's shoulder. Kenna tried to turn as she asked, "What are you doing?" but Meegan held her arms, preventing her from moving anywhere.

"Shield me."

She couldn't hear what Meegan said next, but she recognized the hum of her tone. Meegan was casting an amula.

"Really? Right now? Someone could see you."

"Shh, I'm trying to listen to what they're saying."

"You can do that?"

"Kenna, shh."

Kenna did her best to conceal her friend. Nick only glanced over in their direction once. Not Liam, though. He and Julianna were quietly talking to each other. She couldn't help but wonder if there was more to her and Liam's kiss last night, or more importantly... more kissing in their future.

I want to, yet only if he wants to. Because if he just wants to be friends, then that's cool too. But God, it's been so long. And to be with someone I know I'd get along with... uh, how great would that be?

Meegan stepped out from behind Kenna just as Breyah and Rian finished talking with Ben. In a low voice, Meegan said, "We need to go talk, like, ASAP."

"That bad?"

Meegan nodded.

Breyah quickly called everyone's attention again. "I'm sorry. There's been a development that needs my attention. I'll send for your afternoon meal and will return later to answer all your questions. My apologies."

Kenna watched Breyah leave. The Obard woman and Ben were already gone.

"What the hell was that?" Liam got to his feet and faced the group. "How are we supposed to fight space pirates?"

Kenna wanted to talk to him, to explain that she suspected it was a lie, but Meegan grabbed hold of her arm and dragged her off to their room. Ally was quick to follow. Once the door was shut and the three were alone, Meegan said, "We've got a problem and I don't think they're going to do anything. I mean, I can't say for sure, but I think we have to do something."

"Help who?" Ally asked.

"I overheard the Obard woman, Rian, telling Breyah and that guy Bennach—"

"You mean Ben?"

"Yeah, him. Anyway, I overheard Rian telling them that some archive department, whatever that is, received some kind of secret message asking for help."

"Help? But who…?" Kenna wasn't sure she wanted to finish her question. To be slapped with more alien drama. She nervously rubbed the silver disc on the necklace her mother had given her on her fourteenth birthday. She'd told Kenna that the cluster of circles engraved on the front meant *family*.

That word triggered a memory of her encounter last night with "messenger" Rian—the one from her dream. *"We both have been lied to by those who love us. I've always wanted to know where I belong—do you not want to know where you belong?"*

Lied to by those who love us.

Kenna released the silver disc while Ally picked at her fingernail and nervously finished Kenna's question. "Who needs help?"

"It's Darci, and she's in serious trouble."

50

They didn't speak again of Darci's message until they reached Breyah's office. Breyah closed the doors and activated her Linc's privacy setting so they wouldn't be disturbed while Rian transferred the Archive file request to the glass window behind Breyah's desk. Their silence weighed heavy while Breyah read Darci's message, but it also gave her a glimmer of hope that she'd see her Spiaires again.

Requesters: Darci MaGenach

Request Priority Status: High

File Title Being Requested: Need Immediate Help

Reason for File Request: Athru have taken us captive. Holding us in the old facility. Here with Eryn and Grace. Seph location unknown. Grace needs medical attention. Athru also

> holding two humans: subject ten and an
> unrelated human. They killed subject sixteen in
> docking station. Be advised, one they call
> Quaid is dangerous.
>
> File Request Timestamp: 3577.05.42/26:14:32

"What information can you tell us about this Athru group?" Breyah faced her brother.

Bennach's orange gaze flicked to Breyah before he picked up a plac from his sister's desk. "I need to report this."

Rian snatched the plac from him. "While you're here on Priomh, you'll do no such thing without the Leadess's approval."

He dropped his arms, balled his hands at his sides, and inched closer. "She's not my Leadess."

The temperature in the air dropped. The last thing Breyah needed right now was for Rian to have an episode. Bennach would then have two things to report to his Rhaltan superiors. "Enough!" She forced them apart, giving a slight head shake to Rian before leading Bennach away. "Please, we need your help in getting our people, and the two humans, out of there safely. We can discuss your report after we've gathered more information."

Ben relaxed his stance and nodded. "Fine, but after, I'm required to file an incident report. We've been tracking the Athru on Sendara for years now. At first they were a mere nuisance, bored predults trying to get some attention, but they've changed over the years. We believe three adult Sendarians have taken control of the Athru and have turned this rebel group into an actual threat against the Elemental Council and the royal family."

Why would anyone want to disrupt the entities put in place by our goddess? They're extensions of Isoldesse herself, to see that the Sendarian people abide by the Anumen Doctrine.

"When I called you," Bennach went on, "the day before I left to come to Priomh, my team and I had uncovered the identities of two of the three Athru rebel leaders. Quaid and—and his sister." Breyah caught the hitch in Bennach's voice as he omitted the woman's name. "Since they're siblings, we're assuming the third leader is their brother, Biryn. But we only have his name. There are no other records or images of Biryn. He's done well to stay off the Network, but that makes sense as they're originally from South Sendara."

"The Isle of Awry," Breyah said softly, feeling sorry for those there who had lost their faith in Isoldesse.

"Yes, that's what it's known as, but officially, it goes by South Sendara." With a concerned tone, Bennach continued, "Can you take a guess at which one is wanted by the Rhaltan for murder, theft, destruction...? The list goes on."

Both Breyah and Rian glanced at Darci's message. "Quaid," Rian answered. "Do you have any information on the woman?"

"No," he said without blinking.

He's lying. What is he hiding about this woman?

Bennach then added, "Darci saying Quaid's dangerous is an understatement. His criminal record is probably the longest I've ever seen." He held his hand out, and Rian handed over the plac. After a minute of tapping and swiping, he showed the plac to Breyah. "This is Quaid's official Rhaltan profile and record."

The man's orange eyes in the profile picture looked as if he'd seen his days of blood. Breyah's mind was quickly overwhelmed by the torment of what her friends were going through, how her Spiaires were out there with this man. What state would they find the Spiaires in? They needed to act quickly.

Rian must've been thinking the same thing, because she faced Breyah and said, "Let me take a small team out there. Then, after sunset, when it's dark, we can survey the situation. Once we've determined how many are there, we can decide on how to proceed."

From a clear section of the window, Breyah watched Sendarians talking and laughing in the courtyard below. She couldn't let this Quaid character and his rebels into their compound. There were families here with children and predults.

Rian pulled up an image on a new display screen to the right of Darci's message. "Here's a satellite image of the old facility." She zoomed in. "The most recent aerial image shows there's only one ship. An old decommissioned space-border ship."

"I can see it's old." Breyah peered at the rust-colored patches on the ship from the bird's-eye view.

Bennach assessed the image closer, his arms crossed and feet shoulder-width apart. She knew there was no way he'd pass on an opportunity to catch a bad guy, even if the territory was unfamiliar. When they'd been younger, and their parents asked her to watch him, she'd never been able to keep him indoors. He'd always found a way to get outside and explore the woods and the nearby lake.

She stared at the old facility. Dirt covered the rooftop, and green splotches of overgrowth claimed the corners of the roof. She pictured the old facility in her mind. A building that inspired most of the buildings she and Geevi designed, but on a smaller scale.

Isoldesse has every right to be angry with me. She built that facility for Sendarians to help her. Out of all the worlds she mothered, she chose Sendara, and I brushed it off as not enough. How could I be so selfish as to want more from our goddess?

Bennach pointed to the transport ship parked on the landing pad. "We can take one ship."

And here he goes.

"We?" Rian asked.

"Yes, *we*," Bennach said with a grin. "Now, show me where you keep your weapons."

51

T here was no way they'd be able to pull off a rescue mission without help. Kenna thought Meegan was crazy for even thinking they could do it on their own. Yeah, Meeg had magical powers, but they'd be sneaking out onto an alien moon completely blind as to where to go and how to get Darci out safely. Magical powers might not be enough to keep them alive.

Ally hadn't said a word since Meegan told them what she'd overheard between Breyah and the Obard woman. She'd cozied up in the corner of the two-seater sofa in the room, watching Kenna and Meegan go back and forth about what to do.

"Why wouldn't Breyah and her people send out a rescue team? Why do *we* have to go out there?" Kenna moved next to Meegan, who was staring out the window.

"Kenna, I can sneak us in and out without anyone knowing we're there. Their people may get hurt, but we can do it. You and me."

"*Listen to Fawness. You have loved ones out there who need you. I can sense them,*" Ulissa chimed in through Kenna's thoughts. "*But you'll need help.*"

Kenna dropped her head in defeat. "Ugh," she groaned and plopped onto the couch next to Ally. "Ulissa agrees that we should go."

"See!" Meegan said. "We just need to figure a way out—"

"She also says we're going to need help."

Meegan shook her head and muttered a string of *no*s. "I can't cast an amula if everyone's there, especially Nick."

"If we're going to do this, then we'll need a secret weapon, and that's you. In the event things go wrong, we'll need to get out of there quick. You're our best bet to make that happen, but I'm not going out there unless we bring the others."

"I'm not going at all." Ally curled her feet tighter under her legs.

Kenna wasn't surprised. Ally wasn't the adventurous, outdoorsy type. But Kenna also didn't want to leave Ally by herself. "We need to stay together."

"I'm not going out there. No way. I'd rather lock myself in here and take my chances with these nicer aliens, and not those dangerous aliens."

Meegan pulled Kenna aside. "I might be able to hide her. I can create an invisible wall over there." Meegan pointed to the corner past the end of the bed. "If needed, she can hide behind it and no one will see her."

"Yes! That'll be perfect! Please, don't drag me out there. I won't be any good to you if I'm freaking out the whole time. Might even make things worse." Ally jumped up from her seat and stood in the corner. "How long will the wall last?"

"At least into the night, maybe until morning. I can't say for sure." Meegan touched one spot on the white wall, then dragged her hand through the air in front of the corner and Ally, and before she touched the glass window, she said, "*Ganea troh balla.*"

"What does it mean?" Ally asked, her body slowly disappearing behind the invisible kitty-cornered wall.

"It basically means to create a concealed wall that you can walk through."

Ally stepped forward, and her body reappeared. "How freaking cool is this! Now I can stay here while you rescue Darci!"

"Can I try?" Kenna pushed past Ally and pressed her back into the corner. She faced her friends and said, "Uh, I can still see you. How come it's not working for me?"

"Well, we can't see you." Ally waved a hand in front of Kenna's face.

"Great," Meegan said. "Now that that's done, I think we should figure out how we plan to sneak out of here before telling the others anything."

Kenna stepped out from behind the invisible wall and smiled. "I know just the person to help us get out of here."

52

"**H**ey, Kenna, is Meegan in there?"
Meegan sensed Nick way before Kenna reached the door.
She couldn't hear what Kenna was saying, but it was probably
something to help prolong the inevitable, and she knew it was wrong
to have Kenna constantly be the one redirecting Nick.

She went over to the door, bracing herself for his gaze, then
opened the door all the way. Kenna stepped aside while Meegan's
eyes met his. "It's okay, Kenna. I think it's time we talk."

"You sure?"

"Yeah," Meegan said.

Ally came up from behind and led Kenna out the door. "Come
on, let's give them some privacy. Besides, you need to talk with
Liam and Julianna about that field trip you want to take."

After Ally and Kenna were gone, Meegan gestured with a nod
for Nick to come inside. He was a full foot taller than her. The
perfect height for him to rest his chin on top of her head. Something
he did… correction, he *used* to do often.

When the door shut, he turned to her, but she was quick to walk by and get comfortable in one of the armchairs. "It's good to see you."

He lowered himself into the seat across from her. His hair had grown out since their goodbye at the airport, and she wondered what else had changed over the past few weeks.

"Yeah, it's good to see you too," he said while rubbing the top of his hand. "Though, I wish it were under different circumstances. But here we are. On an alien world, about to fight space pirates."

She couldn't help but chuckle. *Space pirates. Geez, for such a highly advanced race, they're a bunch of shit storytellers.*

They sat there in an uncomfortable silence for a good thirty seconds or more before she finally asked, "How's the residency going? Everyone at the pharmacy nice?"

"Meeg, I don't want to talk about the internship at the hospital. I want to talk about us. You and me."

He's human and you're not. She tried to block out her mother's words, but the truth behind them was too loud to ignore. "Nick, I—"

He was on his feet before she could stop him, kneeling next to her chair. "Before you say anything…" He grabbed her hand, and the moment he touched her skin she almost gave in and tossed all of her common sense out the window. He pulled her hand closer and kissed her fingers. "You have to know that I love you, and I'll always love you. I don't know what happened and I don't care. I just want you to know that I'll always be here for you. Whether we're together or not."

Besides their obvious differences, time was also their enemy. Was she being selfish if she stayed with him for another few years before severing ties for real? He could still be with someone after— someone who could give him a normal life, with kids, and a mortgage, and family vacations. Something she could never give him.

"You don't understand." Her eyes welled, and she swallowed the heartbreaking words before she could spit them out.

I don't know what to do.

"Whatever's wrong, or whoever got into your head, you need to let me in. That's what couples do. They work together. It may not always be easy, and we're bound to have our disagreements, but I know I don't want to be with anyone else. You're it, Meeg. You're my anchor."

She pressed one hand to his cheek, and one after another, her teardrops fell. This was it. Her moment to decide, even though her heart had decided the second he walked into the room.

"I love you too."

His entire body relaxed and dropped two inches before he lunged up to kiss her. He combed his fingers through her long hair, gripping the base of her neck while she wrapped her arms around him. She'd made the decision and there was no going back.

An hour later, their clothes were scattered about, and the sheets on the bed were untucked and rearranged in a new direction. Meegan lay on her stomach, her head resting on his bare chest while he drew circles along her exposed shoulder.

I can't believe we just did that. Holy shit, Kenna's not going to believe me.

He bent forward and kissed the top of her head. "As much as I want to stay in here with you all day, we should probably go check and see what kind of food these aliens are serving before it's gone."

"Did you work up an appetite, Mr. Stempski?"

"Actually, I did. Thank you."

After several minutes of procrastinating, they both eventually crawled out of bed. She peeked a few glances while he dressed; his Florida tan was barely noticeable now and he seemed thinner, not by much but she could tell. Either their time apart had taken its toll on his physical health or the residency program in the pharmacy was more brutal than she'd thought.

Nick pulled her in for one more hug and kiss. "You ready?"

"I'll meet you out there in a second."

"Okay. Love you."

"Love you too," she replied with a smile. A genuine he's-all-mine smile.

When he opened the door, it only took a few seconds before Kenna came running in. She shut the door behind herself, stopping Meegan from leaving. Her gaze darted past Meegan and over to the blankets piled on the floor. "I can't see the bed, but I'm guessing it's a mess."

"Maybe." And then something happened that Meegan couldn't ever remember happening to her. The happiness and love that consumed her flushed to the surface of her skin, and she blushed. "My parents will probably disown me, but right now, I don't care."

"Okay, okay, but more importantly… did you tell him?"

"Does it make me a horrible person"—she emphasized the word *person*—"if I didn't?"

"No, but you did—you know—do it, right?"

They were having a best-friend moment. When you confide in that one person after doing something so special, so life changing, yet for some strange reason Kenna didn't seem as thrilled.

"You disapprove?"

Kenna shook her head. "God no. I think it's fantastic." There was the smile and the reaction Meegan was looking for. "But…"

Why does there have to be a but?

"But he has a right to know."

Meegan leaned against the wall behind her and rubbed her eyes with the heels of her palms. "I know, and I will… tell him. And if he ends up hating me, then we'll cross that bridge when it's time. But not tonight, Kenna. He's so happy and I'm so happy, and my parents aren't here to stop us from being together."

"Okay. You're right. And I'm beyond excited for you two." Kenna's grin grew, and she laughed. "I just wasn't expecting you to round the bases so fast."

"Funny, real funny. But I will tell him," Meegan said as she reached for the door handle. "Tomorrow. I promise."

53

Outside on the balcony, Kenna waited with everyone but Ally. She was in her room playing with Meegan's magic corner. They still had no idea where Xander was or when he would return, but Kenna got the feeling no one really cared. She couldn't blame them. He was an ass, and she'd never understood what Prue saw in him.

During their afternoon lunch, it didn't take much to convince Liam and Julianna to come along on their rescue mission, and Nick had said, "Anywhere Meegan goes, I go." So, they were all in, which eased Kenna's concern about venturing out alone.

"Who's this guy that's getting us out of here?" Liam scratched his arm, squinting in the late-afternoon sun. "And you're sure we can trust him?"

"Yeah, he's cool." Kenna looked past Liam and saw Meegan and Nick quietly talking by the glass railing. *I knew they'd work things out. But now that I know the truth, I can't help but feel guilty.*

He needs to know who and what she really is, especially now that they've crossed that line of intimacy.

Kenna shuffled off the tile she'd been standing on when she heard clicking and beeping from beneath her feet. Meegan and Nick jogged over to see; one of the oversized stone tiles sank and then slid beneath the floor of the balcony.

Matthew popped his head up through the opening. Beads of sweat glistened along his temples. "Ready to go see some real live space pirates?"

One by one, they climbed the retractable ladder to the grounds below. Good thing the balcony was on the second floor of this building. Kenna hated heights and probably would've canceled the entire mission if she had to climb down any farther than one story.

On the ground, Kenna watched as Matthew wiped his forehead. "You nervous, or is this heat getting to you?"

"A little of both," he said, smiling. "I'm used to the warm weather. What I don't want is trouble from Breyah or Rian."

A pang of guilt pinched at Kenna's gut. It wasn't her intention to get Matthew in trouble, but it was a risk she was willing to take to save her friend. To reassure her new friend, she said, "I bet we can get there and back before dark. No one will even suspect we're gone."

"I hope so. Come on, my transport vehicle is this way." Matthew jogged alongside the horizontal wooden slats lining the building. Kenna hurried to follow, as did everyone else, trailing behind in a single line. "Good thing Holt upped my security clearance because the protection barrier is up. We'll have to use the emergency tunnels to get out of the compound."

When Kenna had first talked to Matthew about helping them, she'd used Breyah's space-pirate story but twisted the narrative. She'd told him there were pirates hiding out by some old research facility and they'd taken something from Breyah. Breyah had asked the humans to figure out a way to get out there and retrieve what the pirates had stolen. Matthew was more than happy to help execute their escape.

They continued jogging, and Matthew laughed. "I wish I could see the look on Rian's face when she learns that it was me who helped you complete your Aevo C mission. She'll owe me drinks for a full season."

She was curious to know what an Aevo C mission was, but instead asked, "How dangerous are these pirates?"

"Not that smart. More bark than bite. I've only come across them one other time."

Kenna turned the corner and spotted a large SUV-like vehicle. The thought that Matthew was willing to help them without consulting Breyah first added to her doubts. *But what if the pirate story isn't a lie? What if we're going out there to face a real threat?* She wasn't sure she was ready to put herself or anyone else in danger.

The extended vehicle, with its six wheels and a small open bed in the rear, was parked with its front half up on the grass. Kenna couldn't imagine the Sendarians being happy about Matthew's parking job. As they got closer, Kenna could see that the bottom half of the vehicle was constructed with a dark metallic material while the top portion was framed with plates of tinted glass.

"This road"—Matthew pointed—"is mainly used for the gardeners and the foragers, but we'll use it to get to the tunnel."

"I call shotgun," Julianna yelled and ran to the front passenger side.

Everyone climbed in while Matthew got comfy in the driver's seat. Meegan and Nick sat in the third row while Liam slid over on the second-row bench seat, and when he patted the seat next to himself, Kenna's heart beat faster.

"Come on, Stargirl. I'm excited to see what an alien moon looks like."

His smile brought memories of last night and their kiss. *Oh God, I hope he meant what he said about wishing we lived closer. I think we'd be a cute couple. Something to explore, later... if we survive this.* Kenna pressed her palm to the warm glass of the vehicle. *Oh, please let us survive whatever's out there on this alien world.*

Before she climbed in, she shielded her eyes from the afternoon sun and looked up to the glass wall of their lodgings. Ally was there watching them, and when she waved, Kenna gave her a thumbs-up. She hoped the gesture reassured her roommate that everything would be okay.

No worries, no worries at all. Kenna inhaled and filled her lungs with fresh alien air before letting it all out with a slight shoulder slump. A mixture of excitement and worry swirled inside her gut. *Oh geez, what have we gotten ourselves into?*

After she climbed in and closed the door, Matthew started the vehicle, and they jerked to a racing speed down the dirt road toward an enormous hole burrowed in the side of a hill. There in the dark, a hand squeezed hers, and when they emerged back out into the daylight, the feeling was gone. Though, Liam didn't look as if he'd reached over and grabbed her hand, because he was busy staring out the window, admiring the wooded forest.

"*I'm here with you.*" Ulissa's raspy voice spoke inside Kenna's mind as she squeezed Kenna's hand once more.

54

Gemma sat at the long mess table next to Micah, who was picking at the rust along the crevices. He seemed to be lost without his plac ever since he'd disassembled it for parts to fix Logan's outdated device. The metal bench was uncomfortable and wobbly whenever Gemma shifted in her seat. Logan was on the other side of the room, leaning against the wall, laughing and talking with a few Athru men. One of the men, with long red hair and several broken teeth, was Quaid's pilots. Logan told Gemma he planned to use his comradery to try and weasel out whatever plans the Beast had for them over the next few days. Gemma was almost impressed with his acting skills.

When Quaid strode in with two Athru men tailing him, everyone in the common area fell silent. He snapped his fingers at the pilot and gave him a curt nod. The man acknowledged Quaid's silent orders with a devious smile before jetting out of the common area.

Gemma locked eyes with Logan, who in return feigned the slightest shrug.

Well, he better have learned something useful. All that jibber-jabbering.

"Listen up!" Quaid spread his arms wide. "After tonight's raid we'll return home to the Southern Sendara Isles with our bounty!"

What raid? When did he say anything about raiding the Priomh compound?

The room cheered, and one person called out, "And what of the princess?"

Yes, what of her?

"If the pint-size taut is there, then we'll take her too." Quaid circled the room, dagger drawn and pointed out to his crew. "But I want the transessent bracers and the tools needed to attach them. I've also heard there is a Rhaltan Enforcer in their midst. I want him too—alive, not dead."

The Rhaltan are here, on Priomh? Are they looking for me? What does Quaid want with a Rhaltan Enforcer, and how is he more important than the princess?

Micah side-glanced a questioning look to his sister, and Gemma whispered, "I didn't reactivate my Linc, I swear."

"Then why are there Rhaltan here?"

"I don't know, but we need to—"

"Gemma!" Quaid bellowed. "Fetch me one of your captives. Not the weak Spiaire. A strong one. I think we'll have some fun before we head out. Aye?" Quaid spun the dagger in his hand. When it stopped, he pointed it at Gemma and waved it at her. "Go now."

Thank Isoldesse! Now's our chance to make a run for it. I'm so done with this lunatic.

Without hesitation, she and Micah hurried from the room. The grated floor clanked with each hastened step as they tore through the old ship. Gemma rolled her eyes as she heard Quaid yell, "Who wants the first round?" and a fresh uproar erupted through the ship's corridors.

Outside on the landing pad, Gemma asked, "Did you get ahold of Anora?"

Jogging alongside Gemma, Micah checked his watch. "Yes. She's sending a transport shuttle, and soon. We're to rendezvous out in the clearing. She wants the captives. Cahleen's guarding them out in the woods by the edge of the field. I told her to wait out of sight until we get there."

"Perfect, let's go then," Gemma said, veering away from the old building and toward the woods, but Micah hollered for her to wait.

"I need to grab my bag from the cell corridor and then we can head out there. Logan knows to meet us there."

Gemma turned and hurried to follow Micah into the old research building. "Fine, but we need to be quick. Quaid's waiting for us to bring one of the Spiaires."

They entered the building, and inside the large foyer they ran into Sabine. Gemma had never seen Sabine in pants, but here she was, dressed as if she was ready for a hike in the woods, sporting brown cargo pants with a white shirt that was snug around her midsection, and a khaki-colored vest. A large satchel hung from her shoulder.

"I was just looking for you." Sabine glanced over at the door leading to the subject holding cells. "Where's everyone?"

"And where do you think you're going?" Gemma snorted, eyeing Sabine's outfit.

"Logan messaged me that Anora was sending a transport shuttle. You're not leaving without me."

"You're willing to permanently leave your life on Priomh behind?" Gemma found it hard to believe she'd be willing to walk away from a position she'd held for most of her adult life.

Micah moved past the two Sendarian women and disappeared behind the door toward the cells.

"Packed and ready." Sabine twisted her shoulder and patted her bag. "Anora has opened my eyes to the truth. Sendara has been suppressed for long enough. I want to help restore what Isoldesse would've wanted for our people. To evolve is inevitable."

Gemma crossed her arms and raised an eyebrow. "Yes, you're not wrong, but are you sure you can handle what's expected of you?"

Sabine narrowed her orange eyes. "I thought I proved myself on Earth. I can handle whatever the Athru have got planned." Sabine's plump cheeks lifted, and her white teeth gleamed. "You know, you should be a bit nicer to me, especially because I brought you a gift."

Gemma ran her fingers along the tail of her braid, her interest now piqued. "What kind of gift?"

"The kind that earns me your trust." Sabine spun on her toes and made her way toward the subject cells. "It's this way."

"Trust isn't something you can buy," Gemma retorted as she followed Sabine toward the cell wing. *Though, I do like gifts.*

55

The first half hour flew by with little conversation. Everyone's attention was plastered to the scene outside their window. Kenna wasn't sure what to expect, and even though her mind was compiling a list of potentially dangerous things that could kill them, the scientific researcher in her was giddy to get out there and explore an alien world.

Every so often, she'd glance over at Liam, who was also gawking out his side of the vehicle's enclosed glass top. In the back seat, Nick had one arm around Meegan while she leaned into his body. They were smiling, laughing, and pointing at things they saw as Matthew sped through the forest.

Kenna faced her window again and wondered what life would be like if they lived here. This world didn't seem too different from Earth. The forest outside looked like a forest. The bark of the trees was brown, the leaves green. The two worlds and their similarities continued to baffle Kenna, and she wondered how many other sustainable worlds in the galaxy resembled Earth.

When they approached a break in the forest, Kenna gasped at her first animal sighting. Grazing in the field were deer-like animals with their young. They were big—like, moose big—and had the same light brown coloring with white spots along their hind legs. Though unlike a deer, their bodies were bulkier like an ox, as were their legs and hoofs. A few had short, antlers pointing forward instead of up between their perked ears.

"Maybe we should've brought some weapons," Kenna muttered as the largest of the herd turned his head, locking his gaze on their passing vehicle.

"Yeah," Liam agreed. "I think I saw a black saber-toothed tiger with some serious sharp canines, but like half the size, and it had these white markings circling its neck." He scooted forward in his seat and tapped Matthew on the shoulder. "Hey, did you bring any weapons?"

"Well, Sendarians don't use firearms, and don't ask why. It's a long story. An interesting one, but a lengthy one. It has to do with—"

"Matthew, the weapons? Do you have any?" Kenna politely shouted over the roar of the engine.

"Yeah, yeah, I brought a few things for you guys." He adjusted his hands on the steering wheel, which was more like two curved handlebars connected by a center crossbar, before yelling over his shoulder, "Not much farther. Maybe ten or fifteen minutes."

Almost there. Butterflies swirled in her stomach. Soon they'd be out there, facing who knows what dangers.

Liam nudged her arm with his elbow. "Hey, you're not nervous, are you?"

Her eyebrows tightened together, and she scoffed. "Hell yeah, I'm nervous. If you recall from all those times you forced me to go exploring the fields behind your parents' house in Kansas, I'm not exactly the adventurous type."

He laughed, but his amusement died, and his gaze drifted to the front window. "I'd be lying if I said I *wasn't* scared, but we can do this—together. All of us. We can find your friend and whoever else they took."

And besides scary-ass alien animals, that's the other thing I'm worried about. Who are "they" and why did they kidnap Darci? How much danger are we walking into? I'm crossing my fingers they're the kind of bad guys from a PG-13 TV show and not TV-MA.

Oh my freaking God... What did we get ourselves into?

"I hope you're right." Kenna tipped her head up and rested it against the headrest. Again, she felt a hand wrap around hers, but when she looked, it was Liam's. His touch melted away any nervous thoughts, but a second later, the vehicle dipped and took a sharp left. Kenna's body jerked to the right, hitting the door hard and pulling her hand from Liam's. "Ow! Easy on the potholes!"

"Sorry!" Matthew shot an apologetic look at Kenna through the rearview mirror, which stretched the length of the front window.

She rubbed her shoulder and adjusted herself in her seat again. Liam had returned to the scene outside his window, one hand pressed to the seat in front of him for support.

From behind, Meegan arched over the seat and said, "Nick and I were just talking, and we think later tonight we should all sleep out on the balcony. You know, after we're done rescuing Darci."

"You make it sound like we're running out for a quick errand." Kenna twisted in her seat and faced Meegan. "You're that confident that whatever we're about to face won't be dangerous or get us killed?"

It'd been a while since Kenna had seen Meegan this happy, and it was nice, but also concerning. She'd never known her friend to be this adventurous and wondered if this was another side of her secret Anumen life. All Kenna knew was that they needed to be careful. All of them, even Meegan. They knew nothing about what they were going up against, and that scared Kenna—the not knowing.

"We got this," Meegan said. "Besides, if we need to, we can split up. Then I'll be able to do that thing we talked about."

"What thing?" Liam's attention was now on the girls' hushed conversation.

"What? Oh, it's nothing." Meegan shook a hand at him before sliding back into her seat next to Nick.

Liam stared at Kenna, waiting for an answer. With a shrug, she said, "Ignore her. She's seen way too many mystery movies." It killed her to turn away from him and stare out her window, because she wanted to talk more—to get to know him all over again. To know if his favorite foods were still olives, tacos, and Creamsicles, or if he still only read books with dogs in them. She wanted to talk about anything not related to alien magic or alien worlds. But evading his questions would only fuel his curiosity. So, for now, Kenna stared out into the rhythmic scene of tree after tree.

The sun started to set behind the thinning tree line. It would be dark soon, and she wasn't thrilled about being out in these woods past dark. They needed to get to this so-called old facility, find Darci, and then get the hell out of there before nightfall.

I don't even want to imagine what kind of nocturnal creatures are out there.

To distract herself from overthinking about what could go wrong, she thought about what they'd do once they'd returned. She planned to sit Meegan and Darci down in the same room with her and Ally. No more lies between them, especially if what they suspected was true—that Darci was one of these Sendarians.

Kenna rubbed the arcstone beneath her shirt. If they were going to get Darci to open up, they needed to be honest with her too. That meant Meegan would have to do some revealing as well. Kenna was convinced if everyone shared what they knew, they'd be able to figure out the connection between Meegan's world and the Sendarian world.

No more lies.

That included the truth about where the arcstone had come from, and if their suspicions were right, why Darci had given it to Kenna.

56

"Where are they?" Breyah faced her Lead of Security.

Rian strode in from out on the balcony. "The emergency hatch out there is open."

"What? There's no way they could've known how to access the escape hatch."

Bennach opened one of the bedroom doors. There was a loud crash, followed by the sound of feet running along the hardwood. Once inside the bedroom, Breyah saw a broken mug beneath the provision's alcove.

Bennach touched one finger to the black liquid and then immediately stood. With narrowed eyes he scanned the room. "It's still hot."

Rian walked out of the washroom, shook her head at Breyah, and made her way over to the exterior glass wall. "Linc, show me the video feeds for the common area and all sixteen rooms within the Aevo C subject sector." The window tinted, blocking out the afternoon sun as one by one, seventeen display screens opened along the glass. "Linc, go back one hour."

Nothing.

Rian commanded, "Go back two hours."

Breyah watched the recordings, specifically of the room they were standing in. "There." She pointed to the screen with subjects thirteen, fourteen, and fifteen in it.

Rian closed out everything but the one display screen. She enlarged the perimeters and identified the subjects on the video recording as Ally, Meegan, and Kenna. Bennach approached to watch just as subject fourteen, Meegan, moved one hand across a small section of the room's corner, fingers pinched as if she were stretching an invisible string. A second later, subject thirteen, Ally, who'd been standing in the corner, disappeared. Rian, Breyah, and Bennach all turned their heads and stared at the corner.

"What was that? Where did she go?" Breyah moved closer to the end of the bed.

There was a rustling sound before someone called out, "Please, don't hurt me. I'm coming out now." Ally appeared out of thin air from her hiding spot.

"How did you do that?" Breyah asked while Rian and Bennach inspected the corner area.

"Oh, that. That's nothing. Just a minor trick we humans can do. I didn't want to go with the oth—"

"Go? Where did they go?" Rian cut Ally off while Bennach continued to stick his hand in and out of the cloaked area.

"Uh, well… please don't get mad but… uh, they went to rescue our friend Darci."

Goose bumps pimpled along the girl's brown skin. Breyah grabbed a blanket from the end of the bed and draped it over Ally's quivering body. "You don't have to be afraid of us, but your friends have put themselves in extreme danger going out there alone."

Breyah twisted on the bed and faced Rian with furrowed brows. "I still don't understand how they could've gotten out?"

"They're not alone." Ally sucked in her bottom lip. "Some guy named Matthew is helping them." The human girl was quick to explain after Rian groaned a frustrated sigh. "He only helped because Kenna, well... she sort of lied to him. She told him they needed to get to some old facility and face those space pirates you were talking about. He doesn't know why they're really going out there."

Rian rolled her blue eyes and cursed. "I knew we shouldn't have increased that loggie's security clearance. He's the one who opened the hatch out on the balcony!"

"Yes, I see that now. But in his defense, he was only trying to help."

"This is a serious problem," Bennach said, cutting in. "If the humans try to face Quaid, I can guarantee you things won't end well."

We've already lost one human life, while another recovers from a stabbing. We cannot lose any more lives.

With a decisive nod to her brother, she said, "Take Rian and go now."

Rian explained to Bennach as they left the room that she needed to change. "I'll meet you in the Centrum in twenty minutes."

He nodded, and they were out the door. Breyah leaned in and half hugged Ally with one arm. "Not to worry. Your friends will be fine. Rian and Bennach are two of the best trackers and fighters I know."

She prayed to Isoldesse that time was on their side, and that Quaid wouldn't discover the humans. Ally trembled next to her and Breyah squeezed the girl again, hoping to reassure her. "Now, while we wait, tell me more about this Earth magic."

57

When the vehicle came to a skidding stop, Kenna braced herself by stiff-arming the front passenger seat. Dust billowed outside their windows while Matthew swiveled in his seat. "Everyone okay? Sorry about that! But it looks like the road ahead is blocked off by overgrowth."

The brown cloud surrounding them settled, and Kenna could see out the front window that Matthew was right. They'd have to walk the rest of the way.

Holy mother of... We're really going out there. I swear those scary rhino-looking deer and miniature saber-tooth tigers better stay clear.

Once everyone climbed out of the oversized SUV-glass-tank-like vehicle, Nick asked, "How much farther?"

"Uhm, let's see." Matthew squinted and circled in one spot, taking in their location. There was a field off to their left, but it was the cluster of vines and brush blocking the end of the road that he pointed to. "It's that way... I think. Sorry, I haven't been out this way for a long time."

Meegan turned to Kenna and mouthed the words *he thinks* with a concerned expression.

He then lifted the rear hatch of the vehicle and everyone circled closer. He opened a compartment beneath the cargo-area floorboard and pulled out a black duffel. It was filled with wooden batons and thinner, more flexible sticks that resembled old plastic car antennas.

"Everyone take one," Matthew instructed. "The wooden batons are lightweight but pack a hard hit, while these"—he pulled out one of the antenna-looking sticks—"are lashers." He grabbed the tapered end and bowed it into an arch. When he released the end, it flicked back to its upright position.

Julianna, Nick, and Liam went for the batons, and since Kenna didn't think she'd be able to hit anything hard enough with the baton, she went for the lasher. Meegan was last and picked out one of the lashers too. Kenna wasn't super impressed with their weapons, but on the positive side, it was better than nothing. Also, it was comforting to know no one would be firing bullets or ray guns at them.

Matthew led the way with Julianna close behind. Liam touched Kenna's elbow and said, "Stay close to me, Stargirl. We don't know what's out there."

Her heart did a flip, and she nodded as they walked along the dirt road. Tall grass from the field lined one side of the road, and trees from the forest stretched along the other side. There was a familiar scent in the air, and Kenna wondered if it came from the small green flowers camouflaged among the leaves of the trees.

"What's that fragrance?" she asked Matthew as they reached the end of the road.

He reached up and plucked a flower from a nearby branch. The green flower immediately turned a bright yellow. "It's the Hiccum flowers. They're all over the place. Here and on Sendara."

Meegan came up and held out her hand. Matthew placed the yellow flower in her palm before stepping over a log and into the woods. Julianna, Liam, and Nick followed, and when the two girls were alone, Meegan held up the flower and looked it over. "We had these exact flowers on Anuminis. But we called them *Ittums*. They have special healing properties and…" She pursed her lips and dropped the Hiccum flower to the dirt road.

"And what?" Kenna prodded.

Meegan started for the forest and Kenna followed. The Hiccum flowers, or Ittums, were on every tree. Meegan stopped and whispered, "Those Ittums are the reason Anumens age slower. It took a long time to take effect, but after generations of being subjected to the flower's pollen, our people began to live longer."

"Well, how the heck did these flowers end up here?"

Meegan shrugged. "I'm guessing Isoldesse has something to do with it. Why, though? I haven't got the faintest clue."

"Hey, don't fall behind," Matthew yelled while holding up a branch for Julianna to duck under.

These flowers must be the reason Matthew hasn't aged the past fifty years and still looks like he's in his late twenties.

Nick waited by a fallen log and when Kenna and Meegan reached him, Kenna continued while her friend hung behind with Nick. Daylight was dwindling and so was the eighty-degree heat. A vibrant blueish-green bird the size of a robin sang from a nearby branch. Its beak curved beneath black button eyes.

So far, so good. Maybe this will be an in-and-out rescue.

Kenna picked up the pace and caught up to Liam. He smiled and gestured for her to take the lead. She watched her steps while absorbing their alien surroundings. For such a lush terrain, the lack of bugs surprised her.

Maybe when the Sendarians first built this place, insects weren't on their checklist of animals to move to live on the moon.

But if there are no bugs, then what do the birds eat?

And how long do we have until it's nighttime? How many hours are there in a day on this moon?

I wonder what this moon's rotation is around their sun.

Kenna tripped on a root, but before she face-planted, Liam's hands caught her around her waist. He helped her steady herself before letting go.

Ugh, I wish my mind weren't so all over the place. I'm going to end up making an ass out of myself in front of Liam.

"Thank you."

"Happy to help," he replied with a smile.

Always the gentleman. How was it possible that she could be scared and elated at the same time?

"*You're getting close,*" Ulissa's voice said in Kenna's mind. "*I can sense their essences. All are strong, though there is one that is weak but not life threateningly so.*"

Hold on, Darci, Kenna thought. *We're almost there.*

Ten minutes more of trudging through the woods, and they finally caught sight of the old facility building. They hid behind a cluster of boulders along the forest's edge. The two-story structure looked more like an abandoned elementary school or town hall with its brick-red exterior and wooden-framed windows. Thick, spiky vines crawled up the front walls of the building while roots and weeds claimed the front courtyard.

When one of the large front double doors swung open, everyone ducked behind a nearby boulder. Kenna peeked over the top to see a man with a baseball cap and a backpack over his shoulder. He was jogging in their direction.

"He's coming this way." She motioned for everyone to move around the large rock out of sight.

He didn't seem to notice them as he ran past the rock and out into the same woods they'd just come from. Meegan tugged on Kenna's arm. "Hey, that's the dude who came to Prue's house. The one Ally and I were talking to at the front door. Remember that guy?"

"Yeah, I remember him, but I never saw his face." Kenna watched the man until he disappeared. "You were right—he was lying to you."

"What if Prue's in there too?"

"That would be bad. Very, *very* bad." Kenna surveyed the front of the building again. "We have to get in there and help them."

"What do we do?" Nick moved closer to the girls, one shoulder pressed to the boulder. "Do we follow that guy or go inside?"

"We stick to the plan." Julianna waved for everyone to follow as she took the lead. One by one, they ran across the remnants of a small courtyard that had succumbed to years of neglect. At the front entrance, a layer of caked dirt covered the glass doors.

Everyone huddled close. Kenna lingered behind Liam and Meegan, still questioning if they were doing the right thing. *Maybe I should offer to wait outside. Keep watch or something?*

But then Liam nudged Kenna's shoulder. He smirked and cocked his head toward the doors. "You ready for this?"

She gave him a shaky thumbs-up while Matthew continued talking about the inside layout. "The entryway leads to an open lobby area. We'll have to listen for the pirates once inside. You know what you're looking for, right?"

"Yeah, yeah, we know," Meegan answered before Kenna could confess the truth as to why they were there.

"Remember, stay close," Liam whispered to Kenna while grabbing her hand.

Liam wasn't a big guy, but his grasp felt strong and protective. A sense of security washed over her, easing her jittery nerves.

"We need to watch each other's backs and stay alert." Julianna lifted her baton. "Only use force if needed, and I say we wait until the pirates clear the room before making our move."

I wish I could be as cool under pressure as Julianna. Good thing she's here to help take charge and look after everyone.

"I like that idea." Matthew scratched the side of his buzz cut, and before he could add anything else, a deep, hoarse voice caught them off guard.

"And who do we have here?"

Everyone jumped and scrambled against the doors. Kenna gripped her lasher while Nick and Liam held up their batons. There were four rugged men and two women, heavy on the eye makeup, standing behind a towering man with wide, muscular shoulders. Their mercenary-style clothes were worn with frayed hems and random holes in their shirts and pants. Kenna immediately thought *Irish Gladiator* for the man in front with his red hair pulled into a man-bun and a mix of scars alongside his ear and across the bridge of his nose.

But it was their glaring orange eyes that tipped Kenna's fear. *Oh, shit! Shit, shit, shit! This isn't good.* Her gaze dipped to the different-sized knives and daggers they were holding. *Yup. We're going to die!*

The gladiator-looking man crossed his arms and tsked. "Did the Leadess lose her human subjects? Or has she dismissed you all and sent you to your deaths?"

"These guys must be new," Matthew muttered while stretching a protective arm in front of their group. He glanced at Kenna and stuttered, "Uh, I don't think they're the pirates you're looking for."

"Pirates!" The man bellowed a hearty, pirate-like laugh. "Oh, that's a new one."

"Run!" Julianna yelled before bolting from the group.

"Jules, no!" Liam shouted.

Matthew moved to follow but was met with a long dagger pointing inches from his head.

What the hell? Who runs off and leaves their friends to die? Not cool, Julianna... not cool.

One of the men started after Julianna but stopped when the Irish-gladiator-man barked, "Leave her! We have enough bugs here to play with. Take them!"

The men and women came forward, reaching and grabbing to secure them.

"Let go of me!" Kenna shouted while the others tried to fight their way free, but in the end daggers and knives were more of a threat than their batons and lashers.

We're going to die out here. I knew this was a terrible idea! What if I never see my parents again? We're never going to see anyone again!

The man's thugs restrained them as the towering man moved closer to the doors. "Let me help you inside. That's where you were heading, aye? Well, me too!" He swung the dingy glass doors open and yelled, "Oh, Gemma! Where are you, Gemma?"

58

It surprised Gemma that Sabine's gift made her happy. To see the human she'd grown somewhat attached to standing in the corridor of the holding cells. The moment he saw her, he rushed to her. His arms enveloped her, and for a moment, she wanted the world to disappear.

Isoldesse, please forgive me for the unnatural thoughts I'm having. I know he's human.

"Hello, Xander." She leaned away, trying to hide the glee on her face.

At arm's length, he stared into her bright orange eyes. "So, you are one of them."

"I am." She grinned while running her fingers through his tousled hair. She turned to Sabine, about to thank her when they heard the Beast bellowing her name. "Oh, shit! He's here."

Gemma glanced nervously at Sabine, and then at Xander. *Damn it. I shouldn't have sent Micah to the clearing.*

"Where's Cahleen? We need Cahleen!" Sabine pressed her body to one of the cell doors. "If he sees me, he'll wonder why I'm not at Priomh with Breyah. He'll question—"

Gemma snapped her fingers. "Stop your whining and listen. You only have to tell him that Breyah was on to you. *And* only if he asks. Never offer free information. Understand?" Sabine nodded and Gemma crossed her arms. "I sent Micah to the clearing to meet up with Cahleen, who is guarding the captives. So, we're going to have to get out of here without my sister. I have no idea where Logan is, but that's not our concern right now." Gemma turned and pushed Xander against the wall. "When this door opens, you stay behind it. Do you understand?"

Xander nodded like a five-year-old being told to hide from the bad man.

"What does Quaid want?" Sabine put some distance between herself and the door, cupping her hand over her mouth. "I think I'm going to throw up."

"Hold it together, Sabine. He wants me to bring him one of the Spiaires." She stepped closer to the short woman. "If you have an opportunity to sneak away, take it. Go to the clearing south of here and meet up with the others. Anora's transport shuttle will be here soon."

Sabine nodded while Quaid's voice grew louder beyond the doorway.

Xander reached for Gemma. "What about you?"

"Stay." She shoved him hard against the wall and then kissed him. As she gently pulled her lips from his, she flashed a confident smile. "Don't you fret, sweetie. I can handle myself."

When the door opened, Gemma didn't dare glance to see if Xander was okay.

"There you are." Quaid tilted his head and pointed to Sabine. "And look, your round friend has returned. Excellent!"

"Beannaith, Quaid." Sabine tried not to stammer.

"What news do you have from Priomh?" Quaid waved her to come closer, and when she did, he grabbed her behind the neck and led her out the door. "Come now, and Gemma, bring me my Spiaire."

Gemma stopped in the doorway and under her breath instructed Xander to stay put. Then, at a casual pace with her head high, she followed Quaid and Sabine out toward the open foyer. Occasionally, he'd pull Sabine in close and mutter something in her ear. Words Gemma couldn't hear and didn't care to. She needed to think up a way to distract Quaid. She didn't want to leave Xander behind, or Sabine, but there was no way she was going to miss Anora's shuttle pickup.

At the end of the hall, Quaid shoved Sabine out into the lobby. The open space wasn't as grand as the Centrum but served the same purpose. A cross-space between the research side and the subject side of the building. When the Beast stepped aside, she saw Sabine on the floor struggling to get up, clutching one ankle and wincing in pain.

She'd better be able to run when it's time.

But a new situation unfolded as Gemma entered the lobby. Her feet scuffed to a stop, and her gaze narrowed to make sure what she was seeing was real. A few patches of dirt covered the glass roof lining the vaulted ceiling, but there was enough daylight for her to see five humans lined up against the far wall. Athru men armed with blades guarded behind.

This is going to turn into a massacre.

"Where did they come from?" Gemma eyed each one. Her gaze lingered over one human in particular—Matthew. He was at the end of the lineup, eyes wide and directed at her. He shook his head with pursed lips, disappointment written all over his face.

Well, it's nice to see you again, too, old friend.

"I think they were coming to find…" Quaid turned to Gemma. "Where's my Spiaire?"

"In her cell," she lied.

Quaid pointed to two Athru women. "Fetch me one of the Spiaires."

The one with the shaved head knocked her shoulder into Gemma's while walking by. Gemma ignored the bruising pain in her arm and prayed to Isoldesse that Xander wouldn't be discovered.

A long time ago, there used to be a table in the center of the room, but now the room was an empty space filled with memories of the past. Quaid paced the center in slow strides, and because his attention span was like a child's, he eventually sauntered over to one of the humans.

Quaid stood toe to toe with a man slightly shorter than he. "I don't see what's so special about these bugs." The man's brown eyes didn't break from the Sendarian's. It impressed Gemma that he neither cowered nor spoke.

Smart man. I guess not all humans are as dumb as I thought.

The Beast dragged one of the human girls out into the center of the room. She yelped while slapping the arm that tugged at her hair. Two of the human men lunged forward, but they were quickly restrained with blades against their throats.

"Kenna!" one of the men shouted.

"This one's a pretty one, don't you think?" With a fistful of the girl's hair, he forced her to face Gemma. "Maybe I'll keep her for a pet."

"Quaid!" A man barreled in from the main entrance. Gemma thought the man looked familiar, but she couldn't quite place his name. He raised a shortsword straight at the rebel leader's head. The Sendarian man panted, but his breaths weren't from exhaustion, more like rage as he glared at Quaid.

What do we have here? I think Isoldesse has presented us with the perfect distraction to make our escape. I swear I know him from somewhere. Could it be? No... She cocked her head to the side and thought back to her childhood. "Bennach?"

Bennach briefly gazed in her direction at the sound of his name.

It is Bennach! Look how well he's grown up.

Bennach's gaze flicked to the girl at Quaid's side. "Let her go!"

He seems to have an interest in our damsel in distress. What an interesting turn of events.

From behind Gemma, Xander whispered from the hall, "Hey, *psst*! Tell me when we're making a run for it."

Slowly, she backed up and shushed him, careful not to draw any attention. "What happened to the two women? I for sure thought they would've spotted you."

"I tossed a rock into one of the cells and then locked them in." There was a long pause before he said, "I needed to make sure you were okay."

Her heart thumped an extra beat and the words *Ti amo* recited in her mind. It was no longer a question of whether she should leave Xander.

"Wait for my signal," she whispered over her shoulder. "When I say *go*, help me grab Sabine, and then we make our escape."

When Bennach attacks, we'll run.

Bennach kept his sword pointed at Quaid while surveying the other captives. When he looked over at Gemma again, he held her stare for two long seconds before returning his focus to the immediate threat.

Matthew yelled from the back wall, "Bennach, they're not space pirates or part of the Aevo C. I don't know who they— Ow!" One of the Athru men whacked Matthew's head with the hilt of his knife.

Quaid unsheathed a knife from his belt and held it to the girl's throat. "I couldn't believe my ears when I heard there was a Rhaltan officer on Priomh, and then to discover it was you!" He barked a laugh and tugged at the girl, making her follow his steps. "You! Out of all the gróntahs in the Rhaltan."

I'd forgotten that Breyah's brother was a Rhaltan Enforcer. Was he the one Quaid wanted? Which means the Rhaltan aren't here looking for me.

An empowering relief washed over Gemma now that she knew the Rhaltan weren't there on Priomh looking for her. One problem eliminated. Now she just needed Bennach to make his move so they could escape. Which hopefully he did soon, because they were running out of time and needed to get to the clearing.

Quaid pointed his dagger at Bennach. "If I were ever to believe in that taut goddess of yours, and her blessings, then I guess this would be one of those moments. Too bad Anora's not here to watch you die."

Bennach knows Anora?

Quaid thrust the girl forward, and she screamed. The tip of his knife dragged along her collarbone, drawing a thin line of red blood. "Now, let's play a game, shall we?"

59

The man Ben called Quaid tugged at Kenna's hair and proceeded to drag her about in the center of the room. Her knees were weak, and she wanted to run from this nightmare, but she couldn't. The cut on her neck stung like a giant papercut.

"Ben," she whimpered while she reached up to Quaid's arm to lessen the pull on her scalp. Tears streamed down her cheeks, and her trembling eyes found Ben's gaze. The intensity of his stare gave her a sliver of hope that he'd save her.

The adrenaline coursing through her was a combination of fear and anger as Quaid dragged the cool tip of his blade farther down her neck along her heated skin.

"Let her go!" Ben yelled, sweat beading his brow. "Or I swear to Isoldesse I'll throw you deep in the underground cells of the Rhaltan prison where no one will find you!"

"I don't think I will. I like this one," Quaid taunted and cocked his head. He pressed his nose to the side of her head and inhaled a deep breath. "Though, this one smells too clean. But I'm sure we can fix that."

Kenna couldn't see the evil look on the man's face, but from his insidious tone, she knew exactly what he'd meant. *This cannot be happening. I swear I'll kill this asshole myself if he tries anything.* The thought of this man touching her fumed her fears into anger.

"Release her... Release them all before I invoke Imperilment and skip both the trial and imprisonment."

Quaid barked out a laugh. "Imperilment! That's a good one. Okay, okay. I can see you're not one to play games. Fine, how about we make a deal instead?" He stepped closer to Bennach. "How about you run along with those bugs"—Quaid pointed a thumb toward the back wall—"while I keep this pretty little thing."

The tip of his blade continued south along the front of Kenna's shirt until it reached the arcstone. "What do we have here? Aren't you decorated with a fancy stone?" He lowered the blade beneath the silver chain and tugged, but the chain didn't break. He pulled harder, the chain digging into her skin around her neck.

"Ow! You asshole!"

"I swear, if you hurt her!" Bennach lifted his shortsword and pointed it at Quaid. Quaid laughed, a low, deep laugh as he ripped the arcstone from Kenna's neck. A thin red mark formed along her skin. With a scream, Kenna pressed one hand to her neck. Smears of blood coated her hand.

"No! Not my necklace!" Kenna pleaded. "Please! Oh God, please, just give me my necklace back!"

Quaid tossed the arcstone off to the side and returned his dagger to Kenna's neck. She wasn't sure how long she had before the pain of separation would set in, but she knew it was coming. The arcstone was lying there across the floor, and this asshole wasn't letting her go anytime soon.

"Kenna!" Meegan yelled from behind her. "She needs that necklace! You don't know what you've done!"

The sky was blue, and the clouds were a fluffy white as Kenna stared up at the sky through the dingy glass ceiling above. What a beautiful day outside while they were in here, about to die. Quaid tugged Kenna's hair, forcing her to cry out. His breath wafted over her shoulder and she couldn't help but breathe it in. The stench combined with the growing nausea creeping up her throat was enough to make her throw up, but she didn't. She closed her eyes and focused on Ulissa, on the warmth of the arcstone and the feeling it would give her whenever she was upset, or nervous, or scared. The arcstone wasn't with her, but she could still remember the feeling it evoked.

But it didn't matter. Her vision blurred and a twist of pain curled in her gut. Heat swelled beneath her chest.

Oh, shit. It's starting. The pain of separation.

Quaid ignored the commotion in the room and spoke only to Ben. "What d'you say? Yes? You take all those other bugs while I keep this one insignificant little human bug. Aye? No one will miss her."

Ben shook his head and yelled, "No deal." He then held his shortsword out in front of himself, both hands gripping the hilt. An electric hum filled the air as he separated the sword into two, one in each hand. He struck the narrow blades together, igniting a current of blue energy stretching between the two weapons. When the current disappeared, tiny blue flickers of energy sparked along the silver edges.

Who needs guns when you've got electric swords?

Quaid twisted to face his men, making Kenna yelp. "I knew this would be a blessed day," he exclaimed. "A new bug to play with *and* a new blade! When they're mine, I'll call them my Bennach Blades. Ha! You like that, don't you?" The Athru men laughed and nodded.

Quaid's laughter dissolved, and his amused tone sank. "Kill him."

His command unsettled Kenna. It was slow and guttural. A darker side to this madman. *This is it. They're going to kill Ben and then us. Or worse. And I can't do anything. Oh, I think I'm going to throw up!*

Two men ran past. Ben struck the first attacker's dagger with a wide sweep of his sword, causing the man's weapon to fling across the room. He then quickly spun and faced his second attacker. He slapped his two shortswords together and caught that man's boomerang-looking dagger mid-strike while simultaneously back-kicking his first attacker. The hum of Ben's swords filled the room as he slid the blades down the man's weapon. With a powerful push, he plunged the electrified tips into the man's shoulders. The man screamed and dropped to the ground. Ben quickly withdrew his blades and faced his remaining opponent.

Kenna cringed and forced herself to watch. The tips of Ben's swords were dripping with a shimmering yellow substance.

They don't have red blood.

The first attacker grabbed his dagger and staggered to his feet. He lunged at Ben, who'd reignited the electric current between the tips of his swords. The man ran straight into the searing blue stream, sending volts of energy into his body. He dropped to the floor. His arms and head twitched for a few lingering moments as Ben faced Quaid.

"You leave me no choice. Imperilment it is!" Ben yelled, one of his swords pointed at Quaid. He continued reciting the terms of Imperilment as he reached down and picked up the yellow stone necklace.

Kenna's head was growing hazier by the second and it was hard to focus on what Bennach was saying.

"The only way you're leaving here is by someone dragging your dead body out!" Bennach swung his arm out and pointed one of the swords at the woman with Xander, the one from the outlets. "That goes for you too, Gemma."

"Oh, this is good!" Quaid barked an elated laugh while nodding at the woman. "Makes me like the annoying taut a bit more! What do you say, Gemma? Are we leaving here as corpses?"

Gemma? Her name is Gemma. Did I know that? Okay, well then, who the hell is Anora?

The brute tugged at her scalp, sending a jolt of pain into Kenna's temples. Her vision blurred and large black specks formed along Kenna's peripheral. Knots twisted in her stomach, and she wasn't sure how much longer she could hold on to her consciousness. It scared her to think if she passed out now, where she might wake up, and with whom. Arcstone or not, she needed to stay awake and keep it together.

"If this one's so important to you," Quaid said, vile and harsh, "then you won't mind if I eliminate one of the other bugs." And before anyone could react, he flicked his wrist and the dagger he'd been holding spun through the air. Kenna couldn't see what happened, but she heard the bloodcurdling scream that erupted seconds later. She tried to twist, but Quaid had drawn another knife and the edge was pressed to her collarbone.

"What's happening? I can't... I can't see!"

"Oh, my apologies," Quaid flatly said, and turned Kenna so she had a clear view. Nick was on the ground, his hands wrapped around the hilt protruding from his chest. Meegan was there, on her knees by his side. Nick's eyes were wide open, and he was spitting up blood while gasping for air and staring up at Meegan.

"No!" Kenna cried.

"You see, yes? All good now?" He spun Kenna so she was facing him now, his grip repositioned to the front of her throat. "You know, little bug, I'm getting bored and believe it or not, I've got other people to kill today. A world to overthrow. So, I think it's time we wrap this up. I'd bring you with me, but I changed my mind. I do that sometimes." He positioned the knife so the tip pressed up under her chin. Kenna could feel the prick of it piercing her skin. She imagined what it would feel like when the blade cut up into her mouth.

This was it. The end.

But then his hand loosened from her neck as a voice that sounded like Meegan, but amplified, echoed throughout the room. When he dropped his hand, Kenna fell to her knees. She scooted away while watching Quaid turn and face—Meegan. Behind them, the Athru men who had been guarding their friends were now pinned to the wall, like magnets on a fridge.

From the floor, Kenna watched as Quaid, who seemed unruffled by Meegan's confrontation, stepped closer. "What is this?"

Thunder suddenly clashed as dark clouds clustered over the glass ceiling. The lights in the room went out.

Two glowing white eyes pierced through the darkness.

"Lines have been crossed and now you shall pay." Meegan's voice carried a weight of power through the dark room. Gradually, her body began to glow a soft white, lighting up the center of the room. Black tendrils of smoke evaporated from her skin into the white light.

"What are you?" Quaid asked curiously, still with no sense of urgency.

Kenna stared at her friend in awe and fear. "Meegan, stop!" But Kenna couldn't move to intervene. The pain in her stomach and the heat from the arcstone's absence were too much.

Meegan raised a hand and mouthed unheard words. The arcstone flew from Bennach's hands to the ground before Kenna. She reached for the yellow stone and held it tight.

"I got it! Meegan, stop! I got the arcstone!"

The front door slammed open, and a river of air poured into the room. Meegan's midnight hair danced in the wind as if she were submerged underwater, and her white eyes were now filled with swirls of black smoke.

"Meegan," Kenna whimpered. "What are you doing?" Kenna looked to see if time had stopped or slowed, but it hadn't. Everyone in the room was staring, mouths gaping, as the wind turned into a cyclone and lifted Meegan from the ground.

Everyone stared but Liam. He'd moved during the chaos and slid next to Nick, both hands pressed to Nick's chest. Matthew's eyes were wide as he watched Meegan, then slowly squatted to join Liam and Nick.

"Gemma, let's get out of here!"

Kenna searched the room as she heard the douchebag's voice. The wind whipped at her hair, blocking her view, but she knew it was him. She held her hair from her face and finally spotted Xander running out from one of the side hallways. He was tugging on the arm of the woman from the outlets, Gemma.

How the hell did Xander get here?

"We need to leave!" Gemma yelled to Xander. The two of them shuffled over to help a woman sitting on the floor, holding her ankle. It wasn't long before all three were rushing from the building.

Meanwhile, Ben locked the two shortswords together into one blade again and made his way over to Kenna. With one arm shielding his eyes, he crouched beside her and tried to pull her away, but Kenna refused to leave. To her surprise, he moved in closer, kneeling next to her. He kept one hand on her shoulder while the other held his shortsword out protectively.

It wasn't the first time he'd made her feel safe, and she was glad he was there. But she wished it were under different circumstances. She also wished Meegan would stop and think before she did anything she'd regret. Revealing her powers was already bad enough.

"He's going to kill her!" Ben yelled over the increasing winds.

"Oh, I'm pretty sure she can handle herself," she muttered under her breath.

At the center of the foyer, Meegan cocked her head and held out one open palm toward Quaid. "Who are you to take a life?" She curled her fingers in and raised her hand, commanding the winds to lift the seven-foot Sendarian. He kicked his feet trying to remain on the ground, but gave in and let his feet dangle.

Still, the man smiled and laughed. "Oh, deary. You must be what they're coming for."

Who's coming? What is he talking about? Oh, no. Please—please don't be the Obard! Kenna twisted her body on the floor and buried her face into Ben's chest. *This can't be happening. This isn't like Meegan.*

When she looked up again, Meegan's body wavered into a translucent state. Meegan dipped her eyes and curled her lips up. "Let them come. No one else is dying while I'm here." Her smile spread wider. "On second thought…" Quaid's body launched forward and Meegan plunged her lucent hand into his chest. His long face twisted with pain. Kenna covered her mouth with one hand as her best friend pulled out the man's essence.

No, Meegan. No.

There was no light like Kenna had seen in Liam's essence. Quaid's essence, the color of ash and full of cracks revealing an empty blackness beneath its surface, floated over Meegan's open palm. Meegan's glowing eyes stared into Quaid's as he struggled to breathe.

"You're no match… for… what's coming," Quaid stuttered between gasps of air. It sounded as though he tried to laugh, but it came out more like a weak cough. "They'll take you… and… and kill everyone—"

"Let. Them. Come." Her amplified voice echoed throughout the room.

Kenna had had no idea her friend was this powerful.

Meegan stared at Quaid's rising essence. "You don't deserve a second life either." She opened her hand, spread her fingers wide, and chanted, "*Pyso uharda gahdic tao gohdeo.*" Thick white veins illuminated on the surface of Meegan's transessent stone, as well as on the other transessent stones on Liam's and Nick's wrists.

"What's happening?" Ben asked over the cyclone of wind circling the room. "How is she doing this?"

"We need to help her." Kenna squeezed his arm.

Streams of something thick, like black ink, emerged from within the cyclone. Meegan held her hand up and commanded the streams of blackness toward Quaid's rising essence. The dark tendrils obeyed and moved in, swirling in every direction around the rising essence.

"You don't... have... to do this." But Quaid's pleas were too late. Smoke billowed from Meegan's eyes, and she clenched her hand tight, high above her head.

"Meegan, stop!" Kenna yelled. "You don't want to do this! You're not a killer!"

Her friend dipped her head and blinked several times as if she were processing Kenna's words.

The winds circulating the room took one last turn before whisking out the door, back into the forest. Quaid's body crumpled to the floor. At the same time, the Athru men were released from their invisible bindings against the back wall. They got up and ran from the building without stopping to question if their leader was alive or dead.

The room grew quiet except for the whirring sound above Meegan's head. Everyone except Meegan watched as the spinning black sphere of inky smoke stretched vertically, spreading thinner and thinner until it vanished, taking Quaid's essence with it.

Meegan's shoulders slumped, and her head dropped. Kenna wiggled free from Ben's arms and rushed to her friend. "Meeg, are you okay?"

Meegan looked up. Her eyes had returned to their beautiful shade of brown. "I'm sorry, Kenna. Something... something snapped inside of me."

Kenna pulled her best friend in for a hug, but Meegan pushed her away and rushed to Nick's side. Kenna and Ben hurried to follow. Liam didn't shy from Meegan, but Matthew jumped to his feet and moved away.

With one big heave, Meegan pulled the knife from Nick's chest. Blood gushed from the gaping slice in the upper part of his chest. He cried out and grabbed Meegan's arm while coughing up blood. "Meeg, I'm... I'm s-sorry."

"Shh. I'm not going anywhere. I'm right here." She pressed one hand over the wound. Her voice was low, but Kenna heard her casting an amula. The transessent stone barely showed any glowing veins.

"I need more power!" Meegan yelled and grabbed Liam's wrist. "Don't move." She pressed one hand over the top of his transessent stone and continued chanting her amula.

"What's she doing?" Ben asked, staring at Kenna.

"It's complicated."

Nick struggled to talk. "Meeg, please, look at me." A thin layer of blood coated his teeth. Red blood continued to flow out from beneath Meegan's hand.

"Damn it, Nick. Hold on, okay. I can save you. I need you to be strong and stay with me." Meegan continued chanting. Tears dripped from her eyes, mixing with the blood pooling on his chest.

Kenna wiped her own eyes as she sensed it—Nick's essence. It was weak and about to ascend from his body. "Ulissa! We need to help!" Kenna yelled into the air, not caring about who heard or the puzzled look Ben was giving her.

"*The wound is too severe,*" Ulissa sadly replied in Kenna's mind. "*But I have an idea. I don't know—*"

"Yes! Just tell me, what is it?" Kenna cut Ulissa off in a rush. "Hurry, we're losing him!"

"*Repeat these words: Ogah byoch tao aldach,*" Ulissa instructed.

Kenna repeated the words, again not caring who heard. "*Ogah byoch tao aldach.*"

Meegan looked up. Kenna nodded to her while holding her arcstone and repeating the amula phrase. A weak smile spread across Meegan's face and she grabbed Kenna's hand and joined in chanting. Ben, Liam, and Matthew all watched in silence. They couldn't see what Kenna saw, which was a bright ball of light emerging from Nick's body.

"I love you," were his last words before he exhaled his last breath.

Nick's essence floated upward, but instead of it ascending on, Ulissa appeared and cupped the glowing sphere with her hands. She hugged it close to her body before she, along with Nick's essence, disappeared.

Kenna swallowed and licked her dry lips. "It's done. Or I think it is."

"Nick!" Meegan's hand slipped from Kenna's and she dropped her head to Nick's face. She kissed his lips and rubbed the sides of his face.

"Can someone tell me what the hell is going on?" Liam asked, tears welling in his eyes. "Is he… is he dead?"

When no one answered, Kenna bent down and hugged Meegan from behind. "I'm so sorry, Meeg."

A loud *bang* crashed from the direction of the front doors. Ben raised his sword and moved to protect the group, but lowered his weapon when Darci appeared. She leaned forward, hands resting on her knees as she caught her breath. "There you are."

Darci's forehead had a cut along her hairline, and Kenna immediately noticed her blood wasn't red. Her eyes were also a bright orange. Darci really was a Sendarian.

Darci moved closer but stopped and gasped. "Oh no! Meeg, what happened?"

"Where are the others?" Ben asked.

"Outside," Darci answered while grabbing Kenna and leading her toward the main doors. "You need to go to the clearing. Now. They have Honnah."

"What? How?" Without knowing where the hell the clearing was, Kenna left everyone inside and ran out of the building.

Ben caught up to Kenna and pointed. "This way!" They ran past the boulders and straight into the forest. "The clearing is where our transport vehicles are parked." They raced over fallen logs and under low branches. She almost fell once or twice but didn't stop or dwell on her clumsiness. She needed to get to the clearing—to get to Honnah.

From a distance, she heard what sounded like a helicopter or a large aircraft. When they reached the clearing, a small aircraft was lifting off out in the middle of the field.

"It's a transport shuttle," Ben said while shielding his eyes from the takeoff wind.

Kenna didn't care what it was and took off running with every ounce of strength she could muster toward the ship. She got close, but not close enough. The side door was open, and there holding the railing was Gemma. Standing next to her was a tall woman with long black hair.

"No!" Kenna shouted. "Come back!"

Honnah had something in her hand and let it go right as Gemma slid the side-hatch door closed. Feeling completely helpless, Kenna watched the aircraft disappear into the clouds. Her eyes refocused on the item Honnah had dropped, floating down toward her. A leaf with a yellow Hiccum flower gently landed in her palm. Carefully, she held the leaf to her chest. Her heart ached and her mind spun.

Nothing made sense. Why had Darci lied? Why had she been given the arcstone? Why had the Sendarians brought them to their world? So many unanswered questions—and now this.

Ben ran up and stopped behind her. "What happened? Who's Honnah?"

She turned and faced him. Tears streamed down her cheeks as she leaned into him. At first, she thought he'd push her away, but then she felt his hands slide across her back.

With a sniff, Kenna said, "They took my mom."

60

With everything that'd happened in the last thirty minutes, Kenna wasn't sure what to think, feel, or do next. Her usual racing train of thoughts had been derailed by the mob scene of overstimulated neurons. The one emotion that lingered, compassion, came from the embrace holding her… protecting her. It was exactly what she needed.

She twisted her head from against Ben's chest and looked toward the dirt road. Off in the distance, she saw the silhouette of the new Priomh compound.

This is the field where we first met. From my dream. She turned her head to see the other side of the clearing. *Huh, but where's the white tree?*

"Are you okay?" he asked flatly, as though they'd never met before, but even if he tried, she recognized the subtle twinge of sympathy and concern hidden within his question.

"I don't know. I don't understand what's going on. How did my mom get here?"

His hands pressed firmly to her back, as if to hold her closer. It was an affectionate gesture that confused Kenna, but she chose to not overthink it and to appreciate his condolences. Her moment of peace was cut short when she heard someone shouting her name.

"Kenna!" Liam called from the forest's edge. When he emerged, he ran out to her. His steps slowed as he approached.

Ben released Kenna, cleared his throat, and walked past Liam. "I should help the others."

She opened her hand and stared at the leaf. There was a faint shimmer along the green veins, which she assumed was because it had come from an alien tree. Carefully, she pocketed the delicate item and glanced up at Liam. "Hey, how's Meegan?"

"Not good, but we finally got her to let us move Nick." He wrapped one arm over Kenna's shoulders, and they walked toward the transport vehicles. "So, you never mentioned an *alien* boyfriend."

She bubbled out a laugh. "It's not like that. He was just here and… and I was upset. I don't know how she got here, but they have my mom."

"What? Oh man, I'm sorry. We'll figure it out. We'll get her back, okay?"

"Yeah, okay." Kenna rested her head on his shoulder as they continued to the vehicles. "I'm still trying to figure out what the hell's going on, and the stuff I do know, I can't… I can't talk about. I hope you understand."

Liam pointed to Meegan, who'd just stepped out from the forest's edge. Matthew joined her, cradling Nick's body, and Darci was right behind them. "I'm going to guess the stuff you can't talk about has something to do with your friend over there." Before Kenna could say anything, he added, "It's okay. You guys can tell me when you're ready. I know what it's like to keep someone else's secret. Jules told me before anyone else about her coming out. So, when people asked—"

"Hey," Kenna interrupted, "where is Jules?"

Liam stopped at the edge of the field and scanned the group coming out of the forest. Kenna joined him in searching for his friend and looked toward the two transport vehicles. When neither one of them spotted her, Liam took off running toward the second vehicle while Meegan and Darci jogged over to Kenna.

"What happened? Where's Honnah?" Darci asked.

Meegan stopped in front of Kenna. Her eyes were swollen and red. Nick was gone, or at least his physical body was gone. "I think Ulissa has him," was all Kenna could think to say.

Meegan nodded and dropped her head onto Kenna's shoulder. "I just got him back, and now... and now he's gone."

Kenna lifted her friend's chin. "I don't think he's gone-gone."

"What do you mean, he's not gone-gone?" Darci cut in. "If that's not Nick, then—"

"Darci! Shut up for two seconds!" Kenna shouted, and then said to Meegan, "We need to talk to Ulissa, but not here. Okay?"

Darci waved a hand between Kenna and Meegan. "Can someone please explain to me what is going on?"

"How about *you* explain that"—Meegan slapped Darci's hand and jutted a finger toward Darci's bleeding forehead—"and why *you* lied to *us*? Why are we really here, Darci? How about you do some explaining first!"

Darci sucked in her lower lip. Her strawberry-blonde eyebrows knitted together over her bright orange eyes. "It's complicated, and I want to tell you guys everything. I really do, but I'm not permitted to say. There are so many reasons why, but our goddess forbids—"

Meegan moved from Kenna's side. Her feet shuffled in the dirt as she put her face inches from Darci's. "Your goddess! You mean that piece-of-shit traitor, Isoldesse?" Kenna watched Darci's expression shift from nervous to surprised. Her mouth and eyes slowly widened as Meegan continued to rip into her. "Oh, that's right. I know all about your fucking goddess! And until you tell us what the hell is going on here, we're not telling you anything."

Meegan grabbed Kenna's hand and dragged her away from the Sendarian. As they marched toward the vehicles, and without looking back, Meegan yelled, "And she's not a goddess! So stop calling her one! She's a traitor and a selfish bitch!"

"That was harsh," Kenna muttered.

"Yeah, well, she had it coming. Besides, these people need to know the truth about their so-called precious goddess." She spun and looked Kenna in the eyes. "If they believe Isoldesse is a freaking goddess, then I guess that makes me one too!"

"I know, but Darci—"

"No! Don't do that. Don't make excuses for her. She lied to us, Kenna." Meegan stomped off before Kenna could say anything and climbed into the first vehicle. She slid over to the farthest spot in the third row and touched the seat where Nick had last sat as if she were holding on to their last moments.

How is it less than an hour ago, he was sitting back there holding Meegan? Who would've guessed this was his last day—last moments—with her? With all of us.

What the hell were we thinking trying to pull off a rescue mission without knowing what we were going up against? Stupid, stupid!

Darci walked by, arms crossed and head low, to the second transport vehicle. Kenna felt bad, but Meegan was right. She had it coming. Kenna moved along the vehicle's side and stood at the hood to get a better view of the other vehicle. Liam was there, talking and... and hugging? She rubbed her eyes to make sure she was seeing correctly. He *was* hugging one of the Sendarians.

Huh, if they know each other, I'm guessing that means Darci wasn't the only one pretending to be human.

Curious, she strolled over and asked Liam, "Did you find Jules?"

Liam shook his head, but it was his friend Brody who answered, "They took Jules. Along with Eryn, Honnah, and some tall woman with pale skin and blue hair." Kenna recognized Brody from Liam's Instagram photos. The front part of his dark hair looked matted and hung low over his eyes.

Brody slid into the third row and lay across the seat. Liam hopped into the second row and asked Kenna, "You okay if I ride with Brody?"

"Yeah, it's okay." *But no, not okay.* Kenna returned to her transport just as Ben and Matthew were setting Nick's body in the cargo area of the trunk. From a distance, they seemed cordial, but as she got closer and heard more of their conversation, that wasn't the case.

"Hey, guys," she said. "What's going on?"

Both men went silent. Ben adjusted Nick's body while Matthew continued his protests. "I didn't know!"

"And that's why you should've checked with Breyah or Rian first. This whole thing could've been avoided." Ben, ignoring Kenna's presence, lifted a silicon-like panel up from the bottom end of the vehicle's bed and secured it to the top corners. Along the top, he pressed something that activated a morphing process. Kenna held her hand to the surface and felt the panel transition from a flexible material to a sturdy one that enclosed the open bed. Their version of a pickup truck's tailgate.

Ben turned to face Matthew. "It was a mistake to let you stay on Priomh. You don't belong here. You're not one of us."

You're not one of us. His words stung Kenna even if they weren't meant for her. Though, she wasn't sure why she cared so much. They barely knew each other, and he obviously had strong feelings about keeping to his own kind. But the second his orange gaze flicked her way, along with a tick in his jawline, she sensed something different. Regret? Confliction?

Ben shook his head and through gritted teeth told Matthew, "You can be the one to tell Breyah they've taken her second-in-command, one of her Spiaires, and two humans."

Matthew waved a dismissive hand and moved past Kenna toward the driver side while mumbling, "I still don't understand how they got Rian. What was she thinking?"

"Three. Three humans," Kenna corrected.

"What?" Ben asked while Matthew stopped, the dirt beneath his boots crunching as he twisted to hear Kenna.

"Three humans. Though, I don't think Xander counts as a prisoner. He seemed pretty willing to go with them."

"Who is Xander?" Matthew stepped closer.

"He came here with us. Well," she quickly corrected herself, "not here-here, on our rescue mission, but from Earth. I don't know how he got out to the old compound though."

"Great, so they have three humans, Rian and Eryn." Ben rubbed his forehead and then muttered, "How am I going to explain this to my Rhaltan superiors?"

"I *thought* it was part of the Aevo—" But Matthew stopped himself. "Never mind. I'll talk to Breyah."

"We had to do something!" Kenna snapped at Ben. "It wasn't like you were going to save them, were you?"

Ben lowered his hand from his forehead and stared at Kenna. "How did you know what we were planning to do? More importantly, how did you know Darci was out here in the first place? I'm guessing more of your friend's Earth magic?"

Kenna gasped and tried not to look at the vehicle—to Meegan.

"That's right," Ben said. "We found your other friend hiding in the corner. I can't wait to hear how you and your friend pulled off that trick."

Shit, they found Ally.

"I think we both have a lot to talk about." Hoping to call a truce for now, Kenna licked her lips and with a calmer voice said, "But later."

Ben marched over to the second transport and just before he closed the side door, Kenna glimpsed Liam sitting in the second row. He sat alone, facing the third row, talking to Brody.

Kenna climbed into their SUV-like vehicle and got comfy in the third row next to Meegan. Her friend immediately rested her head on Kenna's shoulder, and they both let the hum of the engine lull them to sleep.

❄ ❅ ❄ ❅ ❄

Once they'd arrived in the docking station, it was well into the night. Holt and his Medical team were there waiting, along with Breyah and some other Sendarians.

With all the commotion, Kenna and Meegan sat on the edge of the vehicle's floor with their feet out the open side door. "You don't want to go with Nick?"

Meegan shook her head. "Why, so I can watch them put his body into a freezer or a locker? I don't think I want to see that."

Kenna hadn't had time to talk more with Ulissa, so she wasn't sure what the amula translated to. "So, what was that amula Ulissa had us recite? I saw her take Nick's essence."

She shrugged. "I don't know. The translation isn't clear. It sounded like *move and stay within temporary*, but I can't be sure. We need to talk to Ulissa. It's unheard of for two essences to reside in an arcstone, so I don't think he's in there."

Kenna rubbed her friend's back and thought it best if they talked about something else besides Nick. "What do you think that maniac meant when he said, 'You must be what they're coming for'?"

"Honestly, I don't even care right now. That's a problem for tomorrow."

Liam was walking past with his friends when he stopped over and said, "I'm going to go with Brody to Medical. I guess when they're done with their exams or whatever, they'll bring us to our rooms. So, you're good if I meet up with you later?"

"Yeah, of course. I'll see you later."

"You sure?" Liam asked. "Because I can stay with you if you want me to."

She did, but it was important for him to be with Brody right now. "Nah, it's okay. I'm good. Meegan's here and I'm sure Brody could use some friends right about now."

Liam squeezed Kenna tight and whispered, "Okay. We'll see you in a bit," before rushing to catch up with the others and the medics.

The hangar bay was filling up fast with more Sendarians. Then, from out of nowhere, Ben approached the two girls.

"You both okay?"

"Fine. We're a bit tired." Kenna stood from the open door of the transport vehicle.

He narrowed his eyes and directed his next question at Meegan. "You're not human, are you? You're like Her, aren't you?"

Meegan got to her feet and looked him right in the eyes. "My boyfriend just died. I'm exhausted. Hungry. And pissed off. Do you think now is the time for an interrogation?"

He softened his expression and shook his head. Meegan moved past him, leaving him alone with Kenna. He stared at her but didn't reask his question. "Your friend will have to explain what happened back there at some point."

Kenna nodded. "Just give her some time, please."

He nodded respectfully. "I guess we can talk later. You know where."

The corner of her lips perked up, and in all this chaos, she couldn't believe he'd made her smile. He walked away to where Breyah and a few others were huddled together. By the look of horror and sadness that formed on Breyah's face, Kenna assumed Ben had just informed Breyah about her second-in-command being taken.

Eventually, Breyah and another woman, a petite woman with thick red hair all twisted up into an elegant updo, approached Kenna. The shorter woman's smile was too big for the situation as her flowing white dress dragged along the stone floor. Cinched strands of fabric crisscrossed over her bodice, laced with thin golden threads.

Kenna stood up again from her seat on the vehicle's edge and quickly said to Breyah, "I'm sorry about Rian."

"Thank you. We'll get them back. All of them, I promise." She then gestured to the woman next to her. "Kenna, this is Princess Emmalyn."

Princess? Oh, you've got to be kidding me. They have kings and queens and royalty on this world?

"Beannaith, Adalyss."

Meegan shuffled closer to Kenna's side, and they gave each other a puzzled look. Kenna then explained to the princess, "Adalyss is my middle name. How do you...?"

"Yes, I know. It's also the name of our queen." The woman reached out and held Kenna's hand. The docking station fell quiet, and all eyes were watching them. "I've waited a long time to meet you."

"Me?"

A man's voice came from between Breyah and Rian. The two women parted, and Kenna's heart jumped.

"Dad!" She ran into his arms. First her mother, and now her father. How had they gotten here? When they parted, Kenna wiped her eyes and said, "Dad, they have—"

"I know. They have Honnah, and I promise we'll get her back."

"Your eyes." Kenna stepped away. "Your eyes are orange."

"There's something I need to tell you about your mother and me. A story you might already know. It begins with a prince who falls in love with a woman from another world, and to be together they have to run away."

"You're talking about your books?" Kenna had read his books hundreds of times, but how much of it was fiction?

Meegan, whose eyes were wider than Kenna's, stared at the man she'd come to think of as her second father. "You're a freaking prince? And a Sendarian?"

Gerard chuckled. "Was. I was a prince."

"Dad," Kenna said, calling his attention back to her, "does that mean I'm... Sendarian?"

Their audience had grown. Ben now inched closer. His gaze narrowed at Gerard. She wished she could read Ben's mind. To know what it would mean to him if her father said yes. But Gerard shook his head. "You are something much, much more than any one race."

Kenna's mind flooded with new questions revolving around her father's words, ...*more than any one race.*

"*I knew there was something special about you,*" Ulissa whispered in her mind.

Everyone is special in one way or another. Meegan's words from earlier echoed in Kenna's thoughts. Learning the truth about Meegan was one thing, but now this. How had she lived with this man her whole life and never known he wasn't human?

She glanced at her best friend and then her father. "No more lies. No more secrets. We need to uncover the connections between our worlds, and you need to know the truth about Isoldesse."

Gerard smiled. "I already know the truth about who Isoldesse is, but it was never my place to reveal that secret. To lead Sendara into a new era of truth." He lifted the arcstone from around Kenna's neck. "I'm glad the bond took effect. We weren't sure."

"You? You gave me the arcstone?"

Gerard nodded. "We have much to talk about," he said while taking and holding both Kenna's and Meegan's hands. "Are you both ready to accept your destinies?"

This seriously cannot be happening.

We have destinies.

I... I have a destiny?

EPILOGUE

Rian skidded the transport vehicle to a stop next to the empty one Matthew had parked at the edge of the open field. She ignored the dust cloud rising into the evening air, obstructing the view, and moved quickly to secure a lasher to her thigh. Her tracking partner, Breyah's brother, Bennach, reached behind the seat for the shortsword Princess Emmalyn had given him. Some sort of new weapon that she'd *borrowed* from Sendara's enforcement agency, the Rhaltan. Rian had her doubts about the princess and the origin of the shortsword ever since Bennach swore he'd never seen or heard of such a weapon in the Rhaltan.

Rian watched as Bennach inspected the shiny blade. *How did the princess really come across such advanced tech? First that fancy pinship that can somehow pinch two points of space together... and... and now this energy-harnessing sword. I swear to Isoldesse that woman is hiding something.*

The loud *vroom* of the solar-powered engine gradually faded, breaking Rian's thoughts and leaving an uneasy silence lingering in the cabin. If her associate felt troubled by their proximity, she couldn't tell.

"You know how to work that thing?"

The corner of his lips inched up as he twisted the hilt. "I'm used to carrying a longer sword, but if this thing does what the princess says it does, then I'll be good. What about you?" He jutted his chin and dropped his gaze to her thigh. "Nothing but that lasher?"

"I prefer to carry light and use the gifts I was born with." She held up a pale fist and matched his sideways grin. "A precise hit with the right amount of force can be quite deadly."

Bennach raised one blond eyebrow. "No argument there."

It felt odd having a casual conversation with a Rhaltan Enforcer, especially since she'd spent most of her predult years on Sendara hiding in the shadows from Sendarians like him. Being an orphan was hard enough, but then to add the unique mutation of the blue pigment in her eyes and hair made life even harder. Raised by her foster mother on a small farm on the outskirts of their assigned community, Rian had rarely ventured outside. When she had, she'd hidden beneath a hooded cloak. Otherwise, she would be a constant target for disgusted glares and ridicule. Also, on more than one occasion, she'd been singled out and brought in for questioning regarding unsolved misdemeanors. Even though her foster mother was the only one who'd ever shown her kindness, Rian never regretted leaving home. The day she'd snuck aboard a supply ship to Priomh had been the best day of her life.

The evening winds picked up once they exited the vehicle. Rian stared out into the trees of the Endless Forest while Bennach crouched and traced his finger along one of the footprints in the dirt.

When he stood, Rian noticed the tic in his jaw. He sheathed his sword and said, "We need to move fast. Hopefully Quaid hasn't come across them yet, because I guarantee you that maniac wouldn't pass on an opportunity to spill blood."

"Is his essence that lost?"

Bennach scoffed. "He's beyond saving. And his brother, Biryn, believe it or not, is worse."

"Well then, we'd better hurry. The facility isn't too far, and we'll get there faster if we run." Rian took the lead and jogged over to the thick brush of spiky vines curling to form a blockade over the remaining stretch of road. Bowing trees from the Endless Forest, blooming green Hiccums on their leaves, lined both sides of the open road.

Rian sent a silent prayer to Isoldesse that the subjects were all safe. She even prayed for the safety of that loggie human, Matthew. Someone she didn't think she'd ever miss but strangely found herself hoping was unharmed.

"Linc," Rian spoke into the air, "report our position to Breyah and tell her we've located Matthew's transport. Inform her that the remaining road near the clearing is blocked by brush and that we're proceeding into the forest on foot."

Rian's Linc confirmed in her ear, *"Communication sent and received."*

This Aevo C has been one problem after another. Let's hope the next world isn't as problematic, but then again, Vennosh's up next. Oh, there's nothing more annoying than dealing with the Vaennians. I've never met a more stubborn or indecisive—

"Hey, you ready?"

Rian's attention veered from future Aevo Compendiums to the spiky thorns catching her sleeve as she followed Bennach into the woods. A few steps in and a strange icy current of air swirled around her body, sweeping over her skin. The white hairs on her forearms reacted with a gentle pull as if being drawn to something off to her left. Whatever it was, it also triggered her dormant counterpart—the numbing darkness she'd learned to suppress over the years. An uncontrollable change that forced her mind to evict her emotions and rational thinking.

No, no—not now!

Beneath her skin, she could feel her bones growing colder by the second, followed by a piercing chill trailing her spine. The last thing she needed was for a Rhaltan officer to witness one of her episodes. She needed to get away before her skin changed and blended in with her hair and eyes.

Off to their left, deep into the forest, the invisible pull that had triggered her episode grew stronger and beckoned her attention.

"Uh…" She swallowed hard. "I'll flank you fifty paces from inside the forest." Rian backtracked and gestured up the clearing. "I'll enter there, halfway up the field, parallel to your position. This way we can cover more ground in case anyone strayed or got separated from the group."

Bennach faced her from under a low branch he'd raised over his head. "We need to stick together. You know these woods better than me."

Rian pointed a shaky finger along the old road but quickly withdrew it when she noticed blue crystals forming along her cuticle. "Follow the overgrowth, along the tree line. This road, or what's left of it, will lead you straight to the old research facility. I won't be far. I just want to make sure the surrounding area is clear."

The moment he turned to survey his intended path, she slipped out of the forest and started up the edge of the field. "Don't wait for me!" She prayed to Isoldesse that she'd put enough distance between them that he hadn't noticed the hint of blue surfacing on her skin.

When Rian heard sticks snapping, she slowed her jog and turned to see Bennach running through the woods toward the old facility.

Good. Now I can focus on subduing this episode before it flares.

With a loud *vrrip*, she unfastened the strip of burr-like material closing the front of her black security vest. She retrieved one of the three slim metal canisters from within an inside pocket. Silently, she thanked Holt for the emergency doses while twisting off the silver cap. This was the not-so-fun part. With an exasperated exhale, she stared at the clear tip with the hollowed-out center at the end of the canister. Pressure injections weren't her favorite, and they hurt like hegah, but right now it was the only thing she had to stop the frigid numbness from taking over. She couldn't leave Bennach to face Quaid alone.

With the bottom hem of her shirt lifted up, she pressed the tip to her abdomen. A second before injecting Holt's serum, she heard voices farther up the field. With the full canister still in her hand, she ducked behind one of the trees. A few seconds later, a group emerged from the woods.

What's this about?

A Sendarian woman with a black dagger shoved a woman with long black hair who was staggering behind the others. Rian couldn't hear what the short-haired Sendarian woman was yelling, but the aggressively waving dagger implied enough.

This can't be good. Do I stay or go help Bennach?

She tried to think but the darkness was encroaching on her already hazy mind.

I need to get a closer look. If only for a second. Then I can decide.

Rian leaned against the tree trunk, lifted her shirt again, and injected the serum. The force sent the contents directly into her muscles and bloodstream, leaving a sizable welt among a cluster of pitted scars.

The effects were immediate. The chill in her bones dissipated and her skin's blue hue receded. Once she felt like herself again, she returned the empty canister to her inside pocket and then peeked out from behind the tree. She counted seven in the group, and now that her head was clear she focused in on their faces.

It's Darci. And Eryn. And… oh no, is that Grace they're holding and carrying? Oh, blessed Isoldesse. She doesn't look so good.

Rian didn't recognize the tall Sendarian man with the hat leading the group. The long front brim cast a shadow over the top half of his face. It wasn't until he tilted his head to the sky that she saw his face, but she still didn't recognize him. He seemed more interested in the sky and his plac rather than the three Spiaires and two humans following him.

Wanting to get a closer look, Rian crouched and ducked through the low brush and trees until she could hear their conversation.

"Hurry up!" the Sendarian woman shouted. The sides of her head were shaved short while dark orange strands along the top of her head were brushed to the center, forming a low narrow strip of spiky hair.

"Cahleen!" the man in the hat turned and called. "Where's our pain-in-the-ass sister? If she's not here soon, she'll miss the shuttle."

Cahleen jogged past the human woman with long black hair and the younger human man with wavy brown hair and tanned skin. Then, as she passed the three Spiaires, she knocked one shoulder into Darci's, forcing the Spiaire to lose her grip on a wilted Grace. Rian shifted her feet in the leaves, resisting the urge to jump out and catch Grace. Thankfully, she didn't have to. Darci was quick to help her falling friend, but only after shoving one hand into Cahleen's back.

Cahleen spun and pointed the tip of the black dagger in the Spiaire's face. "Touch me again and see what happens to that hand!"

Darci said nothing as she looped her injured friend's arm over her shoulder again.

Rian could only hope her Spiaires were thinking clearly enough to remember the survival skills she'd drilled into their heads. *Always be smarter than your opponent. Be aware of your opportunities. Patience and knowledge go hand in hand.*

Cahleen lowered the dagger and snarled, "Stupid gróntah." She muttered a few other curses and continued toward the Sendarian man. Without asking, she grabbed the plac from his hand.

While Cahleen read the plac, the man asked, "Please tell me that wasn't who I thought it was heading into the woods earlier? Because if that was the Aberration, then we need to hurry before she comes back."

Rian narrowed her eyes as she looked out onto the field through the low branches and waited for Cahleen's response. It had been a long time since she'd heard anyone call her that.

"It was, but she's not looking for us. So stop being a little taut and focus on getting us out of here. She's Quaid's problem now. Let him dance with death." Cahleen held the plac out for the man to take while she glared back into the woods they'd come from. "What the hegah is taking her so long?"

Dance with death? What does that mean? What rumors are spreading about me on Sendara?

Rian had never killed anyone on Sendara—well, not intentionally. But still, why would they compare her to death? Were Sendarians using her name to scare their young ones into behaving? Or the Rhaltan to intimidate their captives? *How dare they turn my misfortune into a monster story?*

But then Rian recalled the frigid numbness that had often overcome her during her predult years. The many times she'd blacked out and woken with dried blood on her hands.

Anger boiled beneath her cool skin, but the adrenaline was short lived as a strong gust of wind circled her, lifting her blue hair from her shoulders. The air grazed her arms and pricked at her attention. She crouched low against the base of the tree and studied the group. Her eyes locked with a pair of brown eyes. The woman's thick black hair hung forward, hugging the sides of her face. She stared at Rian while muttering muted words.

Focused on the sky, the two Sendarians herding the group hadn't noticed the discreet interaction. The lure between Rian and this woman grew stronger, and she feared that whatever magic this woman commanded would cause another episode.

Somewhat of her own choice but mostly because of the woman's urging willpower, Rian leapt out from her hiding spot and yelled to Cahleen, "Who are you, and what are you doing with Priomh's Spiaires and these other captives? Where are the other human subjects?"

Rian's gaze flicked to the woman who'd drawn her out and who now watched in silence. Whatever magic she'd wielded was gone. Rian cautiously approached the group, one hand unstrapping the lasher from her thigh. "Answer me!"

On the other side of the clearing, a transport shuttle appeared off in the distance, flying in over the tops of the trees. Rian stopped, still not close enough to strike. The Sendarian man walked behind Cahleen and over to the captives.

"Sorry, we can't stay and chat. Our ride is here," Cahleen said, snickering. She yelled over her shoulder, "Micah, get them to the pickup site! I'll deal with the Aberration."

Hearing the word *Aberration* a second time struck something deep inside Rian's essence. The frigid numbness absorbed her anger, fueling its path to freedom. She wasn't sure how much time she had before the ice buried deep within her bones broke free from the serum's hold. The only way to stop its persistence was to get her emotions under control, but unfortunately, now wasn't the time for Breyah's breathing exercises or calming techniques.

Rian briefly glanced over to her Spiaires. Darci was shaking her head, mouth gaping.

Why does Darci look horrified to see me?

Darci yelled, "Where's Kenna?"

Subject fifteen? Why is she singling out that one human?

The muscles in Rian's forehead strained as her gaze shifted from Darci to the infuriating Sendarian standing across from her. For a brief second, her vision doubled, and she knew the numbness was breaking through. She tried to hold on to her own thoughts. To not give in to the cold emptiness, even though a slim part of her wanted the darkness to take over. Then she could show them the true Aberration they so feared.

"I'm going to enjoy beating the life out of you." Rian forced her eyes to stay locked onto Cahleen's. Her fingers clenched tighter on the lasher's handle. The flexible end pointed out at an angle, ready to strike.

Don't pass out. Don't you dare pass out, she silently commanded. The rage inside feuded with Holt's serum and she struggled to focus.

"I'd like to see you try," Cahleen snarled, holding her position between Rian and the captives.

"Rian!" Darci yelled as she slipped out from under Grace's arm. Eryn and Grace fell to the grass while Darci stepped closer to

Cahleen. She was intercepted by Micah, the broad Sendarian man wearing that stupid hat. But his grasp on her shirt didn't stop her from trying to get answers. "Is Kenna okay? Please tell me she's not out here?"

Without dropping her defenses, Rian blinked several times and then shouted over the incoming shuttle winds, "Yes, the human subjects are out here. They snuck out to look for you!"

Darci's eyes grew wide, and she faced the human woman, the one with long black hair. Darci said something to the woman, pleading words Rian couldn't hear. Micah spun her and, with a firm grip on Darci's shoulder, directed her back to the other Spiaires. Darci winced and then yelled over her shoulder, "Rian, you need to go and save them! Don't worry about us. Go and save Kenna!"

But it wasn't Rian who moved; instead, the woman who'd muttered magical words took off running toward the forest.

Cahleen rolled her eyes. "This shit is getting ridiculous."

"I'm not chasing her." Micah shook his head as his expression twisted from an annoyed look to an exhausted one. He tugged Darci's shirt and dragged her back to the other Spiaires.

It was the perfect opportunity to lunge at Cahleen, and Rian was about to when another Sendarian man exited the forest just in time to catch the fleeing woman. Rian watched the woman's black hair spin as she reached for a nearby tree branch. The branch slipped from the woman's fingers, leaving her with a fistful of leaves, while the Sendarian man hauled the woman back to the group. Her cries echoed over the tall grass and were eventually drowned out by the incoming transport shuttle.

"Well, well. Look who finally decided to show up. Good timing, Logan," Cahleen said with a spiteful grin and then returned her attention to Rian. "Now, where were we?"

Logan, who'd also been holding an unconscious body over his shoulder, walked out into the field in their direction, towing the woman with long black hair by her wrist behind him. The young girl over Logan's shoulder also had long black hair.

Another one of the humans. Shit.

As he approached, Cahleen seemed momentarily distracted and Rian took the opportunity to send Breyah a message.

"Linc," she whispered.

"*Yes, Lead Rian,*" her Linc spoke in her ear.

"Record message."

"*Recording message.*"

"Breyah, Bennach has gone ahead to the old research facility. I'm sorry I left his side, but I came across—"

The moment Logan turned his attention to Rian, she froze. He narrowed his eyes at her. "What's she doing here?"

Rian abandoned the message and centered her stance.

"*Lead Rian, shall I send recording as is?*"

"Yes," she said under her breath. "Send it as is and send it now."

With one hand, Cahleen spun her dagger. "Unexpected hiccup. It's being dealt with. Help Micah get the others onto the ship while I handle the *Aberration*."

I'm going to enjoy beating the life out of this woman. Rian stumbled, but she was quick to center herself again.

"Okay," the tall Sendarian said and with a quick heave, he readjusted the girl's body on his shoulder.

Cahleen's lips curled up and she retrieved another dagger that'd been strapped to the back of her pants. This one was a clawlike blade the size of her hand. Cahleen spun one finger through the hole in the handle before pointing the blade out in front of herself. "I want to see what color she bleeds."

"Oh, I'll show you blood! Your blood!" Rian spat and then sprang into motion. To hegah with the serum and the encroaching numbness fogging her mind. If she didn't strike soon, she was worried she'd black out.

Cahleen's smile grew as she ran toward Rian, one arm low clutching the curved blade, while the other hand gripped her black dagger high in front of her chest. When Cahleen swung the dagger to strike, Rian twisted her body and leaned back, narrowly avoiding contact. Rian reacted and used the handle of her lasher to strike a hard jab into the Sendarian's side. Rian's feet pivoted in unison with her punch, allowing her to reposition herself and shuffle some distance between them.

Cahleen coughed out a ragged breath and stumbled to the side. Rian quickly glanced over at the transport shuttle that had landed in the middle of the field. Micah was directing the captives through the tall grass toward the aircraft's open hatch door.

A whizzing sound sliced through the air and Rian twisted her shoulders and upper body right as something spun by her head. She looked behind to see a crescent hilt sticking out from the ground.

Rian readjusted her feet and shoulders. She kept a watchful eye on Cahleen's hands, shoulders, feet, and hips. She knew the key to a good fight was prediction, but Cahleen stood there like a statue— not giving Rian any indication of what her next move was. The second Rian's fist projected forward, Cahleen sidestepped out of the way.

Rian's head was spinning, and she lost her balance. When she turned to face her opponent, Cahleen's shoulder slammed into her chest, forcing the air from her lungs. Rian tripped over her own feet and fell to the ground. Her hands grasped clumps of grass and dirt. Mouth open, she tried to suck in as much air as she could, but nothing went into her lungs.

The moment Rian finally caught her breath, something snug closed around her neck. Dirt crumbled from her fingers as they grazed the semisoft, pliable material encasing her neck. She rolled onto her knees and faced her attacker.

"What... what is this thing?"

A few paces away, Micah stood next to Cahleen, her curved dagger, covered in dirt and grass, in her hand. Micah tapped his plac and said, "I think that's enough for today. We're on a tight schedule, and it now looks like you're coming with us. So, you two can finish this later. Anora's waiting."

Who the hegah is Anora?

Halfway through his little speech, the pliable material of the collar morphed. Rian stumbled to the side, gripping and pulling at the collar's edge as it got tighter against her skin.

She lunged for Micah but only got a few steps before her feet planted firmly to a halt. Her arms were useless too. It was as though her brain had somehow disconnected from her body. Even the ice coursing through her bones and veins seemed to recede.

What is this thing? And... and how is it controlling me?

When her body turned on its own, without her authority, and began marching toward her opponents, she knew it was over. She'd failed Breyah and she'd failed Isoldesse.

"I'll get her on the transport ship," Micah said to Cahleen.

"Good. Oh, and keep her isolated from the others."

The three rebels walked toward the shuttle. Logan was loading the unconscious girl onto the transport shuttle when Eryn jumped him from the back. She hung on his neck while pounding the side of his head. Micah ran up and grabbed the Spiaire. Meanwhile, Darci and the human man half carried, half dragged Grace away from the shuttle.

Rian was helpless as Logan punched Eryn in the gut and then tossed her into the shuttle. Her body slid across the metal floor, disappearing into the shadows of the transport cabin. Rian's sorrows were lightened as she heard a distant Darci yelling, "Come on, run faster!"

Micah's arm dropped to his side. "Should we go after them?"

But before Cahleen could answer, a familiar voice spoke out from behind her. A voice Rian would've been happy to have never heard again, yet here it was. The oh-so-familiar sound of a spoiled and demanding Gemma Vaudd.

"Let them be. We need to go." Gemma stepped in front of Rian. "Well, well. Isn't this an unexpected gift from our goddess?" She narrowed her eyes and glanced at the collar around Rian's neck. "And you're sure she can't break free?"

"I'm sure," Micah said while reading his plac. "I had to increase the power output so it'll hold."

"Excellent." Gemma spun and followed Cahleen to the aircraft, only to stop and whisper something to the human woman who'd remained. Rian was surprised at the casualness between them and the way the woman nodded, as if they were in agreement.

What is going on? What has Gemma gotten herself into?

"Come on," Micah instructed. He gave a few more taps to his plac, and Rian's body moved toward the shuttle craft.

A second later another human man, dark brown hair hanging low over his forehead, jogged past Rian in pursuit of Gemma.

Where are all these humans coming from? But then Rian recognized him as one of the Aevo Compendium subjects. The unexpected human who'd mysteriously replaced one of the preselected subjects. *Xander, I think that was his name. Gemma must've somehow switched out the preselected subjects. But why?*

It wasn't until the next person hobbled past her that Rian's hopes plummeted.

"Sabine?"

The shorter Sendarian woman ignored Rian as she limped toward the shuttle.

"Sabine, what are you doing here? Please, Sabine. Help me!"

Sabine brushed her light-red hair aside, the roots dark with sweat, and glared at Rian. "Why would I help you? You've never appreciated me or my position. None of you have!"

"I have no idea wha—"

"No more talking," Micah instructed. "I can, if you force me to, restrict you from talking."

Rian couldn't believe Sabine would turn on their goddess. Turn on Breyah. *I might have neglected to show my appreciation to Sabine or flat-out tell her how well she does her job, but I know for a fact that others make it known. Breyah above all. Who is behind all of this? Who is feeding lies and twisting truths to turn devoted Sendarians against their goddess?*

Rian stood there waiting for her puppet master to move her while Micah and Logan assisted an injured Sabine into the ship.

What's wrong with Sabine? Did they—did Gemma and Sabine just come from the old facility? Oh no—Bennach!

"Gemma! Are the humans okay? What of Quaid? What of Bennach?"

Gemma was about to climb into the aircraft when she stopped and faced Rian. The ex-Spiaire brushed Rian's blue hair aside and explained, "Shit's gotten out of control. That's all I can say right now. And... and you may not believe me, but I am sorry you got involved."

"Then leave me."

"That's not my call to make." Gemma narrowed her orange eyes and whispered, "I may not be your favorite Sendarian right now, but I'm the only one you can trust here. Remember that."

Rian didn't respond. Micah stuck his head out from inside the shuttle and yelled over the loud wind coming from the shuttle's jet system. "What the hegah are you two waiting for? Get in here!" He tapped his plac again and commanded Rian to climb in.

Three rows of two seats lined each side of the passenger cabin. Sabine sat alone in one row while Logan and Cahleen occupied the row behind her. On the other side sat the human man, Xander, staring at Gemma like a child waiting for his mother. Rian wondered what attachment Gemma had to the human and how it had come about.

Micah cupped Rian's shoulder and directed her to stand in the corner opposite the open hatch door, next to a short wall separating the loading area from the passenger seats.

By the open hatch, Gemma reached to close the door but was stopped by the woman with the long black hair. Rian couldn't hear what they were saying but noticed how Gemma seemed to grant the woman the moment she requested.

A hard jerk beneath Rian's feet told her they'd lifted off. Gusts of wind blew in from the open hatch, whipping at both Gemma's and the human's hair. The woman then opened her hand and released a Hiccum leaf. She must've held on to it from her attempted escape earlier. Even with the dark strands of hair blocking her face, Rian knew she was looking at something in the field below.

Gemma reached across the woman and grabbed the door handle, then slammed the hatch shut.

How could I let this happen? I should've taken Gemma's absence more seriously. Who knows what treachery she's gotten herself involved in? This whole thing could've been avoided if I'd helped Breyah instead of dismissing her search efforts.

"Don't beat yourself up. I mean, if that's what you're doing inside that pretty little blue head of yours." A slender Sendarian woman stepped out from the shadows of a nearby corridor. Her thick red hair sprouted an abundance of tight curls.

Rian was impressed with this woman's height. She'd never met anyone who came close to being as tall as she was. "And who might you be?"

"Believe it or not, you might actually appreciate who I am and what we're doing here." The woman leaned in, her warm cheek brushed the side of Rian's face, and she whispered in Rian's ear. "What if I could promise a world with no more Rhaltan? No more Elemental Council. And no more royal family." She leaned back and smiled. "A new era is coming. One that is more welcome to change."

She can't be serious. She's planning to overthrow the entire Sendara government.

Though, Rian couldn't help but mentally entertain this woman's proposal.

The woman's plump lips spread wide, lifting her cheeks. "I can tell I've got your attention. Good. Well, Rian, it's nice to meet you. My name is Anora."

THE OBARD ARE COMING IN

FAWNESS

BOOK TWO OF THE

AEVO COMPENDIUM DUOLOGY SERIES

ACKNOWLEDGMENTS

This story has come a long way through numerous revisions and countless drafts. So, starting at the beginning, I'd like to first thank those in my family who took the time to read the first draft version of this book.

Next, I'd like to thank my sister-in-law, Renee Smith. Renee not only read the first draft, but she also did line edits for the entire manuscript. I imagine she'll say that this finished version is nothing like the story she read five years ago.

To my first draft editor, Stacy Juba, who not only helped edit my manuscript, but also helped me grow as a writer, thank you. I couldn't have started this journey without her help. Stacy's constructive feedback helped me realize I had a lot to learn about writing a novel.

I'd like to thank the many writers and authors who share their writing and publishing experiences with others through YouTube, Podcasts, and in books. I learned so much by watching, listening, and reading ways to structure a story, market a book, and how to connect with others through channels like *Jenna Moreci* on YouTube, *Brandon Sanderson* on his podcast *Writing Excuses*, and in books by *K.M. Weiland*.

During the second draft revisions of Isoldesse, I joined a local writing group called *Fantasy, Paranormal, and Science-Fiction Writers of Central CT*. This was my first experience with a critique group, and I learned a lot about reader expectations and the mechanics of story flow. I'd like to thank those in the group that provided helpful tips and direction for my writing: Alexa, Erin, Jeff, Jess, Alex, and Tabitha.

As much as I loved learning how to better my writing craft from the local writing group, it wasn't until I connected with my critique partners that Isoldesse became a more polished manuscript. I cannot thank you enough, Tanni, Cristina, Khalia, and Hayley for all your feedback and critiquing. I look forward to working together on future projects.

I'd also like to thank my beta-readers, Olivia Castetter and Kayla M. Ware. Your thoughts and suggestions from a reader's perspective helped get Isoldesse even closer to the finish line.

And in the last stretch before publication, I'd like to thank my editors, Liz Delton and Nikki Mentges. I cannot thank you both enough for everything you did to make Isoldesse ready for readers to enjoy. Liz is a talented and experienced author who is working on writing and publishing her third series, and who I still cannot believe said yes for taking on Isoldesse one month before her due date! Her line edits and suggestions helped get Isoldesse ready for ARC viewing while the amazing and talented Nikki from *NAM Editing* proofread the manuscript. I can't thank both women enough for all the hard work and time they invested in making Isoldesse ready for publication. I look forward to working with both women again down the road.

My journey as an author is just beginning. To wake up and do something that I absolutely love doing is a blessing, and I couldn't do it without the support of my family. To my children that keep me on my toes when I'm not writing, I love you, Kayla, Abby, and Chloe. Lastly, I'd like to thank my best friend and husband, Jim. I couldn't have done any of this without you. You've listened to me each night talk about my book and have been there for me for every step of the way, and I thank you for that. I love you, sweetie.

About the Author

Kimberly Grymes never imagined she'd take the stories brewing inside her head and put them into a book for everyone to read. Yet here it is! Her debut novel! When she's not writing, reading, or blogging, she's usually hanging out with her husband and kids, baking treats, or keeping busy with crafts. As much as she enjoys reading books, she loves watching movies and TV, and is always on the lookout for the next great sci-fi or fantasy show to watch. Her favorite part of the day is TV time in the evening with her husband and their two min-pins, Jubilee and Cori.

KimberlyGrymes.com
Instagram: @KGrymes.Writes
Twitter: @KimberlyGrymes

PlumReport.com

Plum Report Podcast with Kimberly Grymes
is on Spotify, Google Podcast, Amazon Music, Pandora

CPSIA information can be obtained
at www.ICGtesting.com
Printed in the USA
BVHW081334220221
600770BV00006B/482

9 781736 179307